"Heard you were out on the street making a spectacle of yourself."

That was Matt's opinion. But Kat's other two brothers, Josh and Mark, were nodding in agreement.

"'Spectacle' is a pretty strong word," Kat said. *Or maybe not...* She remembered Slater's kiss. Oh, boy, did she remember it! While she debated whether or not to defend her right to kiss whomever she chose, Matt got into the act again.

"Slater Kowalski's after more than kisses, and we all know that. He wants to pilfer Pop's engineering secrets, so he's hitting on Kathleen. I say it's time we teach that Ridge jerk to keep his hands off Hill women."

The noise level rose as all three brothers and their wives entered into the argument. Kat finally declared enough. Pulling an umpire's whistle from her pocket, she blew as hard as she could.

Having gained their notice, Kat crossed her arms. "As you're all so free with your opinions, listen to mine. Little Kathleen is all grown up, in case you hadn't noticed. And Slater Kowalski is not a jerk." Kat glared around at the stunned faces. "I'm going out with him on Saturday night. A real date, unconnected to work. And it's none of your business. So kindly butt out."

Dear Reader,

I don't come from a large boisterous family. But I always wanted one. I love the dynamics and the interaction, the warmth and the caring. So I've given my heroine such a family. If you've read my previous books, you know I like ordinary people who live in close-knit communities and work at everyday jobs. Therefore I was delighted when my editor asked me to write a story for the new HOMETOWN U.S.A. promotion in Superromance.

Slater Kowalski and Kathleen O'Halloran could live next door to you or me. Because those of us who come from small towns and work at ordinary jobs sometimes think our lives are boring, I've allowed this couple quite an adventure…filled with kites and clouds, kayaks and automobiles. But also romance and mystery! I hope you steal away with Kat and Slater for a while to share their exploits, meet their families and experience their love.

Roz Denny Fox

P.S. I love hearing from readers. Write me at P.O. Box 17480-101, Tucson, Arizona 85731

Books by Roz Denny Fox

SUPERROMANCE

WELCOME TO MY FAMILY

Roz Denny Fox

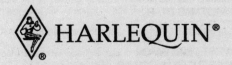

HARLEQUIN®

TORONTO • NEW YORK • LONDON
AMSTERDAM • PARIS • SYDNEY • HAMBURG
STOCKHOLM • ATHENS • TOKYO • MILAN • MADRID
PRAGUE • WARSAW • BUDAPEST • AUCKLAND

ISBN 0-373-70885-8

WELCOME TO MY FAMILY

This edition published by arrangement with Harlequin Books S.A.

® and TM are trademarks of the publisher. Trademarks indicated with ® are registered in the United States Patent and Trademark Office, the Canadian Trade Marks Office and in other countries.

Visit us at www.romance.net

Printed in U.S.A.

To Bernie Sadowski and his lovely wife, Rita.
For their wonderfully positive outlook on life.
For Bernie's stories about his old hometown, and about his
dad and the men who made automobiles. They inspired me.

CHAPTER ONE

THUNDER RUMBLED OVERHEAD. In the distance, lightning cut a jagged swath across the Michigan night sky. Kathleen O'Halloran smoothed a hand over the soft coat of the dog beside her—a young black Labrador retriever who'd just begun to whine. The continual downpour made it difficult to see the road, especially through the waterfall cascading from the tips of two kayaks she had lashed to the top of her aging Isuzu Trooper.

"We picked a beaut of a night to come home, didn't we, Poseidon?" Kat murmured, kicking her lights up to high beam. She slowed to a crawl. Storms worried the dog. Made him restless. Not surprising. Kat had rescued him from a half-submerged log during a bad squall six months back. Hard to say how long he'd been riding the waves. She'd run advertisements in her San Juan Island newspaper and posted numerous handbills around the resort where she'd worked as recreational director. No one had come forward to claim the beautiful dog. He and she had become fast friends. Kat's long trek home from Washington State through the March wind and rain would have been far less tolerable without him.

Certainly she'd enjoyed her freedom out West—who in her place wouldn't if they'd had her bad luck of being the youngest and only girl in a long progression of know-it-all engineers? She often threatened to call herself a recreational engineer just to get recognition in the family. But, the truth was, this past year Kat had grown increasingly more home-sick in spite of Poseidon's company.

Her fingers tightened in the animal's fur. Perhaps her sister-in-law Mary was right when she'd argued last month that blood took precedence over independence. Pop had the whole family in such a tizzy, at least maybe now Kat's brothers wouldn't have time to mess with her love life—assuming any love interest popped out of the woodwork. Kat's family had made sure to keep her apprised of her classmates' weddings. She disliked thinking of herself shelved at twenty-six. But her mother and brothers sure seemed to believe it.

"Uh-oh. Looks like a stranded motorist up ahead." Kat touched her brakes and held her breath against the slight shiver of the precariously balanced kayaks. "Take it easy, Horatio." Her pet name for the vehicle slipped out as she concentrated on her driving. She hadn't seen another car since entering this shortcut. Three years ago, when she'd left Flintridge, only locals used this road. Had that changed?

The car parked on the right shoulder was big and dark. Its hood was raised. As Kat cruised past, her headlights outlined a man wearing light gray slacks and a white shirt plastered to his body by the driving rain. The wind whipped a narrow tie over his left shoulder.

She pulled over a hundred yards down the road and stopped, chewing her lower lip. All the dire warnings aimed at women travelers flashed through her mind. Mama, especially, was big on passing along such dangers whenever she phoned. Of course, the rapes and murders Maureen O'Halloran recounted weren't even close to Flintridge. Nevertheless, there was always a first, and it might be awaiting Kat this very minute.

She backed up slowly, trying to gain a better look at the

motorist in her rearview mirror. After all, she wasn't stupid. Few rapists looked the part.

About then, the man straightened and braced himself against the wind. Kat noted that the deluge had flattened blond hair in what was probably a fifty-dollar haircut across his forehead. From what she could see, he was moderately good-looking. Not a pretty-boy with that stubborn jaw. But clean-cut enough to pass her mother's inspection. Kat set her brake and slid the gearshift into park.

That was when she noticed the car's dealer license plates. Automobile salesman, no doubt. She knew the type. Dandies who worked out in health clubs and dressed for success to give themselves an edge with the ladies. By the time Kat decided to offer help, she had the driver of the stalled car pegged right down to his Cole-Haan loafers and the snowy handkerchief he used to scrub grease off his fingers.

"This one seems harmless enough, Poseidon," she murmured, reassuring herself more than the dog. Flipping on her four-way flashers, Kat shrugged into a bright yellow rain slicker she kept in the car. "Stay, boy," she commanded, opening the door. But for an animal who cowered from storms, this one exhibited uncharacteristic behavior and suddenly bolted into the midst of it. Barking wildly, he splashed through a series of dirty puddles, then took a flying leap at the stranger.

"Poseidon, no!" Kat shouted. "Oh, my Lord." She dashed after her pet and caught him moments after he'd muddied the man's white shirt. It took considerable muscle to force the dog down. Amid garbled apologies, she dragged him back to her vehicle and stuffed him inside. "Shame on you. Bad dog."

The dog nearly escaped again as Kat leaned in to straighten the blanket that covered her seats. Following another stern reminder to behave, he flopped down, looking guilty. His tail drooped. Kat heaved a sigh, rubbed his ears, then closed the door firmly.

"Hey, I'm really sorry," she said, returning to the motorist. "Did he bite you?"

The man settled unfocused blue eyes on her, frowning as if she were an apparition, and definitely an unwelcome one.

Kat winced at his expression—and the muddy paw prints. "I'll pay to have your shirt laundered. My dog isn't...fond of men."

"Not fond of them? Damned animal almost licked me to death. I hope you don't think he's a guard dog."

Partly in deference to her mother's advice, and partly because of his attitude, Kat bristled. "No telling what that animal would do if I was in danger. Kill, maybe. So you'd better not try any funny business. Are you out of gas or something?" she asked, nodding at his car.

Slater Kowalski gaped at the dark-haired, dark-eyed pixie, who, for all he knew, could be telling the truth about her dog's potential to kill on command. But why was *she* acting snippy? He was the victim here. He hadn't flagged her down.

Then, because the woman and her ill-mannered mutt were the last straw at the end of a rotten week, Slater turned and kicked his car's front tire. Not feeling any better, he smacked a hand on the sleek, wet fender. A fender representing the aerodynamic pinnacle of the future. On a car of his own design. So why couldn't his team of engineers make the damn thing run?

His anger drained as it occurred to Slater that the woman was probably questioning his sanity. "I'm not out of gas," he said wearily. "She doesn't even use conventional gas."

"Ah." Kat wiped the rain from her eyes. "I see. Diesel," she stated flatly. "They can be cantankerous if you get water in the fuel lines. All this rain." She shrugged expansively.

"I suppose I can give you a lift into town. Poseidon won't bite…unless I'm threatened," she added for good measure.

Was she kidding? Leave his million-dollar baby? Walk away from his precious prototype on which the future of Flintridge Motors rested? "Uh…no thanks." Slater knew his refusal sounded stiff. "It's not diesel, either. But I really can't leave her out here."

Kat couldn't believe anyone in his predicament would be so stubborn. "I'm sure she represents a hunk of cash to your employer," she said, using the feminine pronoun as he had—the way her dad and brothers all did when discussing automobiles.

"Be reasonable," Kat continued, glancing pointedly up and down the road. "This isn't exactly a thoroughfare. She'll be safe here until you can round up a tow truck."

The man continued to shake his head, and Kat watched his transparent shirt move like a second skin against lean muscles. Quite suddenly she found it difficult to breathe. Darn, she'd always been a sucker for the well-toned look of a runner. And this guy had it all—except brains, obviously. Exasperated, Kat deliberately stuck her head beneath the black car's hood. "I've got a pretty decent toolbox with me. What are her symptoms? If you're not using gas or diesel, then what? Methanol? She looks too heavy for meth. Are you getting spark from the ignition? Have you tried starting her again? Could be vapor lock, you know."

The thirty-one-year-old CEO of Flintridge Motors almost smiled at that. "So, what? Are you a mechanic?" Slater found the possibility intrigued him as he dipped his head and joined her under the hood, out of the rain for a moment.

Kat laughed. "Not by trade. But I'm fair with a socket set. Actually, I grew up near here in a family that eats, sleeps and breathes automobiles. Most are engineers. Combustion, electronic, structural. You name it. One of my brothers builds headers for dragsters in his spare time. If I do say so myself, I'm pretty savvy when it comes to cars."

Slater found himself backing away. After all, his engine was still in the test phase. "You don't say?" He glanced toward her vehicle. "If you're so savvy…why are you driving foreign-built in this town?"

Kat straightened and cracked her head on the hood. Her Trooper—and before that, her Toyota—had been a bone of contention with her brothers, too. "Look, bud, which one of us is stranded by the side of the road? Not me, thank you very much. Ask yourself who built this hunk of junk." She tapped the front grill. "Nobody willing to put their name on it, that I can see."

Nudging her out from under the Special's hood, Slater slammed it closed. "Who'd you say your family works for?" he queried coolly, thinking this woman might be just a little *too* savvy to suit him.

"I didn't."

"What's under those tarps? Hijacked car parts?"

Kat couldn't believe she was standing in raindrops as big as hippos, talking to this insensitive lout who didn't have sense enough to get out of the weather. "Do you want help," she asked tersely, "or do you intend to stand around all night kicking your tires?"

Slater felt a flush creep up his cheeks. He'd been keeping this design under wraps for two years. He had a federal government General Services Administration contract to replace ten thousand agency cars, to be shipped in the not-too-distant future—which meant nothing unless he rolled them off the line on schedule. If not, the company founded by his family might well go belly-up, throwing hundreds of local men and women out of work. The last thing he needed to top off a bad week was some tomboy grease monkey psychoanalyzing him.

Except…that wasn't entirely true; he did need her to deliver a message.

"Look, sorry to sound ungrateful," he said contritely, flashing her a smile calculated to bring her around. "If I give you the name and phone number of my mechanic, would you mind calling him when you hit town?"

Unimpressed, Kat raised a brow. "You have a mechanic on tap at ten o'clock at night? My, my. Yet you don't carry a cell phone? Aren't you lucky I stopped?"

Slater yanked open his car door and dug around in the center console until he found a notepad and a pen. If he answered her sass the way he'd like to, he'd be stuck here forever. He'd been so anxious to test the latest attempt to correct the car's fuel-line problem, he'd dashed out without a jacket, never mind a cell phone. Slater ignored the water dripping from his hair, even though it slid off the hand-stitched leather bucket seats and soaked into the Special's plush gray carpet.

At a glance Kat took in the car's rich interior and the man's obviously expensive gold pen. She scooted in for a closer look and whistled softly between her teeth. Test driver, maybe? They tended to be arrogant, and possessive of their new toys.

Silently Kat accepted the note he ripped out and handed her as he rudely backed her away and shut the car's door in her face. Local phone number, she saw. She hitched up her yellow slicker and stuffed the paper into her back pants pocket. "Who shall I say is demanding this mechanic's lowly presence way out here on such a ghastly night?"

Slater let his gaze travel up a slender denim-covered leg that peeked out from beneath her oilskin slicker. Damned well-shaped for such a small woman, he thought, taking an unexpected jolt to the stomach. Tearing his gaze away, Slater reminded himself she was too smart-mouthed for his taste, even supposing he liked women with boyish hair-cuts—which he didn't. "Name's Slater. Tell Dempsey I'm stalled south of the twelve-mile marker out on the proving grounds with the Flintridge Special."

Kat felt a sudden flicker of interest. He worked for Flint-ridge Motors? Come Monday, she'd be starting there as rec-reation specialist. It was a new position, and the personnel director had hired her from a resume and phone interview. The job had given her a legitimate reason for coming home. Kat was grateful to her sister-in-law for sending her the newspaper ad. Pop was no dummy. Without this job, he'd have known right away that she'd been called home to deal with what the family referred to as his childish post-retire-ment behavior.

"Was there something else?" Slater asked with a faint air of exasperation as he clicked his ballpoint pen.

"What? Oh, no." Blushing, Kat turned and trotted off. "I'll phone this guy the minute I hit town," she promised over her shoulder. Then, because she thought it might be nice to know by name at least one person from work, she paused with her hand on her vehicle's door and called out, "O'Halloran. My name is Kathleen O'Halloran. It's such a small world, I'm sure we'll see each other around."

Before Slater could recover from the shock of hearing a name that stuck in his craw, she'd climbed in her Trooper and tootled off.

Coincidence or fate? Not that it mattered, Slater decided, sliding into the Special to strip off his soggy tie as the truck's taillights disappeared in the sluicing rain. He wouldn't go out of his way to see anyone with that last name. He had enough trouble these days. A revolutionary natural gas engine—great in theory but less so in practice. Employees hounding him to provide recreation opportuni-ties because his competitor across town did. And now his dad's sudden passion for playing the ponies. Ponies and poker. He had an Irish rabble-rouser to blame for *that* particular problem. One O'Halloran. Timothy O'Halloran.

Disgusted, Slater tried wringing water out of his shirt, then gave up and settled back to wait. The most he could hope now was that Miss Fix-it had more integrity than Tim of the same last name.

As GOOD AS HER WORD, Kat stopped at the first convenience store on the outskirts of Flintridge and delivered Mr. Slater's message to Gordon Dempsey. The mechanic swore, then apologized and offered a simple thank-you. He disconnected so fast, Kat couldn't decide if it was the news itself or the name of the person needing his services that had made Dempsey swear. However, she gave only cursory thought to the man she'd left out on the highway. Everything soon took second place to the excitement of coming home.

The big old house with the full front porch where Toby Flanigan had given Kat her first kiss looked exactly as she remembered. And Kat knew before she went inside that in spite of the late hour, her mother's kitchen would smell of coffee and her own favorite raisin-oatmeal cookies. Pop was the only one in the family not expecting her. Kat wondered what excuse they'd made for this evening's gathering of the clan.

Heart filled with joy in anticipation of seeing everyone again, she hauled Poseidon out of the Trooper and burst through the front door.

Her brothers Matt, Mark and Josh—good biblical names as solid as the men themselves—hoisted her off the floor and tossed her from one to the other. She'd always loved this when she was a kid. She hugged each man in turn.

Her poor dog barked and jumped at them until Kat's mother demanded order.

Mary, Kat's most thoughtful sister-in-law, Joshua's wife, relieved her of the wet slicker and thrust a mug of hot coffee into Kat's chilly hands. The other two women, Erin and Shannon, were married to Mark and Matt respectively. All talking at once, the women exclaimed over Kat's new, shorter haircut and how trim she looked. Preliminaries over, the family settled down to ask about her trip.

"Long and boring," Kat replied. "Uneventful outside of a flat tire in Montana. Where's Pop? Did he go to bed?" Kat knew how much flak she'd take if she mentioned her attempted roadside rescue. So she didn't bring it up.

Still, her mom acted uneasy, and Mark scowled as he turned away to pick up the coffeepot.

"It's poker night at Spud Mallory's," Josh explained.

"Ah." Kat nodded. "Well, that's okay, isn't it? Pop and Spud go back a long way. I can remember begging them to teach me how to play poker."

"They never played for money before," Mrs. O'Halloran said, digging for a tissue to hide a sniffle. "I tell you, Katie, your father has taken leave of his senses."

"How much money's involved?" Kat asked warily. "Not high stakes." She looked to her brothers for answers.

Matt squeezed her shoulder as he led her to the table and pulled out a chair for her. "Mom can't get a handle on how much. Pop's gotten secretive about money since he retired. Before, she took care of all the finances. Now he races her to the mailbox for his retirement check and does the banking. Claims he finally has the time to deal with it..."

Kat studied the grain in the old oak table. It had been in the O'Halloran family for generations and had a feeling of permanence. "So, have any of you asked Pop outright what all this means?"

"You know Pop," Josh answered. "He's closemouthed as a clam, unless he wants you to know something. No one

in the family had an inkling he planned to retire early. We
had to read it in the *Motorman's News,* for crying out loud.''

Erin tugged the lid off the cookie canister and passed it
around. ''It's that Louie Kowalski. He's to blame for everything.''

''I know that's what you said when you phoned,'' Kat
acknowledged around a big bite of cookie, ''but who is he?
Where did he come from? That's an important name on the
ridge. Is he a car man?''

Mrs. O'Halloran patted Kat's hand. ''Apparently. We
didn't want to worry you, Katie. About a year ago, Dr.
Shelby told Tim his cholesterol and blood pressure were
up—in the danger range for another heart attack—and that
he needed to lose weight. Doc suggested an exercise program over at the health club. That's where he met Louie,
who was apparently recovering from a recent heart attack.''

Matt broke in. ''For weeks we heard Louie quotes. You
know, Louie this, Louie that—then next thing we know, Pop
and Louie both up and retire. Before the 'good life' passed
them by was what Pop claimed.''

Shannon patted Kat's hand. ''It was like a whole male
club followed suit. Buzz Moran, Luke Sheehan, Spud Mallory. They've all lost their marbles, if you ask me.''

''Well, maybe it's a phase,'' Kat said, glancing around at
the worried faces of her family. ''Have any of you run it
by the psychologist at work? Maybe it's a syndrome or
something. I mean if they all worked at Motorhill...'' She
stopped as they exchanged sharp glances. ''What now?''

Mark, the eldest son, a Rhodes scholar—a man Kat was
convinced knew all there was to know about chemical combustion but often let the real world pass by without notice—
tilted back his chair and frowned. ''Louie worked at Flintridge Motors. Frankly, sis, that's something else that worries
us, Pop's fraternizing with the competition.''

"Great. So, tell me why Mary sent *me* a Flintridge job ad and an application. I thought the old animosity between the two companies had died."

Josh leaned forward. "We got to talking one night. Pop's a whale of an electrical engineer. Retirement doesn't change what he carries in his head, if you know what I mean. Rumor has it Flintridge is having problems with a new prototype. Big problems."

"Come on, Josh. You think Flintridge is trying to appropriate some of Motorhill's technical data? Before I left town, Motorhill tooled down to make only compact cars. Flintridge does luxury stuff, right?" An image of the sleek car she'd seen out on the road flashed briefly through Kat's mind. That car definitely had problems.

"Electronics is electronics," Matt said, polishing off the last cookie. "We've been working on some futuristic stuff at Motorhill. Dad was involved."

"Well, Matt, you moonlight out in the community building headers for the race car set. Do you actually think Flintridge would resort to stealing Motorhill's information?"

"Dragsters tend not to know what day it is, sis."

Mark turned serious eyes toward Kat. "We may be shooting in the dark, kitten. I hope so. But Pop's behavior's shaken us. With you working at Flintridge, keeping your eyes and ears open, you might be able to assess them. We spend so much time cooped up in laboratories, we're like three blind mice."

Mrs. O'Halloran wagged a finger. "Grandbabies. That would keep Pop home. But no. You're all too busy building better mousetraps or whatever to have babies."

All the younger family members grimaced. It was an old, ongoing argument and one that went unheeded as usual.

Kat laughed. "Everything sounds exactly the same around here. Did you ever stop to think you're reading too much into Pop's actions? Flintridge and Motorhill have co-existed for generations. Why steal each other's ideas at this late date?''

Matt laced his hands behind his head. "As Mark said, we stay in our cocoons on the hill. For the record, I wasn't in favor of sending you that job application. But Josh and Mark convinced me that the way Louie's hanging out with Pop is more than a coincidence. And about the time they met, according to the newspaper, there was a change in management at Flintridge. Transfer of power from rich daddy to privileged son. Truth is, we don't know much about folks from the Ridge.''

Kat sipped her coffee. She thought back to high school—to the fierce competition between the Ridgers and the Hillites. The Ridge was largely Polish in origin, and the Hill mostly Irish. The city's business center and a river divided the two communities. Both sides were predominately Catholic, but they maintained separate churches, schools and social activities. Kat wondered why that had never made an impression on her before. In essence they were like two towns in one. Their estrangement was aided and abetted in large part by the two major employers, Motorhill and Flintridge Motors.

Monday, she would cross the bridge and start a new job in foreign territory. The way things sounded, she didn't know whether to consider herself a pioneer or a sacrificial lamb.

"Kathleen looks tired," Shannon said, rising. "Perhaps we shouldn't burden her with everything tonight."

"There's more?" Kat stood as the others began to collect jackets in preparation for leaving. Poseidon perked up his ears. Kat told him to stay. He did, but kept everyone in sight all the same.

Mary pulled Kat aside. "Something I didn't tell you, Kat.

It's rumored that there's worker unrest at Flintridge. The job you're taking is a direct result of pressure put on the new CEO. We hear he's opposed to an on-site recreation program.''

"G-r-r-reat!''

Josh kissed his mother's still-smooth cheek, then turned and enfolded his little sister in a bear hug. "If anyone gives you a hard time, kid...quit. We'll put our heads together and figure out some other way to get our questions answered. I hope you know we're damn glad to have you home.''

Tears sprang to Kat's eyes. She hadn't realized how much she'd missed her brothers until now. Especially as they were also the reason she'd left home. Largely the reason, anyway. "This job sounds like a piece of cake compared to the mess you almost got me into with the infamous Daniel O'Brien,'' she said, punching her brother lightly on the arm.

The exodus toward the door stopped. Erin snapped her fingers. "I told you birdbrains to quit shoving Danny down Kat's throat. He was too slick to suit me.''

Mark dropped a kiss on his wife's nose. "Lord, but she's impossible to live with when she's right." He cleared his throat. "We, uh...do owe you an apology, kitten. Danny-boy is doing hard time now. I think it's safe to say...when you bag a husband, you're on your own.''

Kat grinned. "Hallelujah! You know, this family can be...well...*intense* is a good word. I forgive you for the Danny fiasco. Just remember it, though, before any of you go overboard with this thing regarding Pop. I know you mean well, but—''

Everyone chimed in with opinions at once, the way they always did. Mark caught her chin and shushed the others. "Believe me Kat, not even the people who worked with

Danny knew he had light fingers. And as far as Pop's concerned…he's acting funny. You'll see.''

"All I'm saying," she urged, "is let's not jump to conclusions.''

Her mother stiffened. "Whose side are you on, Katie?''

"I'm not on any side." She opened the door for her brothers and their wives. After another round of goodbyes, Kat was left alone with her mother. Reluctant to continue the subject they'd been discussing, Kat fed Poseidon, then busied herself fixing another pot of coffee. When her mother's silence seemed too overpowering, Kat finally said, "I love you, Mama, and I love Pop. I can't believe the man I remember, pillar of the family, church and community, would jeopardize everything he's worked his whole life for. I'd like some time to make my own assessments.''

Maureen O'Halloran dabbed at her watery eyes. "Tim and I began dating in eighth grade. We married the day after he received his engineering degree. I don't know where the years have gone. But lately, I'm not sure I even know him.''

"How's that?" Kat asked.

"I thought we were growing old together. All this sudden youthful energy of his…well, Sheila Murphy suggested he may be seeing a younger woman." Her tears spilled over and followed the faint lines that bracketed her mouth.

Kat bristled. "Sheila Murphy is a busybody who loves to stir up trouble. Pop's not like that. And you're not old. You're still beautiful, Mama.''

"Oh, I'm so glad you're home, Katie. I love your brothers' wives, but I couldn't have confided in them. They're so…so…organized. They don't seem to believe that women should be allowed human weaknesses.''

"Thanks, I think." Kat chuckled.

Suddenly there was a rattle at the back door. Poseidon raced to the screened porch and started barking.

''What the devil?'' A man's deep voice came through the screen. ''Maureen, where did this mongrel come from?'' Timothy O'Halloran's voice was loud enough to shake the rafters.

Kat ran to the door and threw herself into his arms. He smelled faintly of cigar smoke, Irish whiskey and rain, which brought her comforting memories. Kat smiled through a shimmer of tears. ''He's not a mongrel. And he's mine, Pop. Didn't you see my rig parked out front?''

''Kathleen!'' he said with a lilt as he pried her arms loose, stepped back and stared. Eyes misting, he stammered, ''How? Wh-when? I came up the back road. Lordy, girl, are you a sight for tired eyes.'' He caught her close in a bone-crushing hug. ''Maureen,'' he bellowed, ''this calls for a celebration. How long are you going to be home, kitten?'' Releasing her, he held her at arm's length, obviously impatient for an answer.

''You, may not be so excited when you hear this, Pop. I'm home lock, stock and barrel. In fact, I'm starting a new job on Monday.''

''Nobody tells me anything,'' he accused, glaring at his slender wife.

''If you'd spend more time at home, Timothy O'Halloran, you might pick up some of the news.''

Although it was typical of the heated discussions Kat had grown accustomed to when she lived at home, she didn't want her parents arguing on her first night back. ''It's my fault, Pop. I wanted to surprise you.''

His gaze softened. ''Just tonight I was telling the boys I'd like to check out that great fishing you always bragged about up in the San Juans.''

''Really?'' Kat wrinkled her nose. ''First urge in three years? I distinctly remember begging you and Mama to come after you retired. I could go back, I suppose.''

He looked chagrined. "You've been on my mind a lot lately, girl. I'm the only one in my group with a daughter. The guys don't understand when I tell them a son is a son till he takes a wife, but a daughter's a daughter the rest of her life." He shook his shaggy head and a thick strand of still-dark hair fell over his brow. "I'll always worry about you, kitten."

"Sentimental, Pop? Not you—Mr. Logic, himself," she teased, falling into a brogue the way he did when he got excited. "So tell me about this group. Is fishing what you guys do?" She looped an arm through his and led him to the table, shooting her mother a sly wink. Maybe she could clear things up tonight.

"You don't want to hear about the antics of a few has-beens, girl. Tell me about this new job. Has Josh finally badgered you into joining the secretarial pool at Motorhill?"

"Pop…the job's in my field. I'm not sure you'll approve, though. Flintridge Motors opened up a spot for a recreational specialist. Well, you're, uh, looking at her."

"Flintridge, huh? I used to think that crew was phony baloney—until I met Louie. He's retired from there. Worked for 'em all his life, same as I did Motorhill." Timothy suddenly beamed. "Say, Louie's son still works there. Tell you what, kitten…Sunday, when we go to the track, I'll ask Louie if he'll have the lad show you around."

Kat felt a wave of apprehension. "I don't know. What does he do there?"

"I don't know that Louie's ever said."

Kat reached down absently and stroked Poseidon's soft coat. She wasn't interested in getting entangled with a man, especially not anyone from the Ridge, so she didn't want to encourage her father along those lines. "I hate to cut this homecoming short, but I'm really bushed. Will you help me unload tomorrow, Pop? You'll never believe how much stuff I've accumulated in three years.''

He stood and shifted his weight to one hip and placed an arm around his wife. ''That's why your mother and I never moved. I'm a packrat and she hasn't the heart to throw anything out. We always said we were just going to will this mess to all of you kids.'' The two exchanged soft smiles.

Kat's heart swelled. This was the father she remembered. Handsome, charming, loving. Maybe he was missing his old routines. In time, he'd create new ones, she thought. New routines and new satisfactions.

''You two linger awhile and drink your coffee,'' she said brightly. ''I'm going to bed. And as far as the house goes, you can leave me out of the will. I love this place, but I want to live near the water. Wait'll you see my new double kayaks, Pop. You'll be begging me for lessons.''

''And where did you learn to kayak if not on our river, young lady?''

''Yeah, yeah.'' Kat kissed them each and left them, their arms linked, hands entwined. Not altogether happy at being disturbed again, Poseidon padded obediently after her. He objected to being forced out into the rain, however briefly. Yet once they were upstairs, he claimed a spot on the braided rug beside her bed and the next thing Kat knew, he was snoring.

If she'd counted on her childhood bed to bring instant sleep, she was sadly mistaken. She lay awake staring at the gold and silver glitter she'd talked Pop into spraying on the ceiling when he remodeled her room for her twelfth birthday. Kat remembered crying buckets until he'd promised to add the sparkles. Now it was horribly outdated. Time, she thought, did indeed bring change.

Like her going to work for Flintridge. If anyone had ever

suggested she'd take a job with Motorhill's rival one day, she would've vehemently denied it. Frankly, she still wasn't sure about doing this. After the initial interview, she'd been excited to find a local company eager to use her degree and her skills. Mary hadn't made it sound so great, though. At least not as far as the company's CEO went. Apparently the rank and file would welcome her.

That thought made Kat feel better. It'd probably be months before a busy CEO found time to meet her. By then, she'd be able to impress him with a fully operating program.

Yawning, she closed her eyes and muttered, "Plenty of time."

Meanwhile, maybe she'd bump into the sexy test jockey she'd met earlier. Her pulse skipped a bit before it steadied. Why she'd want to meet His Surliness again was beyond her. Sitting up, Kat thumped her pillow into shape. Speaking of men…She really wasn't looking forward to the prospect of Louie Kowalski's son tracking her down. But suppose he did? There was nothing to say she *had* to welcome him to the family or anything.

Kat whacked her pillow again. Relieved to have a few things decided, she snuggled into freshly laundered linens that smelled of security and home.

CHAPTER TWO

THE WEEKEND FLEW BY so fast, Kat wasn't certain there'd been one when her alarm sounded Monday morning. Groaning, she rolled over, grabbed for it, but knocked the clock to the floor. Poseidon bounded across the room and dragged it, still buzzing, out of her reach. ''Now you've done it, dog.'' Kat crawled slowly out from under the covers. Her body ached from the physical labor of unloading her belongings.

After she'd retrieved and silenced the alarm, she warmed up for the air force exercises she'd done religiously since junior high. Back then she'd had a terrible crush on Ryan Kelley, who'd declared himself academy-bound. As it turned out, he'd become a podiatrist and married a gourmet cook. Last time Kat saw him, Ryan was overweight. Yet she owed him for making exercise and good health her life's passion.

The routine didn't take long. Soon she'd showered and dressed for her first day on the new job.

Breakfast was a quiet affair. Just Kat, her mother and Poseidon. Pop hadn't come in from the races until after 2:00 a.m., Kat knew. But because her stomach was in such a turmoil with first-day jitters, she purposely didn't mention that to her mother.

Leaving an unhappy dog behind, Kat drove the route she'd mapped out. Worried about losing her vehicle in the mammoth parking lot, she checked coordinates, then smoothed her suit skirt before falling in with a throng heading through the main gate. Ordinarily she wouldn't wear a skirt to work, but yesterday all three sisters-in-law had badgered her. Seeing the women here dressed in what she'd term *church dress,* Kat was glad she'd taken Shannon, Mary and Erin's advice.

Outside the personnel office, Kat hauled in a deep breath. A lone occupant in the room glanced up, then away as she entered. Kat figured it was just as well she hadn't expected the red-carpet treatment. She approached the woman with her best smile. "I'm Kathleen O'Halloran reporting for work as the new recreation specialist."

The woman's smoothly penciled eyebrows shot up. "I expected a person with your athletic background to be more…robust." The cool gaze flicked over Kat again as the woman walked toward her. "I'm Wendolyn Nelson, director of Personnel."

Kat made her own survey of the statuesque blonde, who wore cascades of gold chains as if they'd been minted for her. The gleaming chains draped an expensive green silk dress that matched the cold eyes. Kat thought the woman resembled a fishpond and she felt disappointed by Ms. Nelson's cold demeanor. During the phone interview, she'd sounded nice. "Athletics is a matter of muscle tone," Kat murmured. "I assure you, I'm much stronger than I look."

"Yes. Well, we may never know the full extent of your prowess. The position may be only temporary."

"But…your advertisement said the job was permanent."

The director seemed faintly disconcerted. "Maybe you'd rather not take the job? Our CEO sees no need to mix recreation with work, and frankly, I agree."

"Well, perhaps I'll have to change *his* mind," Kat said, with a smile she hoped conveyed the message that she didn't care what this woman thought.

"I sincerely doubt that, Ms. O'Halloran." The blonde pursed her lips. "Anyhow, at the moment you have paperwork to complete. From then, until he decides the program's fate, you'll report directly to our CEO."

Kat gave a low whistle.

"I know it's irregular." Ms. Nelson might have said more, but the door opened then and several women trooped in, chatting and laughing until they glanced up and saw the director eying them in a faintly disapproving fashion. They quickly melted into the seats at various workstations.

"Late again, ladies?" Ms. Nelson made a production of checking her watch. "This gives new employees a bad impression of Flintridge. Lucy..." She singled out a thin brunette. "Start Ms. O'Halloran on these forms." She tossed out a folder, marched into an inner office and slammed the door.

Although Kat was sure she wasn't intended to see the look shared by the four secretaries, it was hard to miss. She wondered if anyone had ever quit Flintridge on the first day. Technically, *before* the first day. The notion surfaced again before Kat had completed the endless forms. She was favorably impressed by the company's generous insurance benefits and profit-sharing package.

The video she'd been required to see was wasted time. Except that it gave her a rough idea why the workers here needed a recreational program. As in most industrial-line jobs, the work was repetitive and boring. Otherwise, Flintridge appeared to run a tight ship. Watching the company video, she observed little or no camaraderie among the workers as they assembled the big luxury cars.

"I'm finished, Lucy," Kat said when the brunette poked her head back into the room. Checking her watch, Kat was surprised to see the orientation had taken more than three hours.

Lucy led the way to the director's office, where she tapped on the door. "Ms. O'Halloran is finished," she said. "Shall I escort her upstairs?"

"Certainly not." Ms. Nelson hurried to the door and snatched the folder right out of Lucy's hand. "Mr. Kowalski is expecting *me* to deliver Ms. O'Halloran. That will be all." She dismissed the young woman with a wave.

Kat shook her head. Had the director said *Kowalski?* Perhaps it was a common Polish name, like Murphy in her community. Kat might have asked, except she barely managed to keep with Ms. Nelson's brisk stride up nine flights of stairs. Eschewing the elevator was obviously how Ms. Nelson got her exercise. No wonder she didn't feel the company needed a recreation program! By the time the director stopped, Kat found herself standing ankle-deep in mauve carpet before a desk labeled Executive Secretary to the President.

"Mrs. Carmichael, I'd like a word with Mr. Kowalski before you send this employee in." Ms. Nelson's tone bordered on brusque.

Kat watched a smile fade from the face of the attractive silver-haired woman who turned from her computer. "Is that necessary, Wendy? He's very busy, and not in the best of moods."

Getting the feeling her presence would add to the boss's bad mood, Kat drifted out of earshot to where she could study a large painting gracing the far wall. Suddenly the door beside her, one marked Private, flew open and a man in a dark suit almost bowled her over. "Hazel, get me the stats—" The man stopped and refocused. "You!" he exclaimed, staring at Kat.

Any air stored in her lungs lodged there as Kathleen faced the driver from the stranded car. "Mr. Sl-Slater," she stammered. Kat quickly thrust out a hand, then withdrew it when he made no move to take it. A niggling suspicion began to emerge. Today her test jockey looked top-drawer in a navy blue pinstriped suit, white shirt with button-down collar and a striped tie with just a dash of burgundy. A matching handkerchief peeked from his breast pocket, along with a familiar gold pen.

Kat decided she'd underestimated the cost of his haircut the other day. Those precision layers, graduating from tarnished gold to sun-bleached white, were more like fifty bucks a whack.

A person who often laughed when she was nervous, Kat couldn't prevent a giggle from surfacing now. She imagined how he'd glower if he knew how she'd labeled him the other day. Salesman...or test driver. She giggled again.

Stung by her laughter, Slater felt his blood begin to heat. "Slater's my first name," he said tersely. "You never asked for a last, but it's Kowalski." He enunciated each syllable as he stalked toward his secretary's desk.

Kat's jocularity died and she practically swallowed her tongue.

"You two have met?" exclaimed his personnel director and executive secretary in unison. The former recovered first. "But...you said you didn't know *anyone* with a degree in kinesiology," Ms. Nelson accused her boss. "This is the new recreation specialist I hired."

"What?" Slater whirled, raking Kat from head to toe with a horrified look. "She's our *what?*" he repeated.

"Honestly, Slater," his secretary chided. "If you're not careful, you'll end up with a bad heart like your father. Wendy asked do you or don't you know Ms. O'Halloran?"

"Yes," he bit out, then as quickly denied it, "I mean, no...I don't." Brandishing the clipboard, Slater advanced on Kat. "When we met, it was raining cats and dogs. One of whom left muddy paw prints all down a new linen shirt.

Where *is* Brutus?'' he asked, deliberately peering behind Kat.

His audience looked baffled, except for Kat. ''Linen,'' she murmured. ''It figures. Poseidon's at home. But I thought you said he only licked you. I did offer to pay the cleaning bill.'' Smiling sweetly, she added, ''Are you thinking of throwing that clipboard in another one of your tantrums? If so, maybe I'll quit now.''

''I think not.'' Slater flung his free arm toward his personnel director. ''Ms. O'Halloran's folder, please.'' His stormy gaze never left Kat's.

Wendolyn Nelson hugged the manila folder to her breast. ''My second choice for the job was a nice young man from Purdue. He'll have his master's degree in three months. Of course, he wanted more money, and he can't start until July.''

''Just give me the damn folder. If I don't have a recreation specialist on the premises *today,* we can expect an employee riot.''

''But sir... Perhaps we should go through the list of possibilities again.'' Ms. Nelson still clung to Kat's folder.

This time Kat deemed it prudent not to smile.

''That's not necessary, Wendy,'' Slater snapped. ''I'll take over from here.'' He pried the folder out of the woman's hand and motioned Kat into his office with it.

''What stats did you want?'' his secretary called seconds before Slater stalked inside after his unwelcome guest.

He stopped, his eyes clearly puzzled.

Kat enjoyed seeing his blank expression. It proved him human.

''I'll, uh, get back with you on that, Hazel. At the moment, will you send out a staff memo letting everyone know Ms. O'Halloran is on board?''

Kat took the opportunity to give his office a thorough

once-over. Three upholstered wing chairs faced a massive mahogany desk. She didn't know whether or not she should sit or remain standing. After finishing with his secretary, he paced back and forth in front of the desk, flipping through her file. This room was okay, Kat decided, but it wasn't him. There was none of Kowalski's restless energy in the muted plaids of the furniture, the hunter-green walls or the pale gray carpets. He needed vibrant colors. Reds, purples, yellows.

But, she thought, pulling herself up short, his office decor wasn't her business. Instead, she drifted over to look out the bank of windows. My, but he had a beautiful view. Gazing at the complex, Kat realized it was a veritable park. Low, angular buildings nestled discreetly among tall trees. Broad walkways would be perfect for jogging. Maybe he did jog. Perhaps that was what kept him fit. She sneaked a peek at his lithe, narrow-hipped profile. *Nice. Yummy.* Feeling her blood sing in her veins, Kat spun away to explore yet another wall—this one filled with awards.

"So," he suddenly challenged from behind her. "Your father *is* Timothy O'Halloran. Damn. I just knew it."

Kat whipped around. "What does my pop have to do with this job?"

"Nothing. You've listed him as next of kin." Slater sat in the swivel chair and picked up a pencil. Gripping both ends at once, he stared at her; she felt like a bug being studied. "You did phone Dempsey the other night. That's commendable. Frankly, I can't help wondering which of your father's bad traits you've inherited."

Kat's initial sizzle of interest gave way to anger that burned a path to her cheeks. "Now, wait a darn minute! If you're in any way related to Louie Kowalski, you have some nerve bringing up *bad traits*. My pop was a respected electrical engineer at Motorhill up until he met Louie."

"Louie?" Slater's face matched hers shade for shade. "My father is called Lou at the country club, L.J. in board of directors meetings and 'Sir' when he strolls around this complex. *Never* Louie. Or not until he ran afoul of Tim O'Halloran, that is."

This information set Kat back on her heels. Somehow, it wasn't what she'd expected to hear. Now she didn't wait for an invitation but plopped down in one of Slater's wing chairs. "Your father's on the board here?" she whispered.

"He stepped down from the presidency last January." Slater shrugged impatiently. "He's board chairman, just like his father was before him. What *isn't* like my grandfather is the irresponsible way L.J.'s behaved since he met Tim O'Halloran and his hoodlum pals. Instead of good works, he spends his spare time on poker or at the track."

"Seems to be a lot of that going around," Kat said, shaking her head. "If it's any consolation, it's not normal behavior for my pop, either."

Slater drummed his fingers on her manila file. "Regarding the job. I take it you're aware of how I feel about instituting this position in my company?"

"One would have to be the village idiot not to pick up on that." Kat looked away and caught her lip between her teeth. "So…" She worked to get a grip on her cartwheeling emotions. "Did you ever figure out what was wrong with your car?"

Slater straightened. Once again she'd thrown him off balance. Damn, but he couldn't stop looking at her lips.… The CEO in him beat a hasty retreat. As he stared at her, he saw that concern darkened her huge eyes, tugging on his sympathy. Plus, Slater noticed an appealing smatter of freckles across the bridge of her nose. "This is not a social chat we're having, Ms. O'Halloran," he said, attempting to regain control. "Nothing about that car concerns you. Got it?"

Kat scooted forward in her chair but felt her skirt catch. It was a curse of being short; her feet never quite touched the floor when she sat in big, roomy chairs. "Got it," she repeated, her reply sounding a trifle breathless, which might have been partly because his eyes followed the tug of her hands on a ridiculously short skirt. "I work here, but I don't ask questions about the product." She returned his frown. "Makes no sense to me."

"Speaking of your job. Is that your normal work attire?" Almost before the remark was out of Slater's mouth, he cursed himself for saying a word.

Kat laughed. She couldn't help it. The family had coerced her into wearing a suit and he didn't like their choice. "At the resort, I generally wore sweats. Weather permitting, shorts."

"No shorts," Slater sputtered. "This whole notion of play at work is ridiculous. I don't know what possessed the other automakers. It only lengthens the overall workday when you give longer lunches and extra breaks to accommodate recreation. Don't workers want to get home to see their wives and kids anymore?"

"Have you talked to staff at Motorhill? Or plant managers in Detroit? Absence goes down and productivity up where they have recreation programs. I interned at a facility where they started a new program. I can personally vouch that it did make a difference."

Slater declined comment. He leaned back in his chair and steepled his fingers against his lips. "What equipment would you need to get something minimal going?"

Kat was extremely glad she'd climbed out of bed last night to draw up a list. She extracted it from her purse and pushed it across his desk.

As Slater perused it, his straight brows almost met over his nose.

~~Kat chewed her lower lip again and waited for him to~~ throw the list in his wastebasket.

But when he spoke, Slater sounded calm enough. "Space isn't an issue. I've got an empty warehouse and plenty of ground to grade for a ball field. Equipment is something else. I think it's only fair to tell you, Ms. O'Halloran, I have an attorney checking for loopholes in the proposal our workers presented to the board. The minute he finds one, your program is history. Surely you understand my reluctance to invest in equipment."

Kat steepled her fingers in a gesture exactly like his. "Do you work out?" she asked bluntly, knowing he had to in order to remain so lean and trim.

"Every day." He glanced up. "I'd go crazy if I didn't. I don't, however, exercise during work hours. I belong to a twenty-four-hour gym."

"Which costs you two thousand bucks a year. Right?"

He shrugged. "More or less."

"More would be my guess. However, the men and women who work here probably didn't hatch from a long line of CEOs. Surveys show blue collar workers eat too much bread and too few fruits and vegetables. Heading in this morning I passed a score of people who were overweight. Exercise lengthens life. That, Kowalski, is fact. Exercise also sharpens mental acuity."

"I'm not disputing the merits of exercise. I just have more important things to worry about. Like if we don't produce cars around here, those same people won't even have bread on the table."

"Then Flintridge *is* in a financial bind."

"Who told you that?" He catapulted from his chair, smacking both hands flat on the desk.

Kat shrank back into the oversize chair. "I heard there's a rumor to that effect floating around Motorhill."

"Dammit," he swore, slamming her folder closed. "Squelch it," he ordered.

"Me?" She leaned toward him. "I'll admit I have family working at Motorhill. But they didn't start the rumor. And I sure didn't."

He eyed her coldly in what became a fierce glaring match that lasted until his intercom buzzed. Shifting his attention to a console on his desk, Slater flipped a switch. "Yes, Hazel, what is it?"

"Have you forgotten you were meeting...someone for lunch?"

He spared a glance at a wafer-thin watch. "Yes. Is she on the phone?"

The response was affirmative.

"Extend my apologies and tell her to order our salads. I'll have a chicken Caesar." He severed the connection with the confidence of a man assured that whatever he commanded would be done.

Kat stood. It would be a cold day in hell before she ordered any man a salad via secretarial request. Or if she did, he'd be wearing it when he did manage to show up. "Does this conclude our discussion?" she asked. "Or shall I return after lunch?" She led the way to the door.

"Let's resume at three. Meanwhile, I'll have Hazel show you the office I've assigned you. It's directly below on level nine." He opened the door and beckoned his secretary.

"If you ask me," Kat muttered, "you take darn long lunch hours for someone who doesn't approve of recreating on company time."

Hazel Carmichael rushed up to meet them just then, so Kat missed the crimson tide that flowed up Kowalski's neck.

"Take Ms. O'Halloran to room 910 before I get into trouble with the employees for firing her, Hazel. I want her back at three, so please clear my calendar.''

"Very good, sir. Enjoy your lunch with Ms. Bellamy.''

Ms. Bellamy. Kat wondered what *she* did for a living since she had time to lunch all afternoon. The notion of him dallying with some do-nothing socialite while she twiddled her thumbs, sitting around waiting for his instructions, stuck in Kat's craw. Then, disgusted to think she cared what he did and with whom, she swept all images of her arrogant boss aside and dutifully followed his secretary. She didn't envy Mrs. Carmichael having to choreograph Kowalski's love life. It seemed a demeaning task.

"Here we are, dear.'' Mrs. Carmichael unlocked a door. "I didn't know precisely what supplies a recreation specialist might require, so I ordered the usual pens, pencils, tape and such.''

Kat stepped inside. "At the resort, I had a fourth of this space, a host of kayaks, paddles, five bags of assorted sports balls, a desk and two file cabinets.''

The secretary looked horrified. "No one mentioned sports equipment, Ms. O'Halloran. I'm afraid nothing's been ordered.''

"Call me Kat. And don't worry. Kowalski has my equipment list. I would like a roster of personnel, broken out into shifts with lunch and break times, if possible.''

"I'll call Wendy after lunch and tell her you need it first thing in the morning.'' Slater's secretary jotted herself a note.

"Lovely,'' Kat murmured. Just what she needed, another visit with the company fashion plate. Especially since she'd be wearing sweats tomorrow.

Mrs. Carmichael homed in on Kat's remark. "If Wendy gives you trouble, call me. *I'll* collect the list for you.''

Kat smiled. So she hadn't imagined the friction between those two.

The woman suddenly checked a watch hanging from a slender neck chain. ''It's our lunchtime, too, Ms....er, Kat. If you haven't got any plans, you're welcome to join me in the cafeteria.''

''Thank you, I'd love to join you for lunch. Let me stow this packet in the desk and I'll be set to go. Will I need to wear my badge?''

''No need. Oh, I almost forgot, these are your office and building keys. Slater will show you the warehouse and give you that key, I'm sure.''

Kat tucked the key ring in her purse, and tossed the badge into a drawer. The badge that Ms. Nelson considered simply a waste—as she'd announced in a snide voice loud enough for all in her office to hear—because it was only temporary.

''By the way,'' Kat asked as they left the room. ''If it's not telling tales out of school...how stable do *you* think my position is?''

Mrs. Carmichael cast a glance up and down the hall. When it appeared they were alone, she said, ''Tool-and-die workers have asked for it every year since Motorhill developed their program. They offered to take it in lieu of a raise. But maybe you aren't aware that Flintridge is family-owned except for a small amount of common stock. Benefits and wages are board decisions. L.J. was scrupulous about keeping up with union salaries, as was his father. But neither was big on frills. I don't know why everyone assumed Slater would be less conservative.''

''He's not?''

Kat's companion rang for the elevator. ''Product-wise, no.'' The elevator arrived, but it was full. Giving a shake of her head, Hazel fell silent and headed for the stairs.

Kat didn't want to pressure her, but she was sharp enough

to recognize when a plum had been dropped into her lap. She might never lunch with the president's secretary again and there were things she wanted to know.

As they left the building by the back door and started down a tree-lined walkway, Kat murmured, "The landscaping here is beautiful. One of the Kowalskis must have had an appreciation for gardening."

"All of them," Mrs. Carmichael said. "At least, the three I've worked for."

"You worked for Slater's grandfather? You don't look that old."

The woman blushed. "Not as executive secretary. I came here in my twenties. The company was smaller then. That Slater was a people person. He got down in the trenches with his employees. He retired soon after I began."

"Ah. So your boss is named for his grandfather, but isn't like him?"

"Excuse me… but I had the impression you knew Slater already."

Kat glanced up and caught the curiosity in the secretary's gaze. Mrs. Carmichael was doing some digging, too. Kat grinned. "Don't tell him I ratted." She explained how they met, finishing the tale before they reached the cafeteria line. Talk shifted as they selected lunch salads and found seats away from the crowd.

Mrs. Carmichael smiled. "Cars," she said abruptly. "The car vision is something all the Kowalski men are born with. Slater's grandfather was obsessed by the Ridgemont. L.J. poured heart and soul into the Ridgecrest. And now Slater slaves day and night on his dream car. Makes for a poor life, if you ask me. Although no one does."

"Those first two cars were wildly successful," Kat allowed. "But when you say obsessed, where does that leave family? Wives, for instance?"

Mrs. Carmichael didn't say anything for a moment. At last she said, with a twinkle in her eye, "Slater isn't married. Every unattached female employed here envisions herself the next Mrs. Kowalski. The most persistent is Wendy Nelson."

Suddenly Kat saw things more clearly. "Well, you now have one employee who doesn't see herself married to the boss," Kat announced. "But what's wrong with your rumor mill? Don't these ladies know he takes three-hour lunches with Ms. Bellamy?"

"Goodness," Mrs. Carmichael exclaimed, "she is Slater's great-aunt. She's eighty. I call her the dowager CEO. If she had her way, she'd still be chairman of the board. Her father started Flintridge Motors. Bless Slater's heart, the boy lunches with her faithfully once a month. L.J. avoids her at all costs."

Kat pretended interest in her food. She didn't want to hear anything redeeming about the current president of Flintridge Motors.

"Is something wrong?" her lunch partner inquired. "I shouldn't be talking out of turn like this. I don't, usually. You needn't worry that Slater will chase you around the desk. He's a gentleman."

"I'm not interested in his personal traits. I grew up in a family of men obsessed with automobiles. They work for Motorhill." Kat shrugged. "If and when I marry, you'd better believe the man will have hobbies. And he'll have time for me."

"Motorhill?" Kat's companion looked confused. "I heard you'd come to us all the way from the West Coast."

Kat wrinkled her nose. "I did. From Washington State, where I went to escape being pushed down the aisle with a Motorhill accountant. As it turns out, his financing was a little too creative and he now resides in a...shall we say, state-owned facility. After that disaster, my family wisely decided to let me find my own husband.'' Kat didn't see any reason to mention that she'd been called home because of Louie Kowalski. It would only muddy the waters.

''O'Halloran. You're of Irish extraction? That explains your beautiful creamy skin.''

Kat blushed. ''Carmichael. Is it possible you're from the Hill?''

''No.'' The secretary's eyes filled with tears. ''My husband was a fuel scientist at Motorhill. He was killed in a laboratory explosion long ago—before our second anniversary. His parents weren't fond of me. So after he died, I applied for a job here and moved back to this side of the river. I've never returned to the Hill. Too many bad memories.''

''I'm sorry,'' Kat said sincerely. Rivalry between the car companies often extended into private families. ''Do you have children?''

The woman shook her head, blew her nose and began to gather her things.

Kat realized lunch was over, as was her informal chat with Slater's secretary. She felt there was more sadness in Hazel Carmichael's life than had been explored, but very likely the woman would keep it locked inside forever.

''Thanks for taking me under your wing,'' Kat said on the walk back to the administration building. ''The first day is the hardest. I believe I'll go familiarize myself with the policy and procedures manual. See you at three.''

''It's been my pleasure,'' Hazel said. ''You're a refreshing young woman, Kathleen—if I may call you that. In my estimation, Kat doesn't fit you.''

Kat blushed again. Another curse of her fair complexion. ''Pop called me kitten. My brothers switched to Kat because of the way I fought them when I was a kid. See you at three,'' she murmured, hopping out of the lumbering elevator on the ninth floor. As the door closed and Hazel rode on up, Kat recalled that the president at Motorhill had a private lift. His secretary had her own electronic card to operate it. The no-frills policy extended here across the board.

The company's three-inch manual was fairly standard. Kat leafed through it, read certain chapters. When she grew tired of that, she prowled her office and inspected the view from her two windows. Her corner office sat directly below Slater's, so she had a similar view. But her other window faced the river. Kat hadn't realized the river flowed through this industrial park. Her mind flashed to her kayaks. What a good inexpensive way to add to her program.

She made a mental note to look up depth, grade and regulations for running the river at this point. To kill more time, she studied the map of the complex Hazel had given her. Even then, Kat still had an hour on her hands. It wasn't her nature to sit idle. Having gone beyond the shock of discovering that her boss and Louie Kowalski's son were one and the same, Kat was ready to just get on with the job.

By two-thirty she was so bored, she actually resorted to reading the yellow pages in the phone book. Perhaps she'd price some equipment on her own. From what Mary had said the other night, Kat expected to have to fight for space, but it seemed Kowalski was going to be decent about that, at least.

At five minutes to three, she again stood in front of Hazel's desk.

The woman glanced up. ''Hello, Kathleen. My goodness. Is it that late already? The boss is meeting with his chief engineer. I'll tell him you're here.''

''Thank you,'' Kat said. ''Maybe I'll look at your rogues' gallery, if you don't mind.''

"Do. Down that hall, you'll find portraits of our current board members. They were just mounted last week and look very nice."

Kat spent some time studying Adelaide Bellamy and Louis J. Kowalski. Both had kind eyes. She observed that Slater's dad looked almost mischievous, which dragged a reluctant smile from Kat. Somehow, she felt like a traitor to her family. Considering this, she wandered into the reception area again. She had backtracked to very near Slater's office when suddenly his door was thrown open and out burst an energetic man about her own age. His shirtsleeves were rolled above his elbows, exposing muscular forearms. Unable to halt his forward motion, he ran right into Kat. The armload of blueprints he carried went flying.

"Excuse me," she gasped, bending at once to help retrieve the scrolls. "I'm so sorry," she said, even though he was the one who had't been paying attention.

"My fault," he declared, ending with a low-wolf whistle. "And who might you be?" he murmured, slicking a hand through nut-brown hair. "I don't believe we've met."

Straightening, her arms filled with his blueprints, Kat blinked. "I beg your pardon?"

Casually, the man leaned against Slater's door frame.

Almost immediately, Slater appeared behind him. He, too, was in shirtsleeves, and he frowned as his engineer said, "I think I'm in love. Somebody introduce me to this woman."

"Seems to me you have enough woman trouble, Scott, without looking for more," Slater said emphatically. In an obvious move, he stepped between Kat and his engineering chief.

The man holding the blueprints widened his eyes. "Why didn't you say she was private stock, old buddy?" He backed away, but his eyes remained curious.

Kat sucked in an audible breath. "I'm no one's stock.

I'm the new recreation specialist at Flintridge,'' she said firmly, stepping around Slater to shove the blueprints she'd rescued into Scott's arms.

"Why were you lurking outside my door?" Slater demanded, again insinuating himself between the two.

"I wasn't lurking." Kat was quick to defend herself. "I was looking at pictures. This man—uh, Scott, flew out the door and…and…" She realized her voice had risen and a group that stepped off the elevator had ears perked. She clamped down on the O'Halloran temper.

Slater dismissed his engineer with a word. He ushered Kat inside his office and forcefully shut the door. "I knew hiring you would be trouble," he said, pushing down his shirtsleeves, fumbling to replace gold cuff links lying loose in a tray on his desk.

Kat fumed silently over the unfair assessment, watching him take his suit jacket off the back of the chair and shrug into it.

"I did nothing," she said tightly. "And your…that poor engineer was just indulging in a bit of harmless flirting. Which, I might add, I would have handled without your help."

"Scott Wishynski is neither poor nor harmless. I pay him top dollar, which he spends on a wife and miscellaneous girlfriends scattered throughout the complex." Slater's eyes roamed over her. "Frankly, I wouldn't have considered you his type."

Kat leaned on his desk and yelled, "Whatever type that is, I'm definitely not it!"

"That's what I said. Scott and I generally agree on looks. Redheads, mostly. The difference is…I don't condone cheating *or* dating anyone on staff. In your position, where you'll be dealing with a lot of men, I suggest you adopt *my* policy, Ms. O'Halloran. Now, shall we get started on your tour?''

His lecture fueled a blaze of temper Kat found hard to control. She longed to wipe that smirk right off his face. Except that he really hadn't said anything she could dispute. Still, he needn't think he could dictate how she conducted her personal life. ''You're the boss at work. But I'll do as I please on *my* time,'' she said, stepping aside to let him pass. Then she had to run to keep up. Slater's longer legs carried him quickly through the corridors, when they'd left the elevator, along the walkway. Kat was definitely not used to shoes with heels.

''I have some bad news,'' he said when they arrived at an open arena mounded with mud. ''That last storm soaked the ground. My grader got stuck today. We won't be able to clear this field for your ball diamond. Not for a few weeks.''

''More than one ball diamond, right?'' Kat asked.

''Isn't one enough?''

''You employ both men and women.''

''I didn't realize ball fields were like rest rooms, where codes require his and hers.''

Kat arched a brow. ''I assumed you'd want to run women's teams and men's teams simultaneously, like they do at Motorhill.''

Slater thrust his hands in his pants pockets and ignored her jab. ''The warehouse I earmarked for your use is there.'' He pointed to a flat-roofed building out in the middle of nowhere.

''I'd hoped for a more central site.''

''Look, it's empty. Take it or leave it.''

''You're being deliberately difficult, Mr. Kowalski,'' Kat said. ''People who work in the south end of the complex, which I might point out is *most* of your staff, couldn't get here in time to use the facility on a regular break.'' She pulled a creased map of the sprawling complex out of her pocket and unfolded it. "What about this building?" She pointed to one in the very center. "I understand it's also empty.''

"At the moment, yes. It's also surrounded by restricted design labs. Would you mind telling me how you knew it was vacant?''

The wary expression on his face reminded Kat of what her brother had said about Louie Kowalski maybe tapping Pop's brain. Were they testing Motorhill's techniques in one of those labs? Was that why Slater wanted her out of reach? Well, Kat sure wasn't going to tell him Hazel had suggested that building. "Are you making some areas off limits to me?'' she asked aggressively.

He frowned down into her eyes without answering. The low-hanging clouds suddenly started to spit rain, and Slater gripped her elbow to guide her back to the path. "I wasn't aware until today that my new recreation specialist had so many family ties at Motorhill. I do expect loyalty from my employees.''

"Loyalty or blind obedience?'' Kat asked. "There is a difference.''

"Loyalty…'' A whistle blared three short blasts just then, cutting off whatever else he might have said.

"Loyalty is earned, Mr. Kowalski. I assume that whistle means it's quitting time. Will that be all, or am I now officially on overtime?''

Slater dismissed her with a curt nod.

Kat spun and marched off toward the parking lot.

In a foul mood now, Slater strode in the opposite direction through intensifying rain. It seemed he was destined to get his suits soaked when dealing with that woman. And yet, he thought nastily, a cloudburst was minor compared to all the other things he found irritating about his newest employee. Her sassy mouth, pixie grin and legs far too long for a woman who couldn't be over five foot two... Those complaints headed a list that ended with the fact that her name was O'Halloran.

CHAPTER THREE

"WHAT IN BLAZES do you think you're doing now?" a deep voice bellowed.

Kat went rigid at a sound that had plagued her all week. Her perch at the top of a twelve-foot ladder was precarious enough without her nuisance of a boss shaking the metal frame. "Don't come up," she warned. "I only have one bolt connected so far. Do you want this backboard to fall?"

"To hell with the backboard! I don't want *you* to fall. I'll ask once more—*what are you doing?* I pay maintenance men to handle chores like this."

Kat ignored him, drilled a second hole and inserted a long screw that would help hold the board steady.

"Well?" he demanded.

"They're backlogged," she said patiently. "By the time I submitted a request in triplicate and it went through the process, I'd have my teams practicing already."

"If you don't kill yourself first. Get down here." His tone did not invite refusal.

The drill squealed again. Leaning away from the ladder, Kat shoved a Molly screw through the last hole, then wrenched it tight.

"Now!" Slater roared. "I want to see your feet on this floor."

Kat rolled her eyes. "Brother," she muttered under her breath, although she did move down a couple of steps. "Shouldn't you be bugging a team of combustion engineers or something, instead of me?'' she asked, carefully drilling two holes in succession along the bottom edge, effectively blocking out his retort.

"What's that?'' she called as she set the last two screws. "You say they've solved the fuel-injection problem on the Special? Wonderful!''

"I said get your carcass down here ASAP or I'm coming after you.'' He placed one foot on the lowest rung.

Kat gave the board a final shake and determined it was solid. She glanced down, then deliberately dropped the small drill, guiding the cord through her hands until it dangled about six inches from the floor. "Oops,'' she said as Slater dodged off the ladder. "Sorr-ee,'' she called, tongue in cheek. She knew exactly how far it came to striking him. Not even close.

"Give me that thing, and be careful.'' He snatched the drill at the same time, bending to unplug the cord. "You're dangerous, Ms. O'Halloran.''

Kat pocketed the last screws and started down.

Slater began wrapping the cord around the handle, never taking his eyes from the faded denim stretched tight across her nicely rounded derriere. He held his breath, fearing the fabric might split from the rhythmic sway of her descent. As she drew closer he observed a small hole under her right back pocket. At eye level, it offered him a tantalizing glimpse of red. Silk, he thought. A shiver ricocheted through Slater's body and slammed into his abdomen with the force of jet propulsion. It didn't help his overloaded circuits that she took the last two steps in a single leap and landed, grinning at him over her shoulder through impish eyes.

Slater grappled with his self-control. "Did you know you have a hole in those jeans?''

"Hey, don't break the drill cord, Kowalski.'' She ripped

the drill out of his hands and loosened the cord, missing the way his jaw tightened.

"The boards look great, don't they?" She tilted her head back and surveyed her handiwork. "You play basketball?"

Having forced himself to concentrate on the short, feathery haircut, which he had the worst urge to touch, Slater was slower to track her gaze to the boards. "Which brings up another point," he said. "I don't recall having authorized the purchase of any equipment."

Kat laughed, a pleasant ripple echoing from the rafters in the big empty warehouse. "You didn't. They were donated."

"Donated? By whom?"

Bending, Kat returned the drill to its case. "Actually, if you must know, I midnight-requisitioned one from my folks' courtyard. No one uses it since my brothers moved out. Spud Mallory came by while I was dismantling it and said I could have the one attached to his garage. His boys are grown, too."

"Are we talking Spud Mallory as in the cigar-smoking gambler who fleeces my father weekly in those ridiculous poker games?"

"My Pop and Spud played poker for years," she said angrily, "and never bet a dime until Louie came on the scene and upped the ante."

Slater loosely bracketed his hips with his hands. "I told you not to call my father Louie. And how did you come by the preposterous notion that it was *his* idea to play for money? Especially as he's so incredibly inept that he always loses."

"A lot you know." Kat matched his stance. "Spud told *me* Louie always wins."

Slater digested this tidbit. Stepping back, he massaged his neck and worried his upper lip with his bottom teeth. "I'm getting my information from our housekeeper. Helen's like family. Why would she lie?''

"Why would Spud? He's known me since I was in diapers.''

"Maybe he's protecting *your* dad. How did the subject come up?''

Kat stared at him for several seconds before she turned and gave her attention to collapsing the ladder. It wouldn't do to let him know her family was worried.

He stepped up to help. ''There's a possibility I'm right, isn't there? You're not sure of your facts, are you? Furthermore, I don't think you're any happier about the situation than I am.''

Kat's fingers curled around the cool metal of the ladder. ''You've got that right. My pop didn't do any wacky things before he met yours. I intend to find out exactly what's going on.'' She grabbed the drill case, shouldered the ladder and started for the door.

"How do you plan to get at the truth?'' Hurrying to catch up, Slater relieved her of both items. Outside, he fell into step beside her.

"Spud's garage has an attic, which is accessible from a huge hawthorn tree. My brothers and the Mallory boys used to sneak up there to drink beer. I'll just check out their next poker party myself.''

"Tell me when and where.''

"I prefer to go alone,'' Kat informed him primly. ''I'll let you know what I discover.''

"What makes you think I'd believe your version any more than I believe Mallory's?''

Kat yanked the ladder from his hands, and the drill. Her eyes glittered. ''Would it surprise you to hear that I don't give a tinker's damn what you think? Why don't you go play with your cars, and take Louie with you?'' Having vented the frustration he caused simply by hanging around, Kat stalked off toward Maintenance.

Three young men dashed from the maintenance building. They vied good-naturedly for the right to help Kat. The minute they spied Slater, all three stopped dead.

Conscious of his position, Slater clamped down the urge to order them back to work. He should be the one to help her, dammit. Then again, she probably wouldn't welcome his help. She barely tolerated him in her *vicinity*. Resigned to this circumstance, Slater gave his men curt nods and strode with purpose into an adjacent lab—as if his intent had been to visit his engineers all along.

Kathleen O'Halloran annoyed him. What did he care that she had big eyes and wore red silk beneath those tomboy clothes? And just what the hell made her think he needed *her* permission to check out that poker party? He was perfectly capable of finding Spud Mallory's house on his own.

THE WEEK WAS EXHAUSTING for Kat. All day Friday, she dreamed of doing nothing more strenuous than going home to soak in a hot bathtub. Tuesday, she'd set up teams and started basketball practice, calling on dormant muscles in the process. Then, because the weather hadn't improved and the rain kept them inside, she also borrowed her brothers' old boxing gloves and set up a ring at one end of the warehouse.

Kat had no doubt the men were testing her when they demanded instruction in using the gloves. She had little choice but to comply. It was one of the few times Kowalski hadn't shown up to bug her from the sidelines. Too bad. She was a fair boxer and wouldn't have minded going a few rounds with him. Especially after Wednesday, when a group of women apparently complained to him that she was doing more for the men. He jumped right on that accusation with both feet, insisting she provide something for the women pronto.

A volleyball net was the one piece of equipment he'd authorized her to buy. But there wasn't one to be found in Flintridge. Kat had scrounged the neighborhood for another donation. After finding one, she spent late nights mending it, installing it and working out schedules fair to everyone.

By the time the five o'clock whistle blew signaling the end of her week, Kat's entire body hurt from physical exertion and her neck ached from the stress of dealing with Slater Kowalski. Oh, he was clever, Kat would give him that. He popped into the warehouse at odd hours, smiling that crooked little smile, asking the employees in his sneaky, subtle way if they thought she was doing a good job. Or at least that was the way it sounded to Kat.

The single women out in the ranks soon discovered that complaining about her was a surefire way to get a few minutes alone with their handsome boss. Each time one of them cried on his shoulder, Slater made a point of suggesting Kat put forth more effort to get along. She wanted to scream, or hit him.

She should make the effort! Really! On the drive home Friday, Kat entertained visions of subjecting him to all manner of medieval tortures.

At dinner Pop mentioned that he'd be leaving soon for his poker party at Spud's; until then, it had completely slipped Kat's mind that she'd planned to spy on the group. "Why don't you cancel?" she implored. "We haven't had a moment to discuss my new job. Maybe later we could rent a video and make popcorn like old times."

Her father paused with his fork halfway to his mouth. "I can't do that, kitten. Friday night is poker night."

Mrs. O'Halloran rose abruptly and started banging dishes around near the sink.

Kat sighed, kissing her dream of a soothing bath goodbye. "I haven't played poker since I left here. Maybe I'll tag along. How much money does a person need to crash this game?" She sent her dad a smile. The kind of smile that had always worked with him before.

He looked uncomfortable. Kat knew perfectly well he wasn't in the habit of refusing her anything. She'd begun to taste triumph when he muttered, "Stay home and keep your mother company, kitten. The game is just for regulars. Besides, you should spend your money on pretty dresses that'll attract a husband. Not on cards."

His wife snorted. "Shouldn't we all."

"Since when haven't you been able to go out and buy clothing anytime you wanted, Maureen?" Timothy clambered to his feet and threw down his napkin. Digging a wallet out of his back pocket, he peeled off several bills and dropped them on the table. "You ladies go shopping. Be my guest. Don't wait up, I'll be late tonight."

The moment the door closed on his heels, Kat's mother burst into tears. Kat was so mad at Pop, she wanted to shake him. "Mom, call Dodie Moran. Take Pop up on his offer. Buy yourself a new dress. It'll make you feel better."

The sniffles slowed. "And just where would I be wearin' a new dress, Katie? When Timothy only goes out with the men?"

"To church, Mama. You and Pop still go to church together."

That seemed to give her mother pause for thought. "Will you come shopping, Katie? He left enough money for two dresses."

Kat glanced away. She hated lying. "I'm really bushed, Mama. First week on a new job and all. Call Dodie. Frankly, I need an evening alone to unwind."

"Well, if you're sure..." Maureen O'Halloran reached

for the telephone. Soon, she was preparing to meet her friend at the mall.

Kat escorted her to the door. "Shop till you drop, Mama. Then you and Dodie treat yourselves to a relaxing glass of wine at O'Toole's."

"Oh, we couldn't. It wouldn't be seemly."

Kat delivered a swift hug. "Sauce for the gander is sauce for the goose. This is a new millennium, Mama. Live a little. I don't want to see you home until eleven. Do you hear?"

A small frown etched her mother's forehead, but she nodded. Kat shut the door and slumped against it. She figured that gave her until ten, at least, to check out this poker game. Kat knew her mother well. She'd never sit in a bar, not even a high-class place like O'Toole's, for more than one glass of wine. Two, max, if Dodie was persuasive.

Kat hurried to load the dishwasher, then went upstairs to dress in black jeans and a black turtleneck. She didn't want any neighbors to see her climbing that tree and call the cops. On her way past the bathroom, she gave the tub a last, longing look.

She parked her Trooper in the lot at the corner grocery store and walked the few blocks to Spud's. Her vehicle still had Washington plates and was pretty distinctive. Typical of her recent luck, halfway to his house it started to rain. Cursing men in general, she hunched her shoulders and jogged the last few blocks. Kat huddled beneath a dripping tree across from the Mallory home and checked out the cars lining the drive. Bridie Mallory's new little Motorhill compact was gone. Kat knew Mrs. Mallory's car because when she'd come by the other day to pick up the backboard, Spud had bragged about the engine he'd help design.

Buzz Moran still had the same car he'd driven three years ago, and Kat recognized Luke Sheehan's sports car. He'd picked her father up for the races on Sunday. Kat had listened to her mother expound for twenty minutes on how those men were all going to hell for patronizing the track on Sundays. That left only the black sedan parked parallel to the house unaccounted for. It didn't take a detective to figure out the luxury car belonged to Louie Kowalski.

As Kat slipped around back and gazed up at the spreading branches of Mallory's old hawthorn tree, she felt more like a small-time hood than a righteous daughter. She considered canceling her plans—until she recalled her mother's tears. Before her courage gave way, Kat jumped to catch the lowest branch. She stifled a groan at the effort it cost her already-aching arms to swing herself aloft and straddle the branch as her brothers had done when they were kids.

"Ouch," she yelped without thinking as a thorny branch snagged her arm. "Damn and blast." It felt as if she'd drawn blood. Kat scrambled to a thicker limb and stopped to check. There was a gaping hole in the sleeve of her favorite sweater. She shouldn't have yelled so loudly, but it had hurt as well as surprised her.

Josh had never mentioned the tree had three-inch thorns. Obviously one reason it served so effectively as a smuggling route. What parent would figure a kid was dumb enough to risk getting stabbed for a snitched beer or two?

Since no one roared out of the garage to investigate the noise, Kat edged up several levels toward a bough that scraped the house. The windowsill was within her grasp when a second thorn gouged her cheek. This time she swore roundly, trusting her voice would be muffled.

No one was more shocked than Kat when an arm snaked out of the attic window, grasped her by the belt of her jeans and jerked her into a black hole. Her assailant immediately clamped a hand over her mouth, cutting off not only Kat's muffled cry but her breath, as well.

She flailed her arms and kicked backward, twice connecting with solid flesh.

"Oof. Stop it, you little spitfire," a low voice hissed in her ear.

Kat went stiff as a board. She knew that voice. *Slater Kowalski*. How humiliating. Identifiable now in the faint light seeping in around a trapdoor that led to the garage, he dangled her a foot off a rough plank floor.

Kat jammed an elbow sharply in Slater's ribs, doing her level best to bite his fingers.

"Ugh!" His breath exploded in a hiss, causing him to release her so fast she hit the floor like a sack of flour. "Shh," he muttered, dropping down on his knees beside her. "Do you want them to hear you?"

"Me? What are you doing here, Kowalski?" she demanded with as much force as she could convey in a whisper, considering that they were both trying to be quiet. "Where do you get off manhandling me?"

He silenced her by pressing a finger to her lips, then he nodded his head toward the square door that sat propped ajar.

Only then did Kat register how loud the music and male laughter was that drifted up from the converted garage.

Abruptly, Slater moved his fingers to her chin and angled her face into the flicker of light. "You're bleeding. What happened?" His voice was rough. His fingers gentle.

Kat jerked her head aside to keep him from seeing. There he sat in his Polo coordinates—bone-dry and not a mark on him—while she was wet and looked, no doubt, like she'd come out last in a cat fight.

Slater tried again to see her face.

"Mind your own business," she said, dodging his fingers. He would have insisted, but all at once there was a lull in the Sinatra song and he heard his father say, "Timothy, you're unusually quiet tonight."

Kat's father answered in a lower tone that sent the two eavesdroppers crawling close to the trapdoor. "I had a hard time getting out of the house," Timothy said. "It took a chunk of my stash to throw Maureen offtrack. I sent her shopping."

Buzz Moran snorted. "Since this whole scheme was your bright idea, Timmy, 'tis a fine thing, you shelling out our profits in an attack of conscience."

Lying side-by-side on the floor above the poker players, Slater felt Kat pull away. He started to nudge her, to claim victory...before he saw the quiver in her lower lip.

A huge tear slipped to the curve of her cheek and she quickly brushed it away.

Slater didn't know which affected him more, witnessing the demise of the fierce faith she held in her old man, or the realization that he was the last person she'd want to see her crumble.

For some reason, he was moved by her attempt to keep a stiff upper lip. Without a word, he cupped a palm around the back of her head and gently guided her face into the protective curve of his shoulder. For one strained heartbeat, he waited for her backlash. When it didn't come, Slater began to massage the nape of her neck. Her skin felt soft and cool. Her perfume wafted up and tickled his nose.

Instinct told Kat to resist overtures from a man who belonged to the enemy camp. But darn it all, this had been such a miserable day. So had the whole week, for that matter. She'd give him this much; he had tranquilizing hands. Warm hands... She hadn't thought anything could chase away her bone-deep chill.

Perhaps her suddenly rapid heartbeat was just a belated reaction to being yanked into Mallory's attic, Kat told herself. Perhaps it had nothing to with the man…or with her father. She'd embrace any excuse to keep from admitting that the father she'd placed on a pedestal for twenty-six years had just tumbled.

It made her shudder to think about the number of people counting on her to put the pieces back together. Her brothers. Their wives. Most of all, her mother.

Slater felt her tremble. His fingers flexed in her soft curls. Why had he ever thought her hair lacked feminine qualities? Damp, those charcoal locks clung to his palm, reminding him of satin. He murmured something unintelligible near her ear and trailed soothing kisses along the curve of her cheek. "It'll be all right, kitten."

Kat pushed him away. Eyes wide, she crawled out of his reach. "Who gave you permission to call me that?" She shook her head and scraped back clinging strands of hair still warm from his touch. Closing her eyes, Kat regretted showing him any chink in her armor.

Slater frowned. *Had* he called her kitten? Maybe he had. Come to think of it, this was the first time he'd seen those tiger claws sheathed. "Obviously a gross mistake on my part, O'Halloran," he muttered. "It won't happen again." His words were barely audible. He felt restless, ready to leave. He had the answer he'd sought. The smoke from Spud Mallory's cigars was starting to make him sick. "I'm outta here," he said, heading for the window.

Kat pulled her knees to her chest and hunched her shoulders, massaging her upper arms. "Go. I'm waiting out the rain."

He couldn't just leave her like this. Sighing, Slater leaned toward her and extended a hand. "Come on," he said, "it's over."

Again the music ended. Nat King Cole's "Black Magic" this time. In the lull, Buzz Moran's voice rose above the others. "I swear, Louie, you win every pot. With your luck, we should ship you off to Atlantic City with all our remaining cash."

Slater's dad laughed. "Good idea. But why don't we all go? I'm free anytime. It's you guys who need permission." Much male posturing followed his statement, with all the others also claiming freedom.

"I can go anytime," bragged Tim O'Halloran. "I'll tell Maureen I'm working on the church carnival. In fact, there it is, if anyone needs an excuse."

"When shall we go?" Louie badgered.

Several dates were bandied about before the music blared again, blocking whatever date they'd selected from the two listening upstairs.

Kat uncoiled from her position near the door. She tendered Slater an I-told-you-so look.

He avoided her eyes. Damn, why hadn't he left sooner? Before L.J. made a fool of himself. Slater would rather not have known about those wins, to say nothing of the proposed gambling trip. Because it meant he had to find time to deal with that issue now. Time better spent solving the car's fuel-injection problems. He crossed to stand beneath the peaked roof and tucked both hands in his back pockets. Well, now they were even. But so help him, if she rubbed it in, if she smirked or laughed he'd—

Far from rubbing salt in his wounds, Kat's gaze suddenly became understanding.

It wasn't pity. That would have allowed Slater to simply walk away. Damn. He felt again as he had when he was a teenager and his boat had been cut adrift in a storm-tossed river. Hurriedly burying that particular bad memory, he extended his hand to Kat again. "Come on, tiger, I'll buy you a drink. I think we both need one."

She shut the trapdoor fully, forgetting it was their only

source of light. Kat gasped as the attic was plunged into darkness.

Slater materialized out of nowhere to grip her arm. He intended to lead the way to the window. It wasn't his fault he picked the arm lacerated by the thorn.

Cringing, Kat cried out involuntarily.

"What's wrong?" he hissed. But by then Slater's probing fingers had found the rent in her sleeve. Skimming lightly, he explored the torn flesh beneath.

"Stop it," Kat breathed, fighting a stab of need that sprang from his touch. "I got in a fight with the tree, okay? Score is hawthorn two, O'Halloran zero."

Slater chuckled.

"Go ahead, laugh." She backed away. "And then let's go before we're caught."

Not normally prone to wild mood swings, he took pride in keeping a cool head. Therefore, he couldn't imagine what craziness provoked him to fracture his own rule about never romantically involving himself with an employee. Shocking them both, he slid his hands through Kathleen's short curls, tipped her head back and kissed her.

Kat could almost feel the steam rising from her still-damp clothes. A kiss from Kowalski was the last thing she'd expected. Furthermore, she never would have imagined he'd be so good at it.

Out of nowhere, it seemed, flashes of light filled the interior of the room. Thunder boomed and shook the rafters. Kat's heart leaped and pounded in tempo. It was as if her knees refused to support her, and several seconds went by before she realized Slater had pulled away and said something fairly benign about the ferocity of the storm.

Kat heard him open the window. A sudden gust of wind cooled her hot face. It was precisely what she needed to plunge her back into reality. The return of sanity enabled her to shake off his mind-numbing kiss. Climbing out on the window ledge unaided, she leaped onto a rain-slicked branch.

Kat told herself that she'd known all along it was the storm and not his kiss setting off all those fireworks in the room. But when her knees gave way and she slipped and would have fallen had he not been there, she revised her thinking and gave credit where credit was due. Kowalski kissed like he did everything else—with complete control, but with purpose.

What that purpose might be in this instance evaded her. She just knew he'd better not try anything like that after she got her feet safely on the ground, or Mr. CEO of Flintridge would be picking himself up in the next county.

Slater felt the change in her. He knew it was because of that unexpected kiss. Yet if she'd asked point-blank why he'd done it, he couldn't have explained to save his life. He hated the fact that he'd broken his own rule. But he'd be damned if he'd apologize.

On the ground, Slater found he didn't trust himself to talk or to touch her until they were both well away from the Mallorys' property. Once they'd walked some distance he exhaled and placed his hand in what he thought was an impersonal gesture beneath Kathleen's elbow. He didn't see her Isuzu, and his car was down the block.

She slapped his hand away. "Hands off, Kowalski, or…"

His grip tightened. "I thought we were going for a drink. You may enjoy hiking in the rain, O'Halloran. I prefer to drive and stay dry."

Kat hadn't realized she'd steeled herself for his apology until it didn't come. And she was at a loss to explain why she felt furious with him for acting so blasé about what had gone on between them upstairs.

"I don't drink, but if I did, you'd be the last person I'd

drink with. I'm going home. To map out a plan to save my pop from sure disaster. I suggest you do the same. Kowalskis may be able to afford an attempt to break the bank in Atlantic City. O'Hallorans can't." Leaving him standing in the rain, Kat crossed the street and started jogging in the opposite direction, in spite of the fact that her cold muscles objected.

Slater shivered as rain seeped through his shirt. Where the hell was she going? Hadn't that father of hers warned her how dangerous it was for a woman to be walking the streets at night? Even in a company town like Flintridge? She'd turned the corner before he realized she meant business. Swearing, he dashed to his car and promptly made a U-turn to go find her.

Pulling alongside Kat midway down the block, Slater rolled down his window. "Enough, O'Halloran. I propose a truce. I don't want it on my conscience if you get pneumonia, or worse, if you get murdered."

"Murdered? By whom? I know almost everyone who lives on the Hill." Kat forced a laugh. Laughing proved to be a mistake. It broke her stride, and the muscles in her right calf seized. She fell instantly to her knees.

Slater was out of his car in a flash. "What happened? Did you trip? I swear, you are the most accident-prone female I've ever met."

That did it! Kat struggled to stand. Only, her leg refused to cooperate. All she could do was fight back angry tears when he picked her up and carried her to his car. She found her voice after he'd stripped off her sneaker and started massaging her foot. "Don't. It…it's a charley horse in my calf. Give me a minute. It'll ease on its own."

"Where's your house? I'll drive you there."

"My Trooper's at the grocery store." Then as pain shot

up her leg, she grudgingly relented. "I suppose you could give me a lift there."

Slater had a sarcastic retort on the tip of his tongue, but curbed it as they passed beneath a street lamp and he saw she was still hurting. Not only that, the welt on her cheek looked red and angry. "I'll follow you home. You can invite me in for coffee," he ordered. Then his voice grew gentle, "I'll tend the scrapes left by that tree."

Kat caught sight of the clock in his dashboard. "No, you can't come in," she said, urgently shaking her head. "It's nearly ten."

He smiled. "Do you turn into a pumpkin at ten?"

That brought the first break in tension since their kiss. Kat's lips curved upward. "My mother's due home at ten. She hasn't the foggiest idea I'm out playing Sherlock Holmes. Give me a rain check on the coffee, please?"

Before Slater could say it always rained when she was around, she directed him into the parking lot at the grocery store.

His heart shot into high gear for no reason at all that he could ascertain as she climbed from his car and limped swiftly to her own. Dynamite came in small packages. Damn, but the woman intrigued him.

Slater drifted in behind her vehicle. He followed at a discreet distance as she zigzagged through the dark residential area that made up the Hill's territory. It was just as well things had worked out the way they had, he thought, nervously rubbing his neck. She was nothing like the women he normally found attractive. For crying out loud! Didn't he have enough problems in his life without deliberately soliciting more?

So why did he hold his breath until he saw her safely inside a sprawling, well-kept house? And why, all the way home, did he plot strategies that involved joining forces with her to save their two fathers from calamity?

What most haunted Slater after he got home and climbed into bed was that damned kiss. He'd certainly kissed less difficult women. Women who'd grown up in the bosom of his community. The only thing his mother had asked of him, before she slipped into a coma from which she'd never emerged, was that her only son marry a nice woman who'd embrace Polish traditions.

Unable to sleep, Slater rose. He poured himself a stiff shot of brandy, and by the time his father sneaked in through the front door at one-fifteen, Slater sat quietly in one corner of the library, reading a book on Ireland's customs.

ACROSS TOWN, Kat O'Halloran feigned sleep when her mother peeked in at eleven. Yet she was still awake watching shadows dance on her ceiling when Pop strolled in at one. At 3:00 a.m., for about the hundredth time, Kat plumped her pillow and covered her head. She resented Poseidon's snoozing so easily at her feet.

"Monday," she groused, "I'm going to march straight into Slater Kowalski's office and resign."

At four o'clock, Kat got up and rubbed more salve on her cuts. "Yes. Resign is the smart thing to do. We're worlds apart," she told her ravaged reflection in the mirror. "We have nothing in common." Kat imagined the furor among her brothers and their wives if she were to date someone from the Ridge. Under the circumstance, resigning was the only choice. No kiss had ever interrupted her sleep before. Nor had any kiss ever left her longing like this. Longing for more of the same...

CHAPTER FOUR

BY SATURDAY MORNING, Kat thought the scratches on her face and arms had faded. She didn't expect anyone to notice them and was alarmed when both parents expressed concern. She mumbled something innocuous about how it had happened when she had sorted old sporting equipment stored in the attic. They accepted her story. Too quickly, Kat decided.

Her parents seemed vaguely preoccupied—a fact that concerned Kat more than the injuries resulting from her encounter with Spud's tree.

The most emotion she'd seen either parent exhibit throughout the day occurred after Kat had wheedled her mother into modeling the dress she'd bought. Pop happened to pass the bedroom, and Kat couldn't fault his response. His eyes lit up, and the kiss he laid on his wife was enough to make a grown daughter blush.

It reminded Kat of Slater's kiss. A memory so real, she left her parents in their clinch and dashed upstairs to revise the resignation letter she had drafted around midnight.

Much later, they'd barely sat down to dinner when Slater phoned. "I intended to call earlier," he said. "But I got tied up running tests on the Special. How's the leg, and your cuts?"

Kat recognized his polite boss-to-employee voice. He sounded distracted, as if he had other things on his mind. His car, no doubt. Obviously *he* hadn't spent time mooning over their kiss. "I'm fine." She kept her response brief and to the point. "You're interrupting dinner, Kowalski. Is an update on my health all you needed?"

"By all means, go eat. I'd hate to stand in the way of your putting meat on those scrawny bones."

Kat sputtered indignantly as Slater clicked off.

"Is everything all right, Katie?" her mother called into the hall.

"Fine," she snapped without elaborating. If the elder O'Hallorans suspected the call was to blame for her moodiness, they let it go. Tim declined dessert. He took off to meet his pals, not offering any excuse for leaving Kat and her mother to spend another solitary evening.

By Sunday, Kat had made up her mind to discuss her resignation with her brothers and their wives. Maureen had planned a family dinner as usual. "Count me out," Timothy announced. "I have a meeting of the church carnival committee. We're considering some changes this year. All improvements—you'll see," he said in an offhand way.

Kat gazed at him suspiciously. Now she'd be distrustful of everything Pop said.

Rightly so. As he passed his sons on their way into the house after church, Tim caught Mark's arm. "Keep an eye on your mama and sister next week, son. My carnival committee's going to Atlantic City to check out new games for our booths," he said evenly, as if his words had nothing to do with the circle of shocked faces. Of course, everyone except Kat was floored by his announcement. But she could tell this wasn't an ideal time to discuss her resignation from Flintridge.

"It's Louie Kowalski's fault," Mark ranted after Timothy climbed into his car. "Why else would Pop's carnival committee entertain the notion of using gaming tables? That man is a bad influence all the way around."

Kat poured coffee and held her tongue, even though she alone knew Mark's statement to be true. Yet it bothered her that Pop hadn't acted guilty. Right before he took off, he'd kissed Mama with gusto—as if nothing was wrong.

Josh turned to Kat, his tone reproachful. "Mama said Louie's son is CEO at Flintridge and that you report directly to him. At Motorhill, our rec director reports to Internal Affairs. I tell you, this is a setup to bleed Pop's mind."

"Kowalski did not recruit me, Josh. Your own wife sent me the job notice."

Josh drummed his fingers on the table. They all studied the spouse under discussion as she helped her mother-in-law place dinner on the table.

Matt's wife unloaded two apple pies she'd baked. "Josh, you can't mean you think Louie Junior would really do something so underhanded? They've been in business as long as Motorhill."

"Slater," Kat corrected. "He's not a Junior."

No one paid attention as Matt continued. "I believe Junior would do anything to save his butt with the company." Matt waited as they all bowed their heads and his brother Mark gave the blessing, then he picked up where he'd left off. "Friday, a car buff who works at Flintridge came by for his headers. He happened to mention Kowalski's flawed engine. I gather it may cost the company a government contract. Major flaw," Matt reiterated, raising a brow. "And a *big* contract."

Mark whistled through his teeth. "Well, it's a cinch a family can't hang on to an auto empire in this day and age by being nice guys. I'll bet they're all tough nuts."

Kat recalled Slater's sympathy and his tender touch that night in Spud's garage. But of course she couldn't bring *that* up to her brothers.

Josh's scowl enveloped the entire clan. "Tough nuts or

not, somebody has to shake Kowalski's family tree. I'll bet dollars to doughnuts Pop's not going to Atlantic City just for the committee. Kowalski probably dreamed this up. What if Pop gambles away his whole retirement fund? Someone has to stop him.''

All at once Maureen, who sat at the head of the table, jumped to her feet, let out a sob and fled the room.

Josh's wife, Mary, ever the placater, followed close behind.

"Dammit!" Mark vaulted from his chair. "Pop never used to be a fool. Kat, you've gotta do something.''

"Me? Like what? I told you, Pop ignores me.'' Flustered, she fed a piece of meat from her plate to Poseidon. He wolfed it down and begged for more. Distracted, Kat stroked his ears.

"Mother O'Halloran has locked herself in the bedroom," Mary announced, as she returned to the dining room. She, too, appealed to Kat. "Your father may ignore you, but you're in a position at Flintridge to hear things. Workers talk. You'll know if Kowalski is pilfering ideas.''

"I tell you, no. I can't do it.'' Kat glanced desperately at her brothers. "I think Pop's going through some male crisis. A postretirement thing. One of you should deal with him, man to man.''

Matt stood and paced around the table. "You've always been his favorite, kitten. Mary's right. You're our best bet.'' Bending, he dropped a kiss on Kat's nose. "I'll go talk to Mama. She shouldn't put her life on hold just because Pop's being an old fool.''

During the time Matt was upstairs, Mark and Josh bombarded Kat with suggestions on how she should go about spying on Kowalski at the plant. She couldn't say she was unhappy to see them pile into their cars and leave.

Kat cleared the table, covered the pies, and then coaxed

Poseidon out for a brisk run. A light, cooling rain not only cleared the air but also her head. She would've liked to spend more time outside, but Poseidon kept slowing and shooting her insulted looks until she turned home.

Back at the house, all of Kat's attempts to cheer her mother failed.

"I'm sorry, Katie, but I'm not good company. I'm going to bed."

"Sure. G'night, Mama." Her heart heavy, Kat took the dog for another walk, a quick one. She toweled dry her hair and Poseidon's fur before turning out all the lights—including the one on the porch. "Let Pop stumble around in the dark tonight. If he breaks a toe, it'll serve him right."

"Men!" she later grumbled around her loaded toothbrush. "Why do women always have to do their dirty work? Answer me that, Poseidon," she gurgled as she rinsed her mouth. "My brothers don't want to step on Pop's toes, but apparently it's okay if I do. That's why this mess got dumped in my lap. Suddenly they've forgotten all about telling me I could leave that job anytime I wanted."

Taking his sharp bark as agreement, Kat threw herself full-length on the bed and unfolded her resignation letter. "Who'll this family get to be their spy when I waltz into Kowalski's office tomorrow and quit?"

This time the dog remained silent. He lay curled on his rug, his eyes closed.

MONDAY, AT EIGHT SHARP, Kat trudged up the nine flights of steps leading to the Flintridge executive suites. Her mind freewheeled over the scene she'd left at home. Pop, bustling around the stove making pancakes and small talk, as if he hadn't ruined Sunday dinner. How could he miss Mama's red, puffy eyes? Sighing, Kat charged up the last two flights. And what about Mama? She exhibited a textbook case of passive aggression, if ever Kat had read of one in beginning psychology.

~~Josh should have been there to witness how many times~~ Pop said things about the church carnival. The man didn't expect his family to doubt his word. After all, Mama, too, devoted countless hours to organizing food for the carnival. The only thing that drew a bigger crowd from the Hill was a Murphy wake.

Kat considered visiting Father Hanrahan. But that would be like airing the family's dirty laundry in public. Something O'Hallorans didn't do. She hoped the frown she'd given Pop on her way out today let her errant father know *she* wasn't buying his hypocrisy. That thought was where Kat ran out of stairs.

She entered the reception area and Hazel turned, a perfunctory smile on her lips. "Kathleen," she exclaimed, the smile now genuine. She reached for an appointment book. "You're not on today's calendar. Did you book directly with his nibs? As usual, he forgot to tell me."

"No. I, ah, something came up over the weekend. Is he in?"

The gray head bobbed. "Poor boy has been here all weekend poring over engine blueprints. The Special left him stranded again. I hope you bring good tidings." She aimed a worried look at the door marked Private.

Kat fingered the long white envelope containing her resignation, and flushed. "I...guess this can wait." Folding the letter, she slipped it into the back pocket of her jeans. "So the motor's still cutting out?" For reasons not quite clear, Kat really hoped Matt's rumor was wrong. She'd hate to see Slater lose that contract.

"More than cutting out. I overheard Scott say the fuel's hanging up in the translator conversion system. Melted one of the aluminum cams. Yesterday they installed a new microprocessor and recalibrated the algorithms—if that tells you anything.'' She rolled her eyes

Kat did understand, but she shrugged it off. ''Think I'll stick to flying kites. That's the activity I scheduled for today.''

''You amaze me. Last week a group in the cafeteria were saying you planned to teach kayaking.''

''Um…later probably. When the river's not so high.''

''Oh. Well, I'm keeping you from your kite-flying.'' Hazel reached for the phone's intercom.

''Hazel, leave the boss to his flow valves and combustion chambers.'' Kat backed away. She ran lightly down the single flight of stairs to her office. What did it matter if she quit today or tomorrow? Luckily, she hadn't left the kites at home.

It occurred to her that Matt had been right about Slater's engine problems. Maybe she should stay on awhile and do a bit of sleuthing. She'd certainly have the opportunity. Scott Wishynski, Slater's buddy and chief engineer, showed up for every sport. He remained an unregenerate flirt, and that made him the most likely candidate to let something slip. Kat didn't care to become part of the rumors floating around Scott, however. Not that he'd put any obvious moves on her—yet. And it stood to reason that if anyone knew whether Pop was being used as a sounding board, it'd be the Special's primary engineer.

After the cold war at her house this morning, Kat had fewer qualms about pumping Scott. Tucking away the idea for future use, she made multiple trips out to her Isuzu to unload a colorful array of state-of-the-art kites. Sport models, stunt kites and parafoils in the shapes of stars, dragons and shields.

Thankfully the wind was perfect. Kat stuffed the lesson sheets she'd typed into a box of spools. While stringing cord for her morning class, she'd rehearsed how to deal with the ribbing she'd get from the macho machinists.

Kat grinned. She'd heard all the excuses before. A favorite was referring to kite flying as child's play. Wait'll these men discovered how much strength it took to fly these babies.

Flying conditions were perfect inside the inner courtyard. The grassy slopes offered the ideal site for liftoff. Plus, the area was free of power lines.

Approaching her SUV for a last load, the very person Kat hoped to see suddenly materialized. "Hey, Scott." She sidestepped the arm he would have put around her waist. "Lend me your brawn."

"Everything I have is yours, baby. Brawn, brain and..." Scott leered suggestively.

Oh, brother! The family had better appreciate her efforts.

"Hey, cool," Scott said when Kat popped the canopy and thrust a large winged glider into his arms. "Wow! When you tell a guy to go fly a kite, you mean it."

Kat laughed. In spite of his insufferable attitude, Scott's teasing manner made superficial interaction easy—as opposed to Slater's raw masculinity, which caused Kat anxiety if he so much as got within shouting distance.

"The trick," she said, "is for a woman to pick sports that keep a man's hands occupied." She started off with her load of kites, hoping her not-so-subtle message would sink in. Scott was forever touching her and Kat didn't like it.

"Ah." He caught up, apparently unfazed. "We'll see if that holds true for kayaking. Think I'll sit aft. If I happen to drop my paddle, it'd leave both of my hands free." He switched the kite to his other hand and hooked an arm around her neck.

"Don't even joke about it, Scott. Kayaking in white water takes total concentration. And...both hands on the paddle," she added sternly. "How is it you have so much free time when the others have to pick and choose which sports to participate in?" she asked, hoping to redirect the conversation. "I heard the Special's engine is causing fits again. I would've thought you'd be working overtime."

Scott shrugged as he placed the kite he carried on the grass beside the others. He crowded Kat while she spaced reels of nylon filament equal distances apart. "Slater's uptight about nothing. I told him all along it's a simple matter of flow adjustment. We'll get it fixed before the bodies roll off the line."

"Really?" Kat tested the direction of the wind, then felt her heart speed as it did each time one of her colorful kites caught the right puff of wind and soared aloft. "So you're saying the engine's really all right?"

"Yep." Looking smug, Scott stepped close. He casually slid his arms around Kat's torso and tried capturing her hands.

"Stop it, Scott. Do you want to learn to fly kites or not?"

He nodded.

Assuming he'd said all he was going to about the engine, and seeing others from her class gathering, Kat quickly explained the process to Scott, then gave him the controls. She wouldn't make a scene here, but Kat fully intended to have a talk with Mr. Wishynski about keeping his hands to himself.

Soon she had a dozen or more kites floating in blustery March skies above Flintridge Motor's rolling green hills. Not one man razzed her or made a negative remark. They all wanted a turn.

SEATED IN HIS TENTH-FLOOR office at a table piled high with dog-eared blueprints, Slater Kowalski folded a schematic that showed the Special's dual-flow fuel system and rose to refill his coffee cup.

If only he could be sure they'd corrected the problem this time, he thought, rubbing his tired eyes. Bright-colored spots appeared the moment he took his hands away. Slater peered out his corner window. *Gray skies.* Last time he'd looked, it'd been dark and drizzling. When was that? Sunday morning—or night?

Yawning, he ran a hand over his stubbled jaw. Lordy, but he was tired. Suddenly, he blinked, then squinted at another barrage of color that made him think his eyes were playing tricks.

"Kites," he whispered aloud, pressing his nose to the glass. Below he could see what looked to be the majority of his workforce dotting the landscape. Faces upturned, they gawked. Clumps of workers stood outside nearly every building. So who the devil was minding the store? What in hell was going on?

Slater's foggy brain still wrestled with whys and wherefores when the telephone on his desk shrilled. His private line. More trouble with the Special? He'd told Hazel to hold all calls except those concerning the engine. He left the window long enough to hit the speakerphone button and bark out his standard "Kowalski here." Yet even as the instrument crackled with static, he was on his way back to check out the kites that dived and swooped at dizzying speeds.

"Yo, Kowalski," a hollow voice intoned. "If kites are your idea of secret fuel for that revolutionary car, man, I hate to tell you, but you're fulla hot air."

Slater registered loud guffaws in the background before the voice taunted again. "You Ridge guys lost it? Newsroom phones are ringing off the hook here. Thought I'd warn you. I'm on my way with a cameraman."

Slater recognized the voice then. Under the best of circumstances he disliked the know-it-all local reporter. Today, especially, he didn't respond well to snide innuendo. Suddenly blood pounded in Slater's ears. He'd just isolated the source of his problem. *Kathleen O'Halloran.* There she stood, smack dab in the thick of the kite fliers. And she had on those damned raggedy, threadbare jeans that drove him wild. The faded ones with the tantalizing hole under the back pocket. Even from this distance he recognized them. This time she'd paired them with an eye-popping red blouse. He should have known she'd be at the bottom of this fiasco.

Slater knew he had to be careful what he told this jerk about his new recreation specialist. "Come off it, Henderson. You, of all people, should recognize sport. Or have you forgotten whipping my rank and file into a frenzy by writing a column on perks that Motorhill had and Flintridge lacked? It's not me keeping the old feud alive!"

Not waiting for a reply, Slater cut him off and sprinted for the door. Art Henderson had been the biggest pain in his neck a few months back. It griped Slater to be in the limelight again. He had vowed the next time he made news in Flintridge, it'd be when he unveiled the first Special as it rolled off the line.

Dammit. What had made him assume that after Friday, Kat would be on his side? The enthusiastic way she'd responded to his kiss? Obviously that hadn't meant much.

As he loped past Hazel Carmichael's computer station, she turned from a side window where she stood. "Aren't Kathleen's kites exciting?" she called. "That must've been what she came to discuss with you this morning."

He skidded to a halt. "She was here? When?"

"Early. Such a thoughtful girl. The minute I mentioned you'd been cooped up in the office all weekend, she decided not to bother you."

"Next time, bother me," he said tersely, dashing a hand haphazardly through already-rumpled hair as he jabbed the elevator button three times in succession. When it didn't come fast enough to suit him, he clattered down the stairs.

On the third-floor landing, Slater ran into Wendy Nelson on her way up. "My phone hasn't stopped ringing," she said breathlessly. "You simply will not believe what that…that O'Halloran woman has done now. Boxing wasn't bad enough." Slater's personnel director shoved a fistful of pink messages beneath his nose. "Kites. In our courtyard."

Shrugging, he continued down the next flight of steps.

Doggedly, Wendy followed, catching up to him on the ground floor. "People all over town are laughing. I certainly hope you intend to fire her."

Her statement came as a shock. Bursting through the double doors, Slater's steps faltered. Frankly, he hadn't thought that far ahead—which was quite unlike him. He always insisted things being well-planned and orderly. And that was why this wild, blood-pumping attraction he felt for his impulsive recreation director made no sense. No sense at all.

Annoyed to have been influenced by one kiss, Slater elbowed his way through the onlookers. He'd put an end to her nonsense this very minute. He'd make a polite request, clear the field, then send everybody back to work. He was the boss after all. Belatedly trying to look like one, Slater thrust out his jaw, buttoned the top button of a wrinkled white shirt and tried to tame a disreputable tie. He stalked up Kat's knoll, prepared to set her straight. It might have worked had he not stopped to admire the way she handled her stunt flier, sending it into a screaming power dive.

During that brief delay, Scott Wishynski's kite collided midair with Kat's. Both kites stalled, fluttered, then nosedived into the ground.

Slater frowned at what he judged an altogether unnecessary display of groping between the two participants who fell at his feet—enmeshed in a tangle of nylon lines and fitful laughter.

Unreasonable anger hurled out of nowhere to race like wildfire along Slater's thinly stretched nerves. "Enough of this sideshow," he bellowed, flapping an arm at those left holding kites. "Reel those damn things in and all of you get back to work."

Having had quite a bellyful of the couple still writhing on the ground, Slater reached down and yanked both participants to their feet. His fingers tightened around Kat's slender arm as he turned his full wrath on her. "Stop this damned charade!"

Kat's face flamed instantly. Surely *he* knew she'd been trying to get untangled. Scott, with his superior strength, had taken advantage of the situation. But before she said something she'd regret later, Kat jerked from Slater's hold and bent to the task of separating a tangle of cord. Scott *had* been out of line, but she would have dealt with him on her own terms. Certainly neither of them deserved this public humiliation. She listened to Kowalski's lecture for as long as her Irish temper would allow.

"Is it me personally or my program you're shredding?" Her jaw matched Slater's. "You sure don't act like a CEO trying to hold up his end of the bargain."

Slater turned his back on her and ordered Scott and the others back to work. Then he rounded on Kat. "How *should* I act, Ms. O'Halloran?" The softness of his words held a sharp edge. "Considering I've just been told by the press that your damned kites have made my company a laughingstock all over town. Perhaps you'd rather I invited them to do a feature story on your orgy with Wishynski on the lawn?"

"Orgy?" Kat began, then winced from the contempt in

his eyes. Backing down, she cast a furtive glance around for a camera. She identified only a couple of dozen malingering employees. Burly machinists shouted support. There weren't many women. Those who hung around Kat recognized as dissidents, hoping she'd get her comeuppance no doubt. Wendy Nelson looked positively smug.

"All right," Kat said, mustering what dignity she could. "Then I imagine you'll be relieved to see this." With shaking fingers, she dug the crumpled envelope out of her pocket and shoved it against Slater's chest. "My resignation," she said. Pride squared her shoulders as she walked into the brisk wind blowing off the river. She didn't even realize that was where she'd headed. Her goal was to put distance between herself and Slater Kowalski.

Kat hadn't gone far when she realized blame for the collision did belong to her. Winner of five national kite-flying championships, she should've been paying more attention and keeping an eye on Scott's kite. Still, it irritated her to see how quickly Slater turned a simple accident into something sordid.

The more she walked the worse she felt. The men, in particular, really liked her program. By resigning, she wasn't punishing Slater; she was punishing *them*. As for Slater, he'd be kicking his heels in the air.

SLATER GAZED AT HER retreating form for a long moment. Then he ripped open and read the letter that had first blown from his hand. He'd had to run to catch it. Her prim resignation was like a punch he hadn't anticipated, and it left him reeling.

But, Slater's attention was immediately claimed by workers shouting that he had no right to fire Kat. "We want her program, or we'll all quit."

"Take it easy." He stepped between Wendy Nelson and

a loud spokesperson. ''No one's been fired,'' he cautioned just as the reporter and his crew arrived.

''Same thing. You made her quit,'' argued a grizzled tool-and-die man.

Tempers flared again. The men involved in the kite adventure crowded him as Slater held up both hands in an effort to gain control. Several claimed they hadn't had such fun in years. Those who hadn't flown the kites now demanded equal time.

Slater passed a hand over his unshaven jaw. What troubled him most about Kat's resignation was that it had Friday's date. Friday, which stood out so vividly in his mind. At least, their kiss did. She must have written this as soon as she arrived home. Did that suggest Kat had judged *his* conduct unbecoming?

He stared at a sea of angry faces, feeling suddenly at fault. He, who preached religiously against office relationships, had come on like a jealous fool. But recognizing the truth didn't mean he was ready to explain to the world. Suffice it to say he might have handled things differently had he not been exhausted from spending the weekend with blueprints. ''Lack of sleep,'' he said with a pained laugh. ''I let this get out of hand. Nothing's going to change.''

Everyone except Wendy seemed appeased. She tried to speak to him again about the young man who had yet to finish his master's. Slater shook his head.

''I'll rectify this matter myself.'' He made a show of tearing Kat's resignation in half. ''You men collect the kites and store them. I'll square things with Ms. O'Halloran.''

''Grovel,'' one of the paint specialists told him.

''I do that well. Had a lot of practice dealing with the board.'' Slater felt guilty when the crew broke into a boisterous rendition of ''For He's a Jolly Good Fellow.'' He wasn't at all. If it was left up to him, he'd have accepted

Kat's resignation, for no other reason than his peace of mind. Instead, he followed the direction she'd taken. Immersed in figuring out what he'd say, Slater didn't realize how close he was to the property line until he caught a whiff of the river.

Crowning the last rise, he stared down on Kat as she climbed into a flimsy-looking kayak. Slater's heart dropped to his toes. "No. Wait!" he shouted, forcing leaden legs into a dead run.

Kat thought she heard someone call. Pausing, she shaded her eyes against a thin shaft of belated sunlight. *What did he want?* To throw her off Flintridge property?

"What in holy hell do you think you're doing?" His breathing was labored from the run. It helped only marginally to loosen his tie and the top button on his shirt.

Kat tapped her wristwatch. "You'll get the two weeks' work I promised in my resignation. Right now it's lunchtime. I'm taking my hour in a relaxing run downriver."

"No," he said, grimly, "You're not!"

"Says who?" They faced off like two boxers.

Slater couldn't bring himself to explain how his best friend had been swept from a canoe a whole lot sturdier than this pip-squeak craft of hers. Jerry Gelecki drowned in a deep whirlpool around the first river bend the summer they'd both graduated from college. It was enough that Slater recalled the agonizing details—which included how he'd almost lost his own life in a failed rescue attempt. No, he just couldn't talk about it.

Donning the stoic mask he wore each time he visited Jerry's mother, Slater calmly grabbed the lift toggle on the curl of Kat's kayak and hauled her, boat and all, back on land.

Surprised, Kat looked for something in his face beyond male arrogance. Seeing nothing in the chilly blue eyes other than a determination to have things his way, she reacted as she would with her brothers. After all, she'd spent years combating their testosterone-driven aggression. Adept at disarming Mark, Matt and Josh with a quiescent smile, she flashed Slater one of her very best.

He immediately relaxed his hold on the kayak.

The moment he did, Kat dug her toes under the footrest, jumped into the well and, with the flat end of her paddle, shoved off.

It all happened so fast, Slater stood on the shore, helpless to do anything but watch her bob into the center of the swift water. His stomach churned. "No!"

Full of herself, Kat tossed a careless wave. But when Slater plunged into the muddy water well over the tops of his Italian loafers, she laughed nervously. "Honestly, it's too cold for swimming, Kowalski."

He ran along the water's edge, ignoring the backwash lapping at the cuffs of his wool slacks. "Come back, you idiot. You haven't the slightest idea what you're doing!"

"*Idiot?* Really? For the past three years, I've taught kayaking in rougher water than this."

His progress was brought to a halt by a granite cliff. He couldn't begin to articulate how he felt watching her disappear around the curve—the very spot which had ended Jerry's life.

Kat's willowy body was like a twig compared to Jerry's oak-solid frame. To say nothing of Slater's own superior strength, which had given out too soon on that terrible day.

Scrambling to the top of the rock, he tried one last time to call her back. "Don't do this, Kat! I've come to talk to you about staying on as recreation director."

Busy setting her course, she shook her head—meaning she couldn't hear what he was saying.

Slater held his breath until she passed the deep and fateful eddy. He turned up his collar against the sharp bite of the wind and remained motionless until she became a dot in the distance. Even then, he couldn't make himself leave. The rest of the world ceased to exist for some twenty-five minutes, according to his precision watch. That was when she reappeared in the distance, allowing Slater's stomach to unclench.

He didn't question the joy he experienced when she succeeded in paddling around the whirlpool without incident. Neither did he stop to think that she might misinterpret his motive for staying.

Totally unaware of another presence on the beach, Kat gasped when Slater erupted out of nowhere, dragged her bobbing kayak ashore, and raised her out of the Fiberglas cockpit into a massive bear hug.

The orange life jacket flattened her breasts as Slater clasped her tight and swung her around in circles. "Don't ever scare me like that again," he said raggedly. "I want you back. The crew…we…all want you."

She struggled to get her feet on the ground—and to breathe. His rough cheek felt cold against hers. "Slater…" She pushed at his solid chest. "What is it with you?" She tried to get a look at his face, but he'd buried his lips in her hair.

"All of this just to keep the recreation program intact?" she teased once he'd finally set her down and held her at arm's length.

"Just the basics," he said, his eyes darkening as they roamed her face. "I'll endorse baseball, volleyball and basketball. Maybe even boxing. No kayaking." In his earnestness, Slater's fingers bit deep into her upper arms.

Any pleasure Kat might have derived from his lusty greeting vanished. "What do you mean?" She wrenched from his hold. "I *teach* kayaking. The employees want to learn."

She stripped off her life jacket and threw it aside. "Besides..." She pulled the one-man craft up next to several others she'd off-loaded here last week. "I already have the lessons built into my schedule."

"Unbuild them. I'll send Maintenance down to carry the boats back to your Trooper."

Kat thought the trace of desperation she heard in his voice might stem from a fear of the unknown. She herself had a healthy respect for the sport and certainly didn't regard anxiety as a weakness. In fact, she'd dealt with larger men than Slater who were afraid.

Wanting to put him at ease, she placed a hand on his tense forearm. "I'd be happy to set aside time on weekends to teach you. I understand why you'd feel that in your position, you can't very well turn up in classes for employees."

Her failure to comprehend the danger froze Slater's heart. "You are as irresponsible as your father," he railed, throwing up his hands. "Hear this, Kathleen—there will be *no* kayak lessons."

"But...but...but..." She couldn't seem to finish her protest. His eyes and voice had turned so wintry.

"Excuse me, I have work to do. It's after one. And you're still on the payroll for eight hours a day."

Kat's eyes narrowed as he walked away. Her hands balled at her hips. "Ooh, you...you officious jerk!" she shouted. The retort rolled off his broad shoulders.

A sudden gust of wind struck her from behind. Kat uncoiled her fingers and rubbed at a peppering of goose bumps along arms that still tingled from his touch.

She dallied, putting away her life jacket, until she was sure she wouldn't catch up to him on the path. His response was typical of someone who'd never tried kayaking. But could she really blame him for wanting to show he was boss? After the way she'd tossed that resignation at him in front of his crew, he probably felt a need to throw his weight around, she thought as she reached her office.

Given time, she could bring him around. Kat stood by the window, gazing out at the river. She knew he'd love the sport if she could convince him to go just once. Kat rubbed away a frown. Considering his current troubles, it was understandable why he'd be testy. He was dealing with his engine problems and probably hadn't even heard that her pop and his had set a date for their trip to Atlantic City.

Hazel said Slater had spent all weekend at the office.

Well, what if she killed two birds with one stone, as that unpleasant saying had it, and helped him out in the process? Since her family had put her in charge of Pop, Slater would probably be happy to let her handle the two sixty-year-old delinquents. Somehow she'd stop them from making fools of themselves.

Grinning, Kat sank into her chair and put her feet up on the desk. Kowalski would be so relieved to have one problem off his plate, she was sure she could talk him into changing his mind about her kayaking program.

CHAPTER FIVE

SCOTT WALKED INTO the makeshift gym after work with three men from the maintenance crew. They were there for intramural basketball tryouts. Scott broke away from the others and hurried over to speak with Kat.

"John told me Slater requested a crew to move your kayaks off the river." He gestured toward the lanky foreman who now dug through Kat's playpen full of basketballs. "I asked John to hold off for a few days. I told him Slater will cool down and forget he ever said anything."

Kat bounced the basketball she held twice before shoving it under her arm. "I thought I might talk him into changing his mind. But I don't mind carting the boats home for the time being."

"That's dumb. Leave them there. Have John and the guys hide them in that stand of trees. They should be out of sight, anyway. It'll keep the kids who sometimes play along the river from stealing them."

"Do you really think it's all right?"

"Absolutely."

Kat felt a little guilty, but on the other hand, these men knew Slater better than she did. Scott, especially. They'd worked closely together on the engine design.

As if reading her mind, the young engineer said, "Right now cost overruns are driving Slater crazy. He'll be a different man once the lines are up and running."

"Of course you're right, Scott." Kat's tight muscles unkinked and she smiled. "Okay, guys. Time to play ball." Kat tossed Scott the ball, hard enough to make him wince. "Line up at the free throw. Let me see your stuff."

She filled her clipboard with names and performance notes before she called a halt and locked up the building for the night.

THE NEXT EVENING, at her second set of tryouts, several additional players showed up. Five newcomers, a team unto themselves, all from the graveyard shift. One of them, the most gregarious, apologized for missing the first tryout. "Our job is to convert the tooling plant to meet specs on the Special's custom space-age engine. Yesterday we came in early and stayed late to iron out a glitch in the system."

Kat already knew that up to now, Flintridge had produced and installed standard Wankel engines in all their earlier luxury cars. Basically the same engine Motorhill used, only with more horsepower.

"You men always work grave?" She tapped a pen on her chin. "I'd planned to start practice and ultimately games at five-thirty. That won't be a problem?"

"We play ball every afternoon at the YMCA now."

"Then I'd be stealing you from another team?" Kat frowned at the crew, two of whom topped six feet.

"We're itching to take on Motorhill. How long before you schedule us some real competition?"

"Motorhill has a regular gymnasium," Kat said, trying to be gentle.

"So?"

"In case you didn't notice, we're playing in a warehouse. I store my basketballs in a cast-off playpen. Inviting Motorhill's teams here to play would get us laughed off the planet."

"When's Kowalski gonna build a gym?" asked the most intense of the five.

Kat didn't feel it was her place to tell them that as far as Slater was concerned, the entire recreation program was temporary at best.

Good thing, too. The great man himself heaved out of the shadows so fast, Kat wondered how long he'd been standing there. Scott Wishynski sauntered along beside his boss. Scott had obviously gone home and changed clothes. Slater had not.

He looked so serious, Kat racked her brain trying to recall if she'd said anything to earn her another reprimand. *Not unless he'd found out she hadn't taken her kayaks home.* As he headed straight for her, Kat figured she'd soon find out.

"Buster, Derek." Slater greeted two of the players as he strode into their midst. "I plan to visit your crew tonight. How's the conversion coming?"

"Slow, big guy. Slow." Derek stared out from under permanently sleepy eyelids. "You heard that five cases of half-inch driveshafts disappeared. Not much we can do to finish the conveyor carousel till they surface."

"Dammit, how can five cases that size disappear? They may be only half an inch in diameter, but those suckers are twenty feet long. The wooden cartons they're packed in need a forklift to move them."

"Yep." Buster scratched a grizzled beard. "We pulled the invoice. Len checked 'em in two weeks ago. Banks and Smitty remember bringing in a crane to unload the delivery truck. I reckon they'll turn up. Just a matter of when."

Slater's expression turned to one of disgust.

He punched a finger in the air. "I'm not buying the idea that five crates just got misplaced. Too many shipments have conveniently gone missing lately. I'll be by tonight and we will check every nook and cranny until they're found."

"You're the boss. Seems like a lot of funny stuff's been happenin' all right," put in a man who'd introduced himself to Kat as Travis. "It's gotta be coincidence. Why would anybody who works for Flintridge wanna slow down a project that feeds their paycheck?"

As if realizing for the first time that Kat's interest had risen, Slater clammed up. "I'd like a private word with Ms. O'Halloran," he announced.

Scott stepped around Slater and scooped the ball from beneath Kat's arm. "You two talk away. I'll just warm up. I know I'm late, but I'll still make the team, won't I, teach?" He aimed a cocky grin at Kat.

She frowned down at her watch as the men from the night shift tossed their basketballs into the playpen and headed for the door. "Don't run off," she called a shade frantically. She'd heard enough stories about the lecherous engineer not to want to be stuck here alone while he got in his practice time. "Counting Scott, you're even up. Let's see a little three on three. Shirts and skins. And don't hold back." She blew her whistle shrilly, making Slater wince.

The men obediently trotted back. Travis and Derek, who both had beautiful ebony skin, unselfconsciously stripped off their shirts. Scott had already pulled off his Polo. While Scott exhibited plenty of muscles and a tan—probably the work of a salon—he had zero chest hair. Kat liked men with nicely dusted pectorals. As she wrote their names shakily on her clipboard, she realized she'd been speculating about how her boss would look sans shirt. She didn't suppose he'd do a striptease to assuage her curiosity. The thought made her grin.

"What are you smiling at?" he asked suspiciously.

"Tsk, tsk. Do you dislike basketball, too?" She moved to where she could watch the skirmish under the hoop.

"I like basketball—when it's not taking my workers'

minds off their jobs. Jobs, I might add, that keep food on their tables and a roof over their heads."

Kat clasped the clipboard to her chest. "Because you run shifts around the clock, seven days a week, does that mean you expect to own one hundred percent of their time?"

"I didn't come here to argue."

"Why *did* you come?"

"My father called to say he's going to Atlantic City. With, and I quote, 'Tim and the gang.'" His clear eyes grew stormy at the mention of Kat's dad.

"I know." Kat rubbed at her temple with the hand holding the pen. She accidentally slashed a blue mark along her cheek. "In fact, I'd planned to drop by your office in the next few days to discuss what to do about it."

"Do? What can we do? They're all of gambling age." Hardly aware of what he was doing, he rubbed at the mark on her face, but only succeeded in smearing it as she jerked back.

"Stop. Is my face dirty?"

He gestured toward the pen. "Ink. You can wash it later. What were you about to propose we do?"

"Not we. I. I want to follow them. If it embarrasses them enough, maybe they'll quit and go home. Before my pop gambles away all his hard-earned retirement funds. Not that money's a big issue where *your* dad's concerned."

"It certainly is. From the time my great grandfather made his first dime in Flintridge, our family has invested generously in philanthropy to the Polish community. How would it look if my father squandered that legacy at the gaming tables?"

"All God's children got troubles," Kat said sarcastically.

"This one didn't until his father hooked up with your old man."

"Look, Kowalski, sniping at each other won't solve anything."

Slater thrust his hands in his pockets. "Much as it pains me to agree with you, O'Halloran, you're right."

A smile twitched impatiently at the corners of Kat's lips. "There, that really wasn't so hard, was it?"

He grinned the devastating grin that always had Kat puddling like a snowball set before an open fire. "I guess not." Tucking his chin against his chest, Slater gazed at her from beneath indecently long eyelashes. "You have a plan, I assume, dear Watson? Embarrass them how?"

Kat laughed wickedly. The teams stopped playing and stared at the couple. Scott broke away and jogged over. He'd worked up a sweat and was breathing hard.

"Hey, coach. We don't appreciate busting our butts struttin' our stuff while you trade jokes with the boss. At least call a recess and let us in on the fun."

Kat shook her clipboard under his nose. "I know exactly how the six of you are stacking up. The shirts drew first blood. They're leading eleven to four. You've tried three shots from the pocket and Derek blocked them all. You've turned the ball over twice and Travis once, trying to grandstand. Neither one of you is a team player, but you'll both be adequate if you ever quit trying to hog the show."

Scott's dark eyes clouded ominously. "Guys like Travis and me have played street ball since we were kids. Maybe rules are different on the Hill," he all but snarled.

Kat realized at once that she shouldn't have taken him to task in front of Slater. "It's more a difference between court rules and street rules, Scott," she said patiently. "Street players usually have rough edges to hone. But don't worry, you'll all get to play. I'll post team lists on the gym door next Friday. We'll start practice a week from Monday," she said loudly enough to carry to the other men. "After I see how the teams shake out, we'll work up intramural games. If all goes well, I'll see about playing some of the other automakers' teams.''

Buster, who'd joined them, turned to the others. ''Tryouts are over, dudes. We all made the cut. Shirt up and let's go to my house for a bowl of *bigos*. Mom and Marianne cooked up enough to feed an army.'' He tossed the basketball in the pen, turned and punched Slater on the arm. ''Wanna come? Best *bigos* in the world.''

''Thanks, it's tempting, but I have some adjustments to oversee on the Special's engine. Ask Marianne and Nona to make some for the festival next month.''

''Will do. Hey, coach, invite's open to you, too.''

Kat shook her head. ''I'm late leaving as it is. I have a dog that'll be gnawing holes in the rugs if I don't get home and feed him.''

As the men trooped out amid much joviality, with only Scott lingering, Kat muttered to Slater, ''What is *bigos?*''

He chuckled. ''Practically the Polish national dish. Hunter's stew is the American name. Sauerkraut, mushroom, ham, sausage, stockpot combination. The old-time stuff like Buster's mom and wife make is almost better reheated. Catch up with him and ask him to bring you a portion for lunch tomorrow.''

''That's okay. I'd hate for him to come in early on my account. If there's a Polish festival next month, maybe I'll go and eat some there. I've never been to one.''

''You *should* go. The Monday after Easter everybody on the Ridge sort of whoops it up after Lent. In the old country, people celebrate at home. Godparents take small presents to godchildren. Generally it would be a lazy day filled with visiting friends, sharing meals and so on. Here the church serves as a central meeting place. Various groups operate food booths and provide games for the kids. The money we collect helps the church minister to the poor. I'm surprised you haven't ever been. We don't advertise, but outsiders smell the food and they show up. I don't mind so much now, because I realize the church needs money. As a kid it used to bother me when strangers horned in."

"Why? You don't strike me as ever having been an introvert."

His eyes sparked mischief. "Oh, I was definitely an extrovert. That's why I didn't like opening the festival to outsiders. It meant our parents put the kibosh on high-spirited kids celebrating Smingus Dyngus."

Kat shook her head. "I'm not familiar with that, either."

"Then I don't think I'll enlighten you," he teased.

She walked over and opened the outer door before shutting off the lights. She hadn't realized it, but Scott must have tired of waiting. "You may as well clue me in, Kowalski. You've piqued my curiosity. I'll run by the library and read up on…how do you spell it…Smingus Dyngus?"

"Oh, ho! See, you're already hooked." He followed her outside and watched her lock up. "All right, then. If you're going to pout."

"I'm not pouting. I never pout."

"Do, too. But I'll take pity on you all the same. The loose definition is, Monday-morning pouring of water. More specifically, you try to catch friends off guard and splash them with water. Balconies, stairwells, trees, rooftops are great hiding places. Boys, especially, get pretty inventive. How would you like to be wearing your best Easter dress and have someone pop out of hiding, shout 'Smingus Dyngus,' and douse you with a bucket of water?"

"No. Not an entire bucket. You wouldn't be so mean."

"We were. I had friends who threw their sisters into bathtubs full of water. All in jest, of course."

"Of course. Now, if you were Irish, you'd blame it on

the leprechaun.'' They glanced sideways at each other and started laughing. "I should have asked Buster to bring me *bigos* tomorrow. Not on your life will I attend your festival now.''

"That's what I was trying to tell you. Smingus Dyngus is off limits during the festival. Because of all the visitors who aren't familiar with the custom.''

"You think I trust *your* word?'' A dimple winked in Kat's left cheek.

Slater placed a hand over his heart. "You wound me, Irish rose.''

He sounded so sincere, Kat sucked in a sharp breath. "Kidding aside,'' she said suddenly. "It's getting awfully late. Before we meandered off track, I was going to suggest I tag after our fathers. The fact that they won't be able to shake me will be embarrassing. I might even lay on a few comments where others can hear—about leaving ten hungry kids at home or something. What I need you to do is tell everyone here that I went to Detroit to buy athletic equipment. I'll need two days. Three, max.''

Slater looked amused. "You switch gears faster than a synchronized sports car.''

"You were the first to digress. I didn't bring up Smingus Dyngus.''

"True. But I hate making snap decisions. Let me think about your idea overnight. Stop by my office at lunch tomorrow, and I'll have an answer.''

"All right.'' Kat dug out the keys to her SUV. "Well, goodnight. I hope you find your lost driveshafts, and that the adjustments you make to the Special's engine correct whatever problem you've been having.''

He studied her so long and somberly that Kat began to fidget.

"Why do I have a feeling you won't lose any sleep worrying about it?'' he muttered, jingling the change in his pants pockets.

A frown streaked across her brow. ''I may not lose sleep, but neither was I being trite, Kowalski. I mean what I say. I *am* sorry you're plagued with these problems. I'll see you tomorrow,'' she said, turning away.

He lengthened his stride a little to catch up. ''I'll walk you to your car.''

''You have a lot of muggings in your parking lot, do you?''

A scowl added deep grooves to his face. ''We've had the same number as Motorhill. Which isn't a lot, but even one is too many. If you object to my company, we can go back to the office and call Security to walk you out. You weren't on staff when I sent the memo to all female personnel. Any woman working late is supposed to request an escort to her car.''

Kat immediately pulled in her horns. ''Flintridge used to be safe anytime of day or night—before the population grew to ninety thousand. It's unfortunate that growth attracts undesirable elements.''

''Bad enough when those elements invade the town. Worse when they strike an industry that's operated like a big family as long as we have,'' he mused almost to himself as they slowly made their way to the employee parking lot.

''I take it you don't think the parts shipment has simply been mislaid.''

Slater thrust out his chin and lightly scraped his fingers along the underside of a jaw beginning to show dark stubble. ''If it didn't make me sound paranoid, I'd say I thought someone had it in for me personally. When Dad ran production, everything ran like clockwork. From the moment I took over and announced plans to retool for the gasless engine, we've been beset with mishaps.'' He looked downcast as he glumly kicked a rock off the blacktop.

They'd reached her SUV, so Kat unlatched the canopy and tossed her jacket and clipboard inside amid the clutter of athletic paraphernalia. ''Oil companies have been buying up plans for alternative-fuel engines for years. They're the only ones I know who have a vested interest in seeing a project like yours die at the starting gate.''

''No indication of that here.'' He shrugged. ''Unlike Motorhill, most of our employees have been with us for years. Some are third and fourth generation.'' Slater took the keys from her hand and opened the driver's door. ''I shouldn't be crying on your shoulder. As Derek said, it's probably all coincidence.'' Handing back her keys, he slipped a hand under her elbow and boosted her up. Unable to kill pure male instinct, Slater leaned backward to fully appreciate the view from the rear.

She felt his momentary hesitation and glanced over her shoulder. ''Did I drop something?'' Hanging there in midair, Kat scanned the ground below her.

''Huh? Oh, no.'' Slater cleared his throat. ''Just wondering when you're going to buy a good set of wheels. Doesn't it bother you to be the only import in the lot?''

Kat grinned. ''Not on your life. This baby has a great tranny. She's no gas-guzzler. Doesn't drive like a tank. When American-built can give me all of this at a price to fit my budget, I'll trade her in. Not one minute before.'' Rolling down the window, she shut the door. Smiling down at him, she added over the sound of the engine coming to life, ''Corners on a dime, yet the wheel base is wide enough to keep her upright in a bad storm. From what I've seen of your prototype, Kowalski, you'll have to burn a lot of midnight oil to make those claims.''

''I'm shooting for luxury and operating economy,'' he

bragged. "And that engine of yours needs a tune-up, O'Halloran. If I were you I'd worry about the ping."

Kat watched him walk away, a jauntier spring to his step. "What ping?" she shouted. But he didn't turn. She listened for any slight variation all the way home. And as she turned into the circular drive, she heard it. So he knew engines. *Big deal.* Hers probably only needed some minor adjustment. She'd look into it after dinner. And she wouldn't tell that smart aleck she'd heard the noise, either.

The house didn't smell like dinner cooking when she opened the back door. Poseidon barked happily and nearly knocked Kat over with his enthusiastic greeting. That or he couldn't wait to go out for a run. She held the screen ajar and let him race around the yard, puzzling over what had happened to everyone.

"Mama? Pop?" Even as the dog ran back to sniff her hand, Kat realized the house was empty. Then she noticed the note propped against the cookie jar.

Have gone to the church for a fund-raiser meeting. Pop says the men are meeting at O'Malley's. If you believe that, I have swampland to show you.

                                        Mama

Crumpling the note, Kat sighed. Didn't Spud's wife object to having all those men underfoot every night? Ten out of the last twelve evenings, Pop had allegedly spent at O'Malley's. From dusk until after midnight. At least, he came home. Surely that was significant. If he were really having a midlife fling, he'd act worse, wouldn't he? She'd read in women's magazines about men who went to the corner store and disappeared, never to be seen again.

Was Pop's trip to Atlantic City a trial run? Worry added to the headache that'd nagged at her off and on all day. No.

She had to see that didn't happen. The family counted on her.

Kat dropped her purse on the counter and went back outside to wait for her dog. She always thought best when she jogged. Since she'd be fixing her own meal tonight, she might as well work up an appetite.

While out on her run, she began to think about what Slater had said concerning his church festival. Funny that both of their churches put on similar fund-raisers every year. Funnier still that she'd lived in Flintridge all her life and had never wondered or cared what the people who lived on the Ridge did in their half of the community. Girls from the Hill didn't look twice at boys living on the Ridge.

That wasn't precisely true, she admitted, her steps faltering. They noticed the good-looking ones at school sporting events and tittered among themselves. But only the wildest Hillites sneaked out to meet a Ridge boy. She wouldn't have considered such a move. Mark, Josh and Matt would have skinned her alive. Yet those same protective brothers had pushed her toward the likes of Daniel O'Brien. Danny didn't only have light fingers; he had fast hands and the word *no* wasn't in his limited vocabulary.

For how many generations had the rivalry between the Hill and the Ridge been going on? Kat slowed at the end of three miles and whistled at Poseidon to turn toward home. She had to blot sweat from her face and neck. Letting the dog set a slower pace on the return trip, she wondered about her pop's budding friendship with Louie Kowalski. Suddenly things seemed clearer. The families were in a tailspin—Slater included—because Tim and Louie had broken some stupid, unwritten social taboo. One that said Hill and Ridge were separate and apart.

"Brother," she panted, feeling a stitch in her side. It was pretty silly for residents of the Ridge and the Hill to keep to themselves in their private lives when they patronized one another's businesses in town. That didn't mean, however, that she wanted her pop to be experimenting with massive social change. From the sound of it, Slater didn't want that for his dad, either.

On arriving home, Kat finally had a solution. Pop was a reasonable man. Reasonable and intelligent. She'd wait up tonight and explain that he and Louie, for the sake of tradition stretching back to the birth of Flintridge, had to cease and desist being bosom buddies.

She fed the dog and fixed herself a salad. After eating it and stowing the dishes, she went up to shower and promptly fell asleep in front of the TV. When she awoke with a start after 3:00 a.m., the house was dark and silent. The television had been shut off and someone, her mother she supposed, had covered her with a blanket.

Darn. Kat had missed talking to Pop. Tomorrow. She'd be up at the crack of dawn and catch him before he took off.

THE NEXT MORNING, only her mother sat at the kitchen table, sobbing to one of Kat's sisters-in-law when Kat tripped down the stairs in robe and slippers to let Poseidon out in the yard. Her heart pounded. Had something terrible happened to Pop?

Shannon O'Halloran glanced up and met Kat's eyes. "You've been home for three weeks now, Kathleen," she chided. "Nothing's changed. Mother O'Halloran! Crying isn't going to bring Papa Tim back. Show some backbone here."

"Bring him back?" Kat whispered through dry lips. "What's happened to Pop?"

"Nothing's happened to him," snapped Shannon. "But if I'd told Matt why I dashed out of the house before breakfast, your father might require a wake. Do you know that he and that perfectly awful Louie character have gone to Atlantic City?''

''Today? I didn't think that was until next week.''

''You knew Timothy was going with Louie Kowalski and not the carnival committee?'' Shannon asked, fury in her voice.

Kat turned to her mother. ''I think Spud, Buzz and Luke are going, too.''

''Oh, oh,'' sobbed Maureen. ''That terrible man is leading all of our devoted husbands astray.''

''Mama! Quit being so dramatic. Pop, Buzz, Luke and Spud are adults. Recently retired adults. They deserve some fun. Maybe it's a show of testosterone. You know, to prove they aren't henpecked.''

Maureen stopped wiping her eyes. Her eyebrows and Shannon's shot up into shocked arcs.

''Shame on you, Kathleen,'' scolded Shannon. ''Maybe men on the Ridge go off by themselves without their wives and waste money at the gaming tables. Men from the Hill are solid, church-abiding citizens. They're loving husbands and fathers.''

Kat threw up her hands. ''How can you sit there and spout such sanctimonious drivel? Daniel O'Brien was raised on the Hill and he turned out to be a total creep. There are some very nice men living on the Ridge.''

Shannon gazed defiantly at Kat. ''How can you say such a thing? Everyone knows the boys on the Ridge run wild.''

''They know?'' Kat demanded. ''Or is it a ploy of parents to keep us on our own side of town?''

Maureen twisted her tissue. ''Your grandmother said the Ridgers couldn't be trusted. She never lied in her life.''

''Nor my mother,'' added Shannon. ''She attended college in New York, so you know how liberal she is.''

"Liberal on matters that don't concern the Hill. Look, this isn't getting us anywhere. If my boss will give me the time off, I'm going to drive to Atlantic City and try to talk some sense into Pop."

"Why didn't you say so?" Shannon let her arm fall from around the older woman.

Kat's mother didn't seem all that happy. "Who will look after your dog, Kathleen? I can't take him for runs like you do. Maybe one of the boys will watch him." She glanced hopefully at Shannon, who was giving a negative shake of her head.

"Oh, good grief." Kat let the dog in question back in from his morning run around the yard. "I'll take Poseidon with me. There are motels that allow pets."

Her mother managed a thin smile. "I feel better already. Just knowing you'll be there with Timothy helps. He wouldn't do anything bad in front of you."

Kat wished she felt as confident. "Don't celebrate yet, Mama. First I have to clear it with my boss, remember?"

"You'll think up something convincing," Shannon said as she stood and headed for the door. "If the men on the ridge are as nice as you say, Kat, he'll understand."

"I hope you're right," Kat muttered to herself as she trudged back upstairs to dress for work. She wouldn't know for sure until lunchtime.

IN SPITE OF THE FACT that she was certain the morning would drag, it whizzed by. It was after twelve when she returned to her office after the last shuffleboard match. Because she was anxious to press Slater for a decision, Kat took the elevator to the presidential office suite rather than climb the stairs as she preferred.

Stepping from the elevator, she sniffed the air. Something

smelled heavenly. Her stomach rumbled, reminding her that she'd skipped breakfast.

Hazel smiled as Kat paused at her desk. "There you are." The older woman stood. "I hoped you'd get here before I had to leave. I'm running errands on my lunch break," she said.

"Mmm. I thought maybe you were fixing lunch in here." Kat sniffed the air again.

"I believe that's your lunch," Hazel said, aiming a smile toward Slater's private office.

"Mine? Oh, no. I'm here to get an answer to one question and then I'm headed for the cafeteria. I'd hoped you'd be free to go with me today."

"Trust me, dear. His nibs is preparing you a feast."

Had Slater found out she'd left the kayaks? "Is this something of a farewell to the condemned?" she asked, growing increasingly skittish.

"Nothing of the sort," Hazel stated, although her smile disappeared as Slater burst from his office. "Where is that confounded woman? It's ten after twelve and the *bigos* is getting cold. Ah…" He swallowed several times when he discovered Kat. "Come in, come in." He covered his bluster with a feigned cough.

Kat's mouth dropped open. "You fixed me *bigos?*"

"Yes. Er, um, I went by Buster's house and sweet-talked his mom into giving me some."

Kat smiled her thanks. She couldn't recall anyone ever having gone to so much trouble for her. Well, no one who wasn't family, anyway.

Hazel shrugged into her jacket and cleared her throat. "Are you just going to stare at her through the entire lunch break, Slater, or are you planning to let her eat the stuff you've been fussing with for the last twenty minutes? The lady looks famished."

Slater beamed like a child who could no longer hide a surprise. "By all means. Follow me, Kathleen. *Bigos* isn't a gourmet meal or anything. But it is better piping hot."

"I...thanks," Kat mumbled. "It was chaos around my house this morning. Hazel's right. I'm starved."

Laughing, Slater waved his secretary away and ushered Kat into his office.

She stopped just inside the door. Not only had he reheated the stew he'd spoken of the night before, Slater Kowalski had set the table in his small conference room for two. Silver gleamed and tapers burned. Rolls sat in a basket beside a tray of raw cut-up vegetables and dip. "You did all this? For me?" she said in wonder.

"Well, we both have to eat," he said gruffly. "It doesn't seem right that you've reached the ripe old age of thirty-two, never having tried *bigos*."

"I'm only twenty-six."

He seemed truly confused. "But Wendy said you were..."

"Wendy obviously read the date incorrectly," she said, knowing full well the woman had deliberately lied.

"Kind of you to give her the benefit of the doubt, Kathleen. Now that we have all the niceties behind us, sit and enjoy."

"Okay, but did you know our fathers moved up the date for their trip? They left bright and early this morning. I'd like to have tomorrow off, and Friday if I may."

Slater stepped into his minuscule kitchen and poured two bowls of steaming, fragrant stew. "I've decided to go with you, Kathleen. Hazel's going to put out a memo that says you're off negotiating for baseball backstops. And as far as anyone knows, I'm going to D.C. for a meeting. I see no sense in waiting to leave, do you? I thought we'd take off at five today if that's all right."

His offer was the last thing Kat had expected. "I'd better drive myself," she said. "I have to take my dog."

"Your dog?" Slater remembered the huge, jet-black animal with the muddy feet and the eager tongue. "You can't board him with a vet?"

"There's no time to arrange it." Kat tasted the stew. Her eyes lit up and she smiled. "This is wonderful."

Mesmerized by Kat's sincere dark eyes, Slater felt the ground give way. "The dog won't be a problem," he hastened to assure her. "It'll be a good test for the Special's interior. So we'll leave your house at five?"

Kat still had grave reservations. But how could she turn down a man who'd just fixed her this nice lunch? She couldn't…wouldn't. If for no other reason than she'd like to see what Shannon would make of her taking off with a suitcase and a man from the Ridge.

CHAPTER SIX

KAT FLOATED ALL AFTERNOON on the force of the good will created by Slater's generosity. *Lunch*. Such a simple gesture to make such a huge difference in how Kat viewed the man. After establishing the fact that they were both going to Atlantic City and setting a time, they'd drifted into discussing topics any couple getting to know each other would discuss. Not intimate stuff, but more personal than stilted talk of work and weather.

Because she thought it was too early to expect any change in his attitude about kayaking, Kat never mentioned her love for the sport, even though they covered favorite college and professional sporting events. She wasn't surprised to learn that Slater had been a hurdler in high school and college. He had the leanly muscled body of a track-and-field athlete. She commiserated when he lamented that a torn Achilles tendon had put an end to his Olympic aspirations. "These last few weeks," he'd said, "working in a handball game at the gym once a week suffices for exercise and entertainment."

Neither of them watched TV much or went to movies. They both enjoyed the mellow sounds of eighties music.

Kat left his office energized. Slater had a keen mind, great body and a wry wit. Three things she found attractive in a man. Added to that, his surprising her with a lunch he'd prepared himself—well, sort of—raised his stock markedly in Kat's estimation.

Scott Wishynski popped into her office as she wound things down early for the day. She'd planned to give herself an extra fifteen minutes at home to pack and be ready to leave when Slater arrived.

"You must have read my mind," Scott said. "I split early so we could get in a private kayaking lesson."

Caught off guard, Kat floundered for a reply. Ultimately she shook her head and said simply. "Sorry, Scott. I'm rushing so I'll be on time for an appointment." Technically, one *could* say she had an appointment—with Slater.

"Well, damn. Tomorrow, then?" he pressed, not missing a beat.

"Not then, either." Kat moved him out the door as she locked up. She offered Scott the excuse she and Slater had agreed on and hoped he hadn't changed their story without telling her. "Tomorrow I'm meeting with an athletic supply rep in Detroit. I'll be gone all day and very likely Friday as well."

Scott wagged his brows. "Need company? I'll call in sick and go with you. I know my way around Detroit after business hours. Hot night spots," he said with a wink.

Again Kat didn't know how to respond. "Like your wife would let you do that," she drawled, putting on a huge smile.

"My wife doesn't tell me what to do." He thumbed his chest. "I'm boss in my household. She accepts my decisions or lumps it."

Kat instantly recoiled. She'd heard talk of how shabbily Scott treated his wife. She hadn't wanted to believe the rumors, but now realized they were probably more truth than fiction. "Maybe your wife would like to learn to run the river. Two-man kayaking can be a lot of fun."

"Tina isn't into sports. She's kind of fragile, you know?"

Kat didn't know. But neither did she want to get involved

in a lengthy conversation concerning Scott's domestic situation. "At the moment I'm concentrating on basketball. I'll schedule kayaking around softball once the weather warms up. The river's running too high right now for teaching newbies."

"I'm not a newbie. A lot of us guys used to run the river when we were younger. Even almighty Slater, until he lost his nerve."

He couldn't have said anything more guaranteed to grab Kat's interest. Scott sounded almost derogatory, but he must have been teasing. He and Slater were good friends. A request for clarification rose to the tip of Kat's tongue. Then, for some reason—probably having more to do with everything she'd heard about Scott—she let the opportunity pass. "I'm going to be late if I don't dash," she said. Opening the door to the stairwell, she set a grueling pace down all nine flights.

Scott puffed to keep up, unable to continue their conversation. Kat had seen him bumming cigarettes from the smokers on numerous occasions. He didn't carry a pack himself. One could read that two ways. Either he was a cheapskate or he was honestly trying to quit. She hoped for his sake it was the latter.

"Sheesh." His chest heaved as they exploded through the door leading into the courtyard. "Must be some important appointment the way you're turning this into a marathon."

"Punctuality *is* important," Kat said primly.

"Yeah? I get there when I get there."

Goodness, she always put her foot in her mouth when it came to Slater's chief engineer. Well, tough. Kat did her best to be on time. If Slater tolerated bad habits in his employees, that was for him to live with.

Was disregard for schedules and appointments a flaw shared by Slater? Well, she planned to be ready to leave at five. If he came late, so be it. Unless he drove like a maniac, she figured it'd be almost midnight before they hit Atlantic City, even if they left on time. Of course, it was a city that never slept. Just as many visitors played the night gaming tables as gambled during the day. Maybe more. She didn't think it mattered when they got in—other than to save her father losing money. But Kat was determined that a late start, if there was one, wouldn't be her doing.

Even though she could tell Scott had more on his mind, she said a firm goodbye and parted from him at the juncture in the path. She took the branch that led to the parking lot.

On the drive home, Kat ran through possible scenarios for breaking the news to her mother—that she as well as Pop would be making the trip to Atlantic City with a Kowalski. She needn't have wasted energy worrying. Except for the welcome yips of her dog, the house was empty.

"Mama's gone nearly as much as Pop," she muttered as she let Poseidon out to roam in the fenced backyard. The dog sniffed around the steps, paying no attention to Kat, who went inside, banging the screen door shut.

In addition to tossing jeans, shirts and underwear in a satchel, Kat packed food and water for the dog. Without stating specifically that she was riding with Louie's son, Kat wrote that a friend was driving and left the note where it could be seen. If Maureen had been home, Kat would have introduced Slater. But considering how high feelings in the O'Halloran family ran toward anyone bearing the name Kowalski, it was a relief not to have to go through the grilling.

The last item on her list, besides snack food, was Poseidon's quilt. She always covered her Trooper's seats with it when they traveled. He knew the quilt meant they were going on a trip. Tongue hanging out after a brisk run around the yard, the dog loped over to stand patiently beside her SUV.

"No, boy. Today we're going in style," she told him. "I want you to be a good dog." The words were no sooner out than Slater's sleek black car entered the driveway. Poseidon lunged happily at the man when he stepped from his car.

Slater windmilled his arms as he was knocked flat against the car. "Hey," he yelped, swiping at his face where the dog trailed a wet tongue.

Kat laughed. "That's his way of saying welcome to my family." She finally got through to the dog and he sat, though he wriggled excitedly all over. "He likes you, Kowalski. He doesn't usually like men."

Looking only mildly rattled, Slater bent and patted the pup's heaving sides. "He could use a manicure," he said, straightening again.

"Oh, no. Did he scrape the Special's paint?"

"To heck with the paint. I think he slashed my throat."

Kat stood on tiptoes to see. No blood, but there was indeed a red scratch that curved below Slater's ear and disappeared under his shirt collar. "Ouch. I'll just get the first aid kit from my Trooper." She wrapped her fingers in the fur at the nape of Poseidon's neck and tugged him with her. He whined, turning sorrowful eyes toward Slater. It wasn't easy, but Kat retrieved the first aid kit and a leash, which she snapped to the dog's collar.

"Why doesn't he like men?" Slater asked, swabbing the scratch with a treated wipe Kat handed him from her kit.

"I figure either a man mistreated him or abandoned him. I found him clinging to a log in the bay after a really bad storm." She fondled the dog's silky ears. "He may have fallen off a yacht. I ran an ad in the local paper for weeks, but of course tourists rarely docked at the island for more than fuel and occasionally food."

Slater's eyes locked on the flexing of Kat's slender fingers in the animal's thick fur. Kathleen O'Halloran had strong hands. Yet they stroked the dog with gentleness. He could only imagine how they'd stroke a man's bare skin. *Not something he should be fantasizing about.*

"Put him in the back seat and you climb in front," he said, more harshly than he had intended as he discarded the wipe in a litter bag built into the car's voluminous dash. The dashboard had enough instrumentation to launch the next space shuttle. "I'll stow your luggage in the trunk." The first piece he picked up was the pet travel pack that held bottled water, dog food and Poseidon's dishes.

"Not that." Kat dived across the dog and relieved Slater of the vinyl carryall. "It's his water and stuff. I'll need it inside." If she sounded touchy it was because he'd cut her off so fast. But then, what made her think he'd be interested in her previous work on the island? Or in anything about her, for that matter?

Slater could ignore the sting of the scratch, but not the sting of her words. "Anything else you want to keep with you?" he asked in a friendlier tone.

"The canvas bag has snacks. Chips, crackers and cheese. People munchies." She grinned. Kat never stayed miffed for long.

"My car is a luxury prototype, not an all-night diner, O'Halloran."

Kat poked her head in through the Special's open window. "With all these electronic gizmos, I can't believe you don't have a built-in vacuum system to take care of the little matter of crumbs."

Slater threw back his head and laughed. "Is that a nice way of telling me I'm overly protective of my baby?" He patted the shiny surface of the car.

"Paternal. Yes, that does describe your actions."

"Hmm. I'll try to tone down bragging for this trip."

"If you're afraid we'll get the Special too dirty, we can always take old Horatio."

Slater paused with his car's trunk half-open. "Horatio?"

Kat inclined her head toward her beat-up SUV. "Captain Hornblower. When I'm loaded down with kayaks, I can't brake real fast. I christened him the first time I resorted to lying on the horn and cars fell away like the parting of the Red Sea. I bought the Isuzu used from a college kid. He'd installed one of those a hoogah, a hoogah horns, and I didn't know it. Hard to say who was most surprised. Me or the drivers who dived for the shoulders of the road." She grinned. "And that's when I knew *this* car was a he, not a she. All the noise and bluster."

Slater tossed her two small bags in the trunk and slammed the lid. "Sounds intriguing, but if you don't mind I'll take a rain check. Think how it'd look for the CEO of an American luxury automobile manufacturing firm to be seen driving a…Horatio?"

"Who says I'd let you drive?" Kat let the question hang as she padded the back seat with Poseidon's quilt, then urged him in. She noticed Slater still had a hand on the trunk and a half-amused look on his face as she closed the back door and climbed into the front seat.

"You really wouldn't let me drive that…toy?" Slater pursued the topic after they were underway.

"That so-called toy has Hemi heads and can turn one hundred in a quarter mile. And no, I wouldn't. We O'Hallorans are possessive when it comes to our wheels."

The saucy lift of her chin made Slater laugh again. Kathleen O'Halloran had a gift for making him laugh. He hadn't done much of that lately. He settled back in the soft leather seat, pulled out onto the freeway and set the cruise control. This trip was exactly what he needed. A break from the burdens at the factory. The Special's engine purred like a well-fed cat. For the first time in a long while, Slater was able to believe his luck had turned around.

Poseidon must have decided they were going on a long trip. He flopped down on his quilt, put his head between his paws and soon snored away.

Kat, who'd been somewhat tense at the outset, snuggled into a corner to watch the wind buffet piles of fleecy clouds around a still-sunny sky. She was a cloud-lover. White, gray, black, she loved them all. But the fluffy cumulus formations overhead were her all-time favorites. "Look, there's a Viking warrior," she said, suddenly pointing out thebroad front window.

Slater followed the line of her finger and saw nothing. They'd just passed an eighteen-wheeler and pretty much had the highway to themselves heading toward Toledo, Ohio. He was reasonably certain Viking warriors weren't commonplace to Toledo. "Oh, you mean a biker? I didn't see him."

"No, silly. I'm talking about cloud pictures. It's gone now, but there were horns on his helmet and everything. It was great." She lifted her sunglasses and peered under the frames at Slater. "Don't tell me you've never looked for cloud pictures on a road trip? My dad kept the four of us kids busy for hours that way when we traveled. Put an end to our squabbling." Dropping her glasses back in place, she smiled fondly as if savoring the memory.

Slater felt as if he'd really missed out on something important. "We didn't take a lot of driving trips," he muttered. "Unless Dad needed to check out performance on a particular car."

Kat folded a knee under her and turned slightly to look at him. "Sounds like a pretty boring life for a kid."

"I didn't think so at the time. Boys and cars seem to go naturally together. When I was older, most of my friends envied me having a new set of wheels every year. I got to fill her up at the factory pump for free.''

Slater couldn't remember a time when his father discussed much other than automobiles. His grandparents were involved in the business, too.

Aware of flickering emotions crossing his face—emotions stealing the lightheartedness he'd exhibited earlier—Kat jabbed his ribs playfully. ''Hey, there's no time like the present to learn about cloud pictures. We still have a good hour of daylight.''

''But I'm driving.''

''True. Drivers can take only quick peeks. But you'll be surprised at how much you can see.''

Taking her at her word, he scanned the towers of clouds. ''There, to the right, a Corvette.''

Kat craned her neck to follow his finger. ''That's a bit of a reach,'' she scoffed. ''Looks more like a dogsled to me. I'll give you two points because you're new at this.''

''Points? You didn't say anything about points.''

''You obviously need an incentive. So, there'll be a reward for the person with the most points.''

''What does the winner get?''

''Oh, we can set any prize. Loser buys dinner or washes the winner's car. Stuff like that.''

''I can handle it. It's your turn,'' Slater said, embracing the game completely. ''Loser buys dinner tonight.''

''Okay. But I warn you, I've held the title of O'Halloran champion longer than you can shake a stick at.''

''Talk is cheap.'' Slater grinned. ''Show me the money.''

Kat leaned forward. ''Straight ahead. A jaguar. The animal, not the automobile,'' she said in afterthought. ''He's stretched out in a full run.''

''I can see it,'' Slater said excitedly. ''That's good. How many points do you get?''

"What do you think? Maximum is four. That's where we need an impartial observer in the car. My dad used to assign points."

"All we've got is Poseidon."

Kat chuckled. "Our impartial observer is sawing logs."

"All right. I'd say three points. There's a notepad in the console if you want to keep score."

She opened the console that sat between the two seats. It was compartmentalized and neat as a pin. "Wow. I'm impressed. Wish I had one of these in my Isuzu." There were sliders for CDs, a pocket for a cell phone and a portable fax, holes for pens, a covered cup for paper clips. "Everything for a traveling office—except a bar. Where's the champagne, Kowalski?"

"Our first contract is with the government. I think they'd frown on providing public servants with bars."

"I was only kidding. You have two points and I have three. Your turn."

A lively hunt ensued. Kat's final turn came when it was almost too dark to see any clouds.

"Are you sure that tree was in the clouds?" Slater demanded. "Or was it a real one in someone's yard?"

"I'll discount the tree if you do the same for that dumb coffeepot. It looked more like an ice cube to me."

"Can I help it if you brew your coffee on top of the stove instead of entering the industrial age? It was a ringer for the coffeemakers I have at home and in my office," he insisted as they left Pittsburgh behind in a blur.

"Doesn't matter. Even if I give you full points, I still won," she said triumphantly.

"There's a calculator in the console. Let me see you add them up."

"You're as sore a loser as Matt," she drawled.

"Who's Matt?" he asked, surprised to feel a twist of jealousy.

"My next to oldest brother. He's your age. Very athletic and very competitive. Matthew likes to be best at everything."

"Matthew O'Halloran. Of course. I should have made the connection before. That first night we met you mentioned a brother who worked on dragsters?"

"That's right. He's best at that, too. People come from five states away to have him do their header work. He has a long waiting list."

"Which means your other brother is the genius at Motorhill." He whistled between his teeth, causing Poseidon to sleepily lift his head.

"That'd be Mark. Although Josh would debate you on that. Everything that Mark is to combustion, Josh is to design. And Matt's no slouch at structural engineering. For twenty-plus years, Pop was Motorhill's lead engine-electronics top dog."

"You don't say." Slater studied her through new eyes. "Did he have anything to do with the alternative-fuel car they're rumored to have in the works?"

"He had a hand in early methanol systems." Kat noticed a sudden chill in Slater's voice. "Why all the interest in Motorhill?" she asked suspiciously, recalling her brothers' charge that Louie was tapping Pop's brain.

"As if you didn't know about the big push to be first in coming out with a successful alternative-fuel automobile."

"Ford's already marketing a natural gas vehicle. Where have you been?"

"No one's produced a luxury model."

"Uh—how did we get onto the subject of work? Want a snack?" At the rattle of the food bag, Poseidon came fully awake. Climbing to his feet, he stuck his nose into the brown paper sack Kat had unrolled.

"Hey, watch it. Some of this is for people." She extracted a dog bone and made the dog climb back onto the quilt before she let him have it.

"If that's your idea of people snacks, I'll pass," Slater said dryly.

Cackling witchily, Kat produced a bright red apple, which she polished on her shirt before cutting wedges with a wicked-looking knife.

"You're nuts. Good thing this road is smooth. Hey, take it easy with that toad stabber," he cautioned as she sawed at a chunk of cheddar next.

She balanced a slice of cheese on the apple wedge and stuffed it in Slater's mouth to shut him up. Then she assembled several more on a napkin and sat it atop the console before she sampled one herself. "Not a great car for lovers," she said out of the blue.

"What?" Slater's head whipped around.

Blushing, she patted the wide console that separated the front bucket seats.

"Ah. But these seats both go completely back. A six-foot man can stretch out easily. I'll show you when we stop."

"I'll take your word for it," she mumbled, helping herself to another slice of apple with cheese.

"Chi-cken," he clucked.

"I can't imagine our public servants will give up hotels to sleep in their cars," she retorted.

"They're only our first targeted audience. A year from now, I hope to have a full range of colors and options available in every showroom that currently handles our cars."

"Pretty big undertaking when you still don't have the engine problem ironed out."

"How many miles have we come? You notice any glitches?"

Kat studied the mileposts whipping past. And the exit ramp for Highway 83 leading to Baltimore. She realized they were within a hundred miles of their destination. "I can't believe it's ten forty-five. Do you need a break from driving?"

"I don't insure other drivers on prototypes. But I never thought to ask if you needed another bathroom break. Sign says there's a rest area in two miles."

"On our family road trips, there were four men to two women. Mama and I learned to drive halfway across the United States without a break. Poseidon has begun to pace, though. If you don't want a stain on the Special's carpeting, we should probably stop."

Slater tossed a worried glance over his shoulder. "Why didn't you speak up sooner?"

"Relax. He's pretty well-trained. There...look. The exit is coming up."

Adjusting the cruise, Slater slowed smoothly into the turn. He found a place to park, even though a lot of motorists obviously had the same idea. Sliding from the car, Slater hurried around to open Kat's door.

She was in the process of hopping out before he got there. He had a hand out for the door, and she poised awkwardly on the balls of her feet as the door she flung open almost hit him. "I'm, uh, not used to gentlemen. Next time I'll remember to wait."

"Blame this habit on my aunt Adelaide. She insists women be escorted from a car. Anything else I can...?" he started to offer, then broke off as he found himself staring at her rear. She had dived over the seat to snap on Poseidon's leash.

She backed out, her hair ruffling in the night breeze. "I'll take him for a quick run in the doggy area. In that pouch you'll find his food, his bowls and a bottle of water. Do you mind filling each bowl half full?''

"D-done," he stammered. "Can I get you anything to drink?''

"No, thanks." Laughing, she took off after a dog bent on chasing shadows.

Poseidon wolfed his food, and they were on the road again in less than fifteen minutes. Kat rummaged in the console, selected a CD and popped it into the player.

"She's one of my favorites," said Slater as the latest Trisha Yearwood song poured from the speakers.

"Mine, too." Kat turned up the volume. They listened in silence for a while. As one tune segued into another, Kat said unexpectedly, "I hope you didn't reserve rooms for us at some swank hotel, Kowalski. I'm a blue-collar girl through and through."

"Hotel?" The word almost wheezed out of Slater's mouth. "I didn't book rooms. This trip was your idea. I assumed you'd handle accommodations."

Kat sat up straight. "Well, you assumed wrong. You're the one with an executive secretary who manages those things, not me."

The shoulder nearest Kat rose and fell. "I've never been to Atlantic City, O'Halloran. But just guessing, I'd say they're used to people checking in and out at all hours of the day or night. Shouldn't be any sweat to walk in and get rooms."

"You're probably right. Only we do have the dog. Not every hotel allows pets."

"There are some numbers taped to the phone in the console. One is labeled AC. That's auto club. Call them and ask for a rundown on places."

"It's eleven-thirty. Do they work this late?"

He rubbed his chin. "Maybe only towing services. Try anyhow. Hazel typed that list for me the day after I was stranded in the rain."

"Wise lady. I admit to holding my breath back there at the rest stop. Hazel said the Special has a habit of not starting once you've stopped."

"She's running like a top today."

"That she is. I'll tell Hazel to eat her words."

"Uh…when will you say you rode in the Special?"

Kat's head snapped up. "Hazel doesn't know we're together?"

"No. I trust her with most things, but not that. She's in a private war with Wendy Nelson, you see. I've never encouraged Wendy, but she has…sort of a crush on me."

"Half the single women at the factory have crushes on you, Kowalski."

He took his eyes off the road for a moment. "Married or single, all women employees call me Slater," he said softly. "All but one."

Kat picked up the phone. "Slater," she said deliberately as she punched in the numbers. "Where does Hazel think you are?"

Slater digested the husky way she said his name and thought perhaps he should have let well enough alone. But damn, he hated the way she said "Kowalski." It reminded him of fingernails grating over a blackboard. His hands tightened on the steering wheel, and he concentrated on the dark highway while she asked questions into the phone and jotted down a few notes.

"Hazel thinks I'm meeting my government contact in D.C.," he said when she got off the phone. "Like everyone else does…"

"Oh. Well, uh…the woman at the auto club gave me the names of two hotels that allow pets. We can check them out when we get there.'' They rode in silence for the last thirty miles. Poseidon's head bobbed between them. Muted music filled the car, alleviating a need to speak.

Slater navigated turnpikes and off-ramps to reach the brightly lit boardwalk in Atlantic City at last. Kat directed him to a side street that flanked the first of the two hotels on her list. ''Wait here,'' he instructed. ''I'll go check us in. They probably have a special entrance for people with pets.''

Kat nodded, removing the CD just before he killed the engine. She wrapped a hand around the dog's collar so he wouldn't jump out when Slater opened the door.

He returned in an incredibly short time, or so Kat thought. And he didn't look happy as he threw himself inside again.

''You will not believe this.''

''Try me,'' she said wryly.

''There are a bunch of big conventions in Atlantic City this weekend. Pharmaceutical, Veterans of Foreign Wars, some cosmetics company, I forget who else. The hotel reservationist said there isn't one room available in this town. Nothing that allows pets or otherwise.''

''What? They have seven thousand rooms here. That's what the lady from the auto club said.''

''Not one free.''

''There must be,'' Kat sputtered. ''We're not talking teeny little hotels.''

''You go ask, then. I'm telling you what she said.''

''What about your pop and mine? Did they make reservations?''

''How the hell would I know?'' Slater bit back.

''Okay, okay.'' Kat put a hand to her head. ''Let me think.'' Silence and darkness swirled around them. ''Let's try a smaller hotel.'' She finally suggested. ''Maybe she just meant the major hotels are booked.''

"She said *all,* but I'm willing to try." Slater turned the key…and nothing happened. He turned it back, jiggled it and flipped it again. Still nothing.

"What's wrong?" Kat slid toward him.

He tried several times and finally threw up his hands. "She's being cantankerous. We'd better sit here and let the engine cool. Sometimes that works."

Kat leaned back. "What other choice is there?"

Slater agreed but said little else as twenty minutes passed. The air began to cool and Poseidon started to whine. Slater tried the key again. "Damn. Dead as a doornail. Zippo. Nada. Shall we hike along the boardwalk and grab a bite to eat?"

"What restaurant would allow a dog? You go ahead. You can bring me something."

"I'm not leaving you here alone. Who knows what kind of degenerates wander these side streets?"

"I do have the dog. And I'll lock the doors. Go, Kowalski. Uh, Slater," she corrected herself.

"No. Look. We're both tired from working all day, followed by the long drive. Why don't we put these seats back and catch an hour or so of shut-eye? I'm sure the Special will start after she cools completely."

"All right," Kat said somewhat reluctantly. "I'll take Poseidon into the alley for a minute while you deal with the seats. Will they work without power?"

"They're independent of the electrical system. One of the innovative perks. But I'll take the dog for his nightly constitutional. See those levers?" At her nod, he explained how to recline the seats.

By the time Slater returned, she had a bed of sorts made up on either side of the massive console. The dog lapped up more kibble and water. Kat and Slater polished off the rest of the snacks, then they all settled down to sleep.

Kat couldn't figure out where she was when the interior of the car was suddenly flooded with bright light.

Groggy, Slater nevertheless awakened suddenly to Poseidon's frenzied yaps. He and Kat stared dazedly at each other, both horrified to find their car surrounded by police.

One rapped a night stick soundly on the window. "Get out of the vehicle," he ordered. "And keep your hands where we can see them."

CHAPTER SEVEN

KAT SCRAMBLED TO AVOID the blinding light. Her hip struck the console hard enough to hurt. Amid the pain she felt Slater's soothing fingers on her shoulder. "Take it easy. Can you tone down the dog? The police want us out of the car. Step out slowly," he said in a gravelly voice.

Grabbing Poseidon's collar, Kat snapped on his leash and did her best to control the rambunctious animal. He bounded back and forth across the console despite her efforts to keep him corralled. Tearing from her grasp, he lunged against the window. The nails of his front paws scraped the glass; his hind paws scrabbled for purchase on the console and Kat's lap.

The two officers backed away. One shouted instructions to subdue the dog. Meanwhile, Slater crawled out the driver's door, taking care to place both hands in plain sight on top of the car. "What's the problem, Officer? I'm not illegally parked, am I?"

Poseidon, sensing freedom in the rush of cool air, jerked from Kat's hold and wedged through the door Slater had left ajar. In a wild dash, the dog nearly upset the officer warily circling the car's grill.

Uttering a distressed cry, Kat all but flattened Slater with the door when she dove after her dog. She righted herself in time to see Poseidon's leash snake along the road. Like a streak, he disappeared beneath the boardwalk. A din ensued—yowling, the likes of which Kat had never heard. She dashed past the second policeman, only to be clasped by the collar and shoved roughly against the car.

"My dog," she said weakly. "He's wearing a leash. I'm afraid it'll catch on something under the walkway and he'll choke."

"He's caught the scent of those damned wild cats that live under the boardwalk. Maybe he'll clean 'em out. Heaven knows, nothing else has worked," said the cop who'd captured her.

As the yapping and hissing rose, the first officer hitched his belt over a slight paunch and ordered his partner to help Kat rescue her pet.

"You," he snarled, turning to Slater. "Tell me why you two are sleeping in a car."

"We arrived near midnight. Left Michigan at five, after working a full day. The first hotel we tried said all the rooms in town are booked with conferences. We decided to grab some sleep and try again in the morning."

"Kind of risky, coming all that way without a reservation," the cop said, flashing his light from Slater's rumpled hair to his bare toes.

"Ms. O'Halloran thought I'd made a reservation. I thought she had."

"You folks figuring on getting married here?"

Kat, accompanied by a whining, bedraggled dog and a muddy policeman, returned in time to hear the question. She sucked in a deep breath. "People do come here for reasons other than marriage. Slater's father and mine are at the casinos...someplace." She ordered Poseidon to sit and treated the men to her best smile. "We intended to surprise them. Turned out the surprise is on us."

"Well, we have tight vagrancy laws. Don't allow sleeping on the street or in cars. Hand over your license, son. I'll write you up a warning, then you'd better hightail it out of here and find your relatives. And keep that dog on a leash.''

Slater dug into his hip pocket. He withdrew an empty hand. At first he looked bewildered, then he snapped his fingers. ''I forgot. I put my wallet on the console, along with my car keys.'' He opened the door and started to reach inside. The policeman hauled him back. ''Hey, no monkey shines. My partner will get your wallet. And the registration while you're at it,'' he told his pal, again flashing his light over the outside of the car. ''Classy wheels. What make?''

Slater's face fell. ''Uh, the car's a prototype. She's not registered. Note the dealer plates.''

The second cop backed from the car. ''Didn't find wallet or keys on top or inside the console.''

''That's impossible,'' Slater protested. ''I put them there myself not more than—'' he checked his watch ''—two hours ago. Wow, I didn't realize we'd slept that long.''

''How about you, little lady?'' The policeman addressed Kat. ''Has your license mysteriously disappeared?''

''Not that I know of. Should be in my fanny pack.''

''Which is?'' The cop began to sound irritated.

''In the trunk with my suitcase,'' Kat mumbled.

The policeman looked grim. ''A trunk that needs a key to open. A key that appears not to exist. I don't know what's going on with you two, but we'll straighten it out at the station. And if we don't get to the bottom of it, you won't have to worry about accommodations. You'll spend the rest of the night in jail.''

''Jail?'' Slater and Kat chorused. ''This is crazy,'' Slater muttered. ''I tell you, my wallet and the keys were there. The way the dog bounced around after you woke us up, he probably knocked them off. Did you check the floor?'' he asked the officer who'd done the initial search.

Unclipping a more powerful flashlight from his belt, the

man did a second sweep inside the car. "I think maybe something's wedged underneath the console. Too far under for me to get a grip. Don't know. Could be leather."

Kat edged closer to Slater. "Pry up the edge of the console."

"It's bolted to the frame," he said. "Seats and carpet go in last. How in holy hell did anything work itself underneath that section?"

"You tell me," Kat muttered. "It's your baby." When Slater merely grunted, she turned to the officer. "He's the CEO of Flintridge Motors," Kat informed the men. "This car is still in the design phase."

"Uh-huh," scoffed the older officer. "And you two just happened to be shaking it out on a four-state jaunt. Sounds fishy to me, Harold," he told his partner. "I say we lock 'em up and sort this out where there's coffee."

"Wait," Kat begged as the one man pressed a button on the control panel that would lock all the doors. "Could I at least get the blue satchel from the back seat? It contains the dog's food and water."

The older cop was already nudging Slater toward an official car parked behind the Special. At a curt nod, his buddy retrieved the vinyl tote. Once he'd checked the contents thoroughly, he motioned for Kat and Poseidon to follow the others.

Kat winced as the door closed, shutting them into a back seat, separated from the officers in front by a meshed steel grate. "What now?" she whispered to Slater.

He stopped rubbing his temples. "Call Bob Sorenson, I guess."

"Who's he?"

"The company attorney."

"What?" Kat gaped at him over the dog's flicking ears.

"And let it get out at work that I'm not in Detroit buying equipment? Can't you think of another way?"

"What would you suggest? I prefer razzing to a police record."

"Quiet," roared the driver. "You'll each get a phone call. Better quit bickering and decide who to contact."

They rode the remaining blocks in silence. Even Poseidon hunkered down, placed his chin on Kat's knee and stared at her with soulful eyes. She gained comfort from rubbing his soft ears.

At the station they were asked to repeat their story to a weary-looking lieutenant.

"Let me do the explaining," Slater instructed Kat.

"Be my guest." She indicated a row of hard-backed chairs. "I'll sit over there and give Poseidon a drink." From her vantage point, she could see Slater gesturing and his lips moving, although she couldn't hear what was being said. Goodness, they weren't criminals! Kat was confident he'd straighten everything out.

By and by, the sergeant who'd brought them in entered the room. He handed Kat's fanny pack to the lieutenant. "Had the car towed in," he announced. "Volchek picked the trunk lock with no problem. Afraid we'll have to take a torch to the console to get to the wallet and keys, if they're there."

"No torch." Slater darted a worried glance between the speakers. "The wallet's there, I tell you. Go ahead, lock me up. I can prove who I am! But I've got deadlines and can't afford to let you tear up the car. Will you give me time to figure an alternative way to retrieve those items?"

"Book him." The lieutenant whisked a hand through the air. He hollered for Kat to take Slater's place. As he rifled through her fanny pack, she sneaked a peek over her shoulder. Her heart fell to her toes. Protesting every step of the way, Slater was fast disappearing down a brightly lit hall, flanked on either side by cops.

"Let the lady go. She's innocent. I'll take full responsibility Kathleen," he yelled, twisting to make sure he had her attention. "Use the station phone to call all the hotels and find your dad. Don't wander the streets alone, do you hear?"

"Ms. O'Halloran?" Whirling, she saw the lieutenant holding her driver's license between his thumb and forefinger.

"Washington?" He arched a brow. "According to Kowalski, you both live in Michigan." He tapped repeatedly on a computer keyboard.

Kat cleared her throat. She thought it best to begin her saga with the first phone call she'd received from her sister-in-law. When she finally wound down, the lieutenant had dropped her license on his desk and held his head between gnarled hands. He'd dragged his fingers through his hair so many times, it stood on end. Comical though he looked, Kat knew this was serious trouble, and she wasn't laughing.

"Too preposterous a tale to be a lie," he said at last when she grew silent and stood biting her lip worriedly. Leaning forward, he tapped her license with a pencil. "If I run you in, I'll have to ship your dog to the pound, even though he's got current Washington tags. But damn, I hate to dump you on the street alone at four in the morning. You say you don't have any idea where your dad's staying?"

She shook her head. "Are you really keeping Slater?" she asked hesitantly.

The man in charge shoved the license back into her wallet. "You have picture ID. Your friend hasn't got squat. He may be who he says he is. Again, he may not. For all I know, you two could be the next Bonnie and Clyde. On this license you don't have any priors. Kowalski, on the other hand, may have a rap sheet a mile long. I ran the name and it checks with the address he gave. But he's a mite young to be running an outfit that manufactures cars like the one we hauled in. According to the report…'' He waved a paper at Kat. ''Our expert guesstimates that vehicle is worth upward of sixty thousand smackeroos.''

''Would you tell Bill Gates he's too young to own Microsoft?'' Kat shot back without thinking.

''Billy boy's picture has been plastered all over TV. Kowalski may be a big cheese in Michigan. But until I get his license, here in Jersey he's just another John Doe.'' The lieutenant laughed at his own joke. Then he sobered. ''You look like a nice young woman. Count yourself lucky this time. We've probably helped you escape the clutches of a flimflam man. Be more careful in the future. Won't always be cops around to save your bacon.''

''So am I free to go, then?'' Kat queried, sounding calmer as a plan to help Slater began to take shape, even though the lieutenant insinuated that she was brainless and naive.

''Free as a bird. But if I were you, I'd hop a bus home, provided they'll let you book passage for the mutt.''

''Thank you.'' Kat avoided eye contact as she took her fanny pack and buckled it around her waist. She had no intention of leaving Slater sitting in jail. But after years of dealing with three lordly brothers, she knew that when men laid down an edict, they expected to be obeyed. So she'd let the lieutenant believe he'd made an impression.

What she really needed was a cup of coffee to clear her brain and a quiet place to drink it in order to puzzle out their problem. If only she had a way to let Slater know she hadn't forsaken him. However, asking to leave him a message would be tantamount to tipping off the lieutenant that she had no intention of taking his advice. She sneaked a last look at his hulking form and conjured up a weak smile and a wiggle of her fingers that constituted a wave goodbye. Collecting Poseidon and his satchel of food, Kat left the warmth of the building.

She tarried a moment on the steps to take a deep breath of sea air and to get her bearings. Then she set off at a brisk walk toward the blaze of light flashing from the row of casinos a few blocks away. Casinos filled with scantily clad hostesses and serious gamblers. She discovered, after wandering in and out of several, that it'd be next to impossible to find Pop and Louie. Who knew what casino or on which floor they'd be? And outside in the shadows lurked street-walkers and down-and-outers. After she was accosted by a third beggar asking for spare change, Kat decided she should have let Slater call the company lawyer. So what if their reputation ended in shreds? Faced with possible mugging or worse, hanging on to a spotless reputation seemed foolish.

Kat's next idea was to phone Hazel and throw herself on the secretary's mercy. She might "tsk" over the fact that Slater had lied about his destination, but she thought the world of him, Kat knew.

But as Kat dug through her wallet for money to buy coffee, she ran across the phone number of Slater's mechanic, Gordon Dempsey. His name and number were written in Slater's scrawl. The guy might work for him, but she'd never seen him at the plant. He probably had his own shop and didn't know anyone at Flintridge except Slater.

Nearly 5:00 a.m. Four at home. An ungodly hour, to be sure. But the mechanic had answered Slater's summons late that rainy night. Kat didn't debate long. She hunted up a pay telephone, dropped in her coins and punched in the long distance number. Kat's call was answered by a woman with a sleepy voice.

Two drunk, scruffy-looking men passed by, giving Kat

pause. They slowed, turned and leered at her. She tightened her hold on Poseidon's leash. "I'm, ah, calling for Mr. Dempsey. Could I speak to him, please?" she asked softly.

The voice at the other end shrieked, "You have some nerve calling my husband at this hour."

Kat's ear thrummed from the bang of the woman's receiver. "Buzz off," she growled at the men. "Or I'll sic my dog on you." They must have decided she wasn't worth testing, because they staggered on. Kat patiently extracted more coins from her billfold and dialed the number again, praying the woman wouldn't ignore the phone.

Dempsey's wife didn't, although she let it ring five times. "Look, you call again and I'll have the police trace this call."

"Mrs. Dempsey, please don't hang up," Kat implored. "I'm calling for Slater Kowalski. He's having major trouble with the Special. I'm sorry to bother you so late...um, early, but it's really important that I speak with your husband."

"Well, why didn't you say so in the first place? I'll be listening on the extension, missy, so you'd better be telling the truth."

Kat had to deposit more coins before a groggy-sounding man came on the line. "Mr. Dempsey? This is Kat O'Halloran. I'm calling for Slater Kowalski. His wallet and car keys accidentally got stuck under the Special's console. No one can get them out. The Atlantic City police are detaining him for lack of ID. I wonder...is there a way to lift the console that doesn't entail dismantling half the car's interior?"

Following a spate of heavy breathing, a confused voice asked, "Who did you say you are? You say Slater's in the slammer? Scott said the boss went to D.C."

Kat's stomach tensed. "I don't have time to explain," she said. "I'm at a pay phone and I'm running out of change. I'm Kathleen O'Halloran, Kowalski's recreation specialist. We're on an equipment-buying trip. Call his secretary. She'll vouch for who I am. I'll give you the number at this pay phone if you want to do that and call me back.''

"No. Say, didn't Slater have you call me once before? He was stuck out by the proving grounds?''

"That's right.'' Kat's voice rose excitedly. "So you'll help us?''

"Damned tootin'. That car's worth its weight in gold to all of Flintridge. Can't tell you how happy I am to know she ran that far without her engine cutting out. So happens I've got a pal who lives in Ventnor City, 'bout a skip and a jump from you. He's got tools, and he owes me a favor or two.''

"That's wonderful, Mr. Dempsey.''

"Name's Gordon, doll. Recreation specialist, huh? Never cared much for exercise myself. But maybe I'll take a look-see into the boss's new program. I recall Scott raving about you. Doesn't take much in the way of a skirt to get him tripping over his tongue, but Slater's a whole different story.''

Kat heard a very feminine shriek, followed by Gordon Dempsey back-pedaling to his wife for all he was worth. "Do call your friend,'' she implored, interrupting the argument. "Tell him I'll meet him in the lobby at the Boardwalk police station as fast as he can get here. Oh, and, Dempsey…I'm sure Slater doesn't want news of this to reach Scott or anyone else.''

The two on the line stopped squabbling. This time, Slater's mechanic sounded angry. "The boss and I go back a long ways. He's four-square. No finer man around. I don't spill his business to anyone.''

Surprised by his vehemence, Kat stumbled around for

something to say. "Uh, I'm certain Kowalski appreciates your loyalty."

"Slater saved my life once," Dempsey told her. "No amount of paltry favors makes up for that. Now if you'll get off the phone, I'll call Troy."

Kat squeaked her goodbye. There was egg on her face and she didn't like the taste. That'd teach her to keep her mouth shut. Phew! Dempsey was Slater's staunch ally. Kat wondered if Slater had literally or figuratively saved the mechanic's life. Gordon could have meant that Slater saved him from a life of crime or something. Although Kowalski had a solidness about him—the deportment of a savior. Look how he'd fished her out of the river. She hadn't been in any danger, but Slater had believed she was. Putting aside such thoughts, she used the rest of her change to try to find her pop—to no avail.

Kat trudged back to the police station, barely noticing the faint pink streaks starting to lighten the eastern sky. As she passed a café, the smell of food made her stomach growl. Even Poseidon whined, and Kat realized how long it'd been since she'd eaten. But securing Slater's freedom took precedence. They'd laugh about this over breakfast later.

Kat entered the police station as the lieutenant's shift was ending. He glanced up and stopped shrugging into his jacket. He seemed surprised to see her. "So was I right, little lady? Greyhound wouldn't let you take the mutt aboard?"

Kat sat her tote down. "I didn't ask. I phoned Slater's mechanic. He has a man coming over to lift the console. Who do I need to see for access to the car?"

"Well, now." The lieutenant appeared to consider Kat in a new light. He trotted back to the desk, said something to his replacement, then pulled a folder from the bottom of a stack. "Kowalski couldn't raise the joker he called. His attorney, he claimed. Wonder why he didn't call his mechanic if he had one on tap.''

Kat shrugged. She was very glad a sleepy-looking, pony-tailed young man, bearing a large toolbox, shouldered his way through the doors just then. ''There's our man now. Will someone take us to the car?''

''I'll do it myself,'' said the lieutenant. ''And I'll stay and run the license. See if we can wind this up or if your faith in that guy's misplaced.''

Kat didn't know what Slater had done to rub the lieutenant the wrong way, but he obviously had. She wasn't about to make matters worse. Instead of replying, she intercepted the bewildered mechanic, introduced herself and thanked him for coming.

''Gordo told me what needs doing. Should take me ten minutes, max. No sweat.''

He was slightly off. It took him half an hour and a lot of sweat and swearing. The console was down solid, attached to the frame. The man finally released it enough for Kat to slip her fingers in and drag out Slater's wallet and keys. ''Wow!'' she exclaimed. ''It's a mystery how this stuff managed to end up so far underneath.''

The mechanic slid out from under the car. He ran a lazy, half-leering gaze over Kat as he wiped grease from his hands. ''Gordo said you're his boss's personal trainer or something. Must've been some fancy contortions going on in the front seat.''

Kat felt the tips of her ears sizzle. ''I work for Flintridge Motors. My relationship with Kowalski is professional.'' She pulled Slater's license from the wallet and handed it to the lieutenant, who also smirked.

The mechanic, Troy Kline, packed up his tools, muttering something about talking to Gordo. ''We've consulted on this baby's engine. If she keeps cutting out, Kowalski ought to have me mill a balanced valve train. That's her problem.''

''I'll mention it,'' Kat murmured as Troy said goodbye.

''You can wait in the station, Ms. O'Halloran,'' the lieutenant said. ''It's a valid license. Running the stats shouldn't take long. If he checks out negative for priors, Kowalski's release will be a formality. I'd fix that snafu with the console and the engine, if I were him. You'd be surprised at how many fancy car owners do engage in, uh, contortions in their cars around this town. The type who buy boats like this are powerful men who don't take kindly to being run in.''

Kat elected to save her breath. The lieutenant and Troy Kline were men of the same mentality. To them, a couple couldn't sleep in a car without engaging in sex. She was too tired to put up a defense. Let Kowalski set his Neanderthal pals straight. She'd done her duty getting him released. The lieutenant's attitude was something else she and Slater could laugh about over breakfast.

But the man who showed up in the station foyer some twenty minutes later, stuffing his wallet and keys back into his pockets, didn't act as if he'd find any aspect of this episode funny. Ever. In fact, he seemed downright surly as he stalked out the door ahead of Kat.

''Hey, wait up.'' She hitched Poseidon's food and water duffel higher on her shoulder, wrapped the leash more firmly around her wrist and urged the dog to leave his spot in front of the baseboard heater.

Ignoring her call, Slater circled his precious car, which a young policeman had just delivered to the front of the building. Once Slater had examined every inch of the exterior and looked inside the trunk, he climbed in to check the console. Only after everything met his approval did he snatch the clipboard from the officer's hand and scribble his signature. Stony-faced, Slater accepted a copy of the impound release. Without a word to Kat, he slid under the steering wheel.

The policeman offered to open her door, but she waved him off and ducked her head inside the back door. "I'm sure it wasn't pleasant spending time behind bars, Kowalski. But I haven't exactly had a ball, either." The roar of the car's engine drowned out her words. Frustrated, she boosted Poseidon onto the back seat and quickly crawled in front. Kat barely had her seat belt fastened before Slater peeled out of the drive.

"Silly me…thinking you'd be pleased I found a way to cut short your stay in the big house," she said testily.

"I didn't ask you to rescue me." Slater stomped on the gas. All he could think about was how his blood had run cold when the lieutenant told him she'd gone off by herself in the dark.

The abrupt surge forward slammed Kat back against the leather seat. "Well, ex-cu-u-use me! Drive like this, and your worries will be over. The police station is not a good place to play Mario Andretti."

"And Atlantic City isn't a good place for a woman to trek around on her lonesome playing guardian angel! I said to use the goddamn station phone and find your dad."

"For your information, according to the lieutenant, a lot of men—big shots—come here for illicit reasons. Hotels probably go to great lengths to ensure their patrons' privacy. Anyway," she declared, glancing at him with a faint grin. "How do you know I didn't use the goddamned station phone to track down Gordon Dempsey?"

"Because the lieutenant said, when he threw me in the tank with a crazy and two drunks, that you'd taken off. I was worried. All right?"

"Worried? About me?" Kat turned that over in her mind. "The lieutenant also made a few ribald jokes and repeated the speculations of Gordon's friend when he came to let me out. Weren't *you* the one who said we shouldn't let word of our being here together get out at the plant?''

Kat hesitated. She let her gaze drop. ''I'm sorry, Slater. I'd hoped Dempsey wasn't connected to the plant. I accidentally ran across his name and number in my wallet. Remember, you gave it to me the first night we met? Anyhow, I did look for Pop and I realized how hard it was going to be to find him. It was scary having nowhere to turn. I figured Dempsey was our best shot. So sue me. It worked.'' She studied him through her lashes before saying, ''I'm really, really glad you're back, Kowalski.'' She couldn't help it that her voice cracked just a bit.

The air escaped Slater's lungs in a rush. Taking a hand from the steering wheel, he covered the hands she clasped in her lap. ''It's okay.'' His tone, though still gruff, was shades softer. ''I guess it just nicked my ego, sitting trussed up like last year's Thanksgiving turkey while you took charge. It's a guy thing—needing to be in the driver's seat.''

Kat shook off his hand. ''Then it's time you learned that women are just as capable as men. I moved halfway across the United States to show the men in my family that I could live just fine without their help or intervention. Did it, too.''

''But…you just said you were glad to have me back.'' Slater swung the Special into a parking place and let the engine idle as he searched her face.

''The fact that I *like* your company doesn't mean I'm helpless. Men and women can have different strengths, you know, different but equal.''

''I notice you didn't mention weaknesses. Women are allowed them? Men aren't, of course.''

''That's archaic thinking, Kowalski. Hasn't anyone told you it's okay for men to need help? To admit a shortcoming or two?''

He simply snorted. "Enough already. Shall we try and find our dads?"

She knew men hated discussing emotions. She'd let it go for now. Because Kowalski actually showed signs of having a heart.

"I don't know about you," Kat said, "but I'm starved. Feed me first, then I'll have the stamina to search all the nooks and crannies in the casinos."

"Good plan. But…" Slater cast a doleful eye toward the dog.

"It's still cool enough for Poseidon to stay in the car. We'll roll the back windows down an inch or so to give him air. I'll leave him kibble and water."

"He won't mess up the car?"

She looked offended. "I told you—he's well-trained. I'll bring him a treat and take him for a run along the boardwalk before we leave again."

"This time you'll hang on to him so he won't chase the wild cats?"

"I may not seem it, Kowalski, but I'm a quick study. You think I want another run-in with the men in blue?"

"Khaki," Slater muttered. "The police here wear khaki."

"You're right, smarty britches." Kat took out a folded brochure she'd found stuck in the phone booth. "Hey, according to this, there's a nice seaside café just down the street. We can stay parked right here."

A seaside café would not have been Slater's choice. However, before he could voice any objections, Kat rolled down Poseidon's window, hopped out and had her door locked.

Slater wanted to object again when she asked the waitress to seat them outside on the deck. "Isn't it too windy?" He hung back, reluctant to tell her the sparkle of sun dancing across the ocean waves, or any large body of water, made him queasy.

Kat spun a canvas chair around so that she had a sweeping view of the white-capped crests. After placing her food order, she again turned her face to the tumbling surf and the seagulls swooping through the sky. "I miss living near the water," she mused softly. "I used to sea-kayak among the San Juan Islands every day if I could. It's lazier than whitewater kayaking. You'd like it. I know you would."

Slater dropped his sunglasses over his eyes and stared past the rolling breakers. He was quite certain he wouldn't enjoy anything involving a kayak. Even now, if he closed his eyes, he could see the vicious white tentacles of the river pulling at him. Sucking Gordon and Jerry under the surface. Gordon Dempsey, always a lousy swimmer, sank like a rock minutes after their canoe broke apart. Slater hadn't had to think twice about diving after Gordon and fighting upriver to get him ashore. But Jerry Gelecki had been an ace athlete. Better at everything than Slater. No matter how much he punished himself for hesitating those few seconds before he went in after Jerry, he'd never know what had gone wrong. A cramp, maybe. Slater only knew he'd no more than crawled up on the bank behind Gordon, who was heaving his guts out, when he heard Jerry's garbled cry. As if in slow motion, the giant whirlpool swallowed his best friend. At first Slater thought Jerry was clowning. Every day since, he lived with the fact that those few seconds' delay might have cost Jerry his life. Slater doubted he'd ever shake this sick feeling around open water. Kathleen O'Halloran didn't think he had emotions. He had them all right. In spades.

Kat didn't notice that she carried on a one-sided conversation until their food arrived. Or that Slater scarfed down his meal and forced her to hurry when she'd rather have lingered. He paid the bill, then paced impatiently while she fed Poseidon crumbles of bacon before she took him for a short run along the water's edge.

"Finally," he exploded when she returned, "we can get on with searching for our dads. If they're here to win big bucks, they won't waste time on the slots. At each casino, we need to look for the gaming tables. Blackjack, poker, baccarat and such."

Kat moved closer to Slater's side as they traversed the noisy play areas. "All this money changing hands upsets my stomach," she whispered.

Slater paused near a roulette wheel where a white-haired gentleman bet stacks of chips representing thousands of dollars. "It doesn't bother me since I'm not the one bankrolling a toss of the dice. But every time I think how your dad and his cronies snookered L.J. into gambling after he retired, I want to wring their necks."

"Don't start that again, Kowalski. We don't know who snookered whom."

"Yeah, well, this is getting us nowhere," he said after they wandered yet another dimly lit corridor in yet another casino. "Eight casinos, and no sign of them. They could be in Joe Blow's back room or in a private game for high rollers."

"High rollers? You mean the type of game if they can't ante up someone named Bugsy Malone pays a visit in a long black limo?"

"Malone? Was he Irish? In that case, Luke Sheehan, Buzz Moran and Spud Mallory ought to fit right in. Not to mention Timothy O'Halloran."

"Don't be ridiculous! Quit talking about my pop like that. And I've known those other guys all my life. They're pillars of the community. Of our church."

"So you say. Look. This is futile. We made an error in judgment. I think we should just head home."

"Fine." Kat didn't argue. All in all, their venture had been depressing. She trailed him to the car.

TEN OR SO MILES AFTER Slater left the turnpike, the Special's engine started coughing and running rough.

Kat sat forward as the car sputtered and began to slow. "What's wrong?"

Cursing, Slater nosed it off the road. He opened the console and picked up the phone. "Dammit," he shouted, pounding a closed fist on the dash. "Someone or something jarred the plug loose. We can't call until the phone recharges."

"Throwing fits won't solve a thing. You'll have to hike to a pay phone. But that isn't the real problem. Why don't you have someone mill a new, balanced valve train for this engine?"

Slater scowled at her. "Valve train? What in hell do you know about it? Wait." His brows puckered tightly over the ridge of his aristocratic nose. "That's a distinct possibility." Clamping both hands around her arms, he hauled her over the console until they were nose to nose. "You hit a little too close to home for comfort. Suppose you tell me how a recreation specialist gets so damned smart when it comes to a one-of-a-kind, highly classified engine?"

"A lucky guess?" His bully tactics sent Kat's temper skyrocketing. She could tell him Gordon Dempsey had consulted with the mechanic from Atlantic City. She could, but she wouldn't. Let him stew and wonder. It served him right for all the rotten things he'd said about Pop and his friends.

Poseidon clambered to his feet and thrust bared teeth in Slater's arrogant face, which brought a huge smile to her lips. He turned her loose fast enough then and slammed out of the car, muttering unrepeatable words.

Kat sat there like a bump on a log. For all she cared, Kowalski could tinker with his precious classified engine until hell froze over. Thanks to her dad and her brothers, she was no stranger to the workings of gasless engines. Maybe not exactly an expert, but she wasn't dumb as a post, either. If Slater wasn't so pigheaded, he could avail himself of her family's knowledge. But he *was* pigheaded. He could damn well beg for her forgiveness. Maybe when they got home she'd call Gordon and let him know what Troy had said about the valve train.

If the banging coming from under the hood was any indication how long they'd be parked at the side of the freeway, Kat decided she'd have time for a nap. Pushing the seat back, she closed her eyes and curled up.

Sound asleep was how Slater found her later when he again climbed into the car, his hands covered in grease. Good thing she'd crashed. He wasn't in any mood to confess that after his tinkering with the valve train, the engine had smoothed right out.

He gazed down on Kat's pretty, innocent-looking face. The lady was obviously more than she appeared. But how much more? Slater had long since come to the conclusion that someone at the plant didn't want the Special rolling off the line on time. Was this woman capable of such skulduggery?

For crying out loud, now he found an enemy in every face. Slowdowns on the assembly lines had started weeks before Kathleen came on board. Besides, there was no way she could have hijacked heavy driveshafts. Taking care to shut the door quietly, he slipped the car in gear and drove off.

Obviously he owed Kathleen another apology. Apologizing to her was getting to be a habit. He quietly rifled through the console, pulled out a CD and turned it on low. What he couldn't bring himself to admit was how much he liked watching her sleep.

CHAPTER EIGHT

REPEATED SIDELONG GLANCES at Kathleen's slightly open mouth had Slater gripping the wheel hard, fighting a temptation to pull off the highway and kiss her awake. Could the music be putting nutty ideas in his head? He punched the eject button, and switched to a CD of a loud rock group. Not his preference—it was a CD that belonged to Scott.

The raucous noise didn't stop Slater from remembering how it'd felt to kiss Kathleen O'Halloran that night in Spud Mallory's garage attic. Her lips had clung to his mouth. Her breath, peppermint-sweet then, puffed out now in tiny whiffles as she slept.

Slater shifted in his seat. This line of thinking was insane. Better to concentrate on his problems at the plant. Problems with the Special's engine. If the engine conked out again, he decided he'd kiss Kathleen into wakefulness before checking under the hood. Dammit, wouldn't you know the car ran like a top when a guy wouldn't mind pulling over?

As if his continued study of her features touched a nerve, Kat yawned, blinked several times, then bolted upright in a guilty start. She linked her fingers and stretched her arms over her head. "Wow! I've been dead to the world. Are we almost home?"

Slater swallowed an involuntary groan. Stretching pressed her breasts against her skimpy T-shirt, accentuating the memory of how she felt crushed against his chest. For a man who spent so little time thinking about women, he entertained a very clear fantasy of her breasts and how nicely they would fill his palms.

Lifting a hand from the wheel, Slater rubbed an itchy palm across the rough denim that covered his knee.

Kat unlinked her hands, reached out and turned down the blaring CD. "This caterwauling would wake the dead. Where are we?" she asked again, fixing him with dark, slightly unfocused eyes.

"Coming up on Toledo," he growled. "I was about to wake you. I think we should stop in Detroit. To buy some sports equipment. It'll curb any speculation at the plant if a box or two arrives on the loading dock as a result of your buying trip."

"Sure. But isn't that silly? Since you plan to drop my program?"

Caught off balance, Slater let the car slow.

"You made your feelings on the subject quite plain at our first interview."

Well, she certainly didn't pull any punches. At least this line of conversation took his mind off other avenues of pursuit. "The Kowalskis aren't coddlers. We're hardworking, task-oriented—to use the current jargon. I'm not against play…outside the workplace."

"In companies with rec programs, they have fewer absences and less time-loss due to illness," she reminded him. "Surely you agree that exercise improves health."

"Yes," he said slowly. "Mainly I gave this a try because workers and staff want what you offered. The jury's still out regarding the statistics you quote. If I'm less than enthusiastic at times, Kathleen, it's because I have a lot on my mind."

"Believe me when I say the last thing I want is to cause you trouble. I know your company is nonunion. Could union advocates be behind the disappearing parts?"

"We've been nonunion from the get-go. Why would organizers suddenly make waves? And wouldn't they take credit?"

"Mmm. Then it's a mystery. Did you fire anyone about the time the trouble started? Disgruntled ex-employees can get pretty nasty."

Slater gnawed on his lip for a moment. "That's just it. Most of our employees have been with us for years. The jobs are more or less handed down from father to son, mother to daughter. We keep pace with scale wages and benefits. Frankly, until Motorhill started their recreation program and news of it reached our plant, our workforce had no complaints."

"Mmm," Kat said again. Then she fell silent. The music from the rock group pulsed and pumped into the void no longer filled with conversation.

"Your choice of…music, and I use the term loosely," she said, "surprises me."

Forced to think of something other than problems at the plant, Slater laughed. "It's one of Scott's CDs. He thinks my taste in music sucks. That's a direct quote."

"Scott appears to live life in the fast lane. He's about the last person I'd expect to find as an engineer."

"Why?"

Kat shrugged. "I don't know. I shouldn't stereotype, but all the engineers I've met work things out logically in their heads before they make a move. They're rarely impulsive."

"In other words, engineers are boring. Thanks a heap."

She laughed. "I forgot you're an engineer. But so are my brothers. And I didn't use the term *boring*. Stop putting words in my mouth."

"Okay, I'll admit I did. We were discussing Scott. I make allowances for him. He had it tough as a kid. Well, maybe not at first. His dad made buckets of money in real estate, but he died when Scott was four. Slipped on a patch of ice and fell off the deck of a house he was showing. Scott's mom already had a drinking problem. She went through all their assets in nothing flat. Ended up in jail for forgery and I don't know what all. Scott became a ward of the court. The state bounced him around Detroit in foster care. Finally a caseworker talked a local family into fostering him. Bob and Bertie Gelecki. Their son, Jerry, was older than Scott.'' Slater's voice dropped an octave. ''Scott worshiped Jerry. Imitated him constantly, did everything for Jerry's approval.'' He shook his head. ''We called him Jerry's shadow.''

When nothing more seemed forthcoming, Kat probed a bit. ''I don't believe I've met anyone named Gelecki. You sounded as if Jerry's the reason Scott became an engineer.''

''What?'' Slater roused from some inner introspection. ''Ye-es. Scott followed in Jerry's footsteps, except Jerry died the summer we...he graduated from college with his engineering degree.'' Slater's lips tightened. Suddenly he waved a hand, drawing Kat's attention to a sign for an off-ramp. ''We take the next exit if we're going into Detroit.''

''Sure. It's your call.'' Kat understood that the discussion of Scott and Jerry was closed. She made a mental note to bring it up again to Hazel, the next time they met for lunch. Or maybe she'd only imagined that Slater had steered them away on purpose. Jerry Gelecki was obviously someone who'd been important to Slater, too.

None of Kat's contemporaries had ever died. Still, in her close-knit Irish community, any death was mourned by all. It was probably the same on the Ridge. Maybe she wouldn't ask Hazel. She'd hate to be labeled nosy.

As the tall buildings of downtown Detroit came into view, talk switched again to work.

''Last week I noticed the baseball diamonds were finally

taking shape,'' Slater said. "If it quits raining, you'll need backstops and base plates soon.''

"A supply of bats and balls, too,'' Kat added. "I plan to stick to slow-pitch softball for men and women. I expect some grumbling from the muscle crowd, but I figure they'll get over it in time.''

"If you asked them, they'd play croquet,'' Slater put in dryly. "The muscle crowd seemed to be out in force flying kites.''

Kat's lips twitched in a grin. "So you *do* think flying kites is for wimps. Let me tell you, buster, flying stunt kites takes strength and coordination. The next windy day I'm going to make you try it. If it's ego you're worried about, we can run out to Clio City Park so no one you know will see you.''

He appeared to concentrate on navigating the narrow city streets. "Next thing you know,'' he muttered, "you'll propose picking mushrooms out in the woods.''

"Now, there's an idea. I've spent some fun summers at the Swartz Creek You-Pick strawberry and asparagus farms.''

"That's not the activity your dad engages in out there. First I ever heard of Swartz Creek, Timothy and his hoodlum pals enticed my father to a weekend of harness racing. Complete with betting.''

"On that score, I'm sure Pop's guilty as charged. He loves horse racing of all kinds. Millions of people do,'' she said defensively. "I do.'' She pointed at herself. "You get in such a snit about their betting. Did you know our neighboring town of Fenton was named after the winner of a poker game? William Fenton's three queens earned him the right to name the town in the late eighteen hundreds.''

"Are you saying our dads' gambling sprees are about renaming Flintridge?'' he asked sardonically. "Somehow I doubt we'll become Kowalskiville or O'Halloran-whatever.''

"I doubt it, too. I'm only wondering if you and my family are making too much of all this. The men have worked hard all their lives. Is it so wrong for them to kick back in retirement and enjoy life a little?''

"Playing poker for beer caps is *fun*,'' he muttered. "You saw how much cash they had on the table the night we spied on them.''

Kat remained stubborn. "My pop took turns sitting up nights with me when I was sick. And if it wasn't for him, I'd have totally flunked math. My brothers could have helped, but they teased instead. Pop spent hours every evening on fractions and decimals. And he bought me a prom dress Mama said was too expensive. Of my entire family, he was the only one who understood my need to live on my own. He's a good, honest, decent man. I don't want that to have changed.'' She blinked rapidly to stave off tears.

Slater guided the car to a stop outside an upscale restaurant. He patted Kat awkwardly. "Don't cry, okay? I know this trip was a bust. What you need is to eat. Dry your eyes. I'll even take the dog into the bushes first.'' He pointed to a neatly landscaped plot. "I'll bring him back a hunk of steak, too.''

Kat caught a glimpse of herself in the side-view mirror. "We can't go in here,'' she exclaimed, tugging at her short hair, fussing with her wrinkled shirt.

"Of course we can.'' Slater dug out a credit card.

"We're wearing the same clothes we had on yesterday. We slept in them. Neither one of us has brushed our teeth. Although,'' she lamented, "I *could* eat. How about a burger place, or a dark bar and grill?''

"You look fine,'' Slater grumbled. Nevertheless he

started the car and meandered the streets until he spotted a neighborhood bar that appeared to fit Kat's description.

They both walked Poseidon down a tree-shaded sidewalk. He padded along happily, sniffing at bushes and telephone poles. Back at the car, Slater rubbed the pup's ears as he lapped up the water Kat poured into his bowl. "This dog really is a good traveler," Slater mused. "Hey, maybe pets are what our fathers need to keep them occupied. Maybe I'll buy my dad a golden retriever."

"Not without asking." Kat bundled Poseidon into the car again and coiled his leash on the floor just before closing him in. "Unwanted gifts become throwaways."

"I thought we started out in agreement," Slater said at the restaurant a few minutes later, where they were waiting in line to be seated. "We both wanted to break up their group. What changed your mind?"

"I don't know. Yes, I do. I keep thinking, what if we're blowing this out of proportion?" She glanced up from the menu she was perusing.

"We saw what we saw. And they were talking about a lot of money."

Kat had already decided on her meal. She ordered the minute they were seated. "I'll take the house burger, with the works. Plus your Popeye steak fries. Oh, and a large glass of milk."

Slater shook his head, wondering where in that petite, compact body she had room to store so much food. "I'll go with your luncheon tenderloin and a mixed green salad," he said. "Coffee, no cream."

"Will that hold you till dinner?" Kat asked. "Or did you change your mind about sharing your steak with Poseidon?"

"He'll get some of mine and probably half your burger. Didn't you notice the size of those portions they were delivering?"

"I'll just double the miles I run tonight." She fidgeted in her seat and tapped her hands on the tabletop in time with the fast tune playing on the jukebox.

"You're burning a lot of calories right now. Don't you ever relax? It suddenly occurred to me that you're a study in perpetual motion except when you sleep."

She stopped, peering at him. "Does it bother you? It used to drive my brothers crazy. My boyfriends, too, except for Danny O'Brien. He kept pace and then some. Danny didn't need much sleep. Midnight to 3:00 a.m, he played cat burglar."

"Cat burg—?" Slater did a double-take. He'd never thought about the type of men she might date. He found he didn't like picturing her with a felon. "You don't still date the guy, do you?"

"Goodness, no." Kat whisked a hand through the air. "You think I knew about his nightly avocation? I only ever dated him because he had my brothers' stamp of approval. Those days my brothers thought it was their duty to choose my boyfriends. But they were so far off base when it came to Danny, they've seen the light. Of course, I rub it in every chance I get."

"So now you choose your own boyfriends?"

Kat fidgeted again. Whatever had possessed her to enter such a discussion with a man who, no doubt, had legions of girlfriends? A man to whom she felt *far* too attracted? *Where was their food?* She almost hugged the waitress, who hurried toward them with steaming platters.

However, after Slater had cut his first slice of steak, he returned to his question.

"Yeah-I-do-my-own-choosing-now," she mumbled around a mouthful of burger. She caught the pickle as it slid from the center and dabbed a napkin at the mustard on her chin. Well, she *would* do her own choosing—if she ever met a man worth choosing. Although that might not be precisely true. She was sitting across from a worthy candidate, if only he'd give her some indication that the interest was mutual. Something more than protectiveness, recalling his admonitions of the previous night. Something more than an impulsive kiss in the dark.

Slater set his steak knife aside. "When we began this harebrained excursion, I never stopped to think how it'd look to your boyfriend."

Kat gagged on a bite of tomato. Again she swiped the napkin over her lips. "I don't recall saying I had a boyfriend, but same goes for your special lady," she muttered. "I arm-wrestled a promise from Gordon Dempsey that news of our night in Atlantic City would go no further."

"That's big of you." Slater smiled as he stabbed at an evasive mushroom skipping across his salad bowl. "Haven't you heard that I'm married to my work? My lady got tired of playing second fiddle to a car. Oh, I'm not blaming Christa. She wanted marriage and kids. She married a mechanic about a year back who'll give her all that."

"Not Gordon Dempsey?" Kat recalled the woman's shrill voice and her hostile accusations. Hard to think of that lady as Slater's type.

"Bonnie Dempsey?" Slater exclaimed. "Uh…no. And don't offer to arm wrestle her. She was a champion mud wrestler at a Chicago bar when she and Gordo met. By the way, she's wife number three and very possessive of her man."

"She…we talked on the phone. I think she has a soft spot in her heart for you, Kowalski."

"Because I pay my bills on time. Gordon runs a loose shop. He extends far too much credit."

Kat fully intended to direct the conversation away from dating partners. Slater had given her an opening to return to the subject of cars. But it wasn't talk of cars that came from her mouth as she dipped a thick fry into a mound of ketchup. "I gather you avoid women who mud wrestle. I know you aren't keen on women jocks, in general. What type of lady does tickle your fancy?" Kat shoved the fry into her wayward mouth, unable to believe she'd asked that.

Slater wrapped the last few bites of steak in a napkin for the dog. He did his best to conjure up Christa Banacek, the tall redhead he'd dated off and on since junior high. She was the woman everyone who knew him assumed he'd end up marrying. Right now, though, the picture popping into Slater's head wasn't of a woman with strawberry hair but one with short dark curls and expressive chocolate eyes. *Kathleen O'Halloran.* Shock battered Slater in unsettling waves. *Marriage…*

Kat dropped the half-eaten fry, pushed her plate away, then wiped her fingers one by one. "That good, huh? So fantastic she's indescribable?" Kat snapped her fingers in front of her companion's distant gaze as she attempted to pull off a joke.

"I, uh, guess I never pigeonhole my dates," he said, feeling his face heat as he looked away from her. "You sound as if you think men stick to a certain category of women rather than responding to a particular woman's individual traits."

"That about sums up what I think, yes. Especially you engineers. Everything follows a pattern. Fits a mold."

Slater slowly brought her back into focus. Now he found he wanted to shake her up. To wipe that smug I-have-you-pegged-right-down-to-your-name-brand-boxer-shorts look from her eyes. "I'm one-hundred percent equal opportunity, Kathleen. Ask me for a date. How about Saturday night? I'll accept."

"Wha-a-a-at?" Kat's jaw dropped. "Don't be silly." She

stacked all the dishes on the table into a rickety pyramid. Clearly flustered, she practically scrubbed the flecks off the Formica tabletop in her need to occupy her hands. Hastily digging in her fanny pack, she pulled out some cash and shoved the bills toward Slater. "Time to quit goofing off and get down to business. I'll check the phone book for sports equipment suppliers while you settle the check."

He picked up the money and reached for her hand. Slowly and deliberately, he pressed the cash back into her palm. "I wasn't goofing off. Consider this our first date. I invited you, so lunch is on me." Somehow it delighted him, knowing he'd thrown her off balance. "We don't go in for gender bias on the Ridge. I'll be more than happy to let you choose the movie Saturday and to pay if you want. Food before or after the flick will be Dutch treat—or Polish-Irish split if you'd prefer." He collected the steak he'd saved for Poseidon, left a tip, and slid out of the booth, leaving Kat to stare at the money she clutched while contemplating his proposal.

She took in a big gulp of air and had to force herself to expel it again. He'd rattled her so badly, even the waitress who returned to clear the table and pocket her tip asked if Kat was ill.

"I, um, am fine." She rose quickly. Was she off stride because it'd been so long since she'd dated anyone that the prospect worried her? Or was it because she'd daydreamed far too frequently about the way a certain CEO kissed? And because a date might just mean a repetition of that memorable event?

Then as she brushed by Slater, who stood in line at the cash register, a cocky grin on his face, the truth slammed into her. It'd been nervy of her to probe into his love life. Strong-arming her into a date was Slater's way of telling her to mind her own business.

Kat angled toward the pay phone in the lobby, feeling

both better and worse for figuring out that he probably had no intention of following through with Saturday. Better, since she could breathe more easily. Worse, because in one fleeting moment he'd opened a window through which she'd glimpsed Slater Kowalski without his executive yoke. Not that he wasn't handsome in his role as executive at Flint ridge Motors. He was a *GQ* fashion statement. Kat happened to like him better a little on the rumpled side, the way he'd been on awakening in Atlantic City.

She shook off a vision of his sun-blond hair that flopped over his brow and got back to leafing through the yellow pages of the Detroit phone book.

"Find anything?" His unexpected closeness startled her. Kat immediately dropped the heavy book and lost her page.

"You are the jumpiest female." A smile, from his eyes directly into hers, shaved the sharp edges off his statement.

"A warning before you sneak up might be nice." Kat hefted the book again and patiently thumbed her way to the beginning of the *S*'s.

Slater eased it from her hands and closed the metal cover. "I asked the cashier for directions. Seems we stumbled into a good area. There are three outfits in this vicinity. Two wholesalers who deal in new merchandise, one in used."

"Great. It's your money, boss. You choose." Calling him boss established the distance Kat sought following their too-personal exchange at lunch.

"I may be boss, but you're head of the program," he said, sounding more the CEO again. "I bend over backward to give department managers autonomy."

"So I've heard. And I'd never take advantage, knowing how you *really* feel. What happens to all this equipment when you decide to scrap the program?"

"Now who's putting words in whose mouth? Dumping the rec program was never a definite outcome."

"No?" Kat tapped a forefinger on one temple and closed her eyes. "Hmm. I'm looking into the past. I distinctly see you warning me during my first meeting in your office, that your attorney was trying to find loopholes. And once he did, my program was history. Or words to that effect."

"Wouldn't you know I'd hire someone who turned out to have a good memory? Back then, I thought taking time out for games would adversely affect production. Figures I received from accounting last week remain steady."

"By summer, I predict you'll see an increase in output."

"By summer, I'd better. A fleet of Specials needs to be rolling off the line all polished and ready for June delivery."

They'd begun to retrace their steps to the car. Kat slowed and hung back a bit. "What made you risk everything on an alternative-fuel car?"

"Risk? It's inevitability. Motorhill has electric cars slated for mass production next year. And I hear they're near completion on a test car that uses ethanol. GM, Ford—they all have A-F cars in design."

"Small economy models. Not for the luxury crowd."

"What's the difference? Americans have long had a love affair with roomy, comfortable cars. The problem in using alternative fuel has been its limited range. I think our fuel cell solves that."

"Perhaps. *If* you can get it to spontaneously combust in the proton-exchange membrane every time you switch cells. Not splitting the hydrogen cleanly and separating out the electrons is one of your problems, isn't it?"

"Who told you that?" Her knowledge of the problem startled Slater. He'd thought it was a well-kept secret. One confined to his office. Not information he cared to have leaked to the board—which included his father. Visibly agitated, Slater fumbled the car door open. He remained stony-faced as he fed Poseidon chunks of steak.

Kat, standing behind and to the left, noticed the tense set of Slater's shoulders. She didn't need his next statement to know she'd overstepped her bounds.

"Until you can show me your Ph.D. in chemical engineering, I suggest you stick to flying kites."

His comment provoked her, and Kat's temper flared easily. "How smart is it, building a car that needs a Ph.D. to make it run?"

"That's my worry."

She pushed past him, retrieved the dog's leash and, with a toss of her head, unfurled it and snapped it to Poseidon's collar. "Indeed it is," she bit back. "I can see that D.C. will have to develop a rapid-transit system to transport all the pigheaded men left stranded along the freeways because the Special's designer is the most pigheaded of all."

Ignoring Slater, she urged Poseidon into a trot. Except, even the mutt betrayed her. Sensing he hadn't gobbled all the steak tidbits, he put on his brakes and practically up-ended Kat in his haste to return to Slater.

"Good boy," Slater purred in his throat. "You recognized her slight to the entire male species." The minute the Lab had devoured the last piece of steak, Slater tugged the leash from Kat's loose grasp and jogged off. The dog, who often dragged Kat, kept perfect pace with Slater.

"Traitor," Kat called. However, there was no malice in her tone.

As she watched Slater make his way back, she vowed to keep chipping away at his veneer. She couldn't pinpoint the exact moment it became important to her to see Slater succeed in his efforts with the Special. Kat knew it rivaled her need to put things at home back on an even keel. But the two goals might be accomplished more easily if they were intertwined. If there was cooperation between Flitridge and Motorhill. Between Kowalskis and O'Hallorans. Of course, that was exactly what her brothers *didn't* want. Which meant there was a lot of persuading to be done.

Slater appeared to have run off his irritation. He greeted Kat with a wide smile. "Your dog's a great running partner. I've always been a solitary runner. It gives me time to work out problems in my head. Voicing them to a canine pal might make solving them even easier."

Kat grinned back. "Tell you what I'll do. I'll share him. You get the 5:00 a.m. shift. Rain or shine, he wants his run. Sometimes half an hour earlier."

"And they call anyone with that disgusting habit man's best friend?"

"Man's—that's the point I wish to make. Nowhere have I heard dogs referred to as woman's best friend. So why do I keep letting him get away with waking me up at ungodly hours?" Laughing, Kat leaned over the seat and ruffled the dog's fur with both hands. He barked three times, thumped his tail and gave her a slurpy kiss. Bounding across the console, he greeted Slater the same way as he climbed beneath the steering wheel.

"That's it," he exclaimed, wiping his cheek and chin. "Deal's off. I was just about sold on him, too. But I prefer to wash my face the conventional way."

"You didn't shower today," Kat pointed out gleefully, getting a huge kick out of watching Slater swipe at the wet streaks left by Poseidon's tongue.

"You'd tell me, wouldn't you, Kathleen, if my breath smelled anywhere near as bad as his?"

"Are you kidding? Three things my mama told me ladies don't talk about in public. Bad breath, B.O. and diarrhea."

Slater's sides shook from laughing. "I swear you always have a comeback. Did no one ever tell you how difficult it is to have a serious conversation with you?"

"My brothers. But they don't count. They told horrible

lies about me so their girlfriends wouldn't pay attention to anything I had to say. Warped my psyche.''

''Life at the O'Hallorans' must have been a three-ring circus. Growing up an only child was boring by comparison.''

Kat sobered instantly. ''What did you and your father talk about? At dinner for example.''

Signaling for a left turn, Slater pulled into the center lane. ''When he was home for meals, you mean? Cars, I guess.''

''Big surprise,'' Kat snorted. ''Who took care of you? Who listened to gripes and stuff when you came home from school?''

''We had cooks and housekeepers. Great-aunt Adelaide popped in and out. She taught me the nuts and bolts of the business. And I had friends. Don't make me out to be a poor little rich boy. Neighborhood pals and I rode bikes, built a tree house, kicked soccer balls. All the things boys do. Hey, there's the warehouse we want.'' Finding a parking place put an end to their discussion.

Nearly three hours and two stores later, they had bats, balls and other sports equipment filling the Special's massive trunk. Plus, they'd tucked boxes and bags into every crevice inside the car. They shipped what they couldn't carry. For a number of miles, they'd chatted about the treatment they received at the hands of various clerks.

Kat flopped limply against the seat. ''Look at all the stuff we bought. I can't believe you authorized spending so much money.''

Slater cast a quick glance at the merchandise. He'd slowed in order to leave the freeway at the outskirts of Flintridge.''Did we buy anything you aren't going to use?''

''No, but…''

''Well, there you go. I've never seen anyone get so pumped up over a few infielder's gloves.'' He reached across the intervening space and traced a finger down Kat's cheek. "Small things make you happy, Kathleen. I like that."

Her eyes twinkled. "Hey, don't go getting the idea I'm a cheap date, buster."

"Ah, but that's a moot point. You're paying for our next date, remember?"

She sat up straighter as he turned onto a familiar street. "Our date next Saturday—you *were* joking, right?"

Slater entered the residential area, known as the Hill. "Not on your life," he sputtered. "Although I'll flip you for who drives. On second thought, I'll be chauffeur." His gaze had drifted to the battered SUV parked between two Motorhill compacts. He drove slowly into the circular drive, expecting Kat to blow off a little steam. But she'd gone unaccountably still. Slater didn't think that boded well.

Kat had been so certain he wouldn't follow through, she had a hard time collecting her gear and her wits.

Slater dug out her duffel bag from under the heap of purchases crammed into the trunk. He held it just out of reach, waiting for her reply. But after she dropped the dog's satchel and almost lost her grip on his leash, Slater took matters into his own hands. "Look, I'm not using my position as your boss to coerce you into this date. If you don't want to go out with me, say so."

Her lashes fluttered up in surprise. "I don't…I mean I do want to go. I never thought you'd use your position to force me into…anything." The words came out in fits and spurts as Poseidon lunged toward the house.

"So, what's the problem?" Slater believed in meeting adversity head on.

"You could date any single woman living on the Ridge, I'll bet. Why choose someone from the Hill? Why choose me?"

Slater burst into peals of laughter. She looked so truly baffled that it delighted him. Scooping her up, he swung her around. As far as Poseidon's leash would allow, anyway. And when he set her feet on the ground again, their eyes met. A rising, nearly full moon sent shadows skittering through the trees, turning her irises dark, almost black. In contrast, her skin appeared winter white. All except her lips. They were full and flushed plum red in the flickering light, and begged for a taste. So taste he did. Without asking, he took what he'd craved all day. Even though he knew from his last miserly experience that one taste would never be enough. But he figured asking would probably have earned him a resounding no.

Or maybe not. This time Kat rose on tiptoes and opened for his kiss like the petals on a rose—until the front door of the house flew open and a strident male voice called her name. Or a semblance thereof.

"Kitten? Is that you? Mama's been pacing the floor for an hour. Who's that you're with? Kathleen?" The voice rose to a bellow and moved closer, at last causing Kat to struggle out of Slater's arms.

Hanging on for an extra moment, he mumbled against her lips, "Whoever that is, he's not your keeper. Tell him to take a hike."

Kat broke the kiss completely. "It's my brother Josh," she whispered in a lengthy sigh. "He's worse than a keeper. Someday you'll meet him, but this isn't a good time. Especially if Pop's not home yet and Mama asked Josh to come over. And Mark. His car's here, too."

"I'm not afraid of the big bad wolves. And whatever happened to choosing your own boyfriends?"

"I know, I know." She gave him a little push toward his car. "But those big bad wolves will want to tear you apart. So you'd better get while the getting's good."

Slater looked unconvinced. At the crunch of shoes on gravel, Kat sprang up and delivered a quick peck on his lips. "Go," she murmured. "Please." She wasn't ready for this. Kowalskis and O'Hallorans. Ridge and Hill. She needed more time. And a plan.

Reacting to the urgency in her voice, Slater went.

The Special's taillights winked past the mailbox at the end of the drive just as Josh strode up to Kat. He wasted at least half a minute tripping over her duffel and tangling his feet in the yapping dog's leash.

"Whoa!" Josh righted himself. "Odd cat-eyed tail assembly on that car. I don't recognize the design."

"Mmm, hmm," Kat responded. "Probably the moonlight." She'd bent to gather her things.

"Who dropped you off? Mama said you went to Atlantic City to find Pop."

"I did, but I never connected with Pop. There were several huge conventions in town. The casinos were packed. Quit bird-dogging that car and help me get this stuff inside. Tell me how to handle Mama. She'll be positive Pop's hip-deep in sin."

Josh stepped into the street, as though determined to run a make on the dark car. "Um. That car... Can't help wondering if Mama's worrying about the wrong O'Halloran."

Pretending she hadn't heard, Kat gathered her own stuff and lugged everything into the house. Once inside, she slipped into the bathroom to repair any damage resulting from Slater's kiss. A kiss she'd participated in wholeheartedly. But she wasn't willing to attract the cross-examination of her family. Not yet, anyway. Their first objection would be that Slater wasn't Irish. Their second objection, that he was their business rival. Their third, that he was from the

Ridge. And they'd think of more. The furor that would erupt once they discovered she planned to date the dreaded Louie's son didn't bear thinking about.

Not yet, anyway...

CHAPTER NINE

SLATER DROVE TO THE END of Kathleen's street, where it struck him that he'd abandoned her. Or at least allowed a faceless man to run him off. Faceless, perhaps. But not nameless. And looking back in the rearview mirror, Slater saw a man step into the street. In silhouette, the guy had the bulk of a fullback.

Forced into a right-hand-turn lane by the one-way street, Slater circled the block. He'd let one woman go, let her believe he cared more for automobiles than for her. Slater didn't know why, but he wasn't inclined to let Kathleen slip away. And she'd probably run, not walk, once she stopped to consider how little it'd taken to get him to leave—the merest suggestion of an overprotective big brother.

As he rounded the corner leading back to the O'Halloran house, Slater caught sight of a dark blue Ridgecrest turning into the drive. His father's car. The Ridgecrest was Louis Kowalski's engineering dream, like the Special was Slater's.

Slowing to a crawl, Slater peered through the darkness. Sure enough, his dad climbed out the driver's side. A shorter man emerged from the passenger door. Three others sat in back, identifiable only because of the Ridgecrest's powerful interior lights—a feature in which the elder Kowalski took immense pride.

From what Slater could tell, all of the car's occupants were laughing and having a high old time. He cruised right on past. Obviously the miscreants were returning from Atlantic City. If they hadn't won big, there was certainly no evidence of major loss in their demeanor. That was encouraging.

Again faced with a turn at the end of the street, Slater decided to head home rather than make another circuit. Bursting in on Kathleen seemed rather pointless. He suspected her brother and mother had an overabundance of hostility stored up for Tim. Furthermore, Slater judged the name Kowalski would be cause for a riot in the O'Halloran household about now.

If he took a shortcut home, he'd be able to catch his own dad when he rolled in...and ask a few questions. Normally Slater steered clear of L.J.'s section of the house. Since graduating from high school, he'd had his own quarters, complete with private entrance to the family mansion. When Slater moved from the main area, his dad's only request had been that they continue to take meals together. As time went by, even that fell by the wayside. Because Slater spent more and more hours at the plant.

Not until after he'd parked and made his way through his quarters into a chilly, dark living room did Slater take a good look at the vast emptiness and wonder if his increased absence was to blame for his father's erratic behavior.

Slater had assumed Louis would handle retirement as Great-aunt Adelaide had. It seemed logical to expect that the current board chairman would accept appointments to philanthropic foundations and spend his days running from breakfast meeting to luncheon meeting, and on to black-tie fund-raisers in the evenings.

Slater quickly lit a fire in the huge stone fireplace to help ward off the guilt that accompanied tonight's chill. Toward the end of the last fiscal year, right after his father had passed the presidency on to his son, L.J. was still showing up at the plant every morning on the dot of seven, as if nothing had changed.

Coaxing a feeble flame to life, Slater thought about that period of time. He'd let the first month slide. Then, because of problems that cropped up, he'd talked with his dad about the fact that his very presence undermined his son's authority. Old-timers circumvented Slater, choosing the more familiar route to deal with their concerns. This would have been fine had L.J. sent the men back to their new boss. He didn't. He interfered and often unknowingly countered Slater's directives. It got so bad that Slater eventually had to ban his father from the premises.

More guilt marched up Slater's spine. He added several sticks of kindling as the fire started to blaze. To let the old man down easy, Slater had agreed to meet him for lunch every day at the fitness club. That lasted two weeks, until the board approved his designs based on the government's interest in the Special's alternative-fuel system.

Slater didn't suffer any illusions. If not for his father's persuasive speech, the board would have voted against funding the Special. Surely his dad knew that was the main reason Slater felt it necessary to work his butt off. To prove himself worthy of L.J.'s faith…

Standing, Slater moved soundlessly around the room. His footsteps brushed against the braided rug his parents had purchased on their last anniversary trip to Poland. The room housed at least twenty display cases of etched crystal and cut-glasswork his mother had bought there. And a collection of chore baskets, also selected by his mother. Her presence in this room so long after her death overwhelmed him.

Frequent disagreements with his dad about redecorating prompted Slater's move to a wing where memories of his mother could be called up on *his* terms. Living in a shrine to a dead person didn't bring that person back. Slater had told Bertie Gelecki and Scott the very same thing. They'd canonized Jerry, the last person who'd have wanted to be made a saint.

The front door opened, bringing a rush of air that made the flames in the fireplace flicker wildly. Slater glanced up as L.J. strode through the door. A rangy six-footer, still rigorously in shape, even after the by-pass, his dad sported a full head of hair, more gray now than blond. Eyes, once the color of cobalt, had faded slightly. It pleased Slater to see a spring in his father's step. Despite the areas on which they disagreed, Slater's heart brimmed with love for his father.

Louis broke off whistling the moment he saw his son. "Well, well. What brings the workaholic home before the witching hour? And warming the hearth already? Is there cause to celebrate?" He nudged the door shut, slipped off his coat and carried it across the wide marble entry to drape it over a chair.

"Suppose you tell me, Dad. You're the one who came in whistling."

"Is there a law against whistling?" Louis paused at the bar, took a glass from the shelf and poured three fingers of cognac. He held it to the light a moment, studying its color. "Smooth liquor, warm fire and good friends is all a man my age really needs. I just dropped off Tim, Spud, Buzz and Luke. But I'm quite certain you're aware that the four of us went to Atlantic City. How much extra do you pay my housekeeper to spy?"

Stunned for only a moment, Slater laughed. "Helen cleans my rooms, too, which is *all* I pay her for. If she happens to let slip some of the cockeyed things you're up to, it's because she's concerned for your welfare. I think working here for the past twelve years gives her the right."

"I don't. I may fire her." Louis downed the cognac and smacked his lips.

"What?" Slater's jaw sagged. Helen had been past her prime when his father hired her. The job kept her from having to accept charity from her kids. "You can't fire her!"

"Can, but I probably won't. Who else would take on such a nosy busybody?" Breaking the tip off a dark cigar, Louis struck a match on his thumb. He watched it flare before applying it to the cigar.

"Dad!" Slater threw up his hands. "I swear I don't know what's gotten into you. The doctor told you five years ago to quit smoking. Since you brought up the subject of Atlantic City, I'd like to point out that it's not only your money you're squandering with those hooligans. A big loss would shake the foundation of Flintridge Motors. I haven't broached the subject with Aunt Adelaide. But maybe I will."

His father slammed the crystal glass down on the bar, and his face became so florid, Slater started worrying.

"Listen to me, you young pup. It's *my* money." He thumped a fist hard against his chest. "Not company funds. And I'll do with it as I damn well please."

"All right. Calm down. Don't stress your heart. Here, sit." Slater patted his father's favorite leather chair.

"I am calm," the old man bellowed as he threw himself into the chair. "If I was riled, I'd toss you out on your ear."

Slater paced before the fire. "Let's try and be rational, shall we? Money aside, there are other things to consider. What about preserving the integrity of our alternative-fuel engine? I wouldn't be half so edgy if you hung out with our retirees. It's like you've forgotten the reasons Ridgers and Hillites don't mix. We each have carefully guarded secret formulas and restricted technology." Slater caught his breath and leaned a hand against the polished mahogany mantel for support. He'd just placed Kathleen in the role of enemy. Was that what he really believed?

"I haven't forgotten, son," his father said softly. "I'm ashamed to say it's taken me sixty years to see how stupid and unproductive it is to divide a town. We're beginning a new millennium. High time we got to know our neighbors."

Slater turned slowly. "Stuff's been happening at the plant. It all started about the time you met Tim O'Halloran. Misplaced equipment, broken parts causing work slow-downs. Our classified design lab has been found unlocked twice. What if your new pals befriended you just so they could worm information out of you? Information that'd let them throw a wrench in my operation and keep us from meeting our government contract?"

Louis stared Slater in the eye. "As if I'd blab. But in case you still think I'm a doddering old fool, let me set your mind at ease. The guys and I agreed at the outset that we'd had a bellyful of eating, breathing and sleeping cars. The subject never crosses our lips. We have other fish to fry."

"Bah! It's second nature with you to talk cars. I hear it is with O'Halloran, too."

"And who'd be talkin' to you about Timmy, I wonder?" Louis asked, affecting an Irish brogue. "Wouldn't be his pretty little lass, Kathleen, now, would it? Of course not. You don't have time for anything but that damned car."

Slater clenched his fists and thrust out his jaw. "It might interest you to know that Ms. O'Halloran isn't any happier about your falling in with that foursome than I am. You obviously know I've hired Timothy's daughter. But she— Oh, what's the use of trying to talk sensibly with you?" Expression thunderous, Slater banged out of the room. To say he was less than thrilled as his father's laughter chased him down the hall would be an understatement. He slammed the door into his apartment, shutting out Louie's cheery sug-gestion that he invite Kathleen to the Easter Monday cele-bration held in Zernik Square.

When *was* Easter? Slater snatched a calendar from his desk. Two weeks. Easter was in three weeks. Thank goodness it was late in April this year, but that still left a scant three months later the first batch of Specials were due off the line.

He didn't have time to attend Easter Monday celebrations.

As if Kathleen would go if he *did* ask. He recalled Kathleen saying, after he'd patiently explained Smingus Dyngus, that she wouldn't ever go with him to the festival. Though at the time they'd been joking around. The truth, however, was inescapable: they came from totally diverse backgrounds.

Why then, when they were together, did he have such a hard time remembering those differences? Kathleen was attractive, yes, but not a raving beauty of the type that scrambled a man's brains. And Lord only knew trouble followed her everywhere.

Did it? Or was he searching for reasons to keep her at arm's length?

Slater picked up a stack of mail Helen had left on the corner of his desk. As he shuffled envelopes, a small blue one addressed in Christa Banacek—er, Christa Minski's handwriting—claimed his attention. He slit the seal and pulled out a card announcing the arrival of a baby boy. Nine pounds.

A tremor shot through Slater's hand. He dropped the card. Not, he realized on stooping to pick it up, because of any lingering regrets. But because the news triggered feelings in him that went along with those he experienced whenever he noticed that his dad was aging. Aging well, but nevertheless growing older.

Therefore, so was he. Christa's announcement drove home, as had nothing else, what a recluse he'd become. Slater hadn't even realized she was pregnant. You'd have thought someone at work might have mentioned it. Surely they didn't think—nah! He'd never let his feelings show.

Crossing the room, Slater switched on a handheld recorder that he frequently used to communicate with his secretary. After noting the particulars concerning the new arrival, Slater requested that Hazel draw a check on his personal account and purchase something appropriate. Releasing the button, he stared at the glowing red light a full ten minutes before he sorted through the rest of the mail and dictated responses.

More times than Slater cared to count, his gaze skipped over his functional yet impersonal surroundings. Each time his mind stalled, he found himself trying to envision what type of home Kathleen O'Halloran would create.

None of the cool blues and nondescript tans he now lived with. He pictured Kathleen living in a profusion of warm colors. Red brick rather than gray marble. He didn't know a lot about fabric, except as it pertained to car seats, but it wasn't hard to imagine her choosing textured cloth of rich shades.

Time and again, he tried placing her among his mother's fussy crystal knickknacks, only to return to the notion that Kathleen would be more apt to have open shelves displaying athletic awards. He could see her filling the corners with potted plants, and maybe in the center of a table, a huge vase of cut flowers.

The vision stayed with Slater. So much so that on his way to work the next morning, he stopped at a florist's shop he passed every day but had never gone inside. He ordered a mix of daffodils, jonquils and Dutch irises, signed his name to the card with a flourish and asked to have the flowers sent to Kathleen at her office.

That stop made him late. Forced him to hit the ground running.

As soon as he hurried out of the elevator, Hazel jumped up from her desk and followed him to the door that led to his private office. "Before you go in," she said, "you need to know that last night, Pat Matejko surprised an intruder coming out of the hydrogen fuel-cell conversion shack."

"What? Why wasn't I notified?"

"I tried to call, but I got your answering machine. I figured you weren't back from D.C. so I didn't leave a message. You never gave me a copy of your itinerary," she chided. Then, as if that was beside the point, she continued. "It was barely dark, maybe about seven. I'd stayed late because Scott asked me to go over the figures on his end-of-the-month budget report."

Slater interrupted her roundabout explanation. "Has anyone run a check to see what's missing?"

Hazel nodded. "Patrick met up with Scott, who was on his way here to pick up his report. According to him, all three tanks of natural gas were punctured. Filters were tossed around. In general the room had been trashed. Scott said nothing was taken."

"Good. What about the design center? Did anyone think to check the new lock?"

"Patrick did. Everything else appeared tight as a drum. It was a fluke that he happened to be going past the conversion shack. The coffeepot in Security shorted out. He saw our lights on and thought he'd see if he could bum some coffee from you. Otherwise, no telling what the extent of the damage might have been. Personnel on his shift weren't due to make security rounds for another hour."

"Did Pat get a look at the intruder?"

"No. But he ran into Scott, who was on his way here. Like I said, they gave chase."

Slater started to instruct Hazel to draft a memo to beef up security yet again, when his office door opened forcefully. Rumpled and bleary-eyed, Scott scowled at his boss. "Where the hell have you been?"

Hazel slanted their chief engineer a stern look of disapproval.

Thrown off stride, Slater adjusted his tie. Then in a voice edged with irritation, he snapped, "What are you doing in my office, Scott?"

"Didn't Hazel tell you about the break-in? Pat and I are waiting to debrief you."

"All right. Debrief and be on your way. Frankly, I think our best defense is to iron out the bugs in the Special's engine and get production underway. I had engine failure again yesterday. I want you to look at redesigning her valve train."

"There's nothing wrong with that valve train. It's my design."

"I say it's out of balance." The two men glared at each other until Hazel plucked at Slater's sleeve. "Uh…Pat's still in your office. He stayed to make his report but could probably use some sleep before coming back tonight. You want to tell me how much overtime you're authorizing? And I assume you want me to notify Wendy Nelson."

"Tell her to have the temporary agency call me. I want experienced guards. I think three for swing and three for graveyard. But Hazel—the fewer people who know we're putting on extra guards, the better. We'll catch this guy next time."

"If it's a guy," grunted Patrick Matejko, who'd ambled to the door of Slater's office. The chief of security might be getting on in years, but his broad shoulders filled the opening and blocked the sunlight pouring through the office windows.

Slater paused in the act of shedding his jacket. "If not a guy, who?"

Patrick deferred to Scott. "I didn't get a good look, but Scottie saw someone running down the path to the river. Someone skinny and fast. We found a partial footprint on the river bank. A small sneaker. A woman's, maybe."

Slater took time to digest Pat's statement. "So what are you saying? That the intruder, possibly a woman, came and went by boat? In the dark? But who would navigate the river at night? It's dangerous enough during the day."

The room grew so quiet, a settling dust mote could have been heard. Neither Hazel nor Patrick met Slater's demanding gaze. Scott did, but shrugged.

Slater didn't like what their silence implied, nor did he like the pictures that had begun to float through his mind. Yet he failed to block out the memory of Kathleen O'Halloran navigating the river as if she'd been born to it.

But there was something Slater knew that no one here did—it'd been almost dark when he deposited Kathleen at her house. He rubbed his forehead as if that would help him remember if her SUV still stood in the driveway when he drove by that second time.

Scott skirted Hazel and clapped Slater on the back. "I know it's hard to imagine a chick with the know-how to pull off the crap that's been going on. 'Course, Pat and I don't have enough proof to lay blame. We're just making you aware, buddy."

The phone on Hazel's desk rang. She ducked out again to pick it up. After listening briefly, she glanced worriedly at Slater.

"Is that for me?"

She covered the mouthpiece and said in a stricken voice. "It's Kathleen."

Slater's brows dipped. "Transfer her to my private line." Turning to the two men, he gestured dismissively. "Thanks, guys. Pat, go home and get some sleep. I'll check with you tonight. Scott, I...thanks for your help. Why don't you take the morning off?''

Scott smiled and whacked Slater's shoulder again. ''For a minute there I thought you were gonna pick up the phone and fire the dame. Should've known you can't afford to cause a riot among the rank and file. Maybe it's smarter to keep her here, where we can watch. I want you to know I'll do my part.''

''Hold it right there, Scott. Kathleen is innocent. I'd stake my life on it, so don't go off half-cocked. Anyway, plant security is my worry, not yours. I need you to concentrate on smoothing out the bugs in that damned engine.''

Scott backed away bowing and drawling exaggeratedly, ''Yes, sir! Whatever you say, sir!''

Slater watched the two men, one big and burly, the other thinner and more than a head shorter. As they hiked toward the elevator, a sudden draft seemed to prickle the hair at the nape of his neck.

''You haven't forgotten that Kathleen's on the line?'' Hazel reminded him.

''Uh, no. Put her through.'' Slater spun away into his office and shut the door with a bang. He paced in front of the phone waiting for Hazel's ring-through. When it came, he lifted the receiver, took a seat and leaned back, crossing his feet on the desk.

Kathleen's lilting voice, praising the flowers he'd sent, washed his mind clean of problems. Slater soon found himself grinning for no reason at all, and he looked forward to seeing her later in the day...in spite of the fact that she took it upon herself to scold him.

''These flowers are beautiful, Kowalski. But whatever were you thinking, sending them here?'' She paused. ''Slater, the driver dropped them off in Personnel. The card wasn't even in an envelope. Wendy Nelson delivered them to me personally. I tell you, if her face had been any stonier, she'd be enshrined at Mount Rushmore.''

Damn! Slater had completely forgotten it was policy to leave packages at Personnel. Berating himself, he snapped forward. His feet hit the plastic chair pad that protected his carpet.

"Did you lose the phone?" Kat asked. "Oh, here I am rambling on, and I'll bet you're trying to catch up after missing two days. Me, too. Plus I have to mark all the equipment we bought yesterday so it doesn't walk off-site. I won't keep you. G'bye. And thanks again. You really know how to brighten a lady's day.''

"No, wait…Kathleen. Don't hang up. How was your evening? I mean," he muttered, "your evening after I dropped you off.''

"Oh, is that why you sent flowers? You saw your pop drive in with mine? I honestly can't say what happened. The family seemed headed for a shouting match, so I left.''

Slater tightened his grip on the phone. "Left? Where'd you go? It was dark.''

"I'm a big girl, Kowalski. I'm allowed out after dark. I've even been known to go into a bar alone.''

"So you went out for a drink? Where? To what bar? How long did you stay?" Slater hated the thoughts that had begun to crowd out his sunny mood.

"Look, Kowalski. Buying me lunch and sending flowers doesn't give you the right to act heavy-handed. Where I go and what I do is my business. Maybe we'd better forget about going out Saturday night. Unless you care to apologize. If so, I'll be conducting women's volleyball in the warehouse.''

Slater winced as she smacked the phone in his ear. He said a few choice words before he hung up. If she had nothing to hide, why didn't she tell him where she'd gone?

His anger cooled as quickly as it'd flared. News of last night's break-in probably hadn't reached her yet. He had probably sounded bossy. And possessive.

Once Slater emptied his mind of the incriminating suggestion Scott had planted, he returned to his first conclusion. Kathleen O'Halloran was innocent of wrongdoing.

He looked forward to their date, dammit. He jumped up, grabbed his jacket and was on his way to ask her forgiveness when the telephone rang. It was the temporary agency that handled security guards. Loosening his tie, Slater rummaged in his desk until he found a clean writing pad. Then he sat back, prepared to discuss his requirements. He didn't want any goof-offs or trainees; he wanted experienced guards.

KAT STUDIED THE TELEPHONE that still quivered after she'd slammed it down. That conversation had taken the oddest turn. The man certainly knew how to push her buttons. A fairer assumption might be that they pushed each other's, Kat thought sheepishly as her gaze lit on the flowers.

Lips softening, she moved the heavy vase out of the sun and into a shady corner. The only other time a man had ever sent her flowers had been for the senior prom. And that was just a corsage.

Touched again by Slater's gift of flowers, Kat admitted she had a bad habit of overreacting. Perhaps Slater had simply been concerned for her welfare. It'd happened before. Look how he'd acted about her leaving the police station in Atlantic City. He'd been genuinely worried.

A glance at her watch told Kat she didn't have time to call him back now and make amends. She'd do it, though. Before the end of the day, she promised herself.

IN THE MAKESHIFT GYM, her situation with Slater took a back seat to a more immediate problem—the rudeness tossed her way by the women's volleyball teams.

Betty Landowska, blue team leader, didn't mince words. "Hope you don't think it means anything because Slater sent you flowers. The men made such a fuss about a rec program, he can't afford for it to fold. Everyone knows he doesn't want a recreation program here. So the women are quitting your fancy-dancy teams. Soon as we talk the guys into doing the same, sister, you'll be out of a job."

Kat had opened the bag of softballs and the one of the mitts Slater had left here for her. She tried hard not to let Betty, who had a huge chip on her shoulder, put a blight on the day. Uncapping a permanent marker, Kat picked up the first mitt and wrote Property of Flintridge Motors.

"Hey!" Rose Gierck, equally obnoxious as Betty and the self-proclaimed leader of the red team, elbowed her way through the other players, who hung back. "Those look like new balls and mitts. Where did they come from?"

Annoyed, Kat didn't even look up. "They came from Detroit, Rose. Now, if you ladies don't intend to play, you may as well go back to work."

Some of the more easily intimidated lined up at the net and began batting a ball from side to side. Kat knew that no matter how the women felt about her, they liked the break from the boring assembly work.

Neither Rose nor Betty was inclined to give in so easily. Rose pawed through the bags. "There must be fifty gloves and a hundred balls in here."

"That's right," Kat said. "And an equal number of bats. Several backstops, batting helmets and other things are being freighted in. All brand-new."

"I wouldn't count on getting reimbursed for all this stuff." Betty loomed over Kat in a belligerent stance.

Rose cracked a wad of gum. "Maybe she doesn't expect to be reimbursed."

Betty's blond brows shot up. "You mean the flowers? I doubt that, and don't let Wendy hear you suggest as much. Anyway, this one's too skinny for Slater's taste."

Not liking the gist of the conversation, Kat stood in order to be on more equal footing with her attackers. "Slater signed the requisition. I'm sure he'll let you see his copy to be sure he crossed his *T*s and dotted his *I*s properly."

"As if he has time for such trivia," Betty sniffed. "After last night's break-in, I kinda think he has more important matters to handle."

"Break-in?" Kat's fingers froze around the marker. "Here?"

"Haven't you heard?" Rose asked eagerly.

Kat fixed her attention on Betty. Rose, Kat knew, loved to gossip and tended to blow stories out of proportion.

Betty pulled a mirror out of her jeans pocket and inspected her hair. "Oh, hey, there's Scottie. I heard he and the chief of Security chased an intruder. Let him tell you the story. Time for us to head back to the salt mines, anyway." She placed two fingers against her teeth and blew an earsplitting shriek that left Kat temporarily deaf.

The news must be true, she thought. Scott appeared more somber than she'd ever seen him. Her heart grew leaden with worry for Slater as Scott stepped aside and let the teams file out.

No wonder Slater had sounded terse and distracted on the phone. Kat started toward Scott. How much damage had the trespasser caused, she wondered? Slater couldn't withstand many more delays. Kat had been around the auto industry long enough to know that the problems plaguing Flintridge could spell the end of a company. Though the Kowalski family held fifty-one percent of the stock, the board of directors, if they heard of the trouble and felt the mischief-maker carried a grudge against the current CEO, could force Slater to step down.

Kat's chest tightened. He was so close to being the first automaker to hit the market with an alternative-fuel luxury car. She wanted that honor for him.

As Scott made small talk with one of the women, Kat's mind kicked into high gear. Perhaps she could help expose the culprit or culprits. After all, she had free access to the complex and often adjusted her schedule. She arrived early in the morning or stayed late at night, what with practice sessions and intramural games.

By the time Scott broke away and advanced again, Kat had promised herself that she'd do her darnedest to help Slater find his saboteur. She'd be another set of eyes and ears for him.

It was the least she could do for the man she'd started to...love.

CHAPTER TEN

"SCOTT." KAT'S VOICE faltered. "Tell me about the break-in. The players who just left were mentioning it. That was the first I'd heard."

He cast a quick glance around the room, then slung an arm around her shoulder and bent his head. "Shh. The less said the better. You want Slater to catch the dude, don't you?"

"Yes. Of course." Kat lowered her voice to match his. "But everyone's talking."

"I know. I told that bunch to cool it." Scott grinned and looped a strand of hair behind her ear. "Naturally, I trust you not to talk about this to anyone but Slater and me, babe. Since I came to steal you away for an early lunch, I'll tell you everything I know." He drew a finger across his chest in an exaggerated *X*.

Kat slid out from under his arm. She had to admit that for the first time, his offer was tempting. The more she knew, the better she'd be able to stay on the alert. "I, ah, got up too late to pack a lunch today. I'm eating in the cafeteria, which doesn't exactly lend itself to privacy."

"You've got that right." Scott jingled change in his pocket. "The sun's out. Too nice to stay inside. Join me at the river? We can sit on the dock and soak some up."

"Sounds inviting, but I get light-headed in the afternoons if I don't eat."

"Never fear. Ol' Scotter thinks of everything. I have a

boss who'd prefer I stay chained to my desk, so my office fridge is stocked with sandwiches and soft drinks. It's right on the way to the river. I'll even let you take your pick of tuna on rye, tuna on white, or tuna on whole wheat.''

He finally enticed a smile from Kat. ''With such a wide variety at my disposal, how can a hungry lady refuse? Except...what happened to *kulebiak* or *pierogies?*'' she teased, referring to some traditional Polish dishes Slater had told her about. ''Or do you have stock in a tuna cannery?''

''Nah. My old lady gets on these kicks. She fixes one thing for a whole month. Next month it might be peanut butter and jelly.''

Kat's smile dissolved instantly. ''Men should speak of their wives with respect, Scott. And now that you've brought her up, I realize how our going off to eat together could be twisted to look like something ugly if anyone saw us and gossiped about it.''

''My wife knows. I phoned her.'' Scott shackled Kat's wrist to keep her from walking away. ''I confess to having an ulterior motive in asking you to lunch. I've decided to buy a kayak of my own for when we start lessons. It was actually my wife's suggestion that I ask you for pointers before spending a lot of money unwisely.''

Kat almost laughed. Who would buy a kayak before knowing if they had an aptitude for the sport? But she saw that Scott was serious. ''No need to go to the trouble of taking me to lunch for that.'' She shook herself loose. ''I have handouts that cover the pros and cons of various crafts. I don't mind giving you one before I start a class.''

''You're sure tough on a guy who's trying to make nice. Kayaking's only part of the reason. I know you're being ostracized because the boss sent you flowers. Happens every time he singles out one woman over the others.''

"Oh?" Scott had Kat's undivided attention at last. "Kowalski sends a lot of flowers, does he?"

"What can you expect from a man who has motor oil in his veins?" Scott shrugged in a helpless fashion. "I'm telling you this because you're an outsider, Kat. A bouquet is Slater's way of giving *atta-girls*. He never sees how envious it makes the other women. Frankly, the boss has tunnel vision whenever problems come up with his car. So if you're counting on him to squelch the talk, I'll warn you right now, he doesn't even hear it."

Scott slicked a hand through his hair. "Some of those gals can get nasty enough to make you want to quit. You're too nice to go down in flames. All I'm offering is a friendly ear, Kathleen. Believe me, the catfights may get worse before they get better."

Kat reconsidered his offer, her initial joy in the lovely flowers somewhat dimmed. She still smarted from the drubbing she'd just taken. "I don't know, Scott. I've heard my brothers and their wives discussing the rumors that float around Motorhill. They say the only way to kill gossip is to ignore it." Despite Scott's assurances about his wife's approval, she could see that a private lunch with him could well give rise to more gossip—which would hardly help her deal with the rumors and envy that already existed. Anyway, the last thing she wanted to discuss was what people were saying about her.

"Suit yourself. Being odd woman out can get real lonely."

"I appreciate the warning, Scott. But I'll still pass. Sticks and stones may break my bones…well, you know the rest." She turned back to her chore. "I can either send the kayak handouts through inter-office mail, or let you know when I'm in my office and you can pick up a copy."

Scott clamped a hand on her shoulder. He'd obviously

been about to say something else when the door opened, and Slater walked in.

"If you're not going to use the time off I gave you, Scott, go recheck the design of the Special's valve train."

"What did I tell you?" Scott muttered to Kat. "If Slater had his way, I'd never leave my desk." Stomping through the bags of gloves and balls Kat had left to mark, Scott angled toward the back door. He turned as he grasped the knob. "Bring that handout to my office later, Kat. It's obvious I won't get out again today." He wrenched the door open, then let it slam behind him.

Instead of asking Kat about Scott's flare-up as she'd feared, Slater stared at the back door. "Who unlatched that entry?"

Kat followed his gaze. "I don't know. Shouldn't it be open?"

"No. Maintenance was told to add a hasp that makes it accessible only from the inside or with a key."

"Maybe they found something in the fire codes. Or perhaps changing locks is way down on their list of priorities. Up to now, there hasn't been much worth stealing in here." Kat nudged the bag of new equipment with her toe. "I can see why you'd worry now. These represent quite an investment."

"Did I say I was worried about theft?" Slater refocused, seeing before him a slender woman with few defenses and too-trusting eyes.

"I...uh..." Kat glanced away from his searing gaze. "The morning crews were discussing last night's break-in. If I were in your shoes, I'd install new locks everywhere."

A jumpy muscle in his jaw relaxed. "At the risk of being accused again of trying to mind your business, I admit to asking Maintenance to add those locks for your safety. I knew you sometimes stay here alone to put equipment away after the players leave.''

Kat studied the toes of her sneakers. ''I'd like to apologize for the way I acted this morning, Kowalski. Do you remember my saying how sick and tired I got of my brothers always looking out for me? Sometimes I pop off without thinking. I realized after I hung up that you have to concern yourself with the safety of all your employees. And, well, I'd have reacted differently if I'd known about your prowler. To tell you the truth, I thought you were being paranoid when you claimed someone was after your designs. Obviously I was wrong. Were the designs that were stolen last night vital?''

''Aren't you aware that last night's break-in occurred in the hydrogen fuel-cell conversion shack?''

Kat frowned. ''I guess no one mentioned which building. What could a competitor possibly gain from a conversion test site? Doesn't everyone in the automotive industry already possess that information?''

''Stealing wasn't this intruder's purpose, Kathleen.''

She waited for Slater to enlighten her. When he said no more but gazed at her as if he expected her to read his mind, she threw up her hands. ''I feel like we've reached round three in a game of twenty questions. What did he take? What's missing?''

''Nothing's missing,'' Slater said gruffly.

''Nothing…?'' Kat put both fists on her hips. ''So it's a case of another door accidentally left unlocked? Now I see your point about the one here.''

Slater just kept shaking his head from side to side.

''No? So, are you going to tell me or do I have to guess?''

''The interior of the conversion shack was junked. Tanks were punctured. Gauges and monitors were smashed. The place reeks of dumped chemicals.''

Kat's eyes widened in shock, then as quickly darkened in sympathy. She closed the distance between them and gripped Slater's forearm. "That's horrible. Malicious mischief. Probably the work of bored teenagers, don't you think? Count on me if you're recruiting volunteers to clean up. Tell me when, and I'll arrange to be there."

Slater was ashamed at the relief he felt on hearing the sincerity in her tone. He'd backed her to the hilt earlier in front of Scott, Hazel and Patrick, and had declared Kathleen unequivocally innocent. But Scott's comments had planted a seed of doubt that had since germinated. "I don't think it was a random act of vandalism," Slater told her. "I'm sure you know there's more to fulfilling a government contract than simply rolling cars off conveyor belts on time. Government purchasers require proof of test hours at set phases throughout production. That data has to be sent to their committee and approved before they'll release funds to continue work. Our energy converters had only three more days to run. Because the system's entirely new, the committee asked to see the physical monitors rather than the usual report."

"Oh, no. Slater…" Adding up what he'd explained, Kat clapped a hand over her mouth, then moved it slowly away. "With the monitors ruined, there'll be no advance money." She'd just summed up his biggest problem.

He heaved a sigh. "That's about the size of it. Ordinarily I'd draw on company funds. But the board was against refitting so many of our lines to accommodate this project, so I initially set it up to pay for itself and promised them it would."

Kat paced the floor, ruffling her short hair with both hands. "How many people at Flintridge are aware of what you just told me?"

"I don't know." Slater tipped his head and rubbed the

back of his neck. "Anyone who took the time to read the fine print in the contract, I guess. Why?"

"Oh. So then a lot of people were privy to that information. Shoot. I thought I might be on to something. If only three or four people had access to the contract, it'd be a simple matter of narrowing your suspects."

"I see your point, Kathleen. I wish it was that easy. But we have twelve on the board and they were all given copies. The government committee, maybe ten in all, probably had multiple copies to sell their supervisors on the plan. Then there's Hazel, and whichever clerk she assigned to run duplicates. All managers got a package. We met and went over time lines and discussed how each phase of production affected the individual manager's department." Slater shook his head. "These are folks whose jobs depend on timely completion of the car. It's crazy to even suggest a saboteur works for Flintridge."

"Who then?" While she found it commendable that Slater believed wholeheartedly in his staff, Kat couldn't shake a niggling concern that security was too tight for a virtual stranger to waltz in from outside. Only someone with intimate knowledge of the detailed workings of the company could manage these disruptions. Based on what Slater had told her, she agreed with his assessment. The acts weren't random. They were too well-timed.

"Believe it or not," Slater said, transferring his hand to her neck, where he began kneading her skin, "I didn't come here to dump my problems in your lap."

"Did you come to apologize to me?" she asked, delivering a soft elbow jab to his ribs.

He reacted as she'd anticipated, expelling his breath in surprise. "As a matter of fact, woman," he growled for show more than ferocity, "that's exactly why I ran you to ground."

This time it was Kat whose senses were scattered. An admission was the very last thing she'd expected. All she could do was stare.

Slater laughed, lifting his hand from the back of her neck, genuine pleasure welling from his belly. "Can't say I like the taste, either," he teased. "But occasionally I'm forced to eat my words."

Kathleen joined in with his banter so easily as a rule; this time she didn't. Slater dropped his amusement immediately. "I genuinely mean it, Kathleen. I had no right to question your activities away from work. What you do on off hours is your business, as you pointed out."

"Let's say that conversation never happened, Kowalski." Visibly flustered, Kat bent, picked up her marking pen and the next softball glove. She'd intended to beat him to the punch and apologize first. And she wouldn't have been as generous in accepting full responsibility.

One more thing to admire about Slater Kowalski. That, and his very appealing tush, she thought wryly, watching him stride across the room to relock the door he'd said should remain permanently closed.

"Hey," she called. "I would've done that."

Shrugging, Slater finished the task. Then, apparently ill at ease after making his apology, he marched out the front door, muttering something indiscernible about needing to see Scott.

And that, Kat told herself, was another kettle of fish. Scott Wishynski seemed determined to pressure her into starting kayaking lessons. They both knew Slater disapproved of offering the sport. And she didn't think either of them had wanted to add to his problems by broaching the subject again. Anyway, it was wrong of her to expect Scott to intervene; this was her program. She needed to find time to sit down with Slater and assure him his employees would be perfectly safe.

Kat shivered unexpectedly and glanced around for the source of the chill. Surprised to find all the doors closed, she set the mitt aside and rubbed her arms. The goose bumps on her skin were slow to fade, as was her unexpected sense of alarm.

Eventually she did shake the feeling, and returned to her self-appointed job of marking equipment. Since it wasn't a job requiring a great deal of concentration, her mind drifted. First to Slater, then to his design engineer. Scott ran as rough with undercurrents as his boss seemed moored and steady. Yet Kat couldn't dispute the fact that the two men were friends.

She wondered if perhaps she should cancel any plans, however vague, for kayaking lessons.

Or should she? Slater Kowalski had hired her to launch a recreational program at his company. She was supposed to have autonomy, wasn't she? She'd been hired to give the workers what they wanted, hadn't she? And according to Scott, they wanted kayaking. She sighed. If only Slater hadn't made all those decrees—no kites, no kayaks. Why—and what next?

A cool breeze prickled her arms, but this time the source was easily identifiable. The men due for the noon session raced through the door.

They worked together to put away the volleyball nets without any of the complaining that was their normal pattern. One group donned orange vests and the other the blue, also without Kat's direction. In fact, they barely glanced at her before grabbing basketballs from the playpen. The building soon echoed with the thunk of their practice shots striking the backboards.

Not until she was forced to exhale did Kat realize she'd

been holding her breath, waiting for them to harass her about the flowers as the women had done. At first she was relieved, thinking the men obviously didn't care that Slater had sent her flowers. It wasn't until their time was up and they'd stored the equipment and filed out, with no one hanging back to talk, that it dawned on Kat. She'd been snubbed.

The women had carried out their threat. They'd convinced at least a faction of the younger men that Kat was some sort of...of piranha.

Shaken, she labeled the last three softballs and locked the new equipment securely in the two chests she'd lugged from home this morning. All the while, she told herself that the more mature workers who were due to arrive shortly for low-impact aerobics would be their normal pleasant and talkative selves.

No one showed up for aerobics. Not a soul.

Kat lost count of the number of times she walked to the door to check. At first she made excuses for the older men— like maybe they hadn't received her new schedule. However, she knew they had. She'd run copies and put them in the office mail herself. In the end, she accepted the truth. They were too gentlemanly to be as rude as the volleyball team or to snub her as the others had. It made their defection hurt all the more.

Lunch, not surprisingly, was a solitary affair. She bolted down a cheese sandwich in the cafeteria. No one joined her or even spoke to her.

She felt like hiding in her office for the rest of the day. Except that O'Hallorans weren't quitters. So Kat showed up on schedule for each session. She accepted the heckling from the women and the cold shoulder from the men. By six o'clock, though, her nerves were stretched thin.

"Childish. That's what they are," she fumed as she finally sought haven in the privacy of her office. The first item she set eyes on after closing the door was Slater's gift—the vase of bright flowers. Flowers whose colors were muted in the waning light. Or maybe they seemed less cheery because of all the animosity they'd inspired.

Kat dropped her key on the desk and crossed the room to stroke the soft petals of the iris. Was Slater really as out of touch with the feelings of his employees as Scott had insinuated?

She reflected on how many times she'd seen Slater take a moment to ask a worker about a spouse, children or elderly parents. She'd hate to think it had all been an act. However, she now had to wonder if he'd purchased all that equipment yesterday in order to make it look like he was supporting her efforts. If, as Scott said, Slater's gifts of flowers to other women had caused jealousy on previous occasions, there was a possibility he'd been aware of the trouble this bouquet would cause her. That way he wouldn't have to ax her program. He could sit back and let attrition spell the demise of her classes.

As Kat pondered this likelihood—was he *really* that calculating?—the telephone on her desk shrilled. Its blinking light flashed brightly through the evening shadows falling over her desk. Just how long had she stood there in the semidark, pondering a problem that still lacked answers?

"He-llo," she said jerkily, stretching the length of the cord as she tried to reach the wall light switch.

"So you are there?" Scott's distinctive voice flowed into her ear. "Buster Dorn phoned. He said the warehouse is locked and the intramural basketball squad can't get in to practice. He said your office was dark. I can't see it from mine, but I told him you wouldn't skip out without bringing me the kayak handout. I suppose you're on your way to open the gym now? 'Fraid I'm stuck here," he complained.

"Drop by with the handout after practice. I'll serve you a cup of Irish coffee."

"Make that plain coffee," she said. "I'll have a cup before heading home."

"You don't drink Irish? Won't you be drummed off the Hill?"

"I have a taste at weddings and wakes. Scott, are you teasing me? The company handbook says there's no liquor allowed on premises."

"You read the company handbook? Those rules apply to the peasants, doll. I'm management."

At times his arrogance was more than Kat could take. "According to Hazel, one set of rules governs everyone on staff," she said coldly. "Hey, I'd better shove off if the guys are waiting. I didn't realize I was so behind. Since practice is off to a late start, I may take a rain check on bringing you the handout. Slater lectured me about not walking out to my vehicle alone after dark."

"I'll walk you to the parking lot."

"I can't take you away from your work, Scott. Especially not when Slater's behind on the project. I'll get you the information before the weekend. I doubt you'll have time to shop before then. Bye." Kat slipped the receiver back into the cradle, but not before she'd heard him mutter a curse. She wiped damp palms down her jeans, not liking his tone. When would she learn to watch what she said? Kat knew he preferred the illusion that he was his own boss.

Personally Kat thought Slater gave Scott a *lot* of freedom. But then, it wasn't her company. Slater had a board of directors to please, but no union as they did at Motorhill. That made a huge difference in flexibility. And Scott did work plenty of overtime. She had to quit comparing Flintridge policy to that of Motorhill's. Kowalski's mode of operation obviously worked. People on the Hill grumbled about their jobs on a regular basis. With the exception of Scott, Kat had rarely heard Slater's staff complain.

Loading her pack with new clipboards and score sheets, she flushed her mind of everything except basketball, flipped off the light, locked her office and jogged back to the warehouse.

"Sorry I'm late, guys," she said, a little out of breath as she joined the men who were milling around the door of the makeshift gym.

Derek Jones, whose dark clothes and skin blended nicely with the night, rose from where he'd been sitting on the path, and dusted off the seat of his pants. "Why's our gym locked? We missed twenty minutes of practice."

"Yeah." Derek's pal, Buster, stepped in front of Kat, a scowl on his freckled face. "If I hadn't phoned Scott, we'd have skipped out. Then we would've lost sleep *and* practice time."

Kat dug a ring of keys from her pack and pushed through the huddle to the door. "Today's been strange," she said. "My schedule has been off all day. Last night's break-in affected everyone."

John Tuttle, the tallest of the players, rejoined the group after he turned on the bank of interior lights. "So that's why Slater has Security checking badges at the gate."

Kat dug to the bottom of the playpen in search of the best basketballs. "I'm glad you told me that, John. I'll have to run by my office after practice. I've gotten into the bad habit of leaving my badge in a drawer."

"Well," another player muttered, "I wish they'd catch the dude. Tighter security makes it damned inconvenient. I left my lunch bucket in the break room. When I went back to get it, one of Slater's new guard dogs jumped me. Hauled my butt into Patrick's office. Lucky for me Pat had just come on duty."

"Slater's added guard dogs?" Kat exclaimed.

"Figure of speech," said the player who'd made the remark. "Kid who nabbed me doesn't even shave. He's impressed as hell by his uniform and his new job."

"I, for one, say more power to the boss," Buster drawled. "All the stuff that's been goin' on is kinda spooky, if you ask me. A lot of guys on the graveyard shift are startin' to say Slater's car is jinxed. So far, no workers have been hurt. But we all know when people start talkin' jinx, accidents happen."

Kat dropped one of the three basketballs she'd tried to juggle. "Did you come here to shoot the breeze or play ball?" she demanded, wanting to squelch such talk. It shook her to hear anyone suggest Slater's project was jinxed. In her neighborhood, superstitions of that nature had been known to kill an undertaking. Kat wondered if Slater knew what was being said.

Not that anything to do with the actual building of the car concerned her. Slater had made that clear the day he'd reluctantly hired her. But things had changed since then. Their relationship had changed. At least, it had for Kat.

She zeroed in on a scramble taking place beneath the basket. Kat blew her whistle, automatically calling a foul on Derek. Her mind was full of confused thoughts about Slater. Feelings, both tender and passionate, caused Kat's pulse to skip erratically when the object of her reflections sauntered through the door. He'd changed from his gray suit to jeans and a short-sleeved Polo.

Oh, yes. Her feelings since that first accidental meeting on the highway had definitely changed. Then, when Slater stood at the roadside, his designer suit soaked through, Kat had judged him harmless. Tonight…he exuded danger. To her heart, her emotions. He rocked her senses with his very presence.

The breath trapped in her throat sputtered weakly into the silver whistle. A lack of air made her light-headed and tele-graphed a very different message to Kat's brain. *She was falling in love with Slater Kowalski.*

She shouldn't. She couldn't. Panic seized her by the throat. There were fifty million reasons why the very sug-gestion was insane. *Her family. The wholesale disapproval of his staff. Slater hated her SUV. Ridge versus Hill.* If she needed reasons spelled out, those were good, solid ones.

Suddenly, Derek's muscular frame blocked Kat's view of Slater. Her panic subsided as she was forced to refocus and meet her top player's curious brown eyes.

"You calling a foul, coach? Or did you swallow the pea outta that whistle?"

Kat pushed the flutter of peculiar feelings into the pit of her stomach to be dealt with later. She'd never been close to being in love. What made her think she'd knew love when she saw it—even if it hit her between the eyes? Maybe she was tired or just needed food. That was probably it. She'd eaten only toast for breakfast and it was hours since lunch today.

"Derek Jones," she finally managed to squeak out. Crossing her arms, Kat cleared her throat. "If you don't recognize goal-tending—as evidenced by the fact that you reached up and batted John's three-pointer right out of the basket—name one reason I should start you next Thursday night in our game against Motorhill."

For a moment her words were lost on the silent group of men. Then bedlam broke out as the players digested what she'd said.

Buster whooped. John let out a yodel. Derek rammed a fist in the air and charged among the other players doling out high fives. "We'll work swing that day, guys," John said. "Shouldn't be a problem." Agreement and more cheering followed.

Such was the milieu Slater entered. "Did someone win the lottery?" he asked when they finally let him get in a word.

"Better!" John, otherwise known as Stringbean, clapped his boss on the back. "Coach just announced we get to whup the shorts off those smug bastards at Motorhill next week."

"Whoa!" Kat twirled her whistle at the end of its cord, gently poking John's chest. "I only recall announcing a match between the two teams. That kind of conceit may get you benched no matter how well you play. There's no place in team sports for personal grudges. You asked to play Motorhill. I made it happen. I don't condone name-calling. I won't tolerate it on the court. Win, lose or draw, I'll expect you to act like gentlemen when the game ends."

John brushed a thumb across his nose. "What if those guys start slandering *you,* coach? Do we still hafta make nice?"

"Why would they slander Kathleen?" Slater asked the question with a decided chill to his voice.

The players looked uncomfortable. Two or three shrugged. No one answered Slater until he turned his scowl on them one by one.

Buster broke first. "Rumbles, boss. Down at the Y. Word is that the guys at Motorhill have been saying things."

"What things?" Kat was quicker this time.

Derek bounced the ball, once, twice. Hooking it into his side, he summarized the talk. "Usual stuff. My brother heard we're supposedly getting pink uniforms." He nodded toward Jim Pike, the beefiest of the players. "Pike plays pool once in a while at an Irish pub. Some dude called our team the Katie Maguires."

Slater opened his mouth to speak. But Kat tossed back her head and hooted. "Excuse me, but I don't think those rumors are bad. Half the families living on the Hill claim roots back to the Molly Maguires. No more rough-and-tumble group of dissidents ever lived. The name struck fear in the heart of every coal-mine owner. I suspect we have Motorhill's team a little worried. Up to now, they've had the basketball field to themselves."

"I wish you were right, coach," John said glumly. "I don't think they were referring to our prowess, calling us that. The Molly Maguires wore hand-me-down shirts and pants. I've seen Motorhill's uniforms. They're fine threads."

"When's the game?" Slater asked Kat.

"Next Thursday."

"If I rearrange these men's schedules, can you get uniforms for our team by then?"

She didn't quite believe her ears. "You're willing to spring for uniforms? They're pretty costly. Motorhill shells out big bucks to get cool outfits, Kowalski."

He managed to look disgusted. "You might know the rules of the game, Kathleen. You don't know squat about how men play. Reputation is everything." Slater checked his watch. "It's after six o'clock. You know a place that's open at this hour where we can order Flintridge the coolest of cool uniforms?"

"Mulligan Sports on Lincoln Avenue is open till nine. But practice has barely started."

"Derek's captain, right?" At Kathleen's nod, Slater said, "So leave him in charge. For this kind of reward, I think we can trust the guys to practice hard and turn out the lights and lock up on their way out."

"You betcha!" John grinned from ear to ear.

Slater lost no time hustling Kat out the door. "Can we

choose our own colors? I'd like black and white or black
and silver. Something classy,'' he said.

''Motorhill has red and black. Joe Mulligan will have
swatches.'' Kat found herself warming to the idea of choosing classy uniforms. Or she did until they reached the path
leading to the main gate and she saw the guard posted there.

''Oops, I left my badge in my desk drawer. John said I'd
need it to go out and get in again tomorrow.''

Slater checked his watch again. ''I sent out a memo about
it. I'd vouch for you now, but it's not good policy to grant
individual favors. Besides…you'll need it for tomorrow.''

''It's okay. Joe will stay open if he thinks he has a sale.
Why don't you go on to Mulligan's? I'll run by my office
for the badge and meet you later.''

''I'm not wild about you going into an empty office alone.
Stop by Security and ask one of the guys to escort you both
ways.''

''I'll be fine,'' she said with a hint of annoyance. ''I
thought we settled this. I can take care of myself. Besides,
break-ins two nights running would be pretty stupid.''

Slater juggled his car keys from hand to hand. ''All right.
But be careful. I'll see you at Mulligan's, then. If you
haven't shown up in twenty minutes, I'll send the dog with
the brandy.''

Their mutual laughter mingled as Kat left him at the fork
in the path. Still smiling, she broke into a jog. The walkways
were so well lit she didn't know why Slater was concerned.
She entered the building and took the stairs two at a time
until she reached her office. The badge was exactly where
she'd left it in the center drawer. Clipping it to her collar,
she reversed the process, clattering down eight flights of
stairs and back along the path. Moments before she came
in sight of the front gate, a dark figure stepped from an
adjoining walkway and blocked her path.

"Scott!" Kat flattened a hand to her throat. "You scared me half to death!"

He grinned. "Are you on your way to my office, sweet thing?" Bending, he pressed a wet kiss to her lips.

Kat had had less sloppy ones from her dog. And the fact that Scott was married and gave out kisses of any kind angered her. "I'm on my way to meet Slater at Mulligan Sports. He's buying uniforms for the basketball team," she said coolly. "We've got a match with Motorhill next Thursday. Do you think you can make practice so I can count on you to play?"

Scott toyed with her middle shirt button. "You can always count on me, doll. Speaking of counting on someone. I thought you said you couldn't bring me the info on kayaks because it'd be too late. But ol' Slater snaps his fingers and you jump."

Kat slapped his hand away. Sidestepping him, she said, "I don't like being manhandled. And don't call me doll. A piece of advice, Scott—you should stick to one sport at a time. Miss three basketball practices and you don't play for me. It'll be next month before I start kayaking—if at all."

Leaving him, she sprinted toward the gate. Once there, she showed her badge to the guard, who let her pass. A moment later, Kat experienced the same uneasy feeling she'd had earlier in the gym. She glanced around and saw nothing and no one.

Wait, was that Scott standing in the trees? No. It was just a shadow cast by a stand of spindly pines. She'd let his sudden appearance out of nowhere—not to mention his disgusting kiss and their subsequent exchange of words—get to her. Scott Wishynski was full of himself. A not-uncommon affliction among certain kind of men. But since he was a co-worker and Slater's friend, she'd have to make more of an effort to get along with him in the future.

Well she could do that, Kat decided, whistling the rest of the way to her SUV.

CHAPTER ELEVEN

SLATER AND KAT WALKED out of Mulligan Sports, satisfied with the deal they'd cut. "That was nice of you to order a slew of basketballs from Joe," Kat said. "And sneakers. Sponsors don't usually buy their players shoes." She paused. "I know Joe appreciates the business. He's had to lay off help since his wife, Maggie, had a stroke, and his two sons trade off keeping the store open on weekends. Still, it costs Joe a bundle for home health care."

"You needed new basketballs. The ones you have are pathetic."

Kat cast a sidelong glance at Slater, wondering why he attempted to play down his act of kindness. "You could have added basketballs to our order from Detroit at half the cost."

"I wish we'd placed that order through Joe. The old guy's shelves are almost bare. He's proud. Not the type to ask for help. He could've scammed us or jacked up prices. He didn't. From now on, buy all your equipment here."

Kat's smile extended to her eyes. "Got time for a cup of coffee? My treat, tough guy."

"Lead the way, O'Halloran. This is your side of town."

Kat mulled that statement over. No matter which café they visited, by tomorrow news of her tryst would be scattered like a shotgun blast across the Hill. It was time for her to deal with her brothers' objections—before Kowalski arrived at the house on Saturday. They could meet at the theater, but she refused to sneak around anymore. She still felt guilty about Atlantic City. "We'll go to Flaherty's Coffee Shop, where River meets Sadler Road. I'll follow you in case the Special up and quits."

Slater clapped a hand to his chest. "A knife to the heart. I may let you buy my dinner Saturday night to pay for that jab."

"Not in my parish. I won't have the Hill a-whisperin' that Kathleen O'Halloran had to buy herself a man."

Slater noticed dancing flecks of amber in Kathleen's brown eyes as her brogue grew thick enough to slice. Driven by a need to touch her, he brushed his thumbs back and forth across a dusting of freckles that sprinkled her classic cheekbones. "Anyone who looks at you and believes you'd have to buy a man's favor is an idiot, Kathleen."

She felt her face tingle and grow warm. The rest of her body froze. Kat wasn't a woman often left without words, but, this time her mind went blank.

Cars whizzed past on the street. Drivers honked. The logical part of Kat's brain knew they stood on a very public corner in the heart of the Hill's industrial area. Her emotional side breathlessly awaited the kiss that her sensitized nerve endings told her was about to be delivered.

She wasn't disappointed. Slater's touch scalded, but his lips felt cool when they claimed hers. For a moment only. Then he took the kiss deeper. When Slater's tongue delved between her lips, Kat felt her blood thunder in her ears. Hot pleasure pumped through her like a cloud of steam.

Time lagged. Sound receded. Sensation magnified as Kat's fingers traced the herringbone pattern of Slater's Polo shirt across his shoulders and down his chest. The imprint of the five buttons on her blouse seemed to drill holes along her breastbone. Kowalski pressed her so close that Kat felt the rapid swell of his jeans zipper. The experience rocked her, and thrilled her. But wouldn't it be terrible if a woman *didn't* have that effect on the man she loved?

Even lost in passion, Kat understood it didn't necessarily mean that Slater felt the same. Hadn't Scott virtually said he handed out bouquets of flowers to every Thomasina, Dixie and Harriet? Stood to reason he'd be equally free with his kisses.

Kat's passion began to blur around the edges. How did a woman know if a man was just being a man or if he had stronger feelings for her? Men, at least those in her family, were miserly with the *L* word. Kat had never seen them neck in public. Did that make her shameless? Rising on tiptoes, she filtered her fingers through Slater's soft, shiny hair. She purposely rejected thoughts of guilt, wanting more of his touch when his fingers found their way inside her blouse.

An insistent horn jerked Slater back from a dangerous precipice. He realized he was one step from dragging Kathleen to the ground and making love with her on a street corner. What in God's name had gotten into him? Public displays weren't his style at all.

Although, this wasn't the first time he'd reacted to the bewitching pull of Kathleen O'Halloran's lips. He'd reflected on this fact for only a few seconds when a car backfired and had both of them panting and diving for cover. Disheveled and unfocused, each peered around the hood of Kat's Trooper in search of a sniper.

Tugging her blouse together with trembling fingers, Kat glanced sheepishly at Slater. ''Aren't we a pair of dopes? That was Mark Shaughnessy's 1972 Moonraker. Talk about a lemon car.''

Slater stood and brought Kat to her feet, too. He glared after the smoking, belching car, trying to settle his jangled nerves. ''The Moonraker. Motorhill's most embarrassing disaster," he said, pushing Kat's fingers aside so he could button her blouse.

"A real dog," Kat agreed. "Pop tried to tell them. The powers that be were enamored of the name. They ignored his warnings."

In spite of the warm evening, Slater zipped her jacket all the way to her chin. It was easier to discuss cars than face what had happened between them. He needed time to analyze his part in the episode, and was happy enough to follow her lead. "So your dad didn't engineer that fiasco?"

"Nope. For which we, his family, are eternally grateful. The engineer got fired. Last I heard, he moved to New York and was driving a garbage truck."

"Still an engineer," Slater said, reaching to keep the conversation alive. "A sanitary engineer."

Kat's knees felt spongy. Wobbly. She didn't laugh at Slater's joke. Couldn't. She marveled at his ability to appear so cool. But if he could act nonchalant, she could, too. "Given the importance of a new car's name, Kowalski, what are you rechristening the Special before she hits showrooms?" she asked casually.

Slater gaped. "But…but…she…*is* special. What's wrong with calling her that?"

Kat took time out to respond to a shouted greeting issued from a passing automobile before she answered Slater. "The name is wishy-washy."

"Wishy-wash—" He broke off indignantly.

"You asked my opinion." She buried her hands in her jacket pockets. "Are we hanging out on this corner all night? Look, it's okay by me if you want to skip coffee."

Slater watched lights wink off in two of the stores. He glanced at his watch and was surprised to see how much time had elapsed. More surprising was his sudden desire to go someplace more private than a café—to explore whatever the hell was going on between him and Kathleen. But she looked ready to bolt.

He shrugged. "Give me a rain check? I need to see what progress Scott's made reworking the valve train. If that fails, our next step is to spread out the engine blueprints on a conference table and examine every single detail. According to Dutch, they're ready to punch out body shells. If the board learns the engine is still on the fritz, my head will roll."

Kat hid her disappointment at the quick way he'd agreed to cancel their plan. But she'd probably expected too much on the basis of a few kisses and a little groping. "I hope you iron out the bugs. It must be nerve-racking, to say the least. Since you're so busy, I won't hold you to Saturday night."

Her eyes had gone black as midnight—unreadable. Damn, but he'd been looking forward to their date. Was she being understanding and accommodating about his work, or would she rather not go with him? Slater decided to test the waters. "I'd like to hear more of your ideas for renaming the Special. At dinner on Saturday, we could discuss them."

"You may not want to mimic Motorhill, but they run a name-the-car contest. Employees submit suggestions. A panel of administrators selects one from the top three. The finalists get a hundred-dollar bonus, the winner five-hundred. There's no need to waste one of your evenings, Kowalski. I'll do up a report."

"I *want* to take you out, dammit. Sorry," he muttered, squinting at the pale outline of the moon now rising in a dusky sky. "You're not misconstruing this as undue pressure or…harassment, are you, Kathleen?"

It took the pain in his eyes to prick Kat's conscience. "I'm not misconstruing if you're not. I wasn't exactly passive during that kiss."

Slater jingled his keys again. "Darn right. It was mutual. So it's settled, then? I'll pick you up at your house. Is six o'clock too early?"

"Six is just fine." A ghost of a smile flickered across her pinched face. "I think we'd better go now or Joe Mulligan will never go home. Have you noticed if he was peeking through the blinds since he doused his lights?"

Slater turned toward the storefront.

"Don't look." Kat grabbed his arm and dragged him to the far side of her SUV. "It's probably better if I don't know. That way I can act surprised when he calls Pop."

Slater pried the ring of keys from her hand and unlocked her door. "And I thought the grapevine on the Ridge worked fast."

"I guess it goes with parenting," Kat said. "And with living in a town where people look out for one another. It used to drive me nuts, all of it. Mom and Dad always wanted to know where I was going, who I'd be with, when I'd be back—and that didn't change when I turned twenty-one. Then Matt, Mark and Josh jumped on my parents' bandwagon, and I moved away. But I got homesick. Funny, I didn't think I would. I still get furious when my family meddles. Does that make sense?"

"Yes." He scooped a windblown curl out of her eyes. "You're grown-up but they still see you as a kid. My dad and aunt are the same. I tell myself its time to move out of the house. But the place is huge, and my father isn't getting any younger."

"I am looking for an apartment." She climbed into her Isuzu, closed the door and rolled down the window. "My brothers are throwing conniptions. They want me where they can check up on me—and they want me riding herd on Pop. Besides, Mark says it would be foolish to move, that my job isn't secure."

A guilty expression dragged at the corners of Slater's lips. "You know I had reservations in the beginning. I can't deny it. It wouldn't do me any good, since there are quotes in the newspaper. You aren't worried now, are you?"

Her offhand shrug accompanied a wry smile. "A little, after today."

"What happened today?" He looked puzzled.

"The flowers. Why did you send them to me at work?"

"Why not?"

"I'm an outsider. The staff got antsy when the boss singled me out. Don't get me wrong. I love the flowers. But if you really want me to stay and do a good job, no more bouquets. Maybe we shouldn't go out, either," she lamented.

"Nonsense. I can see that maybe it wasn't wise to send flowers to the office. But my life outside of work is no one's business."

He sounded sincere. Kat wanted him to be. She wanted to keep her job and pursue an off-hours relationship with Slater Kowalski. "Fine. We're on for a Saturday-night movie. But for now, you have an engine to fix. And I'm heading home to my dog."

Smiling, Slater beat a small tattoo of drumbeats on the edge of her door. "Dinner before the movie. All right?"

"Sure. Yes. Fine," she repeated. He stepped back to the curb and waved as she drove off. Kat mentally sorted through the dresses she had in her closet; because of her profession, they numbered very few. She'd need to buy something. Maybe she could talk Mama into going shopping with her tomorrow night.

There was still a smile on her face as Kat entered the O'Halloran circular drive. "Uh-oh! Another family pow-wow?" she muttered, seeking a place to park among all her brothers' compacts. Sliding from her vehicle, Kat wondered what Pop had done *this* time to warrant a gathering of the clan.

Poseidon's front paws landed on her shoulders and he licked her face repeatedly the minute she stepped through the door. That was when she noticed Matt, Mark and Josh bearing down on her with purpose. She knew from the way their wives busied themselves at the kitchen counter that she, not Pop, was the focus of this meeting. In fact, Mama and Pop were both home; they sat drinking tea, looked worried.

"Any dinner left?" Kat asked, avoiding the furtive glances. "Uh, I think I'll take Poseidon for a run first?"

Matt blocked her exit. "Josh and I walked him while you were out front of Joe Mulligan's making a spectacle of yourself."

"Spectacle is a pretty strong word," she said. Or maybe not, considering the state her clothing had been in when Slater called a halt.

Her mother pushed her cup of tea aside. "'Tisn't like you to be kissin' a perfect stranger in public, Kathleen."

"He wasn't a stranger, Mama." Kat made a futile gesture with her hands. "It was Slater Kowalski. Joe probably told you we'd been in his store ordering team uniforms?"

Some of her mother's tension abated. "I see. A thank-you peck on the cheek is what this is all about?" She shook a finger at her sons. "See, all this concern for nothing."

Kat thought about the kiss—way more than any peck on the cheek. While she debated whether or not to defend her right to kiss whomever she chose, Matt got into the act.

"Kowalski's after more than kisses, and we all know that. He couldn't pilfer Pop's engineering secrets through Louie. So now he's hitting on Kat. I say it's time we teach that jerk to keep his hands off Hill women."

Timothy pushed his chair back and reached for the base-

ball cap he always wore. "The lot of you are paranoid. I'm
going to Spud's. Young Kowalski has no use for my outdated techniques, anyway. And according to Louie, his son
spends twenty-four hours a day, seven days a week at the
plant. Doesn't leave much time for romance, does it? Why
don't you leave him and your sister be?"

The door slammed. For a moment, no one said a word.
There was only the sound of Poseidon's toenails clicking
sharply on the kitchen floor.

"See," Mark told his brothers. "We came here for no
reason. There's nothing going on between our kitten and
that jerk, Kowalski."

Josh and Matt argued to the contrary. All three of their
wives entered the discussion. As did Maureen O'Halloran.
They talked around and over Kat.

When the noise level rose so high that Poseidon flopped
down at her feet and buried his nose under his paws, Kat
declared enough. Pulling one of her umpire's whistles from
her jacket pocket, she blew as hard as she could. The noisy
bunch whirled in surprise.

Having gained their notice, Kat crossed her arms. "As
you're all so free with your opinions, listen to mine. Little
Kathleen is all grown up, in case you hadn't noticed. She's
a woman, not a girl. Or a kitten. Nor is Slater Kowalski a
jerk." Kat glared around at the stunned faces. "I'm going
out with him Saturday night. A real date, unconnected to
work. And it's none of your business. So kindly butt out."
Jamming the whistle back in her pocket, she lifted Poseidon's leash from its peg by the door and snapped it on his
collar. Kat made a dramatic exit, leaving seven silent people
hovering around the table.

She left the yard and ran until Poseidon's tongue lolled.
She didn't slow until her own sides heaved and it hurt to
breathe in the night air. She saw she'd inadvertently chosen

a path leading to one of her favorite places along the river. A place where she used to go to avoid her brothers' teasing. But tonight they hadn't been teasing. They really thought Slater and his father were trying to worm Motorhill formulas out of Pop.

Winded, she sat on a rickety dock. She hugged her dog and cried into his thick fur. En masse, the O'Halloran men were formidable. Kat loved them individually and collectively. But she'd also fallen hard for Slater. Now her family knew it, too. Sooner or later, one or all three of her brothers would pay Slater a visit, which would probably put an end to any relationship before it started. She'd seen it before.

Kat watched the flow of the current until the sky became a network of stars. Poseidon's unwillingness to sit still finally convinced her to go home, and she got to her feet with a resigned sigh. She didn't know if she had it in her to fight the naysayers at work and at home, too.

To her surprise, her brothers' cars were gone and the house was dark. She'd expected a verbal drubbing, and had even prepared her rebuttal. It was silly, but their quiet retreat concerned her. Giving up gracefully was not an O'Halloran trait.

She took time for some reheated Irish stew and a shower, then went to bed, although sleep didn't come easy. Kat heard her pop whistling softly as he plodded up the stairs. She reached for the clock. *Two-thirty.* Sharp but muffled words drifted down the hall shortly after she heard her parents' bedroom door close. She pulled the covers up over her ears, wondering if they were arguing about the lateness of the hour, Pop's whereabouts for the last six of those—or her? Tomorrow, she'd find an apartment and take herself out of the equation. If Mark, Josh and Matt wanted to keep tabs on their wayward father, then one of them should move in here.

In the morning, her parents both left the house before Kat had finished her shower. According to the note on the refrigerator, they expected carnival duties to keep them occupied all day. *The carnival.* Kat recalled what fun it used to be. She checked the date marked on the calendar. The Monday after Easter. Why did that date ring a bell? Unable to pinpoint anything specific, Kat rinsed her breakfast dishes, put out food and water for Poseidon, then left for work.

Thoughts of the carnival and all else blew out of her mind the instant she checked in with the gate guard and heard the latest news. ''There was a fire in the reception area outside the boss's office last night,'' the guard said.

Kat pocketed her badge, shrugged a small rucksack higher on her shoulder and took off for the administrative building at a dead run. She didn't wait for the elevator but charged up the stairs.

As she pushed through the heavy fire door, Kat noticed that the acrid smell of smoke still hung in the air. Hazel Carmichael sat at her desk, typing. Slater paced behind her, apparently dictating. Three of the maintenance crew were scrubbing walls.

Kat rushed up to the desk. ''What happened?'' she asked breathlessly. ''I heard there was a fire. Was it the wiring?'' she asked, her gaze drifting to an electrical outlet on a wall near where the men worked.

''How did you hear about the fire?'' Slater asked, just as Hazel explained it had started in her wastebasket.

Kat glanced from one to the other. She chose to answer Slater before inquiring why Hazel's wastebasket would have been sitting next to his office wall. ''At the gate. It's all anybody's talking about. Surely you didn't expect to keep something like this secret? I mean, with fire trucks and police cars swarming a complex that's open twenty-four hours a day.''

''I called no one,'' Slater said. ''I discovered the fire when I returned after we parted at Mulligan's. The potential for damage was great, but there's really very little. Lucky for me, the match somebody accidentally dropped in the basket didn't catch right away. Maintenance said it probably smoldered for a couple of hours.''

Kat couldn't seem to shake the fear she'd battled from the moment she'd heard about the fire. ''But what if you hadn't returned? What if we'd gone for coffee as we discussed?''

''I have too many problems to make myself sick over one that didn't happen. I'm just happy things worked out the way they did. I hate to rush you, Kathleen, but Hazel and I are trying to prepare a report to the GSA committee asking to extend the date for sending them the monitors. By the way, I had Maintenance clean up at the conversion shack. We've restarted the tests already. Thanks, anyway, for volunteering to help.''

''You're welcome,'' Kat said absently. ''Look, I know it's none of my business, but fire is a serious matter. Considering everything that's happened, shouldn't you involve the police?''

Hazel nodded her head vigorously. ''See, I'm not alone in my thinking.''

''Hazel, you of all people should know what would happen if the board of directors got wind of this. Involve the police, and our problems will be splashed all over the news. The board might scrap the entire program. Virtual-reality tests have been perfect on this engine. We're so close, dammit. I'm not caving in.''

The trio had fallen silent, and all turned in unison as the elevator slid open. Slater's chief engineer walked out, stopped short and wrinkled his nose. "Did somebody burn breakfast?"

'If you'd been at your desk where you were supposed to be last night," Slater said none too pleasantly, "you'd know what happened here."

Kat, who stood nearest Scott, saw the anger ignite in his eyes. Just as quickly he let it flame out. Shrugging, he said, "I finished my assignment early. I brought a copy over here, but you'd already gone. The remark about breakfast was a joke. Buster stopped by the house this morning and told me about the fire. What all did we lose?"

"Nothing. I came back at eight yesterday evening—to meet with you," Slater said. "Instead, I found a blazing wastebasket. I unloaded Hazel's extinguisher into the damned thing." Turning to his secretary, Slater said, "Will you have that extinguisher refilled?"

Scott peered around Kat, at the men painting the wall. "You saved the day, buddy. Looks like a wastebasket's all that was lost. Add another page to the Slater Kowalski book of heroic deeds."

"We didn't lose the basket." Slater grinned. "When Dad redecorated a few years ago, the interior designer talked him into lining the desk drawers, file cabinets and wastebaskets with an extra fireproof shield. Maintenance has the basket. Brock Zeigler is a volunteer fireman. He's going to have the contents analyzed. He believes the fire was set. I doubt it. I met with three vendors near the end of the day, and two of them smoked like chimneys. I think one stubbed out a cigarette in the basket. I didn't see him do it, but we left here together at five."

Scott spun on Kat. "Our Kit-Kat left later than that. Maybe she saw somebody suspicious. Weren't you the last person in the building?" he asked. "We met on the path, remember? Slater had already gone. At least, you said you were meeting him at some equipment store."

"That's right. I came back for my badge. The guys at practice told me nobody was getting in or out of the complex without one."

Scott smiled. "You never struck me as the type to break rules. Why weren't you wearing your badge? Their use is covered in that handbook you like to quote."

Flustered, Kat turned to Hazel. "I...well, the permanent badge clips on. I was afraid it'd pull off and get lost. Hazel said badges were only required in classified areas. At least, that was my interpretation. The upshot is, I kept mine in the drawer."

"I probably did say that," Hazel agreed. "The teeth chew holes in my silk blouses. I rarely wore the dumb thing. Not until Slater added security and had me send out a memo requiring all employees to wear their badges full-time."

Slater regarded his chief engineer with impatience. "What's your point, Scott? I'm busy."

"No point. Don't kill the messenger. It was a simple observation. I was on my way to give you the updated blueprints when I met Kat. I noticed the administrative building was dark except for the security lights over the doors. Jeez, I just thought you might want to ask her if the outer door was locked. If this is the thanks I get, do your own sleuthing from here on. Call me when you have time to look at what I found with the valve train." He left via the stairs rather than waiting for the elevator.

A frown creased Slater's brow. "The outside door was locked, wasn't it?"

"I think so. But I can't swear the whole building was dark. It must have been, since Scott seems so positive." She closed her eyes and let her mind drift back. But she came up empty. It was annoying, especially after she'd promised herself to stay alert.

"Don't lose any sleep over it, Kathleen," Slater muttered.

"We should all pay more attention." Hazel laughed. "We're so busy these days, sometimes when I leave I'd be hard pressed to remember my own name, let alone whether a door is locked."

Kat started backing toward the exit. "You're right—we *should* all tune in more. If someone is trying to make Slater miss his deadline, the closer he gets to completion, the more desperate that person will become. My college roommate majored in police work. I remember her saying that desperate people generally get careless. I sure hope that's the case."

He nodded. "Sorry I'm too swamped to offer you a cup of coffee."

"That's okay. I wouldn't have time to accept, anyway. I'll have to go straight to the gym without stopping at my office. I came here because of the fire. I...I'm just glad you're all right."

Slater favored her with a grin. "Me, too. Remember I told you to have Security walk you out to the parking lot if it's dark when you leave. I'm asking Hazel to send another memo to all female employees. We'll be fine if everyone follows the rules."

Tossing off a wave, Kat slipped out.

Slater stood there, knowing his smile was still wide and a little foolish even though she'd disappeared.

Hazel waited several moments. Her sigh brought Slater up sharply.

"Ahem." He cleared his throat. "Where were we?"

"I'm on the fourth paragraph of a letter to our government purchasing committee. I think your mind was on having more than coffee with Kathleen."

He tried staring his longtime secretary down. Seeing no give in Hazel's eyes, Slater tugged at the knot of his tie. "If you're going to lecture, go ahead. Five bucks says it won't be anything I haven't told myself."

"By now you ought to know I'm not the lecturing kind. At least not on personal matters. I wouldn't, anyway, and that has nothing to do with you being my boss." She gave a light shrug. "Kathleen's good for you. You're too tense. She makes you relax."

"Really? And that's not a lecture?"

"Nope. It's the truth. You know it, too, or else you'd have never sent her flowers and started all that gossip. I think it's a man's way of staking his claim and telling others to back off."

"Who made you an authority on romance?"

"If I'm wrong, I'll apologize. You dated Christa Banacek after you came here to train under your dad. Never sent her flowers."

"All right. I'm transparent." Slater looked sheepish. "I'm sorry I caused Kathleen problems with others on staff."

"They'll get over it. Out of curiosity, have you passed her family's inspection?"

"No. Saturday night we're going out, though. At our age, I don't think family approval is an issue."

"If you're Irish," she said softly, seeming to slip back in time, "family always matters. My Johnny's parents and his sisters never accepted me. They did their best to drive me away once we were married. They succeeded after Johnny died. Yet I wouldn't trade the two short years I had with him to avoid all the trouble they caused. If you love Kathleen, Slater, make your stand and let the O'Halloran family know it up front."

Love? The word set Slater back on his heels. As a child,

his mother frequently used to say she loved him. Since then, the term hadn't held much meaning. Did he love Kathleen O'Halloran? She certainly unleashed in him a lot of the more physical qualities that went with love. And if he stopped to think about it, there were other elements, too. Caring, protective ones. And he remembered the fun he had with her. Cloud pictures and dog walks and crazy conversations. Thoughts of her popped into his mind at odd and not always opportune times. But love? That would take deeper inspection.

"It's probably a wise idea to forget we had this talk, Hazel. Read back my last sentence, please."

As she did, he wrote Kathleen's name all over a doodle pad that sat on Hazel's desk. When he drew hearts around the names, Hazel snickered, bringing Slater's attention to what he'd absentmindedly done. Scowling, he ripped off the sheet, wadded it up and stuffed it in his pant pocket.

"Would you print that out?" he asked, "and bring it to my office for signature. And Hazel…"

"Yes?" she prompted.

"If you breathe a word of this to Aunt Adelaide when she calls today to confirm our lunch date—oh, never mind. I've never been good at making idle threats."

CHAPTER TWELVE

SCOTT WAS WAITING FOR KAT outside the building. He fell into step with her. "Listen, Kit-Kat. I hope you don't think I was trying to implicate you or anything. You can see, can't you, how something really bad is going to happen if Slater continues to ignore these warnings?" His hands were plunged deep into his pant pockets. A light wind tangled black curls longer than Kat's own. He looked repentant as a child caught in a misdeed.

Kat's breakfast flip-flopped in her stomach. "I wish he'd call the police."

"He won't," Scott said quickly. "Hey, the last thing in the world I want is for you to worry about management's problems."

"Stop it, Scott." Kat grabbed his arm. "My degree may not be in engineering, but I'm no fluff-brain. As a department head, I deserve to be treated with respect."

"Sorr-ee, Ms. O'Halloran!" His navy blue tie almost swept the ground as he bowed and pretended to doff a nonexistent hat. "I guess the scruffy jeans threw me."

"It's not a joking matter with me, Scott, so quit fooling around. Since you've finished Slater's project, do you plan on making it to basketball practice today?"

"Sure do. You laid down the law, didn't you? I want to play against Motorhill."

"Next Thursday. Seven o'clock in their gym. Slater ordered uniforms for the whole team last night."

"So you said yesterday. Yup, ol' Slater's a prince."

Resentful of his attitude, Kat increased her pace. "Did you get up on the wrong side of bed, Scott? Be at practice tonight if you want to play on Thursday."

"I'd rather kayak. Ten other guys are ready to start. The weather's perfect. When are you going to schedule those lessons?"

She glanced away. "I have to present the idea to Slater again. That day we flew the kites, he said he didn't want me to teach kayaking."

"I don't know why you'd want to bother him with something so trivial. You just told me you're a department head. Slater likes the people he puts in charge to make those types of decisions."

"You think so?"

"I know so. How long have I worked here, doll?"

"Hmm. Well, let me get the basketball game with Motorhill out of the way. Once we play them, other company teams will work us into their schedules. Eleven for kayaking, you said? That's a big group for beginners. Although I suppose some will drop out. See if they can all meet a week from Monday at three to go over what the course would entail."

Scott gave a thumbs-up. "I'll tell them. Are you going to be in your office during lunch? If so, I'll get the handout and walk it around to the others. If you want to keep the class small, no sense sending a public memo."

"I'd appreciate that, Scott." Here, just when she'd been thinking badly of him, he went and did something nice. Scott was one of those brash people who frequently managed to get her back up. Undoubtedly, underneath it all, he had a good heart.

"See you later, then." Scott broke off from her and started down the alternate path. "Hey, for the record," he called out. "Staff likes the job you're doing. They're behind you one hundred percent."

No more than ten minutes later, the notion of staff being behind her seemed an alien concept to Kat. The women's volleyball teams continued to treat her as if she had the plague. The men's exercise basketball squad ignored her attempts to make them play by the rules.

By lunch break, Kat's shoulders ached from tension. Her jaw, as well.

Back in her office, she sat at her desk, holding her head. The door suddenly swung open, revealing Scott's smiling face. His smile was so welcome, Kat forgot that she usually found him annoying.

"Hi." He approached the desk. "You look rugged. Are you getting sick?"

Her gaze shifted to the vase of still-beautiful flowers. "You've worked with the people here for years. How long do they carry a grudge?"

He followed her gaze. "Ah. The infamous bouquet. I gotta tell you straight. The women on staff dislike a stray dog going after their bone."

Kat opened a bottle of water and took a sip. "That's plain enough. The women are jealous. But how do you explain the way the men are acting?"

"Have you heard the saying If Mama ain't happy, ain't nobody happy?"

"Yes." She recapped the bottle. "And the connection is…?"

"Production lines take teamwork. If Ginny's mad or Jack's hungover, it upsets the flow. The name of the game on the line is to make quota, or supervisors dock pay. As a result, Jack and Ginny get the cold shoulder until they straighten up and fly right."

"Sounds vicious."

"I did tell you the catfights may get worse. If the ladies are pissed off with you, it affects everyone on their lines. Then the guys are mad, too. So, my advice, for what it's worth, is avoid Slater. The fuss'll blow over faster. Quit running up to his office in the mornings. Don't cozy up to him at the gym."

Kat thought about their scheduled date—in a town that loved to gossip. How many people would see them and talk? Plenty, she'd bet. But did she care enough to cancel?

Scott wagged a brow. "Such deep thoughts. You don't agree with me?"

"It all seems so juvenile. This kind of petty jealousy went on in high school. They should grow up."

"Nine out of ten workers on the line started here as soon as they finished high school. The ones who didn't drop out early, that is, because the family needed money."

"I see. I'll keep that in mind, Scott. Thanks for the eye-opener," she said, handing him a stack of stapled handouts. "You wanted these?"

He took them without comment and walked back through the open door. Once he'd stepped into the hall, he turned. "I'll be sure and tell the guys to play it cool when they're sneaking off to the river."

Again Kat debated eliminating plans to teach kayaking. While the war raged in her head, Scott shut the door. Kat heard him clattering down the stairs. Sighing, she let him go.

Her afternoon sessions were a repeat of the morning's. The only friendly faces Kat encountered were those of the regular basketball team. They showed up early for practice and were all in a great mood. Scott arrived just five minutes late.

Slater didn't pop in at all. Though disappointed, Kat overheard enough to know he was busy recalibrating monitors in the conversion shack. As she checked doors and turned out lights after practice, she toyed with the idea of stopping by to see him. Even as she hesitated at the fork in the walkway, someone stepped from the shadows of the maintenance building, giving Kat a fright. "Scott!" she shrieked. "This is getting to be a habit. You scaring me, I mean."

"Hey, I'd gone partway to the parking lot when it dawned on me we'd all left you to walk there alone. So I came back. Do you have to go by your office for anything?"

His earlier advice about avoiding Slater volleyed around inside her head. "Nothing, thanks. And thanks for offering to walk me out. But if you're working late again, I'll manage on my own."

"Shame. Didn't you get Slater's memo? Women are to be escorted to their cars after dark."

"I got it." And Kat didn't see any way out of letting him do it.

There were a lot of clouds tonight. The landscape looked eerie. For the first time, she noticed all the drifting shadows and the blind spots where a person bent on mischief could hide. Buildings not running night shifts were pitch dark. She and Scott seemed to be the only two people out. Kat wondered how often Security scheduled patrols.

"How many kayaks do you have?" Scott asked after they'd cleared gate security.

"Huh?" His question intruded on her preoccupation with burglars and sabotage.

"Kayaks. How many do you have? They're more expensive than I thought. I may hold off buying one."

"I own a couple of two-men crafts and three singles. It'll be a while before anyone in class will be proficient enough to kayak alone. You'll learn how to roll and paddle at one of the public swimming pools. I've already obtained permission to practice at Buchanan's on the Hill. After they close, of course.''

''My brother taught me the basics. I need river time. You know, to learn how to handle the rapids.''

Kat paused next to her truck. ''That presents a problem, Scott. I assumed you were all beginners.''

''I'd pay you for private lessons.''

''Money isn't the issue. There are only so many hours in my day.''

''I'm willing to give up lunch. I'll even bring you a sandwich. Come on. Think how bored you'd be hanging back with first-timers.''

''Why the rush? I mean, if you aren't going to buy your own kayak?''

''I am going to buy one. I thought I had enough saved. I will before summer comes around. I'm counting on spending most of my vacation exploring along the river.''

''Kayaking is my passion, too. How can I say no?'' Even as she spoke, she wondered if she'd just made a mistake. But the chance to go kayaking with a fellow afficionada— she couldn't turn it down.

''Awesome.'' He grabbed her around the waist and swung her off her feet.

Kat's nerves were still jumpy when she climbed aboard her Trooper and drove out of the lot. Why couldn't Slater show as much enthusiasm for her favorite sport?

KAT'S WEEK FINISHED on a lower note than it'd begun. She continued to meet her classes, but by Friday almost everyone had dropped out.

There was one bright spot—the search for an apartment and a dress to wear on Saturday had both paid off. The apartment, neat, compact and affordable, came partially furnished. Thursday, after work, she looked it over and paid the required fees and deposits. She would have liked some family support, some congratulations and excitement. But whenever she mentioned moving, her family balked. Her mother cried. Matt, Josh and Mark made sure she heard about every horrible story of dire crimes committed against young women living alone. Only Pop remained silent on the subject. This was due in large part to his absence. He was generally assumed—by everyone except Kat—to be out doing nefarious things with his sidekicks. Tim O'Halloran, however, insisted all those hours he was gone were connected to the church carnival.

Kat didn't know what to believe anymore. She thought long and hard about how to handle telling them that she was indeed moving. In the end, she decided it might be better to spring one major change on them at a time. They were still reeling from the big announcement about her date.

An hour before he was due to pick her up, Kat's brothers and their wives all showed up. She'd barely stepped out of the shower and finished her makeup when a car door slammed. Worried that Slater was there early, she ran to the dormer window in time to see the three couples file into the house. They had some nerve.

Forgetting the care she'd planned to take getting ready, Kat dived into her clothing. They couldn't be planning to have dinner here. No one carried casseroles or pie dishes. Plainly they'd come to give her date a hard time.

Incensed, Kat flew down the stairs. Her sister-in-law Mary chanced to glance up first. She stifled an expression of shock. "Kathleen, that dress…"

Kat's mother seemed to have difficulty breathing.

Matt's wife, Shannon, pushed her new wire-rimmed glasses higher on her nose. "Innocent…and dynamite. Way to go, Kat!"

Shannon's husband dissolved in paroxysms of coughing.

Erin, the plumpest of the sisters-by-marriage and by far the most conservative of the bunch, blurted, "Is it a dress? Maybe, if they'd used more material..."

The item under scrutiny was kelly-green and sleeveless. Tiny satin bows, set two inches apart, closed the bodice. The fitted skirt clung flirtily midway down Kat's thighs. It was a dress that had probably been designed to stop conversations, but had the opposite effect on her family. The room erupted in explosive chatter.

Kat gripped the newel post at the foot of the stairs, battered by the universal language spoken by big brothers. *Slinky. Sexy. My sister isn't going out of here looking like Lolita. Damned right.*

Poseidon added to the cacophony, dashing from one person to the other, alternately growling and barking. Half an hour ticked by, and the argument grew louder. Again, no one asked Kat's views. She contemplated going back upstairs for her whistle. The doorbell rang, so she hissed instead, "Cut it out, you guys. Slater's here. If you do one thing to embarrass me, I'll never forgive any of you as long as I live."

As she hurried to the door in the unaccustomed silence, Kat wished she could wiggle her nose and spirit herself and Slater away from the house. Heart pounding, she flipped on the porch light and opened the door a crack.

"Hi." Slater caught a glimpse of one dark eye, a wedge of pale face and, below, an arrow of bright green. He expected Kat to invite him inside. When the crack remained immobile, he shifted the box of candy he carried to his left hand and plastered his right palm against the frame. "Am I early?" he murmured. "I heard raised voices. If I've come at a bad time, Kat, I'll wait in the car."

"You're not that early," she croaked, wondering how she should prepare him for what awaited. Finally deciding he'd likely faced worse grillings at the hands of his board of directors, she stepped back and motioned him into the house.

He sensed the antipathy aimed at him from the ring of stony faces. But Slater had eyes only for the woman he'd come to collect. She hit him like a tropical storm, filling his head with thoughts of silk sheets and champagne at midnight. It was to his credit that he managed to keep the lust from his eyes and his jaw off the floor as, one by one, Kathleen introduced her brothers. All had muscular bodies, steely eyes and handshakes to rival sumo wrestlers. Slater refused to flinch at any of the bonecrushing attempts.

Slater handed the box of Belgian chocolates to Kat. "The candy is for your mother," he said in what he hoped was a relaxed tone. As relaxed as he could sound encircled by three hulking men who wanted to kill him.

Mrs. O'Halloran, a woman Slater judged could still light up a room and turn men's heads if she chose, pushed through the wall of beef. Watching the men give way, then close ranks around their mother, Slater knew they loved her. They loved their sister, too. Fiercely and protectively. His resentment at being so rudely met evaporated.

"I'm Katie's mother." Maureen took the box of chocolates and fingered the gold bow. "'Tis far more elegant than the one Tim gave my dear mother when he came courting. This is the first sign I've had since then that chivalry isn't dead." Her half-chiding smile briefly touched on her sons. Extending a slim hand to Slater, she let her smile widen. "Please, call me Maureen." She introduced her daughters-in-law, saying quickly at the end, "Don't let us keep you and Katie. The girls and I were just about to fix potato soup and homemade cheese bread. It's an O'Halloran Saturday night tradition. The men peel the potatoes, don't you, Josh?" she prompted, with a tap of her toe to his shin.

He gave an explosive grunt, but it broke the murderous glare he'd fixed on Slater.

Kat snatched the out her mother had provided. She grabbed a black sweater-coat from the hall closet, patted Poseidon and told him to be good, and all but shoved Slater outside.

"Phew!" The word burst forth from both of them as he bundled her into the Special. They shared a rattled glance when he slid into the driver's seat. Then they both started to laugh.

"If looks could kill," he said, "I'd be a dead man." The growl of the engine cut off Kat's response. "Speaking of looks..." Slater coughed into his hand as he wheeled out of the circular drive. "That dress is... Well, it...packs a wallop."

When all was said and done, Kat guessed packing a wallop was good. She resisted tugging at the skirt. Barely.

Should she compliment him on his khaki linen blazer? He looked more than handsome in the jacket, black slacks and a blue shirt that brought out cobalt flecks in his eyes. *Quietly devastating* came to mind. She slanted him a smile. A confident one, she hoped. She felt as if she'd forgotten the rules—if she'd ever known them. Would he accept a compliment? Or would he turn red and die of embarrassment? Her brothers were unpredictable on that score. What the heck? Her motto had always been Go for Broke. Rearranging herself on the soft leather so that she faced him, she trailed two fingers down his nubby linen sleeve.

"Nice jacket. Takes you right out of the square-peg engineering set."

Slater imagined he felt the soft pads of her fingers caressing his arm. He jammed on the brakes at a stop sign he'd nearly missed. "It's just a regular jacket," he finally managed to say, all the while wanting desperately to pull over to the side of the road and check out what, if anything, she had on under that minuscule dress. He almost bit his tongue in half as he stepped on the gas and joined the heavy Saturday-evening traffic.

Her husky laugh might not be seductive to some ears, but it was to Slater's. For a frantic minute he felt control slipping from his grasp and wondered if he shouldn't have made reservations at a less secluded restaurant. One with better lighting.

Essentially this was their first date. It wasn't his habit to figure on bedding a woman after a first date, let alone before they'd reached the main course at dinner. Yet taking her to bed was very much on his mind. And there were so many reasons he should go slow and easy with Kathleen O'Halloran.

"Where are we eating?" Kat saw he'd pulled onto Highway 75, headed away from Flintridge.

"I thought it'd be nice to drive to Saginaw."

"Good. Great. I doubt we'll run into anyone we know there."

"I'm not trying to hide, Kathleen. It's just nice weather for a drive."

Kat smiled. "And we're only half an hour or so from Flintridge in case the Special quits again."

"Hey, lady. Have some faith here."

"All right. Are you taking me to Holly's Landing? Is it still there, even?"

He'd given some thought to taking her there, but in the end he hadn't wanted to spend the evening looking out over the river. He named another restaurant, that was equally exclusive. Slater was happy to see that her smile remained as bright.

"I've never been there, but I've heard the service and the food are fantastic. Is it your favorite restaurant?"

He thought about that a moment. She was making such casual conversation, Slater wondered if she had any clue about the wayward impulses running through his head. He decided it was just as well she didn't. "It's nice. Can't say I have a favorite. An evening of this type is pretty rare for me."

"Really?" Kat adjusted her seat belt and turned more fully toward him. If that were true, did that mean tonight was exceptional? That she was special? Before she had time to give that question the attention she'd like, Slater had stopped outside a stone-and-wood structure set in a country club atmosphere. He climbed out, handed his keys to a valet and straightened his tie with one hand while opening Kat's door with the other. She swung her legs out. Hearing Slater's breath hiss and seeing the valet's eyes bug, Kat concluded the dress and accessories were worth every penny she'd spent. In a last-minute decision, she left her sweater in the car. The heat simmering in Slater's eyes made her feel plenty warm. Sensing she had that kind of effect on a man gave a woman power. Kat added a little swing to her hips.

A part of Slater rebelled against taking her inside, where he knew she'd catch the eye of every man in the place. He could, he supposed, slip his jacket around her. He wanted to as the maître d' led them all the way through one room to a table tucked in a dimly lit corner of another, and he watched the head of every male they passed turn to follow Kathleen's progress.

Suddenly he had her all to himself, the candle glowing against the tantalizing slivers of peaches-and-cream skin visible only to him. Then he was glad he hadn't covered her up. Glad, even though his tongue felt unhinged.

A hovering waiter whipped neatly folded white napkins off the table and spread them across their laps. He snapped his fingers and someone appeared to pour water. "Here's the wine list, sir." He opened the folder and handed it to Slater.

"What's your preference in wine?" Slater asked Kat.

She knew so little about wine. "You choose. I'm not much of a drinker, but I'll take a taste of whatever you select."

Good thing he hadn't planned to ply her with wine before trying to talk her out of that poor excuse for a dress. Slater ordered a high-end California chardonnay, trying not to indulge in such disreputable thoughts. Once again, he struggled toward loftier goals. Then his companion leaned forward to pick up her water glass, exposing a wider patch of skin between the middle two bows on that damnable dress. Pure lust drove a fistful of need through Slater's gut. The whole time it took the waiter to explain the chef's specials, Slater's mind was focused on untying those bows and kissing a trail from Kathleen's navel to her collarbone.

Not until she opened her gilt-edged menu and closed off his view did Slater rouse from his stupor enough to answer the waiter. "Bring us an appetizer of the crab-stuffed mushroom caps," he said decisively. "We'll order our meal later."

"Very good, sir." The waiter bowed stiffly and backed away.

Slater opened his menu. *Great!* How long had he left the poor man standing there while drool dripped onto the tablecloth? The guy'd probably go back to the kitchen and tell the rest of the staff, and they'd all feel sorry for Kathleen. Either that, or they'd skip straight to calling the cops.

Kathleen peered over the top of her menu. "Everything here sounds so good, I'm sorry we came during Lent."

Slater's gaze jerked back to her face. "They do a great kohlrabi soup. Did you see it?"

"No." She flipped through several pages. "What's kohlrabi?"

With soup the last thing on his mind, Slater said, "It's not cabbage or turnip, but tastes similar. Helen, our housekeeper, uses the recipe from here. It's good."

"I'll try it. What did you give up for Lent?"

"Soda. My big weakness is cola. And you?" he asked, realizing his weakness for her was far more powerful. And she would be a lot harder to give up....

"Dessert. And meat." She wrinkled her nose. "Mama always said we ought to give up a favorite. Yet she used to let my brothers get away with picking cauliflower or eggplant. Stuff they never ate, anyway. Boys get to set their own rules."

"Eggplant, huh?" The right side of his mouth kicked up in a smile. "Tonight I was afraid they they were going to eliminated *me* from the menu. Not so much Mark. Definitely Matt and Josh. Were they arguing about me before I walked in?"

"They'd been arguing about my dress more than anything. It's what I get for always wearing sweats or jeans. They need to learn it's my business what I wear."

Slater understood how a trio of vigilant brothers might object to that particular dress. Its label should have read, Lethal Weapon.

"Guess what?" Laying aside her menu, she sat forward and used her hands to eagerly and intimately illustrate aspects of the apartment she'd found. "It's on the second floor. Tiny, but it has homey fireplaces in both the living room and master bedroom. I'm moving soon. As early as next week if the manager can arrange for a crew to paint the place. He'll call me with the exact date. I haven't dropped *that* bombshell on the clan yet. I guarantee you don't want to be within a country mile when I do."

He didn't agree. A lecherous portion of Slater's mind wished she'd already made the move. Especially to the bedroom with the three full-length windows and homey fireplace. He'd never yet taken a woman to spend the night at his father's house. And he was much too old to make out in the back seat of a car. Even a car as well-equipped for comfort as the Special.

"You're awfully quiet. Oh, you're not siding with them, are you?" In exasperation she grabbed the entire plate of mushrooms their waiter had placed in the center of the table. She stabbed her fork in one and popped it into her mouth. The hot filling seared her tongue and brought tears to her eyes.

Her tears, no matter what the cause, seemed to drive a stake through Slater's heart. Kathleen's reasons for wanting a place of her own had nothing to do with him. She'd never given Slater any indication that she'd invite him into her bed or go with him to his. It was all a fantasy he played out in his head. *His* fantasy. Not hers. And if he stopped to consider all the reasons pursuing a relationship with her wasn't wise, the fantasy didn't even make sense. He went through the lot again, reminding himself. She worked for him. They came from different backgrounds. From distinctly separate parts of town.

"As you pointed out the other day, Kathleen, your private life is off limits." He signaled the waiter. "Are you making that your meal?" he asked her. "I'm ready to order."

Realizing what she'd done, Kat hurriedly pushed the plate of appetizers toward him. "Sorry." She felt a change in his demeanor and wondered if she'd committed some unpardonable faux pas. Her stomach spiraled in a free fall, taking the bulk of her hunger with it.

Quite possibly she'd attached more significance to this date than Slater had. Yes, she'd foolishly imagined him visiting her new apartment. Her imagination had him staying for dinner—and after, till morning. Honesty forced her to admit that outside of a few kisses and this date, all else had been her flights of fancy.

She ordered a bowl of the kohlrabi soup with bread. No amount of prodding by the waiter or cajoling from Slater convinced her to order more. Slater ended by shrugging and saying he'd have the same.

"If you burned your tongue, Kathleen, maybe you should have ordered a cold soup. Here, sip on this chilled wine." Slater filled her glass.

She drank it down. "That feels better. Since you don't want to hear about my apartment, what shall we talk about?" she asked after the waiter set the soup in front of them, topped it with ground pepper, then bustled away.

"Finish describing your place. You mistook my silence for lack of interest."

Kat fanned at the steam rising from her bowl. "I certainly did."

He refilled both glasses. As Slater set the bottle down, she lifted her glass to her lips again. Her cheeks were flushed, her eyes bright. He ran his tongue over a dry bottom lip as he watched the long column of her throat ripple each time she swallowed. "Well," he said hoarsely, "some men might take a detailed description of your apartment as an invitation to drop by anytime of the day or night."

She lowered her glass. "What men? You're the only person other than the building manager who even knows I've rented the place." Kat dug in her purse and pulled out a key. "It's vacant. There's not a lot to see, but I'm dying to show someone," she said wistfully.

Slater's eyes moved left and right and left, tracking the lazy swing of the gold metal key. Saliva pooled in his mouth and lethargy invaded his limbs. She looked so heartrendingly eager to parade someone through the place. How could he resist? What the hell. "Do you want to skip the movie and give me the ten-cent tour, instead?"

"Do you mind?" She reached across the table and clasped his hand. "I'd love a second opinion. Maybe I was blinded by the idea of having my own place. If you think it's a loser, I can tell the manager I've had second thoughts. That way, I won't incur my family's wrath for nothing."

"I'm no structural expert. Did you check for leaky faucets, look into safety features and whatnot?"

Worry darkened her eyes. "No. See, I knew I jumped at the deal too fast."

"Not necessarily. They're only questions. The place may be top-notch."

"And maybe not." She mentioned the very reasonable rent.

"Will they allow you to have Poseidon there?"

"Certainly. That was the first question I asked. They have some land out back, with hiking trails. I just have to pick up after my dog. That's only fair."

"Yes. I agree. Are you going to finish that soup?" he asked abruptly.

She glanced at it as if surprised to see it there. "Probably not. The mushrooms were pretty filling."

He stood, dragged out his money clip and peeled off several bills. "The best way to test a car is to drive it and get the feel. Why wouldn't the same hold true for a house? We'll pretend you're having a housewarming party. A loaf of bread, a jug of wine, a fire in that fireplace, and thou. We'll stop at a convenience store on the way."

Kat clapped her hands. Her eyes danced. "Cheese to go with the bread, and candles for atmosphere."

Slater guided her out, his mind filled with plans for the evening. He was oblivious to the appreciative stares bestowed on Kathleen this time though. Convenience stores probably didn't have pillows, and she might not go for such an obvious touch, anyhow. He did have a plaid lap robe in the Special. It'd double as a picnic cloth, and if he got lucky...

He wasn't in the habit of mapping out seductions. But this course of action with this particular woman just seemed so right. Perfect, in fact. Slater glanced over at her as he drove and smiled. She smiled back. He gathered her hand in his and wished the console to hell.

"Two weeks from tomorrow is Easter," he said. "The Monday after is a holiday at the plant." He brought her hand to his lips. "I've never invited anyone to our festival in the square. Normally it's a family thing. Will you go with me, Kathleen?"

"Yes," she said. "Oh, yes." Then a frown rippled across her brow.

"What is it? Do you think the staff will disapprove?"

"I'm sure they will. But that's not the reason I'm hesitating. I just remembered our church carnival is that same day. Or maybe it's that evening. It's a big deal. Everyone who lives on the Hill participates."

"Is there any reason we can't take in both events? I'm willing to risk crossing the imaginary line if you are," he teased.

His statement forced a chuckle from Kat. "'Tis done, then," she said, sounding very, very Irish.

Grinning like a fool, Slater placed a big kiss in her palm and made a show of closing her fingers around it. Their gaiety carried them into a convenience store, where the patrons weren't used to seeing shoppers dressed in the finery that Kat and Slater wore. Rapt with each other and in the throes of a burgeoning love, they barely noticed the glances and smiles.

But when they were settled in the car and ready to take off, Slater remembered something he hadn't bought. "I need to go back for a minute. I forgot something."

"Sure. I'm not going anywhere without you," she teased.

Slater went straight to the pharmaceutical section and made his choice from the selection of condoms. He didn't let the cashier's smirk faze him. Refusing a sack, he pocketed the small box.

Fortunately, Kat didn't ask what he'd bought, and they drove off with little on their minds save the evening ahead.

In less than half an hour, Kat had directed him to the cluster of apartment buildings. "My place is up there—second floor. I even have a balcony."

Slater, being gallant, piled their purchases of wine, bread, cheese and candles atop the bulky blanket. "You lead the way and open up," he told Kat.

Anxious now for him to see and like her choice, she tugged him up the stairs and along the dim corridor. She hurried ahead, gazing in his direction as she unlocked the door and flung it open. Then ran back to help him. Rising on tiptoes she kissed him on the mouth. Unmindful of her smeared lipstick, she concentrated on rescuing the blanket, which had unfurled and tangled in Slater's feet. Until they both squeezed through the door, laughing and stumbling together, neither realized they weren't alone. All the lights in the small apartment blazed. Kat had company she'd in no way bargained for.

Mark, Matt, Josh and their wives stood in the center of the living room, arms akimbo. All glared fiercely at the disheveled newcomers. Fierceness turned to fury when the three men got a load of what Slater carried.

Kat gaped at each brother in turn. "What? How? Why?" she stammered.

Mark acted as spokesperson. "A man—the building manager, I guess—phoned the house to finalize the moving date. Imagine our surprise.''

''We figured you'd show up here tonight,'' Matt said coldly.

''Pretty sparsely furnished for a love nest, eh, kitten? If this is the best Flintridge Motor's CEO can afford, I think you're being led down a primrose path.'' An unsmiling Josh brushed past his brother and accosted Kat.

''You think *I'm* paying for this?'' Slater started for Josh but dropped the sack full of candles when he tripped over the blanket's fringe. Pink, blue and purple candles rolled to the tips of Josh's shoes. Kat's sisters-in-law exhaled aloud as if on cue.

''Good grief.'' Kat balled her fists. ''Out. Every last one of you *out*. It's my name on that lease, not Slater's. The manager had no right to let you in. If this room isn't cleared in two seconds flat, I'm calling the police.''

The men grumbled and expostulated, but their wives nudged them toward the door. Not, however, before Matt got in Slater's face. ''You lay one hand on my sister, Kowalski, and they'll be wiping you off the streets from here to Detroit.''

Slater flattened a hand against Matt's broad chest. ''I think that's Kat's business and mine.'' He didn't back down, and yet for Kat's sake, he was glad Mark and Josh hustled Matt into the hall.

Another man might have been quaking in his shoes. Matt's threats had no effect on Slater. What bothered him was seeing the joy drain out of Kathleen. He crossed the room, took her in his arms and tried to rub away the chill tracking goose bumps down her arms. Returning a smile to her lips took priority over his other plans.

He built a roaring fire, using wood left by the previous

occupants. It wasn't until they sat before it, Kat snuggled comfortably in his arms, that Slater recognized he'd fallen hopelessly in love with her. Yet the obstacles between them hadn't changed. They'd only multiplied.

CHAPTER THIRTEEN

THE FIRE HAD BURNED LOW. Slater hadn't checked his watch in awhile, but a good guess would be that they'd sat for more than an hour without talking. He rubbed his chin across Kathleen's soft curls. "Will you do as your brothers wish and give this place up?"

She stirred in his arms. "My family is breaking apart." Sadness filled her eyes. "Ever since I came home, everything has been different. Take Pop. He's with his friends all the time, not the family. And yet, who can blame him, considering how everyone's been acting. And now there's me. All their fussing seems so pointless. Pop, me—we're still us."

"Maybe you see that more clearly for having been gone."

She sighed and began gathering up the candles. Slater took the hint and folded the blanket. He raked the coals apart with a stick of wood that remained in a wood box, hating the fact that their interlude was over.

They were settled in the car before Kat spoke again. She gazed out at the brick building, friendly with its glow of lights. "I thought I could walk away and ignore the problem with Pop. I can't. It's why I came home. He's why I am who I am. He's always been the family leader. The one who dispensed advice. Had the final say. Now everything is topsy-turvy. Mama's drifting in the wind. Mark, Matt and Josh are all trying to take Pop's place. So the answer to your earlier question is yes, I'm bending to their will." She sighed. "There'll be other apartments if I let this go. Does that make me a wimp?"

"No. You know why you're caving in. At my house, it's as if my father and I are going down separate paths. I feel the gap widening, but can't seem to change course."

"Have we tried hard enough?" Kat wondered aloud. "Instead of going to the after Easter Monday celebrations with each other, maybe we ought to stick with our families."

Slater felt let down. He wanted to spend the time with Kathleen. "How about if we include them? Unless the rest of your family would be mad at you."

"Mama manages a food booth. My brothers and their wives volunteer. I should, but Father Hanrahan forgot I've rejoined the parish."

At the O'Halloran house, the same assortment of Motorhill cars sat in the drive. "An *un*-welcoming committee. Would you like me to go in with you?"

"No. But thanks. I'm game to ask our fathers to join us at the festivals. Unless they're too busy. Mine's been occupied for weeks with some chore or another related to the carnival. Or so he claims."

"Dad, too. I haven't heard it from him directly, but our housekeeper fills me in. According to her spies, he's been playing the ponies more than he's helped at the church. In her opinion, I should be a more dutiful son and get to the bottom of this. Spending time with him on Easter Monday will make Helen happy, if nothing else. I'll put the proposition to Dad and contact you next week. Otherwise, don't expect to see me around the plant. I'm holing up with the engine blueprints. I'm going to find every bug in that system once and for all, or die trying."

"Nothing so drastic, I hope." She released her seat belt.

"Does that mean you won't be at our basketball game on Thursday, with Motorhill?"

He leaned across the console and nibbled at her lips. "Wild elephants couldn't keep me from that." He drew back. "Can we win?"

Kat had trouble thinking about basketball after that kiss. She managed, barely, using the time to collect herself as she fumbled for the sacks of wine and food and candles. "*Can* we win? Yes. Will we?" She shrugged. "Winning takes teamwork. I'm blessed with some real grandstanders. Here, you keep the bread and wine and cheese. Okay?"

"Fine." Climbing out, Slater circled the car and opened her door. "So you're saying I shouldn't kill the coach if we lose?"

Her laughter cut through the night air. "Not unless you want to find a new date for Easter Monday."

Slater relieved her of the two sacks. Sliding one arm around her waist and up her back, he pulled her against his chest, then claimed another kiss.

Kat didn't resist. A sigh of pleasure let Slater deepen the kiss. They both heard the door to the house bang open and felt the glare of light that spotlighted their actions. Kat made a noise in her throat and started to push away. Slater merely tightened his hold and turned, so that his back blocked the view from the house.

When he was good and ready, he ended the kiss. Holding her close as she tried to slip away, he said firmly, "I'm walking you to the door, Kathleen."

She ran two fingers over his lips and along the crease bracketing his mouth. "I wanted tonight to be ours," she whispered. "I'm so sorry my brothers ruined it for us."

Her honesty touched him. Astounded him. Made him feel ten feet tall. Reminded him that he'd spent far too much of his life on cars and blueprints, and not nearly enough on love. "There'll be other nights, Kathleen. A lot, I hope. After I solve the problem with that damned engine. Can you wait?"

"Um, sure. The Special ran like a top tonight. Maybe your troubles are over."

"We'll celebrate big if they are," he said softly. "Just you and me. A weekend in some hideaway." He grinned crookedly, causing Kat to stumble into a solid chest topped by the stern face of Matthew. Her middle brother deftly separated Kat from Slater's curved arm. In an equally slick move, he handed her to the hulking form of Josh, who whisked her inside.

"Either you got no sense or a lotta balls showing up on our turf, Kowalski."

"At least all my muscles aren't between my ears, O'Halloran." Slater stood his ground. "Kathleen is devoted to you, jerk. But even family ties break like rubber bands if the tension gets too great. I'm not stealing her away, O'Halloran. The big bad brotherhood is driving her out." With a last pitying look, Slater strolled to his car and took his time driving off.

Inside, a furious Kat said pretty much the same thing before she collared her dog and swept up the stairs. Poseidon got an earful even after she'd slammed and locked her bedroom door. The dog flopped down on his pillow bed, chin lowered to his paws, and whined in sympathy.

"This won't end, Poseidon. Not until Pop takes over as captain of this ship again. And he won't do that until the family accepts his friendship with Louie Kowalski."

SUNDAY, KAT ROSE EARLY. She had coffee on and cinnamon biscuits baking as her father came whistling down the stairs. "You're in a fine mood, Pop."

"You're up early for a girl who caused so much ruckus last night—at least that's what I heard."

Kat brandished a wooden spoon. "You're as blind as Mark, Matt and Josh. I'm not a girl anymore, but a full-grown woman."

"Aye. In years, perhaps. You're acting childish, kitten, causing all this worry for your mother."

"Me?" The buzzer on the stove sounded. Kat was so flabbergasted, she ignored its bleat. No words came even as Timothy marched past her and pulled the biscuits from the oven.

He ripped off a paper towel, stacked several biscuits in the center, then continued on out the back door. "If you learn to harness your tongue, Katie girl, you'll make some lucky man a fine wife one day. If you've someone in mind for that position like your brothers believe, I'd better be meetin' the lad."

The man was daft. *She* caused Mama worry, did she? What about him? Kat raced out after him. "You might be meetin' the man if you'd ever stick around." Voice raised, she rounded the house in time to see him hop into Buzz Moran's car. Luke Sheehan and Spud Mallory sat in the back seat. The only one of the old scoundrels missing from this morning's getaway was Slater's dad. "Oooh!" Kat ran back inside and bundled half of the remaining biscuits. Whistling for Poseidon, she drove to the river where they spent an entire day kayaking in one of her two-seater crafts.

She felt much better that night. More relaxed. Pitting her skill against the river's current did that for her. Kat vowed to find more time to spend on her favorite sport.

Driving to work on Monday, she considered running upstairs to see Slater. One reason was simply that she hungered to see him. The other—she wanted to tell him what had happened with Pop. She didn't know another soul who'd see the irony.

When she pulled into the lot, there sat the Special attached to the back end of a tow truck. Her stomach pitched. She didn't have the heart to bother Slater right now. He obviously had major difficulties. Hadn't he, in fact, asked her to wait for awhile? By the look of things, he needed to bury himself in engine blueprints from now until summer.

Judging by the stack of memos in the morning's mail, all on Slater's letterhead, Kat figured he must have spent Sunday at his desk. Hazel, too.

Most of the notices had to do with tightening security. A few didn't. One of those brought a delighted exclamation from Kat. Slater had taken her suggestion about polling staff for possible names for the Special. He offered a generous cash bonus. She reached for the phone to call him, remembered the crippled car and decided just to send him an e-mail. Something she rarely did.

With the advent of good weather, Kat met her first scheduled softball teams. She loved the sport. So did those who'd signed up. All were excited about the freshly groomed diamonds and the new equipment. The morning was a joy— the exact opposite of her experience the previous week. Although, most of the workers were noticeably uneasy about the Special's latest breakdown. This was the car all of Flintridge Motors needed to survive.

Not for the first time, Kat wished things weren't so tense between Slater and her brothers. The O'Halloran men knew automobile engines. Innovative or run-of-the-mill. Too bad they were so blockheaded and uncivil, otherwise.

Predictions grew more gloomy as the week wore on. Kat caught snatches here and there. Scott had reengineered the valve train. The engine had seemed to work for awhile, then soon began sputtering out again. Inconsistently and not at any particular speed. Such bugs, Kat knew, were the trickiest to find. Slater obviously needed help from someone more experienced than Scott and his team. If he'd trust her with a copy of the blueprints, she'd gladly take them home and enlist Pop's aid. The trick would be convincing Slater to set aside his pride long enough to accept outside help.

By Wednesday, Kat had worked out what she considered a persuasive argument. Slater hadn't left his ivory tower or she would have confronted him with it immediately. Between starting softball and basketball practice for the big game with Motorhill, she hadn't had time to do much of anything else. As he planned to be at Thursday's game, she'd talk to him then. Someone had to.

Scott looked harried and showed up late to every practice. Kat made allowances and kept the other players off his back.

Just before noon on Thursday, he sought out Kat in her office. "I'm exhausted," he said, slumping in a chair. "Slater has no feelings. He operates like a machine."

"He has feelings, Scott. Imagine having the responsibility for clients, stockholders and all these jobs on your shoulders."

"Are you kidding? The guy was born with a silver spoon in his mouth. If the company goes belly-up, his family has plenty of investments. *They'll* be fine."

Kat blanched. "Are his problems that serious? USCAR's consortium has been exploring alternative-fuel engines for years," she said, referring to an umbrella group formed by the three leading auto manufacturers. "I thought it was mostly price that was keeping them from mass production."

"Suddenly everybody's an engineer. I come here for a break from talking cars and basketball, and what do I get?"

"Sorry, Scott. We're all stressed. Umm…what shall we talk about?"

"I dunno." He sank even lower in the chair. "Why are you saving those dead flowers?"

Kat glanced at the bouquet from Slater. Yesterday she'd picked off the worst of the droopy blooms. She hadn't been able to make herself toss them all. "The daffodils and greenery aren't quite gone," she said, her expression softening.

"Sentimental slop. You're hanging on to them because Slater sent 'em. News flash, baby. He doesn't care about you."

Kat thought about Saturday night. Slater's attentiveness went beyond kisses. "He's a deep, gentle, caring man." She folded her hands precisely on her desk and looked Scott in the eye. "News flash. Don't call me baby."

"So that's the way it is?" Something flickered in his eyes. Before Kat could read the message, Scott flipped back his perpetually rumpled hair and grinned engagingly. "Street talk. A hard habit to break. I really stopped to see if kayaking class is still on for tomorrow."

She reached for a folder. "Didn't you get your memo? The first three lessons, beginning next Monday, are at Buchanan's pool."

"Kayaking in a swimming pool?" he snorted in disgust.

"We've been through this before. It's the safest way to learn how to roll a kayak. Or how to make the boat work for you if you run into rough water and get dumped or ejected."

"You can learn that on the river."

"Too dangerous. I thought you'd know that—you said you'd done some kayaking."

"Yes. When I was a kid."

"That explains it. Kids are fearless." She glanced at her watch. "Do you have a free half hour? I'll take you for a short jaunt downriver and explain more."

"My time is yours, babe…er, Kathleen."

"Maybe a river run will help you unwind so you'll be loose for our big game. But let's not broadcast this," she cautioned. She hadn't talked to Slater yet. And despite Scott's dismissal of her concern, she did plan to. But it was something that had to be done face-to-face, not via some impersonal memo or e-mail message. Darn, she'd have to find time before Monday.

Scott zipped a finger across his lips, indicating they were sealed.

The first thing Kat did once they'd reached the river was find them both life jackets.

Scott tossed his aside. "I'm a good swimmer."

"No one is that good. The river is cold and the current's treacherous. I'm not interested in watching any of my pupils drown."

His attention seemed to be locked on angry white water that whirled crazily around a protruding rock upriver. "If you had some kayaks crack up, could you save all the rowers?" he asked.

"I like to think so, yes. That's a nasty combination you're looking at. Rock and thick foam. Don't worry," she said quietly. "We're going where the currents aren't as swift."

He pushed one of the double-seaters to the water's edge and climbed into the second seat after grabbing a paddle. "I'm not chicken. I wanna see how you handle swift water."

"Another day, Scott. This run is meant to relax." She smiled. "Not to increase tension." Kat ignored his scowl. She proceeded to take them on a forty-minute ride that she herself found both calming and energizing. Her passenger did well. She felt relieved that he wasn't all talk; he did want to learn her favorite sport.

Scott seemed oddly mute at the end of the ride when Kat hopped out and dragged the boat ashore unaided.

"Kid's play," he muttered during their hike back to the office. "Next trip I'd like a little action."

"High as the river's running, you might get more thrills than you bargained for," Kat said. "See you later," she called, watching him stride past the administrative building. "The uniforms are in, Scott. I'll be handing them out to-night."

Which she did. At the end of practice. Observing the players' delight, Kat wished Slater would drop by. He'd get a kick out of seeing these tough guys strut around, showing off like kids. "Do all of you have directions to Motorhill's gym?" she asked as they began to troop out.

"Sure do," they chorused. Derek and John hung back. "We'll walk you to the parking lot, coach." Kat thanked them but cast a longing glance toward Slater's brilliantly lit office. *Oh, well.* She shrugged and fell into step between her two best players. She'd see Slater tonight at the game.

KAT ARRIVED EARLY for the big match. She fielded the expected gibes from Motorhill's coach. Grady O'Reilly was a contemporary of her brother Matt's. The two were friends, but that didn't stop Grady from giving Matt's upstart sister a bad time.

"What idiot hired a woman to do a man's work?" he said, drawing a snicker from his players, who were warming up.

Kat raised her eyebrows at a hail of shots that all missed the basket. "Slater Kowalski. He'll be here in time to watch our team trounce those losers."

Grady shut up and supervised his men.

Kat's team filtered in, a few at a time. They seemed awe-struck by the size and beauty of the gym, and she had a hard time convincing them to don their new suits. They needed Slater to say a few encouraging words. Where was he, darn it? Kat finally got them out on the floor. She managed to keep one eye on the entrance. But Slater didn't show. The first quarter was total disaster; men she'd watched play fluidly during practice, acted like stumble-bums on the court.

At the half, Flintridge was down twenty points. Scott and another of Kat's guards had fouled out. She hadn't expected to win, but she did think they'd make a better showing. She also thought their fearless leader would keep his word and be here to back his team. Flintridge rooters numbered half a dozen—some wives and a girlfriend or two. One of them was Scott's wife, Tina, a pretty but shy young woman. She barely squeaked hello when Kat introduced herself.

Kat burst into the locker room, unannounced. She had too much fire in her eyes to notice that some of the men appeared to be uncomfortable with her presence there. Scott, who'd jumped in the shower, demanded someone bring him a towel and his clothes. "I'm not staying to watch those dudes mop up the floor with us," he told Kat.

She blistered him with a look as she paced in circles around the players she had left. "You played better at your first practice. What's the matter with you guys? Are you worried about Motorhill's jeers and catcalls?" She didn't point out individual errors. Instead, she listed each man's strengths. All glanced up in surprise when a ref knocked, saying they were due back on court. "All right." Kat stuck out a hand. The players piled on. "Go out there and kick butt."

Third quarter they held their opponents to one basket. Flintridge gained eleven points, and they'd remained foul-free. Kat broke out another round of water bottles. "This is more like it," she said. "Hear Grady O'Reilly swearing at his team? We've got him spooked. Pass the ball more. Draw their fouls. Play smart.''

At the final buzzer, the players trotted off the court, staring at the scoreboard in disbelief. Flintridge had tied the game sixty-eight all.

Two umpires approached Kat. "Sudden death overtime okay with you? First point wins the game?''

She beamed around at her players. "It's up to you.''

They nodded. "Where's the boss?'' Buster scanned the bleachers.

"You know he never wanted a rec program,'' scoffed John. "Guess he doesn't care if we skin the competition.''

Kat was plenty P.O.'d at Slater, but she felt he deserved their loyalty. "Skinning the competition is what he's trying to do, too. If those cars don't roll off the line by June 1, you can kiss games like this, not to mention your jobs, goodbye.''

She shouldn't have said that. Her rapier tongue and Slater's absence dulled the edge they needed to win. Swearing under her breath, Kat sent her five best out on the court. Slater said he'd be here, win or lose. He wasn't, and the team had come closer to delivering a win than she'd ever dreamed. Not come close. *They'd won!*

She flew off the bench, shooting both arms aloft in victory. She'd watched Derek drive down the court at breakneck speed. Kat had assumed he'd try the shot even though his momentum would take him too near the basket. At the last second, without looking, he passed the ball behind his back to John, who slam-dunked it for two points.

O'Reilly and his players were stunned. And he lacked the decency to congratulate Kat. "Lucky shot, kid,'' he said. "Tell you what. Call my manager next week to schedule a rematch. I'll roll out my first-string players.''

"Who's he kidding?'' John raged. "These *are* his first-string players. We don't need to play them again. Can you line up games with some colleges?''

"I think so. But I'll have to ask Slater."

"Like he gives a rat's ass," Buster said rudely.

"He will," Kat assured them, defending him again. "In fact, I believe I'll waltz on over there tonight and jerk him right out of his blueprints with this fantastic news. I'm so proud of you guys I could hire a brass band."

The players insisted on toasting her and recounting their win at a favorite watering hole. It was late when Kat finally left to visit Slater. A few blocks from the plant, a car passed her. Scott's? He hadn't shown up at the pub, but maybe he'd taken his wife home and then discovered Slater needed him back at work or something.

Kat showed her badge at the gate, and bragged about their win to the guard. On signing the log, she didn't see Scott's name. So that hadn't been his car? Normally she had a good eye for detail. Scott's flame-red Ridgerambler was perfect except for what looked like four knuckle prints in the passenger door.

The guard's grin stretched from ear to ear as he hung the log book from a hook in the gatehouse. "'Bout time the boss heard some good news."

Agreeing, Kat sped up the path. She passed the conversion shack, where testing had resumed. Beyond that stood a building, now dark, where day workers assembled instrument panels. A night-light glowed in another small structure where duplicate designs were kept. From there, the cinder path stopped at a brick patio running along the rear of the administrative high-rise.

Kat's key opened any door. Tonight, the back provided faster access. She jammed her key in the lock, craning her neck to peer at the upper windows. Light spilled from Slater's office and from an adjoining conference room—prob-

ably where she'd find him slaving over his engine blueprints
and computer mock-ups. Her heart beat faster as she stepped
into a pitch-black corridor. She should have asked the guard
to call ahead.

Choosing the stairs over the elevator, Kat dragged open
the fire door. Anxious now to see Slater, not only to share
her good news but because she hadn't set eyes on him since
their date, she let a burst of adrenaline send her flying up
the steep steps.

The minute she opened the door on the tenth floor and
saw him at the table in the conference room, she knew he
hadn't missed the game on purpose. His guard was down.
Both sleeves were rolled up, his normally neat blond hair
askew. He cradled his head in his hands. The tabletop was
strewn with rolls and pages of blueprints. At least five coffee
mugs sat before him. Crumpled sheets of paper littered the
floor. Judging by the tired slump of his shoulders, things
weren't looking good for the special.

"Knock, knock," she called softly. Still, her stomach
tightened when his head jerked up and she saw the dark
circles ringing his eyes. The man was in desperate need of
sleep.

"Kathleen." He rose, scattering an array of mechanical
pencils in his rush to pull her into the room for a hug.
"You're the most welcome sight I've seen in days. But why
are you here—so late at night?" Thrusting her away, he
squinted toward the bank of windows. "It *is* night?" he said
in a doubtful voice.

"Ye-es." Drawing the word out, Kat bustled to the table
where she collected the dirty mugs. Her response drifted
back from the sink, where she'd gone to wash the cups and
brew a fresh pot of coffee. "I stopped to scold you for
missing our game with Motorhill, and to boast about our

shocking win. I'll forget the scolding. I take it finding this latest glitch isn't going well.''

"The game! Damn, damn, damn. I'm sorry, honey, I clean forgot. You say we won? I don't believe it.'' He started toward the kitchenette.

She turned toward him and grasped both of his hands. "It's true. Tomorrow you won't be able to live with the players.'' Kat gave him a play-by-play rundown and ended with Grady O'Reilly's closing remarks. Her fingers tightened involuntarily around Slater's palms. "Here I go, rattling on about an insignificant victory. It won't mean anything if your hopes and plans for the Special go down in flames.''

He sighed and made a disparaging gesture with one shoulder.

Kat stepped closer, her jaunty smile fading. "Slater, I can help. Let me take a set of blueprints to Pop. He's a genius when it comes to troubleshooting engines. Before he retired, he worked with alternative fuels. He'll find the problem, I know it.''

"Hush.'' Slater dipped his head and captured her imploring lips in a kiss that got out of hand the minute he wrapped her fully in his arms. Forced to finally breathe, Slater smiled down into Kathleen's dazed eyes. "Scott's a good engineer. So are the men on his team. Hell, I'm good, too. Maybe internal hydrogen combustion using proton-exchange fuel cells just plain won't hold up for the long haul.'' He cupped her face and scraped his thumbs gently over her cheeks. "I want you to stop worrying. Do you know how happy I am just to see you?''

Kat buried her head in his shoulder. She inhaled his custom cologne. Bergamot, smoky sage the merest hint of leather. Faint now. The rasp of a day's growth of whiskers told her he'd probably been at this since early yesterday.

But she didn't mind the whiskers. Or the disheveled hair and rumpled clothes. Kat felt right at home with men who got down in the trenches. "I want to help," she said almost fiercely.

"I know. I can't tell you how much that means." He rocked her back and forth, breathing in the smell of her shampoo, before suddenly leaning away. "I could really use a break. That coffee smells fantastic. How about we take a couple of cups into my office, away from all this mess?"

She disengaged their limbs reluctantly. "Sure. I can use a shot of caffeine before driving home. The team insisted on buying me a beer after the game. Under the circumstances, I couldn't refuse."

"I wish you'd phoned me." He groaned. "I should've been the one to buy the first round."

On her way to the coffeemaker, Kat trailed her fingers over a stack of blueprints. "Don't be silly. A basketball game is pretty insignificant next to working out those engine bugs. Are you sure—"

"Positive," he interrupted. "While you're pouring coffee, I'll run into my office and fold the bedding I have tossed on the couch. I've been sleeping here, if you can call it sleeping," he said. "It means I lie down when my eyes won't stay open a minute longer, and hop up again when a new idea strikes."

"Don't put your blankets away on my account," she called after him. "I've seen unmade beds before."

Yes, she had. But Kat wasn't prepared to walk in on the intimate, rumpled sheets of a man she'd developed romantic feelings for. He'd apparently heard her and left things the way they were. The mugs she carried wobbled as unfamiliar yearnings confused her. Disoriented her.

He smiled and plopped two mug mats on the coffee table.

"Sit beside me," he said, his pleasure at her company shining honestly from drowsy blue eyes.

Her heart thumped louder than when she'd run up the stairs. At least she managed, barely, not to spill scalding coffee as she set the cups on the table. Her interest in sharing a drink with Slater took a back seat to a sudden interest in kissing and being kissed by him again.

As if reading her mind, he reached for her.

"Slater?" There was longing and uncertainty and...more, all rolled together in that one breathless word.

"I didn't plan this," he said, voice not quite steady. "But I want you so bad it hurts." Settling into the corner of the couch, he slowly pulled Kat toward him until she straddled his lap. "Your brothers won't interfere tonight, Kathleen. If you have any reservations about where this is leading, then you'd better leave now." As he spoke, his hands worked her blouse free of her jeans waistband and left fiery imprints on her bare skin.

Kat's needs had been building for weeks. It took little more than feeling the swell beneath his zipper to drench her in heat. When his hands inched up her sides and his thumbs skimmed her breasts, she lost all hope of clear thinking.

Slater meant it when he said he hadn't planned to make love. He'd rather be freshly showered and shaved, and in a king-size bed for their first time. Hell, for anytime. At least he was partially prepared. The box of condoms he'd purchased the other night were still in his pocket. Slipping away a moment, he retrieved the packet. And it was a good thing he did it then, because the minute she unfastened the buttons on his shirt and he did the same with her blouse, allowing their skin to touch, what few faculties he still possessed were lost. Completely gone. "You don't wear a bra," he croaked.

"Too confining," she murmured against his lips. "So are these jeans."

"Ah, Kathleen." His protest, if it was one, exploded from the tiny, rational side of his brain. At the same time, his badly shaking hands divested her of those jeans. Partway. He barely got them past her knees when she released him from his slacks. After some minutes of mutual caressing, she was slick and hot and willing, and Slater was well beyond endurance. He wasted only a moment to determine that she was ready before he settled above her and drove into her with one swift stroke.

Her yelp of surprise and harshly indrawn breath added to his befuddled shock at the brief resistance he met. Slater stiffened the length of his arms and went almost frighteningly still.

The delay allowed Kat time to adjust to the alien sensation. Time to adjust, embrace and revel in the wonder of being joined with the man she'd come to love.

Slater fought against the weakness attacking his bones as she slipped her arms around his neck, smiled a lopsided grin and—as if she'd made love a thousand times—slowly began to rotate her hips. Sweat popped out on his back, his shoulders. He felt it slide along his chest and pool in his navel. "Ah, Kathleen!"

"You're repeating yourself," she whispered. Then her tongue bathed his lips and what remained of Slater's grip on reason fell away. He only prayed he could hold life, limb and libido together long enough to give her some measure of fulfilment. He had no way of knowing that star bursts went off inside her head and that her heart exploded with joy at the same time his body floated free. Nor, in the short aftermath while lethargy stole over them, was he destined to ask how she felt.

Because somewhere near them, a door slammed. The

sharp noise shattered their collective breathing and sent them diving for their clothes.

Rumpled and shaken, Kat struggled to tug too-tight jeans over love-dampened skin. "What was that?" she squeaked. "Did someone see us?"

Slater grabbed his slacks. Zipping up, he stood. Not bothering with his shirt, he left her trying to turn her blouse right-side out. Shoving his feet into his loafers, he raced into the cavernous reception area.

Slower to collect her wits, Kat eventually followed. Knees far from steady, she braced herself against the door casing while Slater checked the stairwell and the two conference rooms.

He came back, rubbing his neck. "Did you use the elevator or take the stairs?"

"The stairs. Why?"

"The door must not have closed tightly. A draft probably made it shut."

"I…er…guess that makes sense." Embarrassed now, because she'd never had to deal with the aftermath of making love, Kat slipped past him into the conference room. There she picked up her purse. "You, uh, had better get back to the drawing board. And—" She avoided his eyes. "—I need to g-go."

Slater reached for her, knowing he couldn't let her go without telling her how important a gift she'd given him. Just then the phone shrilled.

"Wait. Don't leave yet. That'll be Security making their routine check. Let me assure them I'm fine, and then we'll have that coffee we missed."

She nodded. But the instant he disappeared, she bolted. She didn't want to share a mundane cup of coffee, which would lead to analyzing what they'd done. She wanted to go home, crawl into bed and savor the experience again and again. The elevator stood open and waiting. Kat stepped inside and pressed the button for the ground floor. She clawed her way out before the door fully opened and raced blindly down the hall, letting herself out the same door she'd entered earlier.

Her mind was on escape and nothing else. So she'd already passed the design center before it registered—the door, which had definitely been shut, now stood open.

Her steps slowed. Security making their hourly rounds? Kat kept going.

Wait. Where was their light?

Doing a hundred-and-eighty-degree turn, Kat backtracked. She felt a weight lift when she peered through the door and saw the yellow beam of a flashlight darting across rows of blueprint tubes. Relieved, she blurted, "Oh, thank goodness, Security."

The person holding the flashlight spun. *Not Security.* Before the light blinded her, Kat distinctly saw a man dressed all in black. A watch cap covered his hair. She tried squinting past the bright beam and held up an arm to ward it off. The man doused the light and slammed Kat with the metal framework that housed cases of blueprints.

She literally saw stars. Colored stars. Dazed, she lunged at the fleeing figure. Her fingers tangled in the soft wool of a sweater, then slid down to catch on a cardboard tube he carried. All she could think was that while she might die in the process, there was no way she'd let Slater suffer another setback. Not if she could possibly help it. She grabbed the tube with both hands.

Her shoulder smacked the door, but Kat didn't let go. Her feet slipped. She fell as she was dragged outside. Just when it seemed she'd have to release the tube, she heard pounding footsteps along the path.

The man in black loosened his hold on the tube and

melted instantly into the black shadows cast by a grove of pines.

Though undoubtedly bruised, Kat felt her blood course triumphantly as Slater, followed by his chief of security dashed into view.

Patrick Matejko reached Kat first. "Drop it," he ordered gruffly. "And don't move. By damn, this time we've got you dead to rights."

"What? No, you don't understand! I surprised a man. A burglar. He ran off that way." Kat pointed an unsteady finger toward the trees.

Slater approached her warily.

Kat couldn't fathom why the two of them weren't chasing the would-be thief.

"Caught her red-handed, boss," exclaimed Patrick.

"No," Kat said again, this time directing her rush of words at Slater. "A man, dressed in black. He ran... disappeared into the trees."

Slater pulled the tube from her slack fingers. In the beam from Patrick's industrial flashlight, the tube was clearly marked: Flintridge Special Prints. Alternative-fuel engine.

Kat read censure in Slater's eyes. She licked her lips. "You can't think I..." But he obviously did, and that felt like a knife to her heart. Maybe more pain than she could bear. Tears slid down her cheeks.

"Why? Why, Kathleen?" he demanded, scarcely believing the proof he held in his hands after the love they'd shared moments ago. Love on his part, anyway. He shifted his eyes from her tears and focused on Patrick's harsh denouncement.

Kat crossed her arms protectively over her breasts. *How could Slater believe such a thing? How could he?* she cried silently and brokenly.

CHAPTER FOURTEEN

THE MEN ARGUED HEATEDLY. Patrick wanted to call the cops. Slater insisted on handling the situation themselves.

Kat knew the real perpetrator was long gone.

"We're not acting on this tonight." Slater spat out his final decision. "The three of us will meet in my office tomorrow at eight. And I don't want to hear a word of this whispered back from anywhere, understand?" He waited until Patrick and Kat both reluctantly agreed. "Pat, escort Ms. O'Halloran to her vehicle. I'll lock the design center and take responsibility for this roll of prints."

Ms. O'Halloran. How had the most wonderful hour of her life been reduced to this? A dull ache spread from Kat's heart to every part of her. If Slater could believe this terrible thing of her, then nothing else mattered. Yet if he truly thought she was guilty, why hadn't he fired her and called the police? Feeling his heavy-lidded gaze boring into her back, Kat hugged her shivering body and walked slowly beside Patrick Matejko. Then, abruptly, she lifted her chin and squared her shoulders. She had nothing to apologize for, dammit! She wasn't slinking out of here like a common criminal.

"Oh, Kathleen," Slater whispered as he watched her walk away. Several minutes passed before he locked the door to the design center and gave it a firm shake. The more he thought about the situation, the more things didn't add up. Allowing for how quickly he'd followed Kat from the conference room—hoping to talk her into staying at least for coffee—Slater didn't see how she could have unlocked the design building and found the proper tube. Especially as she'd carried no flashlight. If she'd turned on the fluorescent overheads, he'd have seen the glow from any number of places along the path.

She did ask for the prints, though.

Yes, but the attempts to sabotage the Special had begun weeks before she came on board. He'd like nothing better than to dump this in the lap of the local police. However, his reasons for not doing so were valid. To continue with the project, he had to have the government contract, which he would lose if there was any question of criminal activity. Someone knew that, and played him like a fish—a sucker on a long line.

The stone-cold logic had sat there all along, plain as a knot on a log. The person or persons at the bottom of these despicable acts were angling for more than the company's demise. Otherwise, they would have leaked information to the government committee and been done with it. *Who? Why? A conspiracy?* His eyes burned from hours spent poring over blueprints. Now his head throbbed, too.

Slater's heart told him Kathleen wasn't involved. Damn, he didn't *want* her to be. But tonight his emotions were too raw for him to be positive about anything. In the morning, he'd take a closer look at the design center. He'd never been one to sit and wait for the ax to fall.

KAT SPENT AN HOUR SOAKING in the bathtub. She submerged herself up to her neck until the water cooled and she was numbed of all feeling. She crept between her sheets, but lay without sleeping. As a rule, Poseidon wasn't allowed on the bed. Tonight Kat welcomed his warm body and sympathetic nuzzle. She wanted escape, oblivion. Still, she *would* face Slater in the morning, because O'Hallorans didn't run from trouble.

As the clock ticked toward daylight, Kat decided against saying one more word on her own behalf. If Slater didn't freely offer a reasonable and complete apology, she'd accept whatever punishment he doled out. And she'd lock him out of her heart.

Exhausted from lack of sleep but in every other way composed, Kat dressed with deliberate care the next morning. Accepting that Slater might fire her, she nevertheless arrived at his office early.

Hazel Carmichael sat at her desk, fingers flying over her computer keys. She glanced up when Kat stepped off the elevator. Instead of greeting Kat with her usual smile, Hazel rounded the desk and enveloped her in a consuming hug. "Kathleen, dear. What a mess you've fallen into. Pat Matejko's been in Slater's office for ten minutes trying to talk him into calling the police. I feel like kicking Slater's rear until he agrees. High time we find out who's making mischief. I don't for one minute believe it's you."

"Mr. Matejko's already here?" Kat wriggled an arm free and checked her watch. "Slater said eight."

"I guess Slater and Pat both had the same idea of searching for evidence around the design center. They ran into each other and came back together."

Kat's heartbeat speeded. "Did they find proof a man was there?"

Hazel pulled back, eyes downcast. "I don't think so, dear. Pat found strands of hair caught on one of the metal shelves near the door. He swears it's yours."

Swallowing, Kat gingerly touched a spot above her ear. "It probably is. I tried to stop the intruder. He threw me against something hard. The door, I thought."

"Oh." Hazel's eyes filled with shadows.

Kat awkwardly patted the secretary's arm. "Don't worry. Thanks for believing in me." Her gaze skipped to Slater's tightly closed door. "I hope Slater does."

Hazel lowered her voice. "I probably shouldn't tell you. No *probably* about it, I shouldn't tell you." She pursed her lips.

"Tell me what? Hazel, I...I...care for Slater. A lot." She couldn't bring herself to admit how desperately she loved him. Not after his unfair treatment last night. If there was a good reason for it, she had to know.

Crooking her finger, Hazel waited until Kat bent toward her. "I heard Pat remind Slater what they found the night he and Scott chased the suspect who'd broken into the conversion shack. Apparently they followed someone to the river. They found a small sneaker print at the water's edge. A woman's shoe, Pat says."

Kat started to speak, then changed her mind. How would it look if she admitted—two months later—that she hadn't taken her kayaks home as Slater had wished? Brother! If only she'd made time to talk to him about the proposed classes. She'd certainly stepped in it now. Her best defense—her only defense—was silence.

She bit stinging color into her bottom lip. "It all boils down to what Slater wants to believe, Hazel. Shall I barge right in?"

"Oh, I shouldn't have told you. L.J. liked to gossip. Slater hates it. He'll have my head." Hazel's expression was stricken.

"I won't give you away," Kat said, raising a hand to knock on Slater's door. "I wish I could provide answers. I can't. I'm as baffled as anyone."

"Come in," Slater bellowed in response to what he assumed was Hazel's tap at the door. He yanked it open. Kat nearly fell through, surprising them both.

He thought he'd prepared himself for her imminent arrival. He hadn't. Her eyes were huge, her face pale. He wanted to take her in his arms and smooth away the look of pain. But with his chief of Security sitting there, ready to ship her off to the state penitentiary, Slater had to watch his p's and q's. "Kathleen. Have a seat," he said tightly, pointing out a chair.

"I believe I'll stand." She made the decision after seeing Patrick stare coldly from the couch where last night she and Slater had made love. Kat hadn't realized it'd be so hard to return to this room. "I have a session of men's softball beginning at eight-fifteen, unless I no longer work here."

Patrick hopped up and waved a plastic bag under her nose. "See, she's not denying involvement, boss. I know this evidence I collected—this hair—matches hers."

Slater waited for Kathleen to absolve herself of any wrongdoing. She frowned at the wild-eyed Patrick, but said nothing. Slater was taken aback. He'd expected her denial, especially as he had secrets of his own. He hadn't shown Patrick a small triangular piece of navy wool he'd found caught on the lock housing. It proved someone other than Kathleen had been in the design center last night.

He only needed her to give them something concrete. If she'd been close enough to snatch the tube, she must have a better description of the intruder than simply a man dressed in black.

The room remained silent. Was she protecting someone? If so, who?

Taking a seat behind his desk, Slater fought down a lump in his throat. "We're intensifying in-house investigations, Kathleen. From now until we catch the culprit, there'll be no unauthorized overtime. No after-hours rendezvous of any kind. Evening practices are canceled, and everyone is to sign in and out."

In spite of Patrick's grimace of disgust, Slater steepled his fingers and continued. "Breach of this order for any reason will be cause for instant dismissal. Any questions?"

Heat, fanned by anger, sent blood tumbling through Kat's veins. She clenched her hands and unclenched them three times. *Rendezvous.* He'd sullied their lovemaking last night by brushing it off as an illicit *rendezvous.* So be it!

"Your mandate is quite clear, Mr. Kowalski. I trust you'll inform the staff by memo? If so, please tell the guys I'll find another place for the basketball team to practice." Grinding the heel of a sneaker in the carpet, she stormed out, almost upending Hazel, who'd apparently stopped Scott Wishynski from entering Slater's office. Kat didn't slow in spite of the fact that they both called her name.

She didn't escape Scott for long. After her baseball practice, he came in search of her. "Kit-Kat, I told you Slater worries about nothing or nobody 'cept number one."

"I believe you said he only cared about his car. Go away, Scott. I have work to do. Don't you?"

"Slater's bumped me from the project. He thinks he can find the Special's problem faster than his engineers. I'm free as a bird for the time being. Do you have time to kayak today?"

His enthusiasm for her beloved sport dragged a smile from Kat. "I have an hour at noon. If you log us out, we can spend almost the full hour on the river."

Scott looked puzzled.

"You'll get a memo. It's a new rule."

"Leave everything to me. You just be there with bells on." He paused at the door. "By the way, I let my old buddy have it today. I told him you're the best thing to happen to Flintridge Motors in years. I said he was nuts to suspect you of trying to steal our plans."

Kat found that Scott's support in some small way counteracted the letdown she felt at Slater's betrayal. And it wasn't until her next class that she discovered Scott was the only person on staff, outside of Hazel, still in her corner. Word of her fall from grace soon spread. Workers whispered in huddles, breaking off their conversations when Kat drew near.

If not for Scott's bolstering, Kat would have quit and not waited around to be proved innocent. His unwavering confidence in her and their noon-hour jaunts on the river were what saved her, kept her going.

He acted the perfect gentleman. And his never-ending jokes buoyed Kat's flagging spirits. Over the next few days, she decided it only took getting under Scott's tough-guy layers to find the man Slater must have known all along.

THE FOLLOWING FRIDAY, a week to the day from the infamous fallout, Scott asked Kat a question. "Am I good enough now to take a run upriver maybe next week?"

"Are you positive you know stalls and rolls? You haven't made any of the practices at the pool."

"My old lady found out Slater canceled my overtime. It's not so easy to get out at night now."

"Bring your *wife* to practice."

"You gotta be kidding. She's jealous of you as it is."

"Why would she be jealous of me?"

Scott bent over Kat as she pulled the craft ashore. "I wonder? Are you for real? You're a babe, that's why. Ever since she met you at the game, she's been jealous as hell."

"Stop it, Scott. I've appreciated your friendship this past week. But you know there's nothing else between us. I treat you as I'd treat Derek or John. I'm coach to all of you guys, and that's it. Period."

A look that almost frightened Kat appeared in his eyes. "If Wendy Nelson has her way, you'll be history before the

Ridgerunner rolls off the line. Or maybe you didn't know Slater let her rename the Special. You didn't, huh? Well, Wendy and I talked him out of copycatting our competitor's method of naming cars. She told me yesterday the boss is dumping you as soon as some Joe Jock finishes his master's degree.''

The news felt like a slap in the face to Kat. It crossed her mind to leave before Slater let her go. She'd halfheartedly scanned job listings in Sunday's paper. This weekend she'd check them more carefully. Oh, but Sunday was Easter. The holiday had come so fast. And now she wouldn't be spending Easter Monday with Slater.

''Lose the sad face, Kit-Kat. Old Scottie's got pull with the boss. I saved your butt when Matejko wanted to fire you last week. I'll go talk to Slater again.''

''Earlier today you mentioned he isn't any closer to solving his engine problems. Is your job secure?''

''Maybe I don't care. Maybe I'll sign with one of the big three in Detroit.''

''Surely you'll stick by Slater? He'll come up with a new design and eventually recover. Aren't clients still buying Ridgemonts, Ridgecrests, Ridgespinners and Ridgeramblers?''

''Yeah. But you oughta know a manufacturer needs a new car every year. Slater's goin' down with this project. I'm surprised he's hung on this long.''

Kat watched the jaunty swing of Scott's shoulders as he started up the path. If she didn't know Scott and Slater were friends, she'd almost think he sounded overjoyed by the prospect.

At the top of the hill, Scott turned and smiled. For some reason, it set off another alarm in Kat's mind. ''Come on, slowpoke,'' he chided. ''I'm not gonna leave Flintridge. It's home.''

Kat shook off the feeling as she caught up to him. She recognized that her nerves were shattered. Was it any wonder when everyone on staff treated her like Typhoid Mary? She was no longer Slater's friend. Kat wasn't even sure their relationship had lasted long enough to qualify her as an ex-lover. Yet she didn't want to see him fail. If only he wasn't so stubborn, so full of pride... Kat knew Pop could have helped him with that engine.

While she was closing her office for the holiday weekend, Kat began to wonder if she could help Slater in spite of himself. He'd made it plain he didn't want the board of directors to get wind of his troubles. But if she cornered Pop and explained, what would stop him from enlisting Louie's aid? Louie might be board chairman, but more important he was Slater's father.

Once Kat had a course charted, her biggest obstacle was catching Pop. Or rather, catching him alone. Easter weekend on the Hill always kicked off a frenzy of work. Family and friends shared spring-cleaning chores. The men handled the heavy outside tasks. Women saw to the inside, plus they bustled around baking goodies to celebrate the end of lent.

All day Saturday, Kat tried to separate her dad from her brothers. "Pop," she ventured more than once, only to be rudely interrupted by Josh, Matt or Mark. If not them, it was Spud Mallory or Luke Sheehan who claimed they needed Tim to look after something of paramount importance to the carnival.

Easter Sunday was devoted to religious pursuits. Father Hanrahan lumbered up at the close of the ten o'clock mass and took Maureen's hand. He smiled broadly at Kat. "Tomorrow you're all going to be so proud of Timmy. Be near the stage at noon. I'll be making an important presentation."

Neither Kat nor Maureen had an opportunity to question him, as another parishioner claimed his attention. Timothy himself had attended an earlier mass along with his sons and their wives. "What was that all about?" Kat asked. "What's Pop done?" She'd figured on skipping the actual carnival.

Maureen shrugged. "Considering how much your father's been gone, maybe he and his pals formed a band or something, and they've been rehearsing all this time." She smiled wanly. "I suppose we'll find out tomorrow. Speaking of tomorrow...I'll need help at the pancake breakfast. Can I count on you, Katie?"

"Hmm sure. What time?"

"We open at six. But I know that's when you run your dog. Ride in with Pop. I heard him tell Luke they'd meet for breakfast at eight."

Finally a chance to nab Pop. Even if he picked up Spud and Buzz, she ought to have a few minutes alone with him.

After the elaborate Easter dinner that afternoon, with the whole family present, Kat set to work. All evening she drafted her plea, then memorized it. In the morning, she cut short Poseidon's run. She didn't want to miss this opportunity. As she fed the dog, she heard her dad singing in the shower. Kat rushed her own. She threw on one of the two new spring dresses she'd bought last week in her depression over Slater. The soft mint-green fabric was sprigged with colorful flowers that lifted her spirits.

Timothy O'Halloran smiled as Kat hopped down the stairs on one foot, trying to slip into sandals, alternately fluffing her wet hair. "Relax, kitten. All weekend I've had the distinct impression you've got something to say to me. Go ahead. Get it off your chest."

"Slater Kowalski's alternative-fuel engine keeps cutting out," she blurted. "Neither he nor his engineers know why. He's so pigheaded he's going to lose his contract. Maybe even his position as CEO. Fix it for him, please, Pop." That wasn't exactly the carefully worded appeal she'd spent hours on—but what the hell?

"Whoa. Whoa!" Kat had been shoving him toward the door when Tim dug in his heels. "I assumed you'd be askin' me to intervene in the argument with your brothers over wanting a place of your own. This is a horse of a different color. Okay, daughter. Start at the beginning and talk slower. I'll take the long way to Zernik Square."

"Aren't we going to the church? Wait—isn't the Polish festival held in Zernik Square?" Kat felt certain that was what Slater had said. But maybe not. Her mind hadn't exactly been on festivals lately.

"That's a pretty dress you're wearin' today, Kathleen." Timothy held her car door open while she swept the short, ruffled skirt inside. After he closed her door, he got inside and returned the subject to her first question. "Can you get me a copy of your young man's blueprints?"

Kat looked horrified. "Lord, no!" Briefly she relayed the saga of the near-theft of the prints. As she had his ear, she told him about the other incidents, too.

"Hmm. Does Louie know all the trouble his boy is havin'?"

"Slater is determined to handle this on his own. He would, too, you understand," she boasted, "if not for one stupid engine glitch."

"If you can't lay hands on the drawings and if your young man doesn't want me to spill the beans to Louie, how do you propose I *fix* things?"

Kat twisted her fingers in her lap. "I don't know. Wiggle your nose?" she said glumly. "I guess I just thought you'd find a way."

Tim shook his grizzled head and laughed. "Ah, Kathleen. Does the lad know how much you love him?"

"What?" She whirled toward him, only to be brought up short by the seat belt.

"I'm not so old that I don't recognize the look of love when I see it, Katie."

"You musn't say that around anyone who works at Flint ridge. He…he doesn't feel the same about me." Kat turned her head to hide her flaming cheeks.

"Then tell me—why should I go out on a limb to save his sorry skin?"

Kat studied her clasped hands. "Because I'm asking. And because you're a friend of Slater's pop."

"The lad must be daft," Timothy exploded. "What the hell, I must be daft." He took one hand off the steering wheel and patted Kat's knee. "If we can sneak Louie aside at breakfast, will you explain this glitch to him? I'll need him to get those prints."

"Won't he be at his own church breakfast?"

"The celebrations are combined this year, kitten. A move that's long overdue. Didn't you listen to the announcements at church yesterday? Now, what'll it be? Yes or no? Will you speak with Louie?"

"Ye-e-s," she stammered, not clearly understanding why the Hill and the Ridge would merge festivals. Her heart sank like lead. Did that mean she might run into Slater? Probably not. He said he resented outsiders horning in, so it was doubtful he'd attend. Unless, of course, he'd invited some-one else. A vision of a smirking Wendy Nelson mocked Kat. She slumped in the seat, wishing she'd kept her mouth shut. Wishing she'd stayed home.

All too soon, the sound of laughter and the smell of food drifted into the car through the open windows. Never one to stay wretched for long, Kat craned her neck to watch milling families all dressed in their Sunday best. "Oh!" She clapped a hand over her mouth. "A girl hidden behind that big tree stepped out and practically drowned some poor skinny boy with a pail full of water. Smingus Dyngus,'' she exclaimed around a delighted chuckle. "Slater explained it's an old Polish tradition on Easter Monday.''

"Louie mentioned that custom one day when we discussed our wee folk. It's a shame the Ridge and the Hill have allowed business rivalries to so completely divide a town.''

Kat turned in her seat, surprised at the crush of people in the square. "I'd say they're mingling today. Look at all the vendor tents. I've never seen so many.''

"A change of pace always acts like a shot in the arm.''

"Look at that line waiting for pancakes. Mama said they needed help. Wow, maybe I'd better forget about eating.''

Timothy pulled a decal out of his pocket and laid it on the dash. It allowed him to park in a restricted area. He exchanged pleasantries with a policeman whose badge read Sergeant Naslaski. "Have you seen the boys?'' Tim asked.

"Moran and Kowalski,'' the cop replied. "Don't you guys eat all the pancakes before my replacement relieves me.''

Tim clapped the man on the shoulder. "We won't if you promise to have your wife save me a plate of mushroom pierogies. Tell her I'll drop by after the boys and I finish our gig at noon.''

Kat registered the cop's thumbs-up response. "Gig? Pop, have you guys formed some kind of band?'' she recalled her mother's joke—or was it a joke? Did Maureen know something she didn't?

"Wait and see.'' He tweaked her nose, then drew her attention to a man seated at one of the outer tables; he stood up and waved. "There's Louie now and he's alone. Come on.'' Catching Kat's elbow, he guided her through a throng of bystanders.

Kat was out of breath by the time they reached a man she'd have known anywhere. An older iron-haired version of Slater. "Mr. Kowalski." She smiled and extended her hand. "My name is Kathleen O'Halloran. I work for your son."

The elder Kowalski's searing examination of her also reminded Kat of his son. "No wonder Slater spends so many hours at the plant," he said. "Or does he even know you're alive? That boy of mine sometimes can't see beyond the end of his mechanical pencil."

Kat recalled a container of mechanical pencils Slater had knocked over the night they were in such a rush to make love. She drew in her bottom lip and blushed.

"Ah, I see you know his bad habits. No matter. Come, have a seat. I'll set him straight when he returns. He's in line, waiting to get our food."

"Slater's here?" The heat seeped from her face.

Tim turned a chair around and sat blocking the view of a nearby couple. In a low voice, without ado, he plunged right into Kat's request.

Louie's eyes narrowed. His face grew florid. Twice Kat interrupted her father. Once she said, "I wouldn't have said anything if I'd thought his engineers were going to find the problem." Another time, and more earnestly, she added, "Mr. Kowalski. Slater would kill me if he had any inkling of what I've done. Please understand, I've thought and thought, but I can see no other way. He needs an outside opinion."

Slater's father sliced a broad hand through the air. "Young pup's cut from the same cloth as his grandfather. *Stubborn* doesn't begin to describe those two. Thing is, Kathleen, I don't know a damned thing about alternative-fuel engines."

Kat dropped her chin to her chest. At least she'd tried to get help for Slater.

Tim scooted his chair closer. "Katie tells me he's running a proton-exchange hydrogen fuel cell. It's what I worked on my last two years at Motorhill. Unless I've lost my touch, get me an hour with the schematics and I can probably lay my finger on the source of the trouble."

Louie brightened immediately. As quickly, he turned laser blue eyes on Kat. "I'm persona non grata at the plant, as you may know. Any chance of you filching a copy of those prints?"

Kat slanted her father a helpless look. He ignored the sharp squeeze she gave his arm and informed his friend about the attempted break-in.

Louie seemed stunned. "I don't get it. Who would benefit from stealing prints of a car that's already prototyped?"

Kat figured they were already in for a penny. She took a deep breath. "Maybe someone who doesn't want Slater to meet his contract date, Mr. Kowalski. Nothing else makes sense."

"You saw a male intruder, you say?" Louie grabbed her hands.

"I saw a figure. He blended with the night. It all happened so fast. But I have a bad feeling, Mr. Kowalski. I can't help thinking that time's running out."

The old man frowned and started to speak. Suddenly he clammed up and compressed her hands tightly in warning.

Kat already knew that Slater was in the area. Her skin heated, then went cold. The fine hair at the back of her neck tickled. Her reaction to Slater Kowalski was always the same. She pasted a phony smile on her lips and plowed through her brain, searching for an excuse to leave fast.

Slater wove his way back to his father, juggling two heaping plates of food he'd balanced precariously on two take-out cups of coffee.

Easing past a rotund man, he suddenly found himself staring at Kathleen. He stood there in shock. If his father hadn't grabbed the plates, Slater would have dropped them both.

Kathleen jumped up to give him her seat as Louie introduced Tim. Slater barely managed a civil handshake. He hadn't seen Kathleen in more than a week—a deliberate act of avoidance on his part. Running into her by chance, dressed in a filmy nothing of a dress that revealed about a mile of leg, negated a ten-day attempt to deny her effect on his senses. On his heart. On his life.

Introductions were over. Still Slater couldn't take his eyes off her. He couldn't get past the ringing in his ears as he floundered in the memories of the bleak days he'd suffered since Patrick and Scott had talked him into surgically severing his deepening relationship with Kathleen.

"I, um, have to assist Mama in the breakfast booth," Kathleen announced. She fluttered a hand over Louie's sleeve. "Nice to meet you, Mr. Kowalski. And, Pop, I'll see you later." Kat leaned in and brushed a kiss on Timothy's leathery cheek. "Slater, congratulations on renaming the Special. Ridgerunner is very nice. It conjures images of sleekness and speed." Then she sprinted off.

Slater pivoted, straining to follow her progress as she slipped through the crowd. He'd intended to tell her how he'd—surprisingly—liked a name that Wendy Nelson, of all people, had thrown out in a meeting. Ridgerunner. He hoped Kat saw how fitting it was. His father had to clear his throat and repeat twice that their food was getting cold before Slater glanced guiltily at the two men. He finally sat.

Talk immediately turned to cars. The ebb and flow of voices had less impact on Slater than did the lingering scent of Kathleen's perfume. After Luke Sheehan, Buzz Moran and Spud Mallory drifted in and pulled up chairs, Slater tuned the whole bunch of them out. His mind devised possible accidental ways of meeting Kathleen again. Maybe buying a second breakfast…He was so engrossed, his father had to nudge him to awaken Slater to the fact that the discussion had moved onto alternative-fuel auto engines.

They covered the whole range, beginning with electric-powered, then solar, methanol, ethanol and finally to hydrogen fuel cells. Previously it had been Slater's experience that people tended to harp on excessive price. These men were embroiled in a highly technical comparison and contrast. At the height of their exchange, Slater suddenly found himself asking for advice regarding his car's malfunction.

Talk ground to a halt. Louie recovered first. "How long has this been a problem, son?" He gave no indication the revelation wasn't brand-new.

"Too long," Slater muttered. "I'll solve it. Forget I said anything."

Timothy looped his arm over the chair back and tilted on two legs. "Sometimes collective heads are better than one. After today, the boys and I will have time on our hands. We'd be glad to give you a free consultation."

Slater shredded the foam of his empty coffee cup. Glancing across the table, he frowned a bit at his father. "This spare time of yours? Is that because the festival's over?"

A smug look passed from friend to friend. "Be near the podium in the square at noon. You'll see what we've been up to for the past year," Buzz said.

"You were quick enough to discard an old has-been," Louie growled. "Wait till *your* parts slow down and you feel useless."

"You were never discarded," Slater contradicted.

Timothy stacked their empty plates. "Put out to pasture. Same thing. We all retired because our physical health declined. Not our minds. The offer to pool our talent is on the table. Take it or leave it. Makes no never mind to me.''

Slater studied the face of each man. ''I'd want your word that what you see remains strictly confidential.'' His gaze settled longest on Tim O'Halloran.

Louie clambered to his feet. ''Stop. I won't allow you to insult my friends.''

Stubbornly insistent, Slater pounded a fist on the table. ''There's more. Things I haven't told you. I have reason to believe someone's trying to kill this project.''

Kathleen's father bounced the tips of his fingers together. ''Do you have any idea who?''

''I made a list. One by one, I'm scratching off names. Brass from Motorhill. Any one of your sons, Mr. O'Halloran. I even suspected you,'' Slater said, going on to explain how Kathleen had been caught with her hand in the cookie jar, so to speak.

Timothy grew red in the face. He grabbed Slater by the front of his shirt. ''That gal doesn't have it in her to hurt a flea. By God, she ordered me to hold my tongue, but you're blind as a bat if you can't see my Katie loves you.''

Slater leaned into the hamlike fist. ''And I love her. Notice I didn't say her name was ever on my list. But Kathleen is bound by family ties. Your sons haven't exactly welcomed me with open arms. She could have tried to pass the prints to them.''

''My boys are hotheaded. Not dishonest.''

Slater spread his hands. ''Then I'll start a new list. If the offer's still open to check my drawings, I accept. Solving the problem might smoke my enemy out.''

Timothy unhanded his shirt and they shook hands all around.

Spud Mallory tapped his watch. ''It's going on for eleven. Shouldn't we head for the podium?''

The men made haste to leave, but Slater detained Tim O'Halloran for a moment. "One other thing, and you can tell Matt, Josh and Mark. I will be calling on Kathleen."

"First, me lad, you'd better be informin' Katie of that."

Slater wrestled with Tim's candid advice for a while. Perhaps he should get his ducks in a row before he apologized. Someone had involved her in the attacks against him at the plant. Until he knew who, he shouldn't risk placing her in danger. He'd figure it out—later. Just now he was curious as to the men's big surprise. Had they prepared an array of card tricks or what?

Slater wove through the crowd. Maybe the old codgers had rigged an elaborate shell game…for charity, of course. Nothing would surprise him anymore. Whatever else happened, he hoped to wangle another look at Kathleen in that sexy little dress.

He spotted her right away. Ringside. Slater worked his way to within arm's length. He knew she'd seen him. Staring at her, he could tell that the pulse at the base of her neck had quickened and beat faster. Slater suppressed a wicked smile as a hush fell over the crowd.

What now? he wondered when Father Pulaski took the microphone and introduced a Father Hanrahan. The poker partners flanked the priests. They jointly held a large, covered rectangle of cardboard.

Kathleen sought Slater's gaze. After a tense moment, both shrugged.

Father Pulaski tapped the microphone. "Welcome," he said. "My congregation from the Ridge have celebrated Easter Monday in Zernik Square for many years. We represent approximately half a town." He handed Father Hanrahan the mike.

"The other half of us live on the Hill. We don't know a lot about our neighbors on the Ridge and they don't know much about us. We on the Hill host a similar yearly carnival to raise funds for charitable works. We've each hoarded our money and stubbornly clung to cultural independence—to the detriment of greater prosperity.''

Tim O'Halloran stepped forward. ''Last year the state inspected our high school and said for safety's sake our parish needs to provide a new building.''

Louie Kowalski leaned over Tim's shoulder. ''They said the same to the Ridge diocese. The perfect site for a new school is a piece of property that sits in the valley between the Ridge and the Hill. Both our dioceses tried to buy the land.''

''To our dismay,'' said Father Pulaski, ''neither Ridge nor Hill had sufficient funds.''

''That's where we came in.'' Timothy indicated the five. ''In the process of dickering, it became evident that one facility, sharing costs to install the latest computers and equipment—would better serve both communities. We all want a good education for our kids and grandkids. We also realized that involving everyone in the early stages would have sparked old animosities and caused delays, so we purposely kept the group small. The long and the short of it is…we five set out to earn enough money to purchase the land. We present to you this symbolic check.'' He tore the covering off the cardboard that had been made to look like a check. A very substantial check. ''Money raised here today will kick off the building fund.''

Kat's mouth fell open as people shuffled closer. In a ripple effect, they began to clap. Jostling against Slater, she hissed, ''They raised that money by gambling.''

''The point is, they did raise it for a good cause.''

''Yes. But why were they so secretive? My dad has company funds available for community projects.''

''That's Ridge money. This check represents joint funding—Ridge and Hill. They're wily but smart. What's done now is done. See how they've united the town.''

"They didn't go off the deep end like we all feared." Kat threw her arms around Slater to express her glee.

He held her tight, enjoying the feel of her body. Caught up in the craziness of the moment, he forgot his vow to keep his distance. Swinging her off her feet, he slammed right into Scott Wishynski. "Hey, Scott!" Slater set Kat down and looked puzzled as Scott all but knocked them aside.

Kat clutched Slater's arm and they both gazed after him for a few seconds. "There's so much noise, he must not have heard you," she said, shaking her head.

Slater absently rubbed her arms. "Scott's just moody sometimes."

"Hmm." Kat strained to see where Scott had gone in such a rush, but he'd disappeared. "I'm off to congratulate our pops. Come on." She shot away like a rabbit freed from a snare.

But he'd remembered his pledge to keep her safe, by keeping her apart from him. Slater sucked in a deep breath and remained where he stood.

CHAPTER FIFTEEN

KAT EXPECTED SLATER to follow her. He didn't, which told her his hug had meant nothing. He'd been taken by surprise, that was all. Though she meandered through the craft and food booths for the rest of the day looking for him, Slater never put in another appearance. Because her pop was pressed to stay for an impromptu meeting with other school supporters, Kat rode home with her mother. Maureen chattered happily all the way to the house, where they were met by Kat's brothers.

"I hafta say Pop had us all snookered." Grinning, Matt twisted the top off a beer. "At least now, I understand why."

Josh rocked back in one of the kitchen chairs. "Looks like we had you leave Washington for no reason, sis."

"At least now you can quit that crappy job," Mark said, tugging at one of her curls.

"You don't know anything about my job."

Mark's wife, Erin, chortled. "Don't let them give you a hard time, Kat. They've been ribbed by people at work ever since your basketball team beat Motorhill."

"It's more than that," Josh added. "We don't like the rumors floating around about the break-ins and all that extra security Kowalski's hired. The dude's got trouble. Big trouble. The kitten's better off outta there."

Mark grabbed both brothers by the back of the neck. "Pop said for us to back off and let Katie be. He told me that he, Spud, Luke and Buzz are meeting Kowalski later this week to help debug his engine. Doesn't sound like Slater's trying to steal from Pop. Not if the guy came out and asked Pop for help.''

"He did?" Kat frowned. "Are you sure he said Slater asked?''

Mark nodded. "Right before he reminded me what would happen to the town's economy if Kowalski's operation topples.''

Their conversation progressed to encompass other changes they could expect in Flintridge. Kat didn't comment. She groped through her mind for a reason Slater would deliberately leave her in the dark. She came up with one. Or rather it was a reason Scott had suggested. With Slater, his car always came first.

THE NEXT DAY AT WORK everyone buzzed about the school merger. Kat wasn't surprised. The story, complete with pictures, had made the newspaper's front page. Even though her father was a big part of the news, no one asked Kat anything.

Scott had been so distracted yesterday, she wasn't at all sure he'd show up for their lunchtime river run. He did, but fifteen minutes late. He still seemed not quite himself.

Kat supposed it had to do with the school merger. She'd heard enough to know that not everyone approved of uniting the town. Not interested in conversation, Kat motioned Scott into his normal back seat and said, "I'm counting on peace and quiet. I don't want to discuss the school consolidation, okay?" She already wore a life jacket and handed him his.

He slung the vest negligently over a shoulder and stared at her strangely. They settled in and shoved off.

"Your old man and Slater's dad are upstairs reengineering my drawings. The cat'll be out of the bag soon enough. Time's up for everyone. Turn upstream.''

Frowning, Kat twisted around to gaze into Scott's slightly glazed eyes. ''What are you talking about? Scott, are you all right? We're not going anywhere until you put on that life jacket. And definitely not upstream. The rapids are still too rough.''

His spurt of laughter seemed uncontrolled. But Kat had to face front again as he'd turned them upstream and they hit a cross current that sent the boat into a spin. She cut her paddle deep, trying to set them straight, parallel with the shore, and headed downstream again.

Scott reached around Kat and knocked her paddle aside. The boat lurched. Scott paddled fast until they were once more pointed upstream.

''Scott, take it easy! What are you…?'' Kat's words petered out as he ripped the double paddle from her hand. She lunged for it and missed. Kat felt the front of the kayak dive; it dipped into a deep trough and moved toward the swirling waters of the big eddy. Hands gripping the sides of the craft, Kat swung around to lecture Scott.

''I said we're going upstream today, doll face,'' Scott yelled over the noise of the water. ''But only one of us is coming back.''

Kat stared into a face she didn't recognize. Into the face of a madman. ''You! You broke into the design center. You're trying to ruin Slater. Why, Scott? Why?''

''It's always been me, Kit-Kat. I did set out to ruin him. Now I've found a better way. An eye for an eye. So shut up and turn around. Poor little Kathleen's going to meet with a horrible accident. I'll be out of town before anyone finds your body.'' Scott raised his paddle and tried to strike Kat in the head. The blow glanced off her shoulder, instead. She gasped as he whacked her again.

"I TELL YOU, THIS MAKES no sense." Slater strode around a table in the largest of his three conference rooms, peering over the shoulder of each man as he went. "My set of blueprints doesn't match the ones I ran off Scott's computer this morning."

All the men sat with shirtsleeves rolled up and jackets draped over the backs of their chairs. Timothy O'Halloran snaked a hand through a handsome shock of hair. "Blocked emissions outlet in one. Hydrocarbon leak in another. Scored linkage now revised. And so on and so forth. Each snag stalled your engine, boyo."

Spud darted a glance from Louie to his son. "No offense, men, but where did your engineers get their degrees? From sending in cereal-box tops?"

Slater's hand was already on the phone. "Hazel, get Scott on the line." He fidgeted until she buzzed back. "No answer, boss. He must be out to lunch."

"Permanently out to lunch, based on these mistakes," joked Buzz Moran.

"All the engineers can't be at lunch," Slater said. "Let's pay a visit to the team. We can grab a bite in the cafeteria after that. Scott's probably there."

The men rose, shook down their sleeves and trudged out.

Two design engineers sat at their desks, various stages of blueprints spread out. Slater walked up to one. "Jim, did either of you do detail work on the Special's power plant? Er...the Ridgerunner, I mean."

"Are you kidding?" the man called Jim snorted. "Nobody but Scott touched that baby. He wouldn't allow it."

Slater pulled at one earlobe. "That crazy guy never had help? What in hell was he thinking, trying to do it all alone? Shall we take a quick gander at Scott's computer drafting center? There must be some error in his program." Slater explained that his chief engineer preferred to work in solitude. "We converted an outbuilding into his office. It's just down the path."

The men followed Slater. They clustered around as he booted up Scott's computer. Just as it came on, Luke Sheehan bumped a partially full coffee cup, spilling the contents. Slater jerked open a bottom drawer in search of napkins or something to wipe up the spill. All that was in the drawer was a navy blue sweater. He snatched it out, letting the spilled coffee run over the edge of the desk. Rage overwhelmed him as he plunged two fingers through a good-sized, triangular tear. "Why, that son of a bitch."

"What is it?" Louie asked.

"This sweater. I found the missing piece caught on the design center lock the morning after Kathleen surprised an intruder."

"You think Scott... But why?" Louie seemed to have a hard time coming to grips with the notion.

Slater ran for the door. "Scott's the only one who can answer that. And we won't know until we find him."

As the men exploded out of the office into the brilliant noonday sun, Slater's chief of Maintenance drove up in a truck filled with flats of blooming geraniums. "You men headed to a fire?" he teased.

"We're looking for Scott. Seen him around?"

Pausing in the act of unloading the wooden flats, John Tuttle scratched his chin. "Don't know for sure, but my best guess is he and the coach are paddlin' the river."

"Paddling...? Impossible," Slater snapped. "Didn't I ask you guys to help Ms. O'Halloran load her kayaks so she could take them home? That was weeks ago."

"Yep. But some of the boys wanted kayaking lessons. Scott said he'd talk to you and get back to me. Next thing I heard, the class was meeting at the indoor swimming pool in town. I figured Scott had talked you around."

''Well, he didn't.'' Just the thought of Kathleen on the river with Scott made Slater's blood turn to ice. ''Quick,'' he shouted at John and the others. ''Let's unload these plants. Then give us a lift to the river.''

Seven sets of hands made short work of the job. As the pickup bounced and jounced down the hill, Slater huddled in back, fretting. ''Her first week on the job, I made it clear to Kat that the river was off limits. As if shooting those rapids in a kayak isn't dangerous enough, now she's out there with a possible thief…or worse.''

Timothy linked his fingers. ''Katie's an experienced river-runner, lad. To watch her skim along the water, you'd think she was part of the boat. Matt taught her. He claims she outdistanced him in one summer. Don't worry.''

Slater lifted his head and gazed at Tim O'Halloran through bleak eyes. ''I was good, too. Or so everyone thought.''

John leaned out the open window. His words blew back on the wind. ''There's the river, boss. Looks like they're out on the water, like I said.''

Louie Kowalski bent over the side and slapped the driver's door with his hand. ''Drive us to the bank, John.''

Moments later, as the men vaulted from the truck and stumbled to the rocky shore, it was evident to everyone that the two kayakers were in trouble in the center of the river. They fought a dragging current and white water slamming over the boat's bow.

Louie held out a shaking hand. ''The girl has no paddle. And what's Scott doing? He's raising his oar so far out of the water, it looked to me as if he hit her in the head.''

OUT ON THE RIVER, Kat was fighting more than a swift current. Fear had her by the throat. The two-man craft was long and unwieldy without the benefit of a second oarsman. Her muscles strained each time she tried to turn and grab Scott's paddle.

Each time he fought her off, he ordered her to climb out of the craft. He cursed loudly when she deflected his blows, hung on and refused to jump.

If she went overboard, she'd be dashed against the jagged rocks. But the angrier Scott became, the more likely they'd both die, anyway. He wasn't a strong-enough kayaker to keep them out of the massive whirlpool. And that last strike he'd delivered to her head had almost knocked her senseless.

The water was deeper here. Kat determined she had one chance to overtake Scott. But if she didn't succeed…

ON SHORE, SEVEN HUFFING, puffing men thrashed their way around brush and boulders, hoping to get closer to the bobbing boat. Slater, who led the pack, feared that the combined stress of the pressure and worry would prove to be too much for his father's heart and Tim's. Slater hadn't even had time yet to spare for Kathleen's plight. He only knew that she was drawing ever closer to the dangerous whirlpool that had claimed the life of his best friend. And with her was Scott, who had serious charges to answer. Slater wondered how he could sweat when he felt so icy cold. Yet sweat dripped into his eyes.

Forced to stop by thickening underbrush and a narrower coastline, Slater stripped off his shoes, his shirt and tie. "John," he panted. "We're the youngest and strongest. If you swim well, we've got to go after them. Once they drift around that bend, the rapids will suck them in."

Timothy had bent double trying to haul in large draughts of air. "Wait! Look, they've turned over," he managed to wheeze.

Slater's insides twisted and heaved. He'd known fear before. Had flirted with death himself. He'd never felt such stark terror. "Oh, God, Scott's out of the kayak. He's caught in the eddy. I'll get him, John. You go after Kathleen."

Slater didn't wait for a response. He made a shallow dive under the surface of the frothy water.

"Look!" Spud Mallory said in a panic. "Katie's up! She's still in the kayak. See there, she's trying to grab hold of the paddle."

Tim all but hopped up and down. "I told you she was good! When she was just a little kid, I saw her roll a kayak time after time. Enough to frazzle a man's nerves."

"I'm not sure she'll reach the paddle," John said. "You fellows stay here and help pull Slater ashore when he brings Scott in. I'll run around the bend and throw a rope out to Kat when the current sweeps her past the final land hook." He raced back to his truck and grabbed a rope from inside the vehicle.

BELOW, IN THE WILD SURF, Kat had bobbed up from the kayak's full roll. Surprise had been on her side. She'd braced for the three-hundred-sixty degree revolution, as she'd taught at each practice. Scott had missed those sessions. Furthermore, he hadn't a clue what was about to happen.

Kat leaned forward to avoid his flailing paddle as they went under. She held on as he began to struggle. She felt the moment he was pulled free of the kayak. The sudden buoyancy fishtailed the long hull, nearly ejecting her. It took all her experience to right the craft and complete the roll. Though she was very glad Scott had missed the practices at the pool, Kat would never deliberately let anyone drown. The number-one question in her mind when she broke the surface was how could she save Scott and keep both of them from being sucked into the horrendous whirlpool?

''You bitch!''

Kat heard Scott coughing, swearing and floundering in the waves. Too bad the force of the roll didn't knock him out. In her courses, she'd covered the rescue of an unconscious person. Never, though, the rescue of someone who wanted her dead.

When Kat realized there was a second swimmer thrashing around in the water, it was maybe two seconds after a brilliant sun flash from the nearby bluff drew her attention to a small audience standing there. But they weren't just standing. They were waving, gesturing madly and yelling, although the crash of the white-water rapids muffled any sound.

People, any people, meant help. And she could use help to extract herself from this fix. The tremendous tension she'd been under for the last half hour had sapped her energy. Exhausted, disoriented, Kat wasn't sure she could outwit the insidious pull of the vortex. Especially without a paddle.

Her stomach bottomed out in panic. The swimmer couldn't save her and Scott. Caught in the pounding waves surrounding her craft, Kat screamed at the swimmer to concentrate on rescuing Scott. ''Get him,'' she yelled, trying to point.

Kat got a fast look at the swimmer before she attempted a second grab for the oscillating paddle and missed. *Slater.* Oh, God, no! Slater, who hated the river. She hadn't listened when he'd told her not to give lessons, and now he could very well lose his life due to the very thing he'd warned her against.

Her heart in her throat, Kat felt the current whisk her away. Spinning and whirling, her kayak raced toward the river's bend.

Over the churning whitecaps, Kat saw a man leaning out

from a section of sandy beach. *John Tuttle*. Her lanky basketball forward. What was he doing here? As the current swept her closer, he yelled at her to grab the rope. It flew out at her. For a second she had her hands on it. But they were slick with water, and she felt the burning rope slip free. "No!" she screamed in her throat when she saw John kick off his shoes and leave the safety of the shore.

By not making that appointment to talk to Slater about her classes, she'd caused this mess. John, Scott, Slater— they could all die. And so could she.

FIGHTING THE STRONG UNDERTOW that tossed Scott around like a rag doll, Slater glimpsed Kathleen's kayak hurtling out of sight. For an awful minute, he envisioned history repeating itself. To stop and go after Kathleen, to turn his back on Scott, would be to sign the young engineer's death warrant. Scott still wore all his clothes, including jacket and shoes. He'd undoubtedly swallowed water during the kayak's roll. His struggles grew increasingly more feeble. Slater was close enough to see the terror in Scott's eyes.

Determined there'd be no life lost this time, Slater made his choice. He'd save Scott first. Then he'd do whatever it took to rescue Kat.

Hoisting Scott in a fireman's carry, Slater kicked toward land. He'd gone no more than four strokes when Luke Sheehan met him. They redistributed Scott's deadweight and cut in half the time it took to reach shore.

On their knees in the shallows, the two men heaved Scott into waiting arms. "Pound the water out, but hang on to him," Slater said hoarsely. "I'm going after Kathleen."

"John already did," his father said. But the knowledge didn't deter Slater. He knew those jeering, thundering rapids well. So many nights after Jerry had drowned in this very spot, Slater had heard those dreadful sounds in his sleep. On the nights he managed to get to sleep.

"Yo, Slater!" John's shout penetrated Slater's numb brain. "Give me a hand."   .

Treading water he peered around an outcrop of rocks. His stomach turned inside out. Not five feet away in the swirling water, John had a hand clamped to the O-ring at the front of Kat's boat. Looping his arm around the largest of the freestanding rocks, Slater was able to stretch out his other arm and catch John's hand during their next revolution. Slater's first real moment of peace since he'd discovered the navy blue sweater in Scott Wishynski's desk drawer came when he had both Kathleen and John beside him on the shore.

John spoke first because Slater and Kat were wrapped in each other's arms. "That was a pretty piece of seamanship, coach. Ranks right up there with our big basketball win."

Kat still clung to Slater, but when she got her breath back, she asked, "What happened to Scott?"

"Luke helped me wrestle him out of the water. We dumped him with my dad and yours. What in hell were you two doing out there?"

"It all seems so crazy. Like a bad dream. I don't know how to tell you, Slater, and maybe you won't even believe me. Scott's behind every last shred of vandalism that's happened at Flintridge."

"I do believe you, Kathleen. The morning after the design center break-in, I searched the building and found a piece of sweater wool caught on the door lock. Today I found the sweater in Scott's desk. That was after your dad and his friends figured out that every set of engine blueprints had been sabotaged in a different way. He was clever, I'll give him that. As soon as I found and corrected one problem, he'd subtly design in another. What I don't know is why,"

Slater said, sounding truly baffled as they came abreast of the older men, who were holding Scott captive.

Timothy O'Halloran clasped Slater's hand tight, then John's, before he turned to envelop his daughter.

Scott sat hunched on the ground. Louie's jacket hung loosely from his slumped shoulders.

Slater dropped down on his knees in front of his one-time friend. "Why, Scott? You had a good job. Good pay."

Scott looked up, his gaze slowly circling the ring of pale faces. "Why did you rescue me? Why, when you let Jerry die?"

That knocked the wind out of Slater's lungs. "I didn't let Jerry die. I pulled Gordon from a boat that broke apart on the rocks. Gordy couldn't swim. The river was even higher and swifter than it was today. I thought Jerry…he…swam better than me. He…must have developed a cr-amp." Slater's voice broke even after all the years. "Don't you know I almost died trying to find Jer? Two fishermen pulled me out and hogtied me, or I wouldn't be here today."

Kat left her father. She sank down beside Slater and flung an arm over his shaking shoulders. "If you know anything about Slater Kowalski," she yelled at Scott, "I can't imagine how you'd ever think he could do such a wicked thing. That's what you meant when you said Slater would pay an eye for an eye, wasn't it? You thought taking my life would hurt him as much as losing your foster brother hurt you?"

Scott covered his face with his hands and started to cry. "Jerry's mom and dad, my foster folks, were never the same after he died. I did it to square accounts for them. I knew Slater loved you as much as we all loved Jerry. And yes, I wanted him to pay."

Kat drew back, shaking her head. "Oh, Scott. How wrong you are. Slater doesn't love me. And…"

Slater grabbed her by the shoulders. As quickly, he softened his hold and gave Kat a gentle shake. "That's where you're wrong, Kathleen. You may be the last to know, but you mean the world to me. I love you."

"Really?" Eyes bright with tears, Kat lifted a trembling hand and ran her fingers over his damp cheeks and chin. "I thought...I...well...I mean...really?" she stammered again.

"Really, Kathleen." Slater's hands slid up and down her arms, "Before all these witnesses, I'm asking from my knees. Will you be my wife?"

Her eyes overflowed. Tears mixed with the river water running down her cheeks, and she buried her face in Slater's sun-warmed shoulder.

The men hovering around exchanged happy grins. Timothy cleared his throat first. "Can anyone foresee a better way to cement the union of this town than a wedding celebrated jointly by the Ridge and the Hill? Say yes, Katie-girl, so that Father Hanrahan and Father Pulaski can both post banns."

"Yes," Kat said loud and clear. Then she added, "Yes, yes, yes," in case they hadn't heard. In case Slater hadn't heard. "The wedding date is up to Slater. If it's all right, though, I'd like us to be married in Zernik Square."

His method of agreement was to capture her trembling lips in a long, long kiss. And now that he had her back safe, he had a hard time turning her loose.

All but Scott whooped for joy. He spat at their feet.

Louie hoisted the young engineer by the scruff of his shirt. "Lotta work to be done, my friends. A wedding to plan and a car to fix. Let's start by emptying the trash."

Scott looked like a miserable piece of humanity as the men hauled him off.

Kat knew that after all he'd done, he didn't deserve pity. But she thought of his poor young wife, and of Jerry Gelecki's parents, who'd already tragically lost one son. She held Slater back, curling her fingers lightly around his strong, tanned forearm. Her eyes were dark with compassion.

"I know what you're going to say," he breathed. "Scott needs psychiatric help. He won't get it if we charge him with attempted murder."

"You read my mind." Standing on tiptoe, Kat looped her arms around his neck. She planted a warm kiss of thanks on his lips. "Blessed be, say the Irish."

EPILOGUE

KAT STOOD AT ONE END of Zernik Square clutching her father's arm. She gazed at the horde of people lining a long burgundy runner rented for this happiest of occasions. Her wedding to Slater Kowalski. Old and young, from the Ridge and the Hill, waited to hear them exchange sacred vows. Two priests. One covenant.

Nothing about the wedding was conventional. Much to her mother's dismay, Kat had on a white cotton peasant dress, topped by a hand appliquéd Polish vest—a gift from Louie. The vest had belonged to Slater's mother. Kat wore it for her father-in-law.

The entire basketball team stood up with Slater. Minus Scott Wishynski. He'd already begun receiving treatment in a small, private psychiatric facility. His foster parents were saddened by what he'd done. They said they'd always known Slater had tried his best to save their son.

Kat's slender body trembled. "Can you believe Slater asked Josh to be his best man?" she whispered to her father.

Tim patted her hand. "Slater's a man in love. Are you happy, daughter?"

"Deliriously so, Pop."

The piano rippled. Kat's bridesmaids started the walk. "I hope no one notices that Slater has more attendants than I." She blew kisses to each of her three sisters-in-law as they passed. Then to Hazel Carmichael, her matron of honor.

"Believe me, kitten," Tim murmured, "people aren't counting noses today."

Kat's eyes never left Slater as she started her walk. At the dais, Timothy placed his daughter's hand in that of his soon-to-be fourth son. Smiling through tears, he stepped back to join his wife. As a hush fell over the crowd, the clear contralto strains of Wendy Nelson singing "Be My Love" filled the square.

Slater kissed Kat's fingertips. No one heard him murmur, "Who knew Wendy could sing? You're the one who figured that out with the recreation survey you did. You discovered all kinds of hidden talents in our workforce." He paused. "You amaze me, Kathleen. I hope to be amazed for the next fifty or sixty years."

Father Pulaski and Father Hanrahan appeared in all their impressive raiments. The service that followed was solemn; the promises repeated with conviction.

A cheer greeted the last "I do."

After shaking hands and kissing strangers for the better part of two hours, Slater and Kat tried to sneak away. By then the band had started. Friends of each family kidnapped first the bride then the groom to dance Polish polkas or Irish jigs. Pots of *bigos* simmered on picnic tables, next to tubs of Irish stew. One thing the Ridge and Hill had in common—both factions loved a party.

"Enough, already," Slater protested about the time a full moon started its ascent. "My wife and I—" he smiled into Kat's eyes when he said *wife* "—have wine chilling at a cabin near…well, now, only a foolish man would tell you jokers where."

That prompted a rumble of laughter.

Kat, who'd changed into jeans, hugged each of her brothers. Matt got a special thanks for going home to retrieve Poseidon.

Looking smug, she told Slater where she'd parked her Isuzu. They'd plotted this escape for weeks, positive not a soul would expect them to take her SUV on their honeymoon.

Louie crooked a finger at his son, beckoning him aside.

"What now, Dad?" Slater sounded cheerful enough, but everyone could see he was itching to grab Kathleen and flee.

Tim and Maureen joined Louie. They waggled a shiny car key at the newlyweds. Caught off guard, Slater and Kat—who had a firm grip on Poseidon—followed the trio and a trail of onlookers to a side street. There sat a gleaming white car with gold wire rims.

"A Ridgerunner," Kat exclaimed.

"Yes and no," cackled Slater's Great-aunt Adelaide. "A souped-up Special. The first car off the line." Accompanied by a loud drumroll, she unveiled the front license plate. Scrawled in fourteen-carat-gold letters, it read Honeymoon Special.

Matt O'Halloran slapped Slater hard on the back. "Take it easy on the straight-of-ways, bro. She has precision-milled hemi heads. Made 'em myself." He blew on his fingers and scraped them across the lapel of his tux.

A crush of well-wishers forced Slater, Kat and their dog into the car.

Kat's brother, Mark, was pelted by a hail of rice as he busily affixed strings of tin cans and old shoes to the bumper. Josh tied navy knots in the nylon cord.

Slater kissed his bride full on the lips before shooting away from the curb.

Turning inside her seat belt, Kat glanced back. Poseidon burrowed into the plush rear seat. He whined and covered his head with his paws. "Poseidon hates the sound of those tin cans," Kat murmured. "Stop and I'll take them off."

Slater leaned across the console to kiss her again. "Let's leave them until your brothers can't hear us anymore."

"Okay, but why?"

"It's a subtle thing, Kathleen. But I believe it's their way of welcoming me into the O'Halloran family."

"Hmm. Well, I have a better way of welcoming you to the family. You'll see when we get to the cabin."

Slater laced their hands. "'Tis only fair to warn you, Katie," he said in a fair rendition of the O'Halloran brogue. "The last thing your dear mother said when she pulled me aside…she's counting on us for grandbabies. A lot of grandbabies."

Kat gave him a cheeky grin. "Then, by all means, I think we should oblige."

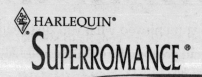

HARLEQUIN®
SUPERROMANCE®

Another wonderful new book from

Judith Arnold
DR. DAD

Sometimes...a man needs help learning to be a dad. That's what the Daddy School is all about.

Widowed pediatrician Toby Cole is finding his soon-to-be teenage daughter, Lindsey, increasingly difficult to deal with. His woes magnify after beautiful Susannah Dawson, burned out from her job as star of a television soap opera, moves in next door, and he and Susannah fall for each other. Lindsey needs Susannah to be *her* special friend, not her dad's. Soon, Toby needs the Daddy School to help him cope.

On sale February 2000, and look for another Daddy School book later in the year.

THE DADDY SCHOOL
Don't skip it!

Available wherever Harlequin books are sold.

HARLEQUIN®
Makes any time special ™

Visit us at www.romance.net

HSRTDS

If you enjoyed what you just read,
then we've got an offer you can't resist!

Take 2 bestselling
love stories FREE!
Plus get a FREE surprise gift!

Clip this page and mail it to Harlequin Reader Service®

IN U.S.A.	IN CANADA
3010 Walden Ave.	P.O. Box 609
P.O. Box 1867	Fort Erie, Ontario
Buffalo, N.Y. 14240-1867	L2A 5X3

YES! Please send me 2 free Harlequin Supperromance® novels and my free surprise gift. Then send me 6 brand-new novels every month, which I will receive months before they're available in stores. In the U.S.A., bill me at the bargain price of $3.57 plus 25¢ delivery per book and applicable sales tax, if any*. In Canada, bill me at the bargain price of $3.96 plus 25¢ delivery per book and applicable taxes**. That's the complete price, and a saving of over 10% off the cover prices—what a great deal! I understand that accepting the 2 free books and gift places me under no obligation ever to buy any books. I can always return a shipment and cancel at any time. Even if I never buy another book from Harlequin, the 2 free books and gift are mine to keep forever.
So why not take us up on our invitation. You'll be glad you did!

135 HEN CQW6

336 HEN CQW7

Name	(PLEASE PRINT)
Address	Apt.#
City	State/Prov.	Zip/Postal Code

Return to the charm of the Regency era with

GEORGETTE
HEYER,

creator of the modern Regency genre.

Enjoy six romantic collector's editions with forewords
by some of today's bestselling romance authors,

**Nora Roberts, Mary Jo Putney,
Jo Beverley, Mary Balogh,
Theresa Medeiros and Kasey Michaels.**

Frederica
On sale February 2000
The Nonesuch
On sale March 2000
The Convenient Marriage
On sale April 2000
Cousin Kate
On sale May 2000
The Talisman Ring
On sale June 2000
The Corinthian
On sale July 2000

Available at your favorite retail outlet.

HARLEQUIN®
Makes any time special ™

Visit us at www.romance.net

PHGHGEN

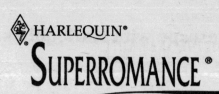

Welcome to cowboy country!

MONTANA LEGACY by **Roxanne Rustand**
(Superromance #895)
Minneapolis cop Kate Rawlins has her own reasons
for wanting to sell her inheritance—half of the
Lone Tree Ranch, Montana. Then she meets
co-owner Seth Hayward and suddenly splitting the property
doesn't seem like a good idea....
On sale February 2000

COWBOY COME HOME by **Eve Gaddy**
(Superromance #903)
After years on the saddle circuit, champion bronco
rider Jake Rollins returns home—determined to find
out whether his ex-lover's daughter is *his* child.
On sale March 2000

Available at your favorite retail outlet.

3 Stories of Holiday Romance from three bestselling Harlequin® authors

Valentine Babies

by

ANNE STUART

TARA TAYLOR QUINN

JULE McBRIDE

Goddess in Waiting by Anne Stuart
Edward walks into Marika's funky maternity shop to pick
up some things for his sister. He doesn't expect to assist
in the delivery of a baby and fall for outrageous Marika.

Gabe's Special Delivery by Tara Taylor Quinn
On February 14, Gabe Stone finds a living, breathing
valentine on his doorstep—his daughter. Her mother
has given Gabe four hours to adjust to fatherhood,
resolve custody and win back his ex-wife?

My Man Valentine by Jule McBride
Everyone knows Eloise Hunter and C. D. Valentine
are in love. Except Eloise and C. D. Then, one of
Eloise's baby-sitting clients leaves her with a baby to
mind, and C. D. swings into protector mode.

VALENTINE BABIES

On sale January 2000 at your favorite retail outlet.

HARLEQUIN®
Makes any time special ™

Visit us at www.romance.net

PHVALB